# HARBINGER

## Nova Online #3

## ALEX KNIGHT

Editor: Brook Aspden-Li

Copy editor: Laura Hughes

# Chapter One

"So, let's talk."

Thorne spoke the words but Kaiden still didn't believe they weren't some sort of trick. How could they not be when they came from the very woman who'd hounded them all this time? The Party agent who'd hunted them in Nova and in the real world. Who'd gone after their families. Who'd nearly caught them in that fateful raid on the resistance bunker. She'd been their greatest enemy from day one. A direct manifestation of everything that was wrong with the Party.

Kaiden looked over to Zelda. She was frowning, still angry, but something else too. Confusion, maybe? Or suspicion?

Titus' feelings were clear. Fists balled and eyes wide, he looked like he was about to step into a boxing ring, about to fight for his life. Which, considering the circumstances, he probably was. They all were, seeing as they were trapped in a van with Captain Ava Thorne herself.

*This is a trick. It has to be.*

"You expect us to believe you're here to switch sides? Just like that?" He shook his head. "No way."

Thorne sighed.

"This looks crazy to you. Believe me, I know. But if I weren't genuine, why haven't I arrested you already? Why play games?"

She nodded to the database behind Zelda. "The Party's willing to kill for that. Do you really think you'd still be holding it if I'd come with them?"

"She... has a point?" Kaiden said, none too happy to admit it.

"I don't care if she has a point. She's with the Party," Titus growled. "There's nothing complicated about this. Either she has police waiting outside to take us in or she's bluffing to buy time until they get here."

"Time. Right," Thorne said as if she'd just remembered something. "This van is barely shielded. My handheld console picked up your signature as soon as I was within a mile. The police have much better equipment. We need to turn off those VR headsets, disconnect from the internet, and get moving. We need to get somewhere safe and somewhere rural."

*'We'? What 'we'?*

"There's no 'we' about this," Kaiden said. "There's us and there's you."

"We don't have time for this." A hint of anger crept into Thorne's voice. "A friend tipped me off that you were here but information like that doesn't stay quiet for long. The police are likely already on their way. It'd be best not to be here when they arrive."

Kaiden peered out one of the front windows, but saw nothing out of place.

*This doesn't make any sense.*

"What are you playing at?"

Thorne let out an exasperated groan, then started talking rapidly.

"While hunting you three, I've seen a side of the Party that I didn't know existed – wouldn't have believed existed had I not seen it for myself. Commander Moran, Agent Werner, and I don't know how many others, are running things behind the scenes. A shadow government, a secret oligarchy – call it what you will, but they're in control and I'm worried there's no line they won't cross to keep things that way. We already saw what they're capable of when they took your parents," she said with a quick nod toward Zelda. "And that's hardly the worst of it. That's why we have to move. You three can't get caught. That database can't fall into Party hands. There's so much more at stake than I ever realized."

"My parents?" Zelda said, speaking up for the first time. Her expression was pained, suspicious.

"They're dead," Titus growled. "Because of the Party."

"No," Thorne cut him off. "They were taken into custody just before the bombing. They're in prison, but I don't know which one."

*Hold up – what?* Kaiden recoiled at the news. Zelda visibly balked.

"Playing games with my emotions isn't helping your case," she said, her words dripping with venom.

"You don't trust me. I get it, and I don't blame you. But we *do not have time for this.*" Thorne reached for her pistol.

*This was a trick! She's attacking!*

Kaiden made to lunge forward, but the weapon was already drawn. Except she wasn't pointing it at him, nor at Titus or Zelda. Instead, it was pointed down at the floor. As Kaiden watched in disbelief, she reversed her hold on it, then held it out toward him, grip first.

Titus lunged forward and snatched it up. He flicked the safety off and the pistol came to life with a high-pitched whine as he turned it on Thorne.

She held up her now-empty hands. "You have the database. Now you have my weapon too. I have no leverage over you anymore. I won't ask that you trust me right now, but I will ask that you listen. For your sake as well as mine, we need to move."

A knock on the van's back door made Kaiden near jump out of his skin.

"Police! Open up!"

Titus cursed and jerked the gun toward the door. "That'll be her backup."

"No, no!" Thorne whispered, then waved for everyone to stay quiet. "I got this."

"I'll get us out of here," Kaiden said, then crept toward the driver's seat. How many police were outside? How long could Titus hold them off? *Could* he hold them off? And what about the database? They had to hide it before—

The groan of the rear door opening echoed through the van. Light flooded in, but only a crack as Thorne kept the door mostly closed. She pressed her face to the gap.

"Metro police, ma'am. I need to search this vehicle."

"No, you don't." Thorne reached into a pocket and withdrew a badge. "This is an ongoing operation, officer. You need to leave before you blow our cover."

Kaiden eased into the driver's seat. The windows were still in opaque mode, so no one could see in, but he could see out.

"With all due respect, Agent, this vehicle showed up on my scanner. I have to take a look."

Kaiden raised a hand to the ignition switch but didn't press it yet. He looked back to Titus and Zelda.

"Buckle up," he whispered.

"Of course we came up on your scanner," Thorne said, getting angry now. "What use would a stakeout be without surveillance equipment?"

"Agent, I need you to step out of the vehic—" The voice cut off as Thorne threw a punch. Even from up at the front of the van, Kaiden heard the officer's nose break.

"Stun him!" Thorne shouted, then swung the door wide open and ducked for cover.

Titus hesitated, blinded by the sudden bright light, maybe, or unsure what to do. The police officer was bent over, hand to his bleeding nose. He looked up, saw the three of them inside, then went for his gun.

Titus flicked Thorne's pistol into non-lethal and pulled the trigger. There was an electric pop and a knockout round caught the officer in the chest. Electricity ripped through him, then he collapsed to the pavement with a thud.

"Now can we leave?" Thorne asked, pulling the door shut and turning back toward them. "Before—"

There was a second electric pop as Titus fired another knockout round, this one into Thorne's chest. She spasmed, then collapsed to the floor.

"Move over, Kai," Titus said, tucking the pistol into his belt. "I'll drive."

## Chapter Two

"All right, this is officially bad news," Titus said, easing the van to a stop, then flinching and nearly kicking it back into motion as another wave of police cruisers zipped by just overhead. They were everywhere around the city, moving in numbers as if a manhunt was on. But was it a manhunt for them, or for Thorne? Kaiden wasn't sure anymore. He didn't trust her, not by a long shot, but now he was wondering what had happened with her. What had changed that she'd go so far as assaulting a police officer to help them escape?

"Is this hidden enough?" Zelda asked. Titus had landed them somewhere in the suburbs, in the parking lot of a busy mall.

"Hiding in plain sight," Titus said. "It worked last time."

"Until Thorne found us."

"I don't know where else to go. King Street won't take us, we can't go home, and if we park in an alley or something that'll be even more suspicious. Here, at least, we blend in."

"As long as we keep the headsets offline," Kaiden said, nodding to the pile of them on the back seat. After Thorne had gone down and Titus had started driving, he and Zelda had switched the headsets off, disconnected from the internet, and essentially ensured the entire van went dark. They'd also cut seat belts from the back seats and tied up Thorne. She was still unconscious from the knockout round, but she would wake up eventually, and it was a safe bet she wasn't going to be happy when she did.

"So, what's our next move?" Kaiden asked. "As if we weren't wanted enough, we shot a police officer and kidnapped an agent. Though, she might be a fugitive now too? I honestly don't know what to believe right now."

"She did try to send that cop away," Titus said, thinking aloud. "But it could still be a trick. Even if it isn't, that doesn't make up for everything else she's done. She had Bernstein's database in the first place."

"Bernstein's database!" Zelda exclaimed suddenly. "It still has that video file Bernstein left. Maybe it can help us."

*Right!* In all the chaos Kaiden had forgotten about it.

"Video file?" Titus asked.

"'You're probably wondering why I made you do all that,'" Zelda said, reading the name of the file as she accessed the database via her handheld console. "It looks like a video message Bernstein left for us. Or, well, for whoever managed to open the database. I need to play it. Was just about to before *she* showed up." She frowned at Thorne.

"Do it," Titus said, leaning in close.

"Wait, are we sure she's fully unconscious?" Kaiden asked, looking at Thorne. "I don't trust her. Anyone know how long that knockout round is supposed to last?"

"I can hit her again," Titus suggested, reaching for the pistol.

"Is that safe?"

"Do we care?"

"Don't," Zelda said, holding a hand out to stop Titus. "She's unconscious." And with that, she pressed play on the video file.

Her handheld console flashed to life, then spewed a rain of brightly-colored pixels into the air. They swirled and spun like so many motes of glowing dust, then, all at once, resolved themselves into the shape of a man.

Bernstein.

He stood there, a fully realized projection, if not looking a bit odd considering he'd materialized in the back of a dingy old van.

*He looks like he always did. Just like the last time I saw him. Before...
before the Party killed him.*

What remained of his thin white hair had been brushed back,
but rose in a poofy, rebellious mess as always. His blue eyes
were bright and seemed to shine with that look he'd get when
on the verge of solving some new puzzle. Even his clothing
looked real; a faded old polo tucked into khaki shorts, and a case
on his belt holding pens and the assorted tools he'd never been
caught without.

For a moment, Kaiden wanted to reach out and touch him as
if he were there in the flesh. But that'd be ridiculous. They
hadn't been as close as that. It was just the terrible thought of
how the man had spent his last moments that made Kaiden want
to reach out, as if he could perhaps still save the eccentric old
man. But this wasn't Bernstein; just a recording of him. Just a
recording of a man that had been dead for so long now.

Except it hadn't been that long. It just felt like it, what with
going to prison, breaking out of the warden program, being a
captive of the rebels, hiding with the King Street gang, not to
mention the mad scavenger hunt they'd gone on just to unlock
the database. It hadn't been forever – but man had it felt like it.

The projection flickered once, then jumped into motion. And
just like that, Kaiden could almost, if just for a moment,
convince himself that Bernstein was still alive.

"Well, uh, if you're watching this, that sucks," Bernstein said,
a slight frown pulling at his features. "I mean, you solved my
clues and found the database, so good on ya! But also, I'm likely
dead, so, well, I guess I should have been more careful? I wonder
what I got wrong? What tripped me up?" He waved the thought
away. "Bah, no reason to get caught up in what-ifs. It's just as
likely no one will ever watch this. I've made it this far, haven't I?
But, on the off chance someone is watching this, I suppose I owe
you an explanation."

"Yeah, I'd say so," Titus said with a disbelieving laugh.

"You, uh, have the database now, so obviously you already
know what's in it: the sum of my decade's worth of research
into the Party's egregious abuses of power, complete with

evidence enough to prosecute most of their leadership. I would say I hope you use this wisely, but, you see, I designed that scavenger hunt to ensure I wouldn't have to hope. In order to solve all of those riddles, to unlock all of those passwords, you needed to know me. And I don't mean 'know me' like old man Gerald two doors down. I mean *really* know me. Like that kid, Kaiden. I let him get closer than I should have, but you can't beat a decent gaming buddy. Nothing like a good puzzle to give you insight into a man's mind, eh? Yes, if I were to keel over tomorrow, he'd have a decent chance of finding this. Great lad. Lot of potential."

Kaiden's mouth fell open at that.

*I didn't know he thought that highly of me. Though, considering I did help get this database and open it, I guess he was right. Maybe I don't think highly enough of myself?*

"Actually," Bernstein said, stroking his mustache. "Zelda would probably find and unlock this thing first. She's a clever one."

*Hey!*

Bernstein faced where the camera must have been, as his eyes turned right toward them. "Zelda? That you watching this?"

Kaiden looked over at her. Her jaw was clenched but there was no visible expression on her face to betray what she was feeling. Was that a tear creeping into the corner of her eye, though, or was he just seeing things?

"Anyway, whoever you are watching this, you must have been someone I knew and trusted. But why the lengthy scavenger hunt to unlock it? I know it probably felt random, but let me assure you it was anything but. In fact, I specifically designed that hunt so that it could only be completed once you were at a sufficient level. And if you weren't, then you'd be forced to power level before being able to open the cipher and access the database. Ooh, did you have a good time against the grachnids? That part was one of my favorites. I love those big creepy crawlers." He had a childish grin on his face as he said the last bit.

"But the hunt, right." He cleared his throat. "It was designed to power level you so that when you hear the rest of my plan you won't say it's impossible." He laughed. "Just *mostly* impossible."

"What's he on about?" Titus asked. "What rest of the plan?"

"He's getting to it," Kaiden said, all too familiar with the way Bernstein liked to draw things out for drama. Apparently, it persisted even when he was recording critically important videos meant to be played in the event of his untimely death. Had to hand it to him, the man was consistent, if nothing else.

"All right, so back to a question I've wrestled with for a while now," Bernstein said. "How does one spread the critical information I've gathered – information that will see justice brought upon the Party – without getting caught? Furthermore, how does one spread it to enough people that it'll actually make a difference?" Bernstein started pacing, the projection wading through the front seats of the van as he did.

"The obvious answer would be the internet. Of course, the Party has censored that to the point of crippling it. Their AI censor programs are so effective you wouldn't get one megabyte into uploading this database before they stopped it, identified your IP address, and dispersed some Party thugs to your house. Everything after that – well, let's just say it wouldn't be pretty."

Kaiden couldn't help but wince. Bernstein had found out exactly how bad it could be when Party thugs turned up at your door. He'd deserved better.

"So, what to do, what to do? How do you disperse information to the masses when the entire government is set against you doing that very thing? You go through a loophole. A particular loophole that's been a thorn in the Party's side for years now." He drew out the moment, then smiled. "You go through Nova Online."

The projection of Bernstein was getting excited now, talking more quickly.

"Nova Online, the only place they can't censor... yet. That makes it the perfect loophole. Slowly and secretly, I uploaded the database to Nova, bit by bit and hidden inside innocuous files. Then, once it was in-game, once it was safe from the censors, I put it all together. Assembled my masterpiece!" He cracked his knuckles. "Then, I just needed to weaponize it. To disperse it to the masses. But... again we come to the question of 'how?'"

"This guy likes to hear himself talk," Titus remarked.

"He was brilliant," Zelda retorted.

"But a bit eccentric, you have to admit," Kaiden said.

Zelda looked offended.

"What? I loved the guy, but it's true," Kaiden said by way of clarification.

"You're being thick. Just hear him out. His plan will be perfect." She turned back to the video projection.

"Trading was my first thought," Bernstein continued, oblivious to their disagreement. "But as I'm sure you know, files in Nova Online can't be duplicated." He waved his hand as if exasperated. "If you can't copy a file, then the information contained in it is valuable, making the file a sort of in-game commodity. Yadda yadda. It's a nice thought, but I'm not sure it ever panned out. Anyway, exact copies of files can exist, but only if they're uploaded individually into the game. Seeing as it took more than a year to upload the first database, byte by byte so it went undetected, you can understand how that wasn't a feasible option. And besides, trading wasn't big enough. It couldn't be scaled. In theory, I could trade the database to another player, have them download a copy, then pass it on. But having a physical copy of the database doesn't do much. Keeps it safe, I suppose, and allows you to replicate it offline, but you'd never be able to physically disperse enough copies. No, I needed a way to get the database to as many people as possible and before the Party could react. By the time they figure out what the database is, it needs to be too late. The information contained within it needs to have spread as far as possible. To every player in the game, ideally. Millions of players.

"But again, we're faced with the same problem. How to send a file to every player in Nova at once?" He left the question hanging for a moment, like he didn't have an answer. Kaiden knew better, however. Bernstein always had an answer.

The projection smiled knowingly.

"The answer is the warden All-Frequencies Broadcast

System. You know, that system they use to send a message to every player in-game at once? Surely you've seen it before. Probably received a message or two from it. But did you know it can host files as well? Files that can be downloaded from it by everyone who receives the message?" Bernstein smiled wider. "The AFBS as they call it, is a direct line to hundreds of millions of people. Can you imagine if this database – this evidence – were sent to each of them? Why, the Party's crimes would be undeniably exposed. That many people with evidence can't be stopped. Change would be inevitable." He paused for a moment, smiling directly at them, then nodded.

"Though, of course, there are two challenges that must be overcome for this plan to succeed. First, the AFBS can only disperse files that have been uploaded to Nova Online – I've taken care of that one for you. The second problem is the one I'm still trying to solve. It's the reason you needed to power level – and will likely need to do so again. It's the reason I've been trying to gather allies and confidants. It's the reason I haven't done all this myself yet."

"Well, get on with it!" Titus said.

The video projection couldn't hear him, obviously, but it paused momentarily before continuing.

"The AFBS can only be accessed from the heart of Warden Headquarters. Now, I doubt the Warden Corps would react kindly to my request to borrow their system for a quick broadcast. That's why I – er, I guess now you – have to take it by force."

## Chapter Three

"Take Warden HQ. By force." Zelda repeated the words for a third time. It still didn't sound any easier.

"Just that, huh?" Kaiden said, feeling the words constrict in his throat. He didn't know much about Warden HQ, but from what he knew about how well defended even a single carrier like the *Anakoni* was, he couldn't imagine HQ would be exactly a walk in the park. Zelda's shock only reinforced that idea.

"Oh, come on," Titus said, looking at them both. "After everything we've done, is this really that big a challenge? We'll need some muscle to help us, but how bad can it be? It's not like they have an army there."

Zelda winced and Titus frowned.

"Wait, do they? Do they have an army?"

"There aren't that many wardens," Kaiden said, thinking aloud. "There are millions of players in Nova. The Warden Corps is nothing compared to that number."

"We're not going at this with all of Nova at our backs, Kai," Zelda said. "Currently, the entirety of our force comes to a sum total of three. Besides, you both saw the fleet guarding the void tear. That was only forty, maybe fifty percent of the Warden Corps' navy. There's a lot more ground forces too." She paused, clearly thinking. When she spoke again, there was the slightest hint of hope in her tone. "Given, most wardens are usually on rotation, dispersed across the universe and working wherever they're stationed, so we have that going for us. As long as they're not tipped off that we're coming, the full warden force won't be waiting for us at HQ. That's... something."

"Okay, good!" Kaiden said, trying to be positive. "That's one advantage in our favor."

"It's still nowhere near enough." Zelda shook her head. "Look, I can't fault the logic of Bernstein's plan. As far as I can tell, it would work – in theory. But that's only if we could make it to the AFBS control panel. It only exists in-game and can only be accessed by a player standing directly in front of it. I just can't see a way for us to get to it. Not unless you two have a personal army I don't know about. And we don't even know what will be waiting for us at Warden HQ. I mean, the place could be a fortified maze. Say we did fight or sneak our way in, how would we find the AFBS? And how do we use it?"

"Storming Warden HQ and taking it by force? That'd be pretty much impossible," a voice chimed in from the back of the van. "Unless you had the help of a high-ranking warden with detailed knowledge of how the Corps operates and how HQ is laid out." Thorne struggled into a sitting position. "Oh, that's right, you do."

*How long has she been awake? How much did she overhear?*

"Though if you keep shooting me with knockout rounds and tying me up with – what are these? Seat belts? – I might have to reconsider my offer."

"We didn't ask for your help," Titus growled.

"But you do need it."

"Do we, though?" Kaiden asked. "We took the database despite your efforts to stop us. We unlocked it despite the entire Warden Corps hunting us."

"That's right. You did." Thorne nodded. "And I'm still impressed. But imagine how much easier all of that would have been if, instead of working against one another, we'd worked together." She drew out the last word. "I'm not your friend. Far from it, in fact. I get that. You don't know me; I get that, too. But consider this. Kaiden, you want to clear your name, be free again. Zelda, you want to free your parents, want to expose the Party's injustices. Titus, you want... well, I don't exactly know, but it probably starts with not being labeled a terrorist and actively hunted by the Party, yeah?" She looked at each of them in turn. "You'll get what you want – what you need – to carry on with your lives if that database gets dispersed to everyone." She nodded as if to the world beyond the van. "All I've ever wanted was to protect people. To make sure something like the Great Test never happens again. But the Party has become something just as bad. I can't let it continue like this. You don't have to trust me, because dispersing that database to the masses gives you what you want and gives me what I want. Why do we need trust when we have mutual self-interest?"

Silence followed her words. Kaiden bit his lip.

*She has a point. But, what? She just shows up after hunting us all this time and wants to switch sides? Wants to help us bring down the Party?*

"I don't buy it," Kaiden said, shaking his head.

"I agree," Zelda said, staring at Thorne as if she were a puzzle to solve. "We're missing something here."

Titus huffed. His mouth worked like he was chewing the inside of his cheek and contemplating something he didn't much care for.

"Mutual self-interest is how a lot of things got done on King Street," he finally said. "You don't have to like or trust who you're working with on a job as long as you both want the same thing."

"She's from the Party," Kaiden said, gesturing toward her. "They killed Bernstein, the rebels, Zelda's parents."

"Arrested Mr. and Mrs. Yoshida," Thorne corrected.

"Oh, great. Only arrested. Disappeared and taken to some unmarked prison. Much better."

"Kaiden's right," Zelda said. "This database Bernstein compiled, it's full of horror stories of what the Party has done. I haven't even dug that deep into it and already I can see that."

"And that *sickens* me," Thorne said, a hint of a growl creeping into her voice. "I've dedicated most of my life to the Party." She gritted her teeth, lips pulling into a scowl. "I fought through the

Great Test, that hellacious war, all for the ideas of the Party. I watched people I knew, people I loved, die in that hell. And then when peace – blood-soaked, hard-won peace – was finally achieved, I gave years of my life to building the Party. I've spent the last decade protecting it. People I loved died to put the Party in power, and now, after all that, I find out it was all a lie? All to put power-hungry maniacs like Moran in charge? No. It requires an answer. It *demands* a response. You don't understand the betrayal, the loss I feel right now.

"So, I get it. How could you possibly understand why I'm here? But I'm not asking you to understand my reasons and I'm not asking you to trust me. I'm asking you to let me help you, because right now, you're the best way I see to right the greatest wrong in this world since the Test."

Silence, then, for some time. Kaiden looked over to Zelda, then Titus. Both were frowning, and he didn't blame them.

"I... uh, well," he said, then stopped. Trusting Thorne felt wrong in every way. Working with her felt even worse. But was there a chance she was actually genuine? Had she really come to help?

A police siren sounded outside. Thorne looked toward the windshield, then cursed.

"That officer you stunned – you tied him up, right? Restrained him before you left so we'd have more time before he blew our cover?"

*We were in a hurry...*

"Well, we—" Kaiden began.

"Oh my god. You didn't." Thorne shook her head. "How have you three not been caught yet?" She cursed, then sucked in a deep breath. "You're wanted fugitives. Hunted in-game and out. You're living in a van that's hardly even shielded. You're low on food, you have no place to go, and you have barely enough money to even gas this thing up. Did I get all that right?"

Zelda reluctantly nodded.

"So let me help you." Thorne struggled against the seat belts binding her, then sighed. "Hell, keep me tied up if you want, but we need to move, *now*."

Another police siren outside, this one drawing nearer. Kaiden peered out a window and cursed.

"They're headed this way." And they were. At least four squad cars were zipping through the traffic lanes, lights flashing and sirens blaring. An armored SWAT vehicle followed them, heavily armed soldiers crouching in its open side door, guns in hand.

"I have reserve accounts, money I've tucked away under different names," Thorne began, speaking rapidly now. "Most of all, though, I have a place we can go. Somewhere secret, somewhere safe. But we have to go now. You can't delay any longer. You have to make a decision: work with me and bring down the Party, or let me the hell out of here. I'm not going down because you three couldn't get your heads straight." She took a deep breath and the glare on her face eased slightly. "So, what's it gonna be?"

# Chapter Four

"All right, make a turn northeast," Thorne said, directing Titus with a gesture from her recently unbound hand. "Not too much… there! That's the heading."

"This is it?" The big man slowed the van to a stop. Around them, wetlands stretched into the distance in all directions. "You're leading us into a swamp."

"Yeah, pretty much," Thorne said. Technically, around these parts they called it a bayou, but she'd never really seen the difference. All that mattered was her bunker was off the grid and hidden well out of anyone's way.

Thankfully, they'd made it out of the city and were now well beyond its suburbs. Basically in the middle of nowhere. There wasn't likely to be anyone around to recognize their vehicle, but all the same, they needed to get hidden.

"Hold this direction for two miles, then we'll come to an acre of trees blackened by fire a year or two back. I'll show you a good hiding spot for the van once we're there."

"I'm sorry, am I driving a getaway vehicle or exploring a new continent?" Titus asked. "You know we have GPS to give us exact directions? Don't need all this orienteering crap."

"Where we're going has no address," Thorne said. It was safer that way, after all.

"Okay, sure. But it has coordinates, right? I could put them in the van's computer and we can head right to it."

"The best way to make sure information stays safe is to keep it up here," Thorne said, tapping a finger to her forehead. A fact she'd learned all too well during her years tracking down dissidents for the Party. Everyone thought their offline databases were safe, but anything could be hacked. Anything except one's memory. No computer was breaking into that.

Titus grumbled, then called to the others who were huddled in the rear seats.

"Is it too late to change our minds about this?" he asked. "We can still ditch Thorne in the swamp and find our own hiding place, yeah?"

Neither Kaiden nor Zelda responded. They were too occupied with the database. Zelda had it open on her handheld console and they were flicking through it like mad, thoroughly exploring its contents.

"This thing is loaded," Kaiden murmured, clearly awed by the information Bernstein had acquired. Sooner or later, she needed to get a look at that database, Thorne knew. Realistically, she didn't need any more prompting to see what the Party had become, but all the same, she wondered just how deep the corruption ran.

"I'd be more excited about everything Bernstein gathered here if it all wasn't so terrible," Zelda said, opening another file on her console's screen. "Extortion of private customer data from just about every company of significance. Mass surveillance well beyond what's legal..." She spoke the crimes as she read them, glancing at the evidence coupled with each accusation before moving on. "Taking bribes from criminals. Extrajudicial imprisonment of citizens—"

"Well, that one sounds painfully familiar," Kaiden chimed in.

"Murder," Zelda read, the list growing still more severe. "Extreme collateral damage when responding to rebel activities."

Thorne winced at that accusation specifically. She couldn't help but think back to the day she'd gone to talk to Zelda's parents; to Werner busting in and arresting them, and then the bombing. How many innocents had died that day?

"Disappearing 'political radicals' and their family members. Operating black site detainment centers." Zelda shook her head. "It just goes on and on. If even half of this got out it'd be enough to bring down most of the Party's leadership. I knew Bernstein had dirt – we dug a lot of it up together – but I didn't know he had stuff like this."

"This the fire-damaged place?" Titus' question pulled Thorne's thoughts from the database. She glanced out the windshield.

"Yeah, that's it. See the old cypress tree just ahead? To the left? Yup, that one." She nodded as Titus angled the van toward it. "Take us just beside it, then ease us into that thicket. We can hide the van there. The bunker's just a short walk."

Walking through the swamp wasn't the most pleasant of experiences, but the further they kept the van from the bunker, the better. A lone vehicle abandoned in the swamp wouldn't raise too many eyebrows, but one parked next to a semi-hidden structure? That'd be a big fat red flag.

"Huh. Look at this." Zelda said, pointing something out to Kaiden on her screen. "Another one of those broken links. It's pointing to something that's not on the database again."

"Something Bernstein deleted, maybe?" Thorne asked. "Or was this still a work in progress? He didn't finish it?"

Kaiden and Zelda looked up at her in unison with less than friendly expressions on their faces. Clearly they didn't care for her listening in on the conversation.

"Forget I said anything," she said, holding up her hands.

*You're going to have to trust me eventually, though,* she added internally. They were right to be suspicious. Honestly, she couldn't blame them. But she was also experienced enough to know that when things were dire, you didn't turn down help, especially when you were desperate for it. Probably the trio didn't realize how much trouble they were in. They'd been in hot water when they'd had the locked cipher. Now, however, they had the unlocked database, and by slipping past Moran's fleet in-game they'd pissed him off. No doubt he was personally on their case now. She'd always known he was a man not to be trifled with, but with what he'd told her on the *Anakoni*, with what he'd revealed about his little shadow government... suffice it to say, if there was an embodiment of what was wrong with the Party, he was it.

"How's this?" Titus asked, easing the van to a stop tucked well into the trees.

"A bit further," Thorne said, waving him on. The branches were in close now, some scraping against the outside. A draping of stringy Spanish moss ran across the windshield as Titus really squeezed them in tight.

"Perfect," Thorne said when the branches scraping on the side sounded like they'd started taking the paint off. "Shut her down and grab your stuff. We're hiking from here."

"This is it?" Kaiden stared at the entrance to the bunker and slapped at a mosquito making a feast of his elbow.

"Doesn't look like much," Titus agreed.

"That's the point, guys," Zelda said, rolling her eyes. Thorne had to suppress a smirk. That was very much the point. Realistically, she hadn't expected to ever truly need the bunker, and she'd definitely never thought she might bring others to it. But now they were here, she found she was actually eager to show off her hard work, and maybe just the slightest bit proud. Sure, they were all fugitives at the center of the massive manhunt, but she'd prepped this bunker, bit by bit, on her days off for years now. She had been ready for war, famine or nuclear winter. All that preparation, all that paranoia, was finally about to pay off. It was a good feeling. Although, she had never expected to use it to hide from the Party itself.

"What is this place, anyway?" Kaiden asked, looking around at the small island. Though, it wasn't really an island so much as an acre or so of ground that was raised enough above its surroundings that it didn't flood every time it rained. Or rather, didn't flood entirely.

"The bunker's an old remnant from the Test," Thorne

explained, pushing through palm fronds and Spanish moss as she approached the entrance. "There's hundreds of them scattered throughout the country. Nearly all have been abandoned."

"Uh, yeah. I can see why," Titus said, waving away a banana spider the size of his hand.

"I've heard of these places," Zelda said, sticking close to Titus and letting his larger frame push the spider webs out of the way. "But they're super bare-bones, just designed as temporary shelter from the bombing raids that were common back then."

"Yeah, well, I've done some work on mine," Thorne said.

The entrance to the bunker was all that was visible above ground, and it was just a bunch of slate-gray concrete stained slightly green from the various plants and funguses growing up it. The door was metal, but looked just as dull and disused. Intentionally, of course.

Thorne leaned down to the rusty old combination lock. It clicked quietly as she turned the dial first one way, then back the other, then once more back again and stopped on the last digit. The lock came open with a click and the panel it'd been keeping shut slid open with a slight hiss. Thorne entered the quick fourteen-digit code on the keypad contained within, then stepped back with a nod.

The door groaned, bolts retracting inside as the passcode was accepted. A moment later, it swung open on creaky hinges. She'd like to have oiled them, but in the interest of keeping up the bunker's neglected appearance she'd been forced to leave the hinges in something approaching a state of disrepair.

"It's a bit damp," she warned, then led them inside and down the front stairs. "Hard to keep it dehumidified, and being below ground level in a swamp means it's a constant battle to keep the water out. But the air conditioning keeps it cool, there's plenty of food, and a fair bit of space." She gestured to the interior of the bunker like a parent showing off a child.

"Well, look at this," Kaiden said. "There's a whole apartment down here."

"Not bad," Zelda agreed.

Thorne felt a smile pull at her lips.

"In that corner there's the kitchen," she explained, pointing out the minute amount of countertop space, miniature sink, and a few cooking appliances. Really, the appliances were excessive considering the built-in pantry was filled with salvaged army rations that chemically boiled to heat themselves when dunked in water.

"There's also a low-energy fridge," she said. "Which is really just a fancy way of saying 'a box that's slightly darker and cooler than the rest of the bunker.' Got some bottled water reserves in there, but most of what's drinkable comes in through the exterior filtration system. Completely clean, just smells a bit of eggs thanks to all the sulfur in the swamp."

Thorne turned next to the corner across from the kitchen, which contained what she liked to think of as the living-dining room combo. Really, it was just a big, wooden table pushed up against one wall and with space for four chairs. Only one was set out at present.

"There are more chairs," she said. "But, well, I wasn't expecting company, so we'll have to dig them out of storage."

The last two corners of the room were taken up by the work-space: a desk she'd laboriously dragged down into the bunker, a few blank notebooks, and her backup VR headset. She'd never really used it – hadn't exactly slunk off into the deep swamp to work – but being disconnected from her job wasn't a luxury she'd been afforded. As a full-time warden, if something were to happen, she needed to have access to Nova no matter where she was – at work, at home, or in her hidden swamp bunker.

"We have a steady internet connection here, believe it or not," she explained. "Had to set up signal boosters in a chain, one every mile, all the way out to the nearest signal relay. Pain in the butt, tell you what. But it works. And unlike your van, every-thing here is properly shielded. And any incoming or outgoing data is redirected through the next town over so it looks like normal traffic."

"This is insane." Zelda looked dumbfounded.

"Yeah, man. Is doomsday prepping like your hobby or some-thing?" Titus asked.

She was so accustomed to this being her hobby that she'd forgotten it wasn't exactly a normal thing to do. Most people went to the beach during their time off, or hung out with friends – drinks at the bar and all that. But the Test had changed her, Thorne knew. How could she relax after the things she'd seen? How could she just trust that humanity would continue as normal and not break down into another world-rending war? No, some scars couldn't be forgotten. She'd seen the world go to shit once before. If ever it happened again, well, she'd made sure she would be ready.

"With the situation we're in right now, I'd say it worked out," she said, sparing them the sorry backstory.

Kaiden nodded. "Can't argue with that."

Thorne smirked, then pointed out the last feature of the bunker. Cut into the wall between the kitchen and dining room was an in-set doorway.

"Hallway to the bedrooms and bathrooms," she said. "Nothing fancy. Two in total with bunk beds in each. They're bolted in place so there wasn't much I could do about swapping them out, but I did update the mattresses, at least. They're... almost comfortable."

"Do the spiders get in frequently?" Titus asked with a shudder, still pulling webs from his face and neck.

"Just the small ones," Thorne said. "Though those are the most venomous."

"Well, that's just *fine*. You know, I've always wanted to die in some random swamp via spider bite."

"Oh, and make sure to check the toilets before you use them. Found a frog or two in there before..." She felt herself frown. "Still can't figure out how they're getting inside..." Bothersome little things had been plaguing her since day one.

She shook the thought away and looked back up at the wanted fugitives she was bringing into her emergency shelter.

"So... what do you say? Think this'll do the job?"

Kaiden shook his head disbelievingly.

"Seems as good a place as any to bring down the Party, I guess." He shook his head again. "Home sweet swamp bunker."

## Chapter Five

As it happened, the bunker wasn't so bad – for a place in the middle of a swamp and all.

Kaiden found himself pleasantly surprised. It took a few days to get the bunker fully functioning – not that they were in any particular hurry. Titus had died in their battle against the Void-lord and still had a few days left on his respawn timer. It gave them plenty of time to plot and plan while they fixed up the bunker.

All in all, Thorne had kept it in good shape. Even still, it had needed a bit of work before going fully online. The tech side was the most important to cover. They had to double check the internet connection was secure and ensure the system was holding a stable connection that would support four people online at once.

There were also more mundane things, like figuring out sleeping arrangements and rationing the food responsibly. Through it all, Kaiden kept a close watch on Thorne. She hadn't given them a reason yet to distrust her, and considering Zelda and Titus had agreed to let her watch Bernstein's message, it seemed like she was becoming part of the team. But that was a ruse; he knew it was. He'd let her get comfortable. If she was comfortable, she'd be more likely to make a mistake. To slip up and reveal what she was truly after.

"The AFBS can only be accessed from the heart of Warden Headquarters. Now, I doubt the Warden Corps would react kindly to my request to borrow their system for a quick broadcast. That's why I – er, I guess now you – have to take it by force," Bernstein's video message repeated. Kaiden stared across the bunker's table to where Thorne was seated. She nodded, apparently taking in everything Bernstein had said.

"I caught bits of it when waking up in the van but really wasn't cognizant enough to understand it all," she said, shooting an annoyed glance at Titus. Still sore about being stunned, undoubtedly. *Probably that hadn't felt very good*, Kaiden thought, remembering when he'd been tazed by the rebels.

"If keeping my gun makes you feel safer, that's fine," Thorne said to Titus. "But in the interest of us working together, don't shoot me with it again, yeah?"

The big man shrugged. "Don't give me a reason to."

"All right, all right. Everyone play nice," Kaiden said, giving them both stern looks. "We've agreed to join forces for the time being – as strange as that feels. But if this is going to work, we need to be focused on the same objective, not picking at one another." He looked at Titus. "Let's not stun Thorne again." He turned to Thorne next. "Please don't give us a reason to stun you."

"Seriously, though," Zelda added. "We don't have time to bicker, especially not with what I'm seeing online. The Party's stepped up their raids, searching for us no doubt. And word is there's a blanket curfew on the way. That's just speculation for now, but I wouldn't put it past them."

"No, that sounds right," Thorne said, leaning back in her chair and blowing out a breath. "Moran's sure to be pissed the database slipped through his fingers. If anything, this is just the beginning. The longer we hold the database, the more pressure he'll feel. His actions are only going to get more and more severe in response."

*That doesn't sound good.* Kaiden frowned. "How severe are we talking here?"

Thorne crossed her arms.

"Hard to say exactly, but if his shadow government is as powerful as he implied it was, then he can bring to bear the full power of the Party. And I don't see why he would hesitate to do so, considering that database," she nodded to the hard drive at the center of the table, "will bring down the Party if its contents are spread widely enough."

*It's past time the Party answered for its injustices.*

"We're on a timer, then," Zelda said. "We don't know how long, but every day we don't execute the plan to get this evidence out to the masses is a day the Party gets more desperate and more dangerous."

"Exactly," Kaiden said, nodding along. "So, let's get to work." He turned to Thorne. "What's it going to take to get us into Warden HQ and send the database to everyone in-game?"

*She's not actually going to answer truthfully, but let's hear what she makes up anyway.*

Thorne shook her head, then chuckled softly to herself.

"This isn't a joke," Titus said, scowling.

"No, I know it's not. It's just... this idea is insane. Possible, just maybe, but for the most part, insane. Bernstein was ambitious, you gotta give him that, eh?" She looked up at them, then cracked her knuckles. "But let's talk shop." She typed something into her handheld console, then projected a hologram into the air above the center of the table. It was an asteroid, vaguely transparent and with large, rigid structures seemingly jammed on to its surface.

"This," Thorne said, working her console's controls to adjust the view of the asteroid, "is Warden HQ. It's built on the asteroid Custos, which circles the known game universe in a forced orbit. It's big enough that, as you can see, considerable infrastructure has been built up on it." She tapped the screen and the view of the asteroid zoomed in on what appeared to be dry docks, vehicle garages, and bunkers complete with a frankly worrying amount of ground-to-air missile launchers mounted on top. The bunkers and the rest of the structures protruded from the surface of Custos as if half-sunken into it.

"The majority of Warden HQ infrastructure is beneath the

surface. The barracks, living spaces, training rooms, armories, and – of course – the command center where the highest-ranking wardens operate, are right in the center. The AFBS is housed in the next room over."

"Can you show us a schematic of that?" Kaiden asked. Seeing the outside of the base was good, but having knowledge of its inner workings would be even better.

"No can do," Thorne said. "That's not publicly available. But I've been there more than a few times. I know the inside of the rock well enough to guide us through it."

*Oh, well, isn't that convenient?*

"You're gonna need to teach us the route," Zelda said, squinting at the hologram asteroid as if she could peer inside it and see the way. "Fighting our way in is gonna be risky. If you die, we need to know where to go."

It was a test, Kaiden knew. If Thorne really was going to work with them then she needed to prove her worth.

"Plot out the route as simply as possible and we'll work on memorizing it. We're also going to need to know how to work the All-Frequencies Broadcast System."

"It's not complicated, really, but I agree," Thorne said. "Still, all this is well and good, but I think we're jumping the gun. None of this happens unless we can get into Warden HQ in the first place. That's not going to be easy."

"What about sneaking in?" Titus asked from across the table. "Don't get me wrong, I'm all for going in guns blazing, but why make things harder than they have to be?"

"This isn't a movie. There's no way to do that. No conveniently large enough air vents, no droids that can hack into the base's system and open doors for us. There're no backdoors, no side hallways. If we want in to this base, Bernstein's right. We have to do it by force."

*Damn.* Kaiden withheld a sigh. He'd expected that would be the case, but hearing the details of Warden HQ's defenses wasn't exactly encouraging. Assuming Thorne wasn't lying about everything, that was.

"And we're sure there's no other option?" Kaiden asked. "No other way to access the AFBS?"

"Bernstein would have accounted for it," Zelda said. "He knew what he was doing, and if this was the plan he settled on, then it must be the best one."

"She's right. And Bernstein was right." Thorne idly flicked her finger across the screen of her handheld console and set the hologram of the asteroid to spinning in a mad frenzy. "The Warden Corps knows how powerful access to the AFBS is. Nothing about it works remotely. It can only be operated from inside the command center."

"All right, so we go guns blazing. What kind of resistance should we be expecting?"

"And be as specific as possible, please," Zelda added. "How many wardens? How many ships, etcetera? We haven't even touched on how we're going to find allies to help with this, but before we do, it'll probably be good to understand what sort of firepower we need to bring."

"We need enough soldiers to punch a hole through the base. It doesn't have to hold long, but long enough for us to get to the AFBS and send a message. The soldiers with us are going to need to be pretty much max level. And, for that matter, so are we."

*That's a good point,* Kaiden thought. He'd had just about enough of being under-leveled in every fight. That they'd made it this far was a miracle, but they couldn't rely on luck and creative strategies to win every battle.

"The in-game level cap is sixty," Zelda said, running the numbers in her head. "We're all what, thirty-one right now?"

"Thirty-four here," Thorne added.

"So we need to gain twenty-six to twenty-nine levels before we even attempt this," Kaiden said. "That's a lot of grinding. And, as you said earlier, every day we waste is a day the Party grows more desperate. More dangerous."

"It sounds like we need a training montage," Titus said, grinning a little. A bit more like his usual self, then. Being around Thorne clearly had him on edge, and Kaiden couldn't blame him, but he had missed the levity the big man often brought to their otherwise dire situations.

Titus looked around the room as if waiting for something, then sighed.

"No upbeat rock song? No quick cuts to all of us killing countless mobs as our levels skyrocket? Dang." He huffed. "I guess that means we're doing this the hard way. One level at a time."

"The hard way, certainly," Zelda said. "But that doesn't mean we can't do it the smart way, too. We don't have time to waste just mindlessly grinding. Being max level won't count for anything if we don't have the allies to storm Warden HQ, so we should do both at once, or as much as we can."

"Like we did when preparing to attack the freighter," Kaiden said, thinking back to their strategy then. "Everywhere we go, we pick up as many missions as possible, then complete them while en route to where we need to be next."

"Exactly," Zelda said. "But this isn't a few levels we're talking about. We need to max our characters. We need to be on this grind hard."

"All right, then." Kaiden nodded. "Sleep is for the weak anyway, right? We'll push through until we hit max level. That's only one part of the solution, though. We still need to find allies. Other players crazy enough to attack Warden HQ with us – and a lot of them."

"Bernstein had some names in the database, didn't he?" Titus asked, gesturing toward the hard drive containing it. "A list of potential allies?"

"Some names of sympathetic individuals, some notes on powerful players he thought might be able to help, even some contact info for them, but nothing concrete," Kaiden said, remembering what Zelda had shown him. "It looked more like the result of a brainstorming session, but I don't think he made much headway on it."

"That's a good start, though," Thorne said, leaning forward. "We can work with that. Who'd he list?"

Zelda pulled up the database on her handheld console,

opened her mouth to speak, then stopped. She squinted at Thorne with suspicion.

"We're literally talking over the specifics of this plan in a bunker I own," Thorne said, rolling her eyes. "The database is here and so are you. If I wanted to call in the Party, don't you think I'd have already done it?"

*She has a point. Again.* Kaiden was getting awful tired of that being the case.

"This is all happening very quickly," he said, looking at Zelda, then Titus. And finally, Thorne. "You were the enemy for so long, it's hard to think of you as an ally now."

"Exactly," Zelda said, then shook her head as if pushing away the thought. "Trust isn't an easy thing to just hand out. Not after what we've been through."

"I get it," Thorne said, and her expression said as much, for whatever that was worth. "But I can't help you if we're not all on the same page."

Kaiden looked to Zelda. She met his eyes, and he nodded. She sighed, then did the same.

"There are four groups whose support must be won in order to take Custos by force," she said, reading from Bernstein's notes. "The first is Maximus."

"Yeah, that makes sense," Thorne said. "Top PVP guild in the game. If you showed up to a battle with them at your back, you wouldn't just be bringing fighters. You'd be bringing the most experienced PVPers."

"That sounds real good to me," Titus chimed in. "Everything is easier when you have the proper muscle backing you up. But how do we set up a meeting with the head honcho? He's the one we have to convince if we want them with us."

"Any chance you have a back channel or something?" Zelda asked Thorne.

"I've got nothing," she said with a shake of her head. "Shackled a few of his boys over the years – mostly when their PVP battles got out of hand – but beyond that, I might as well be a stranger to them."

"They have recruitment officers listed on their guild

website," Kaiden said, searching with his own handheld console. "We can friend one in-game and reach out."

"It's not ideal, but it'll have to do." Zelda looked down to Bernstein's notes again. "The second group we need on our side is the free wardens."

"Ooh, now that one I can do," Thorne said, leaning forward again. "They aren't organized or anything, but I've seen plenty of wardens graduate out of the program. Can pull up contact info for most of them, too. I know a few of them resent the Party, even if they did complete the program. With a bit of prying, I'd wager I could uncover more than a few whose interests would align with ours."

"Now we're talking!" Kaiden said. Considering the daunting obstacles ahead, a bit of progress was a huge relief. "But we have to be careful. If any are loyal to the Party, they could blow the whole plan."

"I'm not going to tell them specifics," Thorne said as if that should have been obvious. "Not until it's too late for the Party to react, at least. Do you know how many operations I've set up where secrecy was essential? Trust me on this one, Kaiden."

*'Trust' is a word getting thrown around an awful lot these past few days.*

"The third group is, well, not a group at all, but a single player," Zelda interrupted before Kaiden had a chance to respond. "I've heard of him before: 'Odditor.' Wasn't aware he ran any factions, though. And Bernstein didn't list, or didn't know, which they were. All the links to them in the database point to empty folders."

*Odditor? What kind of player name is that?* Kaiden wondered. Though, to be fair, when it came to anonymous online accounts, people had a penchant for coming up with the strangest names. In comparison to some he'd seen, 'Odditor' was pretty tame.

"Who is this guy?" Titus asked. "And what does he do that makes him important enough to be on the same list as the top PVP guild and free wardens?"

"Odditor is kind of a figure from Nova folklore," Zelda explained. "He's been playing since the beginning. Max level now, and all that, but mostly a hermit. A lot of people know him because he streams these crazy obstacle course type events using a menagerie of monsters he keeps on his private moon."

"He makes the monsters run obstacle courses?"

"He makes players run the obstacle courses... while trying not to get eaten by the monsters."

*Huh. Kind of like Marty's arena, maybe a bit more sadistic. Does sound kind of cool, though...*

"Really, I don't know who would tune in to watch it," Zelda said. "People are weird."

"Oh, yeah. Totally." Kaiden nodded profusely. "I don't know who would want to watch that."

"Anyway," Zelda said. "Bernstein seems to think the guy is important. Says here: 'Odditor lives up to his name. An odd fellow, to be sure, but one with numerous connections. On top of the guilds he runs (link), I believe he's also a member of The Syndicate (link), and a highly ranking one at that. Perhaps even a founding member.'" Zelda cut Titus off as he tried to speak. "I know what you're going to ask, but the links are broken. There's been a few like that throughout the database. Stuff Bernstein didn't finish, I guess. It's possible he hadn't finished this data-base before he got caught. Probably, it was never meant to be totally completed, but was continuously growing as he learned more."

"What's 'The Syndicate?'" Titus asked.

"More folklore, but this time it's nonsense," Thorne said. "We always heard rumors about 'The Syndicate' in the Corps. They're supposed to be some secret group of powerful players. Puppet masters, pulling strings behind the scenes." She laughed. "They're just a myth the criminal NPCs prattle on about when they get caught, which has got the players thinking they're real. There's no evidence to support any of it."

"Maybe they're just really good at staying quiet," Titus said with a shrug. "That's the smart way to run an operation."

"If there was a secret group of powerful players running things behind the scenes, the Warden Corps would know about it."

"Well, you're not going to like the last name on this list, then," Zelda said, frowning at Thorne.

Having seen the database on the flight over, Kaiden knew what came next.

"The Syndicate," he said.

Titus laughed and Thorne rolled her eyes.

"Yeah, okay. Well go ahead and strike that one off the list," she said. "We'll brainstorm a different faction to replace them. Maybe even to replace all of these, if necessary. There's still a chance none of these people are crazy enough to join us."

"Bernstein said these were the best options," Zelda said. "We need to listen to him. He's gotten us this far."

"*We've* gotten us this far," Titus said.

Zelda looked offended. "With essential help from Bernstein."

"I'm sure that's the case," Thorne said, focusing on Zelda. "But all I'm saying is everyone is fallible. Everyone makes mistakes. We can't just take Bernstein at his word during every step of the process. There needs to be room to adapt, to change as circumstances dictate."

"That sounds like a whole lot of uncertainty to me," Zelda fired back. "Bernstein knew what he was doing."

"Bernstein's dead," Thorne snapped, then winced. "I didn't mean it like that."

But Zelda was red in the face, nostrils flared.

"He's dead because of the Party. Because of *your* Party."

"We've all made mistakes. I'm owning up to mine and doing something about them." Thorne spoke calmly, precisely, but there was clearly a restrained anger beneath the surface. "And I'm not about to let this plan fail because of some blind devotion to the memory of a man. A smart man, undoubtedly, but we have to trust ourselves to make the right decisions going forward."

"You sure bring up 'trust' a lot for someone who still worked for the Party less than a week ago."

Thorne clenched one hand into a fist, then exhaled a long breath through her nose.

"Guys!" Kaiden shouted before she could stoke the fire

anymore. "Calm down." He gave Thorne a long look, then a similar one to Zelda. "This is stressful. Believe me, I know. This plan is damn near impossible. But it is a plan. A way forward. With the Party crackdown going on outside and the manhunt for us all not slowing down anytime soon, we don't have time to spend here bickering." He tried to soften his tone. "There's a ton of stuff up in the air still. I get it. But the framework Bernstein set up is our best place to start," he said, nodding toward Zelda. "Even if we need to adjust on the fly." He turned to Thorne. "But we'll discuss and agree on those decisions as they arise."

Thorne gave a stiff nod at that.

"Good," Kaiden said. He took a deep breath, then tried to shake the tension from his mind. "Guys, we can do this. I know we can. It's not going to be easy, but when has it ever? We've made it this far, right?" He gave a small smile, hoping someone would join him. Titus, at least, gave a small nod. The big man had been locked out of the game for a week and was eager to jump back it, despite the daunting task ahead.

"Then let's get to work. We need to log back in, group up, and get this plan going." He clapped his hands together, trying to get them excited. "So, who's ready? Let's go kick some ass!"

Thorne held up a finger.

"That's all well and good – and I'm all for it. There's just one small complication."

Kaiden frowned as she spoke.

"The last time I logged off was on the *Anakoni*, surrounded by wardens. When I get back in-game, there's a good chance there's going to be a welcoming party waiting for me – and not the happy sort."

## Chapter Six

"Remember, if you don't hear from me within an hour, I've likely been Shackled. One of you will need to log out and disconnect my headset, otherwise I'll be stuck in there," Thorne said, feeling the gravity of her words as she spoke them. Odds were this would be the last time she logged in to her character. If the wardens Shackled her – and there'd certainly be an attempt to – there would be no rescue. She'd have to make a new character. Start over from scratch.

"We'll be ready," Kaiden said from across the room. He, Titus, and Zelda were booting up their headsets around the dining table. Thorne was at her desk doing the same.

She took a deep breath to steady her nerves.

"All right, then. See you on the other side, eh?"

Kaiden and Titus nodded. Zelda ignored her, still hot from the argument. Admittedly, that could have been handled better, Thorne knew. She hadn't meant to belittle Bernstein – clearly Zelda admired him – but they also couldn't risk—

Thorne stopped herself. There wasn't time to get into all that now. She needed to be clearheaded for what was to come.

"Good luck, everyone," she said, then pulled on her headset.

~

**Welcome to Nova Online.**

The text faded into view, then back out. Next, it would drop her into Nova. She'd seen the welcome screen so many times it all felt natural; the few seconds' pause after she launched Nova, then the welcome text, then the game. The world would materialize around her, would build itself up pixel by pixel in the blink of an eye, and she'd be in Nova Online once again.

Except that didn't happen. The darkness surrounding her remained until another message appeared.

**Log in unsuccessful. Account has been locked.**

*Locked? What the hell?* In all her time as a warden she'd never had trouble with this sort of thing.

**A password reset has been sent to the email address on file along with instructions to unlock your account.**

*You're kidding me, right? I don't have time for this!* But there was no way around it. Thorne grumbled as she minimized the game and used the VR headset to find the email, follow the instructions therein, and unlock her account.

**Welcome to Nova Online.**

The message faded into view as she relaunched the game. A moment later, it was replaced with a familiar view: the hangar of the *Anakoni*. A place that had, for some time now, felt like home. From the looks of things, though, that was no longer the case.

"She's here! Hammers at the ready, everyone!"

A line of wardens stood waiting for her. Seven in total, fully armed and armored. Thorne shook out her arms and reached for her hammer.

*Two blasters, two shielders, and three power wardens,* she thought, taking in their numbers. *Levels twenty-nine, twenty-eight, thirty, thirty-four, twenty-one, twenty-five, and thirty-five respectively.* Some lower than her, one higher. Mostly that was thanks to the *Anakoni* being in a low-level system. Not that it made much difference. Odds of seven to one were pretty much insurmountable even without taking levels into account.

And then there was the problem of the shuttles.

Thorne grimaced as she looked up at them. The side of the hangar she was on had been cleared, which left her no place to hide from the two shuttles hovering above. They were each tilted down, weaponry at the ready while their pilots watched through the windshields.

"What's this all about?" Thorne asked, trying to look surprised.

*The shuttles look like the strong point, but they're a weakness,* she thought, a plan already forming. A desperate one, and not likely to work, but a plan nonetheless. *There's no winning this fight on the ground, but if I can force my way on to a shuttle it's my best chance to make it out alive. Heroic Leap will get me up to one of them, then I just have to bash open the door before the other shoots me off…*

The plan was ridiculous, but it was the best she had.

"You know very well what this is all about," a voice shouted, pulling Thorne from her plotting. It was a voice she recognized. Thorne looked toward it with a frown.

**Dawson**
**Warden Drill Sergeant**
**Class: Power Warden**
**Faction: Warden Corps**
**Level: 32**

Dawson. A proficient leader, talented drill sergeant, and as loyal to the Corps as any. She'd marked him for promotion for his excellent work thus far, though the way things were shaking out, she didn't see herself handing out any more promotions in the future. His addition to the enemy ranks made it eight against one, not counting the two shuttles. The already insurmountable odds were being stacked even more against her.

One of the blast wardens fired a shot and Thorne ducked

behind her buckler shield. Her health bar flashed and a bit of damage trickled through, but that wasn't the point of the attack. You couldn't log out of Nova when in combat. The attack officially marked the start of a combat session as far as the game was concerned.

*They don't want me leaving. I'm sure they'll go for Shackle as soon as my health is low enough.*

"You'll have to forgive us, Captain, but orders are orders," Sergeant Dawson said.

"Don't waste time explaining yourself to her," another warden said.

**Tarsin**
**Warden Colonel**
**Class: Blast Warden**
**Faction: Warden Corps**
**Level: 21**

*Colonel Tarsin? Who the heck is that?* Colonel wasn't a rank frequently handed out in the Corps. Thorne knew all the ranking officers of note and she'd never heard of a Colonel Tarsin. Especially not at such a low level.

He was a wiry man, with long hair tucked into his helmet but still sticking from beneath it in several frazzled strands. His expression looked equally frazzled, though he was trying to hide it behind what Thorne figured was supposed to be cool confidence. Looked more like he was suffering from indigestion.

"You have your orders. Now see to them," the colonel commanded.

There were several grumbles, and Thorne cocked her head to the side at that. That was strange. Since when did wardens complain about their orders?

"Don't question me!" Tarsin barked. "Do your jobs!"

Several of his soldiers shook their heads, but Dawson clapped his hands and they fell into line. The shield wardens locked their shields together, the blast wardens took aim, and the power wardens, including Sergeant Dawson, raised their hammers.

"You're wanted on charges of treason, aiding and abetting known terrorists, and endangering the safety of the public," Sergeant Dawson said.

*So that's what they're pushing, huh? Straight from Moran, no doubt.*

"Quite a list there," Thorne fired back. "Apparently I've been busy."

"Apparently."

*I need thirty charge to Heroic Leap on to the closest shuttle. Any extra charge I'll dump into breaking down the door and getting inside.*

She checked her charge bar. Her shield had gained five charge from the shot the blast warden had taken to trigger combat.

*Twenty-five to go, then. If I get in close to the wardens, the shuttles will have to hold fire. That'll be step one. Hopefully I can live long enough to make it to step two...*

Thorne raised her hammer.

"Well, what are we waiting for? Let's do this."

Chapter Seven

**Welcome to Nova Online**

"Finally!" Kaiden almost shouted as he loaded into the game and spawned inside the *Veritas II*. Titus and Zelda appeared next to him a moment later, their characters glowing for a moment as they finished loading in.

"My account was locked," Kaiden said. "What was that all about?"

"Same," Titus said, a frown plastered across his face.

"That makes three of us, then," Zelda said. "That sounds coordinated. Almost as if—"

"Captains!" a friendly voice called out. "It's a pleasure to have you back."

Acton was striding toward them from the cockpit. It hadn't been that long since he'd seen him last, but given everything that had transpired, it sure felt like it. Not to mention it just felt good to be back in Nova Online. In the real world it was all hiding and plotting, running and looking over his shoulder. In Nova, he could defend himself. In Nova, he was strong. Strong enough to maybe – just maybe – bring down the Party.

"The ship wasn't the same without you," Acton said, gesturing to the room around them. "For one, we haven't had to do anything even remotely suicidal."

"Yeah, well, don't get used to that," Kaiden said with a laugh.

"He's right. We've work to do," Zelda added with a sharp nod.

The first officer straightened at the mention of work.

"Of course. Very good," he said, then gestured out the cockpit windshield. "If you look outside, you'll notice absolutely nothing of distinction. That's because, per your last orders, we've taken the ship 'somewhere out of the way.'"

"And where is that?" Kaiden asked, peering out at a vast expanse of featureless, empty space.

"Dead space. Away from any relevant stars, out of the shipping lanes, and far from any combat zones. We are, functionally, in the middle of nowhere."

*Yeah, I guess that qualifies as safe.*

"The ship's still a fair bit banged up from the excitement at the void tear," Zelda said, reading the information displayed on the monitor on the near wall. "We're going to need to get that repaired. What's the nearest station that could handle it?"

Acton narrowed his eyes.

"With all due respect, Captain, but we're not expecting any more... excitement, are we? Or should I ready the crew?"

Kaiden chuckled at that. "Nothing so crazy as playing bait and flying between two warring fleets," he said. "All the same, I can't promise easy flying either."

Acton nodded. "In that case, we'll set course for the nearest station," he said, then patted the pilot on the shoulder. "See it done, yes?"

"Yes, sir!"

"Actually," Kaiden said as a thought occurred to him. "Set course for the nearest turen station. Our good standing with them might be necessary. We'd like to avoid any run-ins with the Warden Corps."

"Very good, Captain."

"Oh, and Acton?" Kaiden asked after a glance toward Zelda. "Which of our current crew would you say is the safest?"

"The safest, sir?"

"Least likely to die," Titus corrected.

Acton seemed confused at the thought, and Kaiden found he couldn't blame him. To be fair, it was an odd question. But the request attached to it was going to be just as odd.

"Well, I suppose if the ship were to be destroyed, we'd all die. Disregarding that..." He thought for a moment. "Were the shields to go down, the cockpit would be a prime target for an attacking ship. Sias," he said, nodding to the pilot, "and I would be in a high-risk area. Likewise, were we to be boarded, the remains of our own boarding crew – much depleted from our previous *adventure*, I might add – would engage the trespassers. Thus, I suppose our 'safest' crew members would be the mechanics and core engineer. Their stations are deep inside the ship and their roles do not require them to participate in active combat."

"But an unstable core is volatile and prone to exploding, right?" Zelda asked. "So I wouldn't want to trust our core engineer with this job."

"That just leaves the general ship mechanics, then," Kaiden said.

"All right, then," Titus said and gestured toward the exit of the cockpit. "Let's go have a chat with them."

"Braker, Johnson," Kaiden said, making sure his words were very clear as he spoke to the two NPC mechanics. "You understand what we've told you, right?"

"Got a ship needs fixin', I'm your man," Braker said in what seemed to be his favorite of his extremely limited programmed responses.

"We'll keep it shipshape down here, Captain," Johnson said.

Titus laughed. Kaiden sighed.

"Lighten up," Titus said. "It's never going to come to this. You really think someone's going to not only manage to find this ship, but also board it, defeat us, *and* have the good sense to check the crew for the database?"

"I really hope not," Kaiden said with a glance toward the mechanics.

To be fair, it was a good plan, though it'd sounded better when Zelda pitched it. There was only one copy of Bernstein's database in-game and it had to be kept safe. Taking it into a PVP zone would mean if its keeper died, the database could be looted. That was an unacceptable risk. So, the answer was clear: keep the database out of PVP zones. But how was that possible when everyone was going to be needed in the days to come? Well, why did a player need to hold the database? Why not give it to the least likely of the crew to die? It made good sense.

Looking at Johnson and, specifically, Braker – who they'd entrusted the database to – Kaiden was starting to think maybe it wasn't the best plan after all.

*I don't have a better one, though.*

"Even if we get boarded, and we get defeated, and whoever does all that thinks to search the crew, they still won't be able to loot the database unless the ship is in a PVP zone," Zelda said. "And Acton won't let that happen. He has his orders. He'll self-destruct the *Veritas II* long before any boarders take control of it."

"No, no, I get all that," Kaiden said, swallowing his doubts. "It's just..." He gestured to Braker. "I'm worried he doesn't understand everything we've told him. It seems a bit... above his pay grade."

Braker gave a sharp nod. "Ship's running just fine, Captain," he said.

"Braker," Titus said, leaning in close. "All you have to do is your job. Don't worry about the item we traded you. We'll come get it back whenever we need it. Got it?"

Braker nodded again.

"Got a ship needs fixin', I'm your man."

"See?" Titus held out a hand. "He's got this, no problem."

Kaiden sighed and started back toward the bridge.

"I hope so. It just feels wrong, giving up the database."

"We're not giving it up. We're protecting it," Zelda said. "Trust me, I don't love the idea either, but you know what I like even less? Carrying that database into a PVP zone."

*Fair enough.*

"Anyway, we can't worry about it now," Zelda said. "We have to keep thinking ahead. You all sent friend requests to Maximus' head recruiting officer, right?"

"Sent," Kaiden affirmed, then checked in the game's social window.

**Friend request to Recruz: sent**
**Status: awaiting response**

In the interest of protecting players' privacy, you couldn't directly message someone in Nova unless they were on your friends list. Well, you could, but it'd go to their spam folder, and considering the amount of spammers advertising mostly less than legitimate services, who checked their spam folder these days?

"No response here, either," Titus said. "You think maybe he didn't see the request?"

"I think he's a busy guy," Zelda said. "Remember, we skipped the regional recruiters and went straight to the head recruiting officer for one of the biggest guilds in-game. He'll get back to us, but it probably won't be quick. Don't worry about it. In the meantime, let's get this ship fixed." She peered through one of the hull windows and toward the approaching cluster of lights that was a turen space station. "And then grab any quests we can. While Thorne's figuring out her... situation on the *Anakoni*, we might as well get a head start on some grinding."

"I wonder how she's doing?" Kaiden mused. From how she'd described things, it sounded likely she was going to be making a new character. "I can't imagine she logged on to many friendly faces."

## Chapter Eight

The shuttle on the left opened fire. Thorne sprinted forward; shield raised to block what little of the damage she could. Except, it wasn't firing at her.

*Huh?*

She looked up to find the shuttle on the left had turned its guns on the one on the right. The wardens seemed caught by surprise as well, their eyes wide as one shuttle obliterated the other.

The defending ship's shields flared to life, flashing with each impact as round after round screamed through the hangar. Under the direct barrage and from so close, the shields didn't hold out long. Just about long enough for the pilot to spin the shuttle to face the assault, then catch the full force of the attack on the nose.

Chunks of armor and metal were blasted off the shuttle, and as Thorne watched, the health bar above the ship ticked away in a constant stream of damage. She could imagine the alarms going off inside it.

*Shields offline! Hull integrity low!*

"Who's piloting that thing?" one of the wardens shouted. "Do we fire on it, sir? Sir?"

Sergeant Dawson wasn't responding, though.

"Lieutenant!" Colonel Tarsin shouted up at the firing shuttle.

"What the hell are you doing? I demand you stop!" Clearly this hadn't been part of the plan. "Stop firing!"

*All the better for me.* Thorne tightened her grip on her hammer, then continued her charge toward the distracted wardens. She didn't understand what was happening, but it didn't take a strategist to see she could bend it in her favor. Maybe her odds had just become a bit less insurmountable.

"Sir!" One of the blast wardens was up in Sergeant Dawson's face now. "Orders, sir?"

A message appeared in Thorne's vision.

**DM from: Dawson**
**"Good to have you back, Captain. This'll take just a moment."**

*What?* Thorne hesitated, trying to understand the message. A moment later, its meaning became clear.

Sergeant Dawson swung his hammer in a rising blow and caught the blast warden in front of him right under the chin. The surprised soldier staggered back, then raised his hammer-gun and fired.

Sergeant Dawson blocked the blast with his buckler-like shield, then swung again and again, driving the warden back.

"This is treason, Sergeant!" Colonel Tarsin shouted, then gestured to the rest of the wardens. "Take him in, too."

The wardens seemed to hesitate again, but the sight of Dawson attacking one of their own spurred them to motion a second later.

Thorne didn't waste any time trying to make sense of everything. Clearly circumstances here had changed, but the pressing matter was to attack, so she did.

The wardens were just starting to respond to Sergeant Dawson's surprise onslaught when Thorne reached them. She tore into the back of Colonel Tarsin first, landing two solid hammer strikes to the back of his helmet.

**Critical hit!**

**+50% damage (Headshot)**

**Critical hit!**
**+50% damage (Headshot)**

The colonel's health bar flashed, then dropped to around sixty-five percent, but Thorne wasn't interested in the damage so much as the charge she gained with each strike. Her passive ability, Improved Aggressive Mindset, gained her charge equal to fifteen percent of the damage dealt in each attack.

Colonel Tarsin spun and fired a Scatter Shot full into Thorne's chest. She moved her shield to block as much of it as possible. Lasers exploded against her, draining her health bar, but those that hit her shield filled her charge bar as well.

Another attack from the blast warden landed, and Thorne watched her health bar drain even further at the impact. Not much, though; Tarsin was several levels below her.

She doubled down on her attack, trying to throw off her opponent's aim. That was the key to beating blast wardens – you had to stay right up on them. Their attacks were all long-ranged and they usually took a moment to fire. In comparison, swinging a hammer took no time at all. And for whatever reason, this Colonel Tarsin was only level twenty-one. That didn't make any sense, but it did make him an easy opponent to kill.

Sergeant Dawson was surrounded by his own wardens now, taking attacks from all sides. He was getting buried under a barrage of Scatter Shots and Improved Chain Furies. Lasers exploded around him and hammers fell in a constant stream of damage. Dawson's armor was crackling with energy and his own attacks lashed back at his numerous assailants in a frenzied blur.

*He's activated Through the Breach*, Thorne figured. *Doubles movement speed and reduces damage taken by thirty percent for ten seconds.*

Even still, that wouldn't be enough. No one could survive the onslaught he was facing.

The shuttles were exchanging fire, but not for much longer by the looks of it. The one that had attacked first still had its shield active while the other was missing large chunks of its hull. What was still attached looked like swiss cheese.

Throne glanced down to her charge bar. Fifty-four percent.

*Plenty for Heroic Leap. Time to book a ride out of here.* She looked up to the shuttle which had attacked first and began to line up her jump.

An explosion shook the hangar as the damaged shuttle hit zero percent hull integrity. It fell out of the air and slammed into the deck, then exploded in a crackling blue ball of energy as its core detonated. Thorne flinched away from the blinding light as splash damage tickled her health bar. The rest of the wardens had been closer to the blast, though, and took fifteen to twenty percent damage each.

"Now the rest of 'em, El!" Sergeant Dawson shouted.

*El?* Thorne paused at that. *Who's El?*

Sergeant Dawson leapt into the air and raised his hammer high. *Heroic Leap,* Thorne thought at first, then recognized the collection of energy crackling in his hammer.

*No.* She smiled. *Much better. Earth Shatter.*

Sergeant Dawson came down like a meteor and his hammer with him. When it struck the ground a shockwave burst outward, sweeping over the wardens surrounding him. They took no damage, but the attack knocked them to the ground.

"My turn," she said, then called to mind what was sure to be a devastating ability when used against stunned foes.

**Ability: Improved Chain Fury**
**Your combat prowess allows you to chain attacks together. For the next 5 seconds, each attack deals an additional 20% damage for every successful attack before it.**
**Cost: 50 charge**
**Cooldown: 2 minutes**

Thorne activated the ability and her hammer began to shimmer as energy manifested around it in the form of glowing chains.

"No!" Sergeant Dawson rushed toward her.

She took aim at him on instinct, but he slid into place beside her then raised his shield toward the stunned wardens.

"What're you—"

"Hit 'em, El!" Sergeant Dawson shouted.

The still-flying shuttle turned its guns on the wardens – who were trying to climb back to their feet – and let loose. The hangar resounded with screaming lasers as the twin six-barreled guns mounted under the wings of the shuttle held nothing back.

The health bars of the stunned wardens plummeted in unison as metal and smoke was blasted into the air. The floor of the hangar itself buckled and groaned as it started to glow a molten red.

**Blast Warden Tarsin assisted kill - 2,000 EXP gained!**

The message flashed on Thorne's screen as the health bar of the colonel dropped to zero. At the same time, the others died as well. Thorne hadn't actually engaged them so the game didn't give her credit for the kills, but six more death notifications trickled in across her screen.

When the last of the wardens went down, the shuttle let off its guns. Their spinning barrels slowed, then stopped.

"Ha! Now that was a thing of beauty!" Sergeant Dawson cheered, pumping a fist in the air.

The shuttle spun around, then lowered to the deck and opened its rear door. A moment later, a figure stepped into view.

**Ellenton**
**Warden Lieutenant**
**Class: Blast Warden**
**Faction: Warden Corps**
**Level: 29**

"Enjoy the show, Captain?" she said, a smirk stretched across her face. "Took you long enough to log back in. We were starting to wonder if you ever would."

Thorne lowered her hammer, frowning at the lieutenant. She looked at Dawson next and started to piece things together.

"Why help me?" she finally managed, asking the first of the many questions swirling in her mind.

"Things have gotten... weird around here lately," Lieutenant Ellenton said.

"We'll explain on the *Borrelly*," Sergeant Dawson said. "Best get moving before reinforcements show up."

## Chapter Nine

"I suppose I should say thanks," Thorne said as the *Borrelly* rocketed into the abyss of space. "But you realize what you've done, right? Turning on the Corps like that, killing a colonel?" She shook her head. "There's no going back from this."

"We're well aware," said Sergeant Dawson. Or was he just Dawson now? He produced a sleek black shard from his inventory and inserted it into the collar all wardens wore around their neck as part of their armor. He turned the key with a click and the collar fell away. As it did, his character's status updated.

**Dawson**
**Free Warden**
**Class: Power Warden**
**Faction: Unaffiliated**
**Level: 32**

Dawson looked down at the collar lying on the floor.

"Never thought I'd do that. Always thought the Corps was my calling." His voice hardened with his next words. "But this isn't the Corps I signed up for. Not anymore."

"Things have changed since you disappeared during the battle at the void tear," Ellenton explained, still piloting the ship but craning her neck to one side so Dawson could unlock her collar as well. It clattered to the floor and Dawson kicked it under a seat, then offered the key to Thorne.

A week ago, she would have hesitated to take it. Would have had to stop and consider the consequences of using the key and becoming a free warden. But not now. She'd committed herself to this course, had joined up with Kaiden and his friends, and now – well, now there was no room for uncertainty. She took the key and broke her vow to always support the Warden Corps.

Her collar fell away with a soft click. Anticlimactic, almost. Probably she should have felt more emotional about it, but knowing what the Party had done, what it'd become, there was no doubt this was the correct course. She might have made a vow to the Corps, but first she'd made a vow to serve the people. When those two conflicted, picking between them wasn't much of a choice at all.

**Congratulations! You have been released from the warden program and are now a free warden. You retain your character, along with all gear and experience collected. The *Anakoni* will no longer be your respawn point upon death, but the last large city, outpost, port, or settlement you visited prior to dying. Welcome to the full Nova Online experience!**

"You feel any lighter?" Ellenton asked from the pilot's seat.

"I feel like I've just declared war against the Party and all of its supporters," Thorne said. "And so have you. But why? That's what I don't understand. Why did you help me?"

"It's like Dawson said earlier," Ellenton answered, talking over her shoulder while flying the shuttle. "The Corps has changed. You know Moran's always been the power-hungry bureaucrat. More concerned with moving up in the Party than running the Warden Corps. But hey, fine by me, I always said. We still got the job done when we needed to, for the most part. But when Kaiden and his friends attacked you on the *Anakoni*, something changed. The Party branded them traitors, rebels, terrorists."

Thorne could only see the profile of her face, but it was enough to see a questioning frown stretch across the pilot's features. "Now, I hadn't known them long, but they struck me as a pretty alright bunch. Rebels? Doubtful. Terrorists? No way, Jose. That didn't sit right with me, but hey, I was just a lowly lieutenant, right? What do I know? Then there was that nonsense at the void tear – you know, when the dark turen decided to play demolition derby with our fleet? Yeah, ever since that happened and you disappeared in the middle of it, Moran's gone off the deep end. Says you're a traitor now." Ellenton laughed and shook her head. "Then the story came down the line that you let yourself be bested by Kaiden and his friends to cover their escape. And with classified information, no less. They said you were working with the resistance the entire time. Now, I didn't think Kaiden and his bunch were terrorists, but I knew for darn sure you weren't. So I said to myself 'El, this has the stink of Party politicking all over it.' From then on, things only got worse."

"Worse is being too gentle," Dawson said, then cracked his knuckles angrily. "Moran started showing up in-game all the time. Wanted to be a hands-on leader all of a sudden. Wanted to bring his own personal henchmen with him, too." Dawson hiked a thumb over his shoulder. "That *colonel* you saw back there? Tarsin?" He laughed. "That moron hadn't played Nova for more than a week before today. Hadn't joined the Corps either. Then, all of a sudden, him and a ton like him – not even worthy to be ensigns – start popping up. Came 'highly recommended' by Moran, too. Got appointed officer ranks right away. Ranks they didn't – and don't – deserve. They've been superseding the authority of every warden from lieutenant to general since. It used to be rank counted for something. Was a thing to be respected. But now, all that seems to matter is whether you kowtow to Moran or not."

*Colonel Tarsin? That level twenty-one's the captain of the* Anakoni. *And Moran expects experienced career wardens to take orders from him?*

Dawson was pacing now, fists clenched. "Now, I like to think of myself as a tolerant individual. I try to be reasonable. Undermining the integrity of my Corps, though? That's a fine way to piss me off. And then there's..." He paused and the anger drained from his face a moment. Looked like he was caught up in a memory. "And then there's the crackdown."

Ellenton nodded solemnly as he said it.

"They haven't just gone after people close to Kaiden and the others. The Party's using this crackdown as an excuse to go after anyone and everyone. They took my neighbor's kid a couple nights ago. Now, I'm not gonna say the boy was a saint, but he wasn't a danger to anyone. Just stupid kid stuff, a bit of anti-party graffiti – typical rebellious phase. Happens to the best of us. Didn't stop him from being disappeared in the middle of the night, though." Dawson shook his head. "I'd always heard rumors of that sort of thing happening, but rumors are rumors, you know? And besides, if it did happen, the criminals that got brought in probably deserved it. But this? This was different. They damn near took the whole family. And for what? Didn't even have a warrant. Seems they don't need those anymore."

"Things are changing, and fast," Ellenton said. "Worst they've been since... well, since the Test, I figure. Dawson's not the only one who's seen these new abuses of power. Hell, I saw a guy arrested just for being a patron of that restaurant you liked. You know, that soup and sub place? Since you went dark, anyone who knew you – or was what they considered 'too close' – was at the least taken in for questioning. We both certainly were."

"Who took you in?" Thorne asked, mind reeling with questions and struggling to keep up with everything she'd missed in the last few days.

"Some ass named Werner," Ellenton said with a shrug.

"Things are changing, and very much not for the better," Dawson grunted.

"How deep does this sentiment run?" Thorne asked, mind filling with more questions by the minute. She'd expected Moran would have labeled her a traitor and figured some wardens would find that suspicious, but it seemed like things were considerably farther along than that. Not to mention the Party acting against their own laws, taking in anyone even suspected of something illegal. Since learning Werner and Moran's true nature she knew such things were possible, but even then, they'd been subtle. Kept quiet.

And what was the deal with these jumped-up officers? The whole thing sounded like a takeover of the Corps. No doubt these new 'officers' were people like Werner, loyal to Moran and actively serving the interests of his shadow government.

"I couldn't say for certain how many others share our point of view," Dawson said. "Few are willing to speak out of turn, what with the purges and all."

*Purges? What?*

"Oh yeah, that," Ellenton said. "Speak out against Tarsin or the goons like him and you'll find yourself reassigned. Or that's what they're calling it. Far as we can see, anyone that steps out of line logs off and doesn't log back on." The implication hung in the air, all the more worrying for its ambiguity.

"Moran caused this divide," Dawson said. "He made it clear. You're with him or you're against him. When given the choice between him or you, well." Dawson stood up a bit straighter. "That was hardly a choice at all."

"I'm... honored," Thorne said, the words catching a bit in her throat. "And seriously concerned. Don't get me wrong, I couldn't be happier to have you two with me, but do you understand how bad this could be for you? This goes beyond Nova. Beyond the Warden Corps. You need to protect yourselves. Need to hide. Moran is powerful in the Party. More powerful than I thought possible. He will send people after you. He will—"

"Yeah, yeah. We're aware of that," Ellenton said with a dismissive wave, her tone of voice entirely too unconcerned. "But this isn't just about Nova. Word on the street is that whatever Kaiden, Zelda, and Titus stole, it was big. Big enough to cause a bit of a scene if it got out."

Thorne found herself nodding at that.

"That's, uh, putting it gently."

"So you've seen them, then? The files they took?" Dawson stepped forward. "Is it as bad as the rumors say it is?"

Thorne nodded. "Worse. What they're trying to expose

would change everything. And, as far as I can tell, for the better. I hadn't realized how bad things were. Hadn't realized Moran and those working with him had deceived all of us."

Dawson sighed at that. Ellenton gave a sad sort of laugh.

"Dawson," she said. "I told you, didn't I? Way back when. I said I thought something was wrong. Said too many things weren't adding up."

He nodded at that, a sad, slow sort of nod. "I didn't want to believe it then. Hell, I don't want to believe it now." He looked up at Thorne. "But if you're saying this is real, this is the point we're at? Then I believe you. And I'm ready to do what I can to make it right."

"*We're* ready," Ellenton corrected him. "As evidenced by the fact that we just sent a superior officer and a bunch of fellow wardens to respawn," she said with a disbelieving chuckle. "Whoo, boy. We're in a heap of trouble."

"You really are," Thorne said. "Look, if you're with me on this, I am eternally grateful. But you're no use to anyone if Moran's goons find you. You have to get somewhere safe. Somewhere hidden."

"We didn't exactly wing this, you know," Ellenton said, too casual as always. Sounded more like she was talking about having planned a party than attacking her own government.

"We have a plan to get hidden," Dawson explained. "Everything's ready for us to disappear. We just needed confirmation what we were doing was right. And you're telling us it is?"

"I am," Thorne said, praying she wasn't ruining their lives. She'd chosen to walk this path herself, but she hadn't expected anyone else to follow. Definitely hadn't expected to lead them into it.

"Then that's that." Ellenton stood up from the pilot's seat. "You're working with Kaiden and the others, yeah?"

Thorne nodded.

"Take the shuttle, then. Group up with them." She left the cockpit and slapped Dawson on the shoulder. "Sarge and I will take care of ourselves in the real world. Once we're settled, we'll be in contact, yeah?"

Dawson gave a firm nod, then logged off.

Ellenton watched him disappear, then looked back at Thorne.

"Oh, and Captain? Be gentle with my baby. She's a good shuttle." With that, she logged out.

Thorne was left alone in the *Borrelly*, thoughts spinning to make sense of everything that had just happened.

"I hope you know what you're doing," she said to herself. "Because your life isn't the only one on the line now."

Chapter Ten

A burst of light exploded from Kaiden's shield as he used Flash Bang.

**Ability: Flash Bang**
**Discharge an intense light from your shield that blinds opponents within 10 feet for 5 seconds. Has a 3-second cast time.**
**Cost: 25 charge**
**Cooldown: 5 minutes**

The pirates closest to him stumbled backwards, hands over their now burning eyes.

*No time to waste.*

Kaiden darted in and brought his hammer down on the first of them. His first attack missed the headshot he was aiming for, but the aim on his follow-up strike was true.

**Critical hit!**
**+50% damage (Headshot)**

The pirate's health bar flashed with each attack, then drained. One more blow and it emptied entirely.

**Pirate Lackey assisted kill - 800 EXP gained!**

**Achievement Unlocked!**
**Swabbing the Deck - 200 EXP!**
**Clearing pirates from a system is always welcome. The righteous will thank you for your efforts. The less than righteous will... well, you'll find out.**

Kaiden turned to the next pirate, who was a half-dozen paces away, and activated Hammer Toss. The throw was on target and slammed into the opponent's chest, dropping her health into the red. An Improved Burst Arrow from Zelda came in over Kaiden's shoulder to explode against the pirate and finish her off.

**Pirate Lackey assisted kill - 800 EXP gained!**

"Hey! Fight your own pirates," Kaiden shouted jokingly.

"Already finished all of mine," Zelda retorted. "Looked like you needed the help." She smirked.

"How smug you all are!" The shout caught Kaiden's attention. The pirates' captain was striding toward them.

**Argos Andros (NPC)**
**Pirate Captain**
**Faction: None**
**Level: 35**

"Who sent you?" he shouted, the veins in his neck visible as his voice echoed through the cargo hold. "Answer me! Who sent you!"

Kaiden hesitated. "Uh, that's a good question." He racked his brain. "Hey, Titus. Was this the quest we picked up from the station security chief or that merchant captain?" They'd grabbed so many at once it was hard to remember.

Titus shrugged. "Does it matter?"

Kaiden turned back toward the pirate captain and raised his hammer. "Guess not."

"Such insolence!" The pirate captain flung back the folds of his haggard trench coat to reveal an extra set of arms – robotic and melded on to the sides of his torso. "I'll teach you to cross Captain Andros!"

Kaiden ducked behind his shield as each of the captain's four hands drew a pistol and started firing. His charge bar filled more with each blast that he blocked – a good thing, considering he'd been just about empty.

"This guy's got four levels on us," Zelda said while doing her best to bob and weave through the hail of blaster fire. "Let's not underestimate him."

"He might not be our only problem," Kaiden said as the captain turned and instead of shooting at them, fired half a dozen rounds into the lock of a door at the rear of the room. The door hissed and smoked, then slid open. A roar echoed through the cargo bay and then a massive beast clawed its way out of the too-small room it'd been crammed into.

It looked like some foul cross between a rhinoceros and a camel. Thick brown fur covered its body, retreating only around its two humps and nose where a bramble of horns jutted from the creature's flesh.

**Enraged Ceraphalodon **Huntsman****
**Level: 40**
**Quick facts: Captivity has left this creature wounded and weakened. It cannot heal to full health while captive.**

Kaiden read as much about the beast as his visor would tell him, focusing specifically on the "Huntsman" tag next to its name. What was that about? The Baboulian Manhunter they'd fought way back in their early days in Nova had been marked "Elite," he vaguely recalled. It'd been a tough opponent. But what was this "Huntsman" tag?

**Creatures in higher level areas can spawn with an additional status attached to them.**
**"Elite" represents a general increase to all of their stats.**

**"Tenacious" means the creature will deal more damage the lower its health is. "Huntsman" means the creature will always attack the highest-level opponent in the vicinity.**

Kaiden relayed the information to the others as the Enraged Ceraphalodon shook its head and took in the room. Its eyes scanned over everyone.

"It'll attack the highest-level opponent in the room?" Zelda asked, frowning. "But that would be…"

The NPCs in Nova were well programmed, but there were some areas where they fell short of human intelligence. The Enraged Ceraphalodon gave a roar, then lowered its head and charged Argos.

It slammed into him, leading with its foremost horns. The captain was flung backwards to slam into a wall. He grunted as he hit it, then slid to the floor.

"Suppose I deserved that," he mumbled. "Oh, well. It was worth a shot."

He raised all of his guns and fired a flurry of rounds into the Ceraphalodon. The creature's already low health drained. It roared and charged again. Argos kept shooting, and all at once the Ceraphalodon collapsed to the floor, the momentum of its charge causing it to slide several extra feet.

Argos pulled himself to his feet and dismissed the beast with a curse.

"Wasn't being paid enough for you anyway."

"Can we get back to our fight now?" Titus asked. He stepped out from behind his shield and the captain opened fire. Several shots hit Titus in the chest and shoulders. His health bar flashed and dropped to forty-five percent. The big man seemed unconcerned.

**Ability: Energy Grip**
**The warden can unleash an energy coil to lasso targets and pull them closer.**
**Maximum range: 50 feet**
**Cost: 10 charge**

**Cooldown: 20 seconds**

A coil of energy whipped out and wrapped around one of the captain's arms. Titus pulled hard and the pirate was dragged forward, flying through the air to land at Titus' feet. He tried to pull himself up, but Titus had another ability at the ready.

**Ability: Shield Slam (Replaces Shield Bash)**
**The warden slams their shield into the ground, stunning enemies in a 5ft radius.**
**Cost: 15 charge**
**Cooldown: 2 minutes**

A small shockwave rushed outward as Titus brought his shield down and the captain stumbled a half-step back, then teetered in place, seeming on the verge of collapse.

"There's your window!" Titus said, then started in with a barrage of hammer strikes.

Zelda focused all her fire on the captain and Kaiden darted forward as well, making the most of their precious seconds against a stunned enemy. The assault sent the captain's health plummeting into the yellow.

"I like to call that little combo the grab and smash," Titus said, still admiring the one-two punch he'd thrown to stun the captain a moment ago.

"Ha! Have a taste of *this!*" the captain shouted, then spun down in a circle, arms windmilling around as his blasters shifted into full auto. The attack poured out a stream of damage, but rather than blocking it, Kaiden continued his attack.

*Sixty-five percent health. I can take it,* he thought, then lashed out with a hammer strike at the captain's head.

**Critical hit!**
**+50% damage (Headshot)**

He swung again and landed another critical hit, then took careful aim and scored another.

*Two more to activate Onslaught. That'll finish this guy off nicely.*

"Let's finish this up. Still more quests to get to," he shouted, then took aim for the last two criticals he needed. The captain lunged forward and Kaiden swung for another headshot – but it was a feint. The captain backpedaled instead and Kaiden's attack missed the head and glanced off the shoulder instead, breaking the chain of criticals.

*No! Darn it.*

It was more annoying than anything, but a setback none-theless.

"Ooh, almost had Onslaught there," Titus said, wincing. "That would have been cool."

Kaiden grumbled in response and pursued the captain, who was yelling again.

"You'll regret this day! No one crosses—"

Something huge and molten roared over Kaiden's shoulder and slammed into the captain, cutting him off. He didn't explode so much as disappear entirely as the attack caught him full in the chest and kept on going. What was left of the captain and the attack blasted through the far wall and punctured the hull of the ship.

**Pirate Captain assisted kill - 3,400 EXP gained!**

"Ha. I love Inferno Shot," Zelda said, admiring her handiwork.

"A bit of overkill, don't you think?" Kaiden asked, surveying the remains of the battlefield. All the enemies were dead and now the cargo bay was rapidly depressurizing as the air escaped out of the newly created hole in one side. Debris and corpses were being sucked toward it in a swirling vortex.

"Overkill, maybe." Titus was grinning. "But that was awesome. Is that what it looked like when you killed the Void-lord and me with it?"

"Kinda, except with a bit more screaming and a lot more sizzling ooze."

**Quest Complete: Capture or kill the pirate crew of the SS**
*Walrus*
**Reward: 5,000 EXP, +2 faction prestige, 1,000 credits**

"All right," Titus said, clapping his hands together. "That's another quest down. What's next?"

"Hold up a sec." Kaiden had noticed something. A notification he'd missed during the fighting.

**Friend request from:**
**Thorne**
**Free Warden**
**Class: Power Warden**
**Faction: Unaffiliated**
**Level: 34**

**Accept?**

"Guys!" He waved them over. "I got a friend request from Thorne. Check your social window, see if you did too?"

*This is good news, right? Means she must have made it out.*

Kaiden accepted the request and a direct message immediately followed it. He read it aloud.

**DM from: Thorne**
**"There was a greeting party. Made it out, though, with help from unexpected friends. Headed your way now in the**
*Borrelly.* **Will explain once there."**

"The *Borrelly*?" Zelda asked. "Where did she get that?"

"I mean, it's stationed out of the *Anakoni,* so maybe she took it?" Kaiden said, still processing everything.

"Ooh boy. Ellenton's gonna pissed when she finds out," Titus said with a laugh.

"But she made it out!" Kaiden said. "And she's headed here. That's better than we expected."

Zelda nodded.

"Means we don't have to give her a week-long migraine by forcefully disconnecting her headset from the game." She paused. "How close is she? How long will it take her to get here?"

Kaiden hovered over her name on his social window and additional details appeared.

"She's two systems over. Covering that kind of distance in a shuttle is gonna take forever. Better part of a day, at least."

"That's fine," Zelda said, turning to leave the cargo bay. "We have more quests to complete. Come on. These levels aren't gonna grind themselves."

Kaiden composed a response to Thorne as he jogged after Zelda. How had she made it out? He wanted an explanation. Something to convince him the Party hadn't just let her escape so she could act as a double agent.

**DM to: Thorne**

**"Understood. Interested to hear that explanation."**

Titus brought up the rear, and as they worked their way out of the pirate ship, Kaiden found Thorne's escape just sounded a little too good to be true.

## Chapter Eleven

The *Borrelly* was docked inside the *Veritas II*. From where they were standing – in the hallway of the light cruiser – they could see out of a large window that looked into the cargo bay. It gave an unrivaled view of the sleek shuttle, tucked snugly into the docking station. Kaiden still couldn't believe it was here.

Logistically, it made sense. The *Veritas II* was a light cruiser and as such had a docking bay for a shuttle. They'd talked before about acquiring one to keep in there. But having a shuttle docked with them wasn't what was so strange. It was *which* shuttle was docked with them.

*The* Borrelly, he thought. *The shuttle we started this whole crazy adventure on.* Just having it so close was making him nostalgic. For simpler times, maybe. But also for a time when it hadn't felt like him, Titus, and Zelda against the whole of the world. Though they had Thorne now, right? And from what she was saying, Dawson and Ellenton were also on their side. That sounded good enough that, for a moment, Kaiden started to believe they could actually pull off this whole mad endeavor, despite his ongoing reservations about Thorne.

"Ellenton and Dawson?" Titus asked, smiling wide. "That's awesome!" He swung his arm as if practicing with an imaginary hammer. "Man, can you imagine having Dawson on our side to help bash some Party goons? That's going to be sick!"

Admittedly, it was a pretty awesome thought. Harsh as the man had been, Kaiden had always had something of a soft spot for the scream-happy drill sergeant. Having him on their side was an unexpected comfort. Assuming it was true. And then there was Ellenton. Kaiden hadn't realized how much he'd missed her until now.

"I want to give Dawson an offline copy of the database," Thorne said, shattering the good mood.

Titus' smile faded and Kaiden felt his own hopes falter at the words. He couldn't help his suspicion. Thorne continued speaking, clearly aware of the direction of their thoughts.

"Dawson is going to try to sway as many free wardens as he can to our side. Having the evidence from the database would help him immensely." She held up a hand to stop any incoming protests. "In the real world, we're not restricted by Nova's limitations. We can make as many copies of the database as needed, so we're not losing anything. I'll make a copy and leave it in a hidden location somewhere in the city. Then I'll contact him and let him know where it is. This way, there's no chance he leads me into a trap – which I am completely confident he would never do. If anyone can be taken at their word, it's him."

"And what about you? We're supposed to take you at your word? What if you're smuggling a copy of the database to the Party instead?" Titus asked, arms crossed. "How can we trust you?"

"He's got a point there. Not that it would be much use to them beyond preparing some kind of propaganda to counter the accusations," Kaiden said, then shrugged. "Look, if Dawson's helping, I'm ecstatic to hear it. But at the same time, it feels bad to just hand out copies of the database. Even if you're not betraying us in some convoluted manner, taking a hard copy of the database into the city risks it falling into the Party's hands."

"But what difference does that make?" Thorne asked, looking earnest. "If they get a copy of it, is it really that bad? It doesn't affect us at all. They capture one hard copy, so what? We can make more. The end game here is sending it out to every player in Nova. That's going to be a lot easier if Dawson can bring powerful free wardens to our side."

God, but Kaiden was tired of this situation. Wanting to trust Thorne but not feeling able to. It was like being stuck in a permanent limbo. A purgatory of suspicion.

"Thorne's right," Zelda said, finally joining the conversation after having sat in a thoughtful silence thus far. "It feels strange to say it, but she's right. Dawson turned on the Party, so I think we can assume he's being truthful. Unless this is all some ruse they're putting on to make us trust him. Either way, it doesn't matter. We don't need to trust him. We don't need to give him anything more than one hard copy of the database. If he is being truthful and can use it to recruit wardens to our cause, that's excellent. We need the allies. If he's being deceitful and working with the Party, then they get a copy of the database. They can read through it and then – what? Tremble at the thought of what would happen once the information in it gets out?"

Zelda shook her head. "If we suspect there's the slightest chance Dawson is working with the Party then the solution is we don't give him any leverage over us. Giving him a hard copy of the database is low risk with the potential for high reward. Even if he betrays us, as long as he doesn't know our endgame of taking the AFBS, how much damage can he really do? We'll keep him at arm's length and only trust him as much as we need to."

"That's a cold way to think about a man who just gave up his livelihood and put his life on the line to help us," Thorne said. She sighed. "But if that's what it takes to make this happen, so be it."

"So that's what we'll do, then?" Kaiden asked, looking at them all.

Zelda and Thorne nodded. Titus hesitated a moment, then relented with a shrug.

"I want to believe he's with us," the big man said. "I just hope he really is."

"Well, we're giving him the chance to prove it," Kaiden said.

"When we log out next, Zelda will make a copy of the database and I'll fly it to the outskirts of town," Thorne said. "I'll keep away from the population centers, leave the copy some-where hidden, then hightail it back. Won't take more than half a day."

"All right, that's settled then," Zelda said. She lead them back toward the main quarters of the ship. "Now we need to talk about what comes next. What are we doing to keep this plan rolling? To gain more allies, and level ourselves?"

"Well, we kicked the crap out of those pirates," Titus said, walking in step beside Zelda. "And saved that crippled explo-ration vessel, and delivered those medical supplies, and…" He paused. "Maybe it'd be easier to say we raked in some serious mission EXP."

"I can see that," Thorne said as Zelda led them through the halls of the *Veritas II*. "You've leveled, I notice."

Kaiden nodded at that. As a result of the rush of missions they'd done while waiting for her to arrive, they'd each gained two levels, putting them all at thirty-three – just one level below Thorne.

"Picked up a new ability each, too." Kaiden pulled up his character sheet.

## Character

*Name:*
Kaiden
*Race:*
Human
*Level:*
33
*Class:*
Enhanced Warden
Attributes

*Strength:*
48 (+2)
*Intelligence:*
42

*Endurance:*
47
*Perception:*
42
*Dexterity:*
116 (+2)
*Unassigned:*
0
**Abilities**
*Kickback*
*Shield Bash*
*Hammer Toss*
*Lightspeed*
*Improved Enhanced Senses*
*Riposte*
*Flash Bang*
*Improved Blur*
*Onslaught*
**Enfeebling Strike**
**Slayer (passive)**
**Hamstring**

**Perks**
**Turen Tinkering**

He dug through his messages to get the screenshots they always sent to one another. "Hold on. It's probably best I forward these to you." Now that she was on his friends list he could send her images, which is exactly what he did. First, the one he'd taken:

**Ability Unlocked!**
**Hamstring: Charge is redirected into your hammer. On your next successful critical attack this charge cripples your opponent. Their movement speed is reduced by 50% for 10 seconds.**
**Cost: 60 charge.**

Cooldown: 2 minutes.

Then, the screenshots Titus and Zelda had taken:

**Ability Unlocked!**
**Shield Link: Your charge is redirected to flow into a nearby ally. For a duration of 15 seconds, all charge you absorb is sent to a warden ally within 50 feet.**
**Cost: 30 charge.**
**Cooldown: 2 minutes.**

**Ability Unlocked!**
**Lock On: You direct charge into your hammer-gun. For 5 seconds, as long as the last target you damaged is within your line of sight, your attacks will not miss. You cannot attack any other target. If you take damage this effect deactivates.**
**Cost: 30 charge.**
**Cooldown: 30 seconds.**

Thorne eyes were distant, no doubt reading the abilities he'd sent her. "Yeah, I'm familiar with these. Shield Linking with a blast warden is a classic strategy," she said, speaking to Titus and Zelda at the front of the group. "The shielder absorbs the damage and the blaster spews it right back out at the attacker."

"Pretty much what we were thinking," Zelda agreed.

"Just need a target to practice it on." Titus cracked his knuckles. "Can't wait."

"Hamstring is also essential," Thorne continued. "Allows an enhanced warden to operate a bit more in a rogue-like capacity. Get in behind the enemy, then hamstring their important players. Makes it far easier to take them out of the fight."

"I haven't tried it yet, but the potential is definitely there," Kaiden said as he imagined using the ability in combat.

He was dragged back to the present as they arrived in the main section of the ship. Acton stood there, waiting for them.

"Acton," Kaiden said, nodding to him. "This is Thorne. She's a guest of ours. Going to be helping us."

The first office gave a half bow, then extended a hand.

"Caesarius Acton, ma'am. It is a distinct pleasure to meet you. If there's any way I can be of service, please don't hesitate to call on me."

Thorne hesitated a moment, seemingly taken aback by his overly formal manner.

Kaiden leaned over with a whisper. "He's always like that. You'll get used to it."

"Huh." Thorne clasped Acton's hand and gave it a shake. When that was done, Acton straightened back into his usually rigid posture.

"The repairs to the ship are complete, Captains. We're back in perfect working order and the crew stands ready. Additionally, we've replenished the numbers of our boarding crew, as requested. Seeing as this is a turen station and not exactly at a prominent crossroads, the only option available was turen marksmen. You'll find our barracks now occupied by them and the survivors from our last... adventure, who have tiered up thanks to the hell you put them through. After these expenditures, our credit balance is at 20,230."

As he spoke, Kaiden pulled up a menu detailing the specifics of their ship. Sure enough, it was fully repaired. And under 'boarding crew' it now listed their new hires and veteran survivors.

**Boarding Crew (6 human marines), Journeyman, tier 4**
**Boarding Crew (14 turen marksmen), Journeyman, tier 3**

There was more specific information available on the units themselves, but Kaiden wasn't interested in that at the moment. For the time being, it was just important they had boarding crew.

"Very good, Acton," Zelda said. "Let's put those remaining credits to use, huh? I was perusing upgrade options for the ship.

I saw there's a more efficient shield system we could pick up. The Mark 5 All-Stops, I believe."

"Very good, Captain."

"And there was some turen hull armor in stock, I noticed. Let's refit our hull with it." She looked at Kaiden and Titus. "It'll give the ship a ten percent armor increase while slimming down our profile, reducing the range at which we can be spotted on radar."

*When has she had time to go through all of that?* Kaiden shook his head, amazed as usual at her foresight.

"Absolutely," Kaiden said looking at Zelda, then to the first mate. "Let's do all of that."

"Most assuredly, sir. Though that will deplete our account almost entirely."

"About that," Thorne said, then shrugged. "I've a fair few credits lying around. Easy to stockpile when the Corps was paying for everything," she said with a sheepish grin.

"How much?" Zelda asked.

"It's not a limitless amount," Thorne said bluntly. "But it's enough to help us kit out our army, once we have one. Or buy some last-minute upgrades for the ship, once we know better what it'll need."

"Fair enough," Zelda said.

*Good to know we'll have some additional funds to fall back on should we need it,* Kaiden thought.

"Purchase those upgrades, Acton," Zelda said.

"Very well, Captain," Acton said, then returned to the cockpit. As he did, a message appeared in Kaiden's vision.

"Guys, I have good news," he said, smiling as he read the text.

**Friend request to Recruz: sent.**
**Status: accepted.**

# Chapter Twelve

"Yo, what's up?" Recruz's voice came through the call as the video clicked on and an image resolved from a blurry picture into something more coherent. A projection of Recruz's head, the tops of his shoulders, and a bit of background hung in the air in front of Kaiden.

"Hey there, uh, Recruz. This is Kaiden," he said, trying not to act nervous and failing spectacularly.

"He knows who you are. The magical technology of caller ID exists in Nova, believe it or not," Zelda whispered sharply.

"I know, I know," Kaiden said, shooing her away then turning back to the video call. Recruz stared back at him, seemingly unimpressed. He wore a helmet with a tinted glass front that made it difficult to make out his exact features. In the background, it looked to be chaos. At least a dozen or so figures were duking it out in a battle, abilities and explosions firing off left and right.

Recruz didn't even wince as steaming soil and a few pieces of what might have once been a voidspawn rained down on top of him.

"Hey, uh, so. It looks like you're busy. I just wanted to call and see if we could maybe, uh, set up a meeting with…" Kaiden hesitated. *Really should have thought this out more. God, this is going to sound stupid.* "With the leader of Maximus?"

Recruz must have hit a setting in his helmet as the glass front de-tinted, revealing his face. It was laughing, deep and long. He shook his head and caught his breath.

"Hey man, good one." He glanced over his shoulder, then ducked as another player flew through the air just past him. He turned back to the video call.

"Look, Kaiden. If you want to join Maximus, that's cool. I don't need to give you the spiel, I'm sure you know who we are. But we do have level requirements. And look, dude, I know who you are. You're wanted by like every warden in game – and hey, that's kinda cool. Tons of great opportunities for PVP there. But dude, seriously." He set his features in a stern expression. "You're level thirty-three. That's like, not even a good joke. You need to be at least level fifty before you can hope to do anything relevant in hardcore PVP." As if to punctuate his statement, something exploded in the background, but Recruz hardly even flinched. A shockwave washed over him and for a moment the video was obscured by a storm of dust and debris.

"I'm not trying to join Maximus," Kaiden said, brushing off the attack on his ego. *Only level thirty-three? Come on, man. I know that's not anywhere the level cap, but I worked hard for this!* "My friends and I, we need to talk to your guild leader. He's going to want to hear what we have—"

"Nah, he's probably not," Recruz cut him off. "Anyway, good talking to you, Kaiden. Send us an application once you hit level fifty. We'd love to party up sometime and gank some wardens or something."

"Wait, Recruz! You—"

The call ended abruptly. Kaiden looked up at the others who'd been gathered around watching the call.

"So... that didn't exactly go to plan," he said.

"You kind of failed to mention the part where we're in possession of a top-secret database and on a mission to bring down the Party but need their help," Zelda said.

"Yeah, well... he failed to let me get a word in," Kaiden retorted.

"Hold up. I'm gonna call his ass," Titus growled, then started a video call.

"Yo, what's up?"

"Listen here, punk. You just hung up on my friend, but if you know what's good for you, you're gonna listen to what he has to say." Titus gave a stern look, then moved toward Kaiden as if to include him in the video call.

"Nah, I'm cool." Recruz ended the call.

Titus cursed, then a moment later, cursed again. "He blocked me!"

"Yeah, kind of saw that one coming," Thorne said, grimacing as she leaned back in her seat. "Those Maximus guys don't take well to authority. Only really listen to orders from their guild leader and his officers."

"Oh, so you're an expert on them, then?" Titus retorted, but there wasn't much malice in it. Seemed the big man was more embarrassed than anything.

Thorne raised her hands in a gesture of peace.

"Just trying to help," she said.

"Then help us figure out what to do next." Titus turned toward the others. "This guy's not listening to us. We should go around him, find another way to set up a meeting with Maximus' guild leader. What was his name again?"

"PlayaSlaya," Kaiden answered, calling the popular figure to mind. Aside from being the founder and leader of Maximus, he was one of the game's most successful PVPers. Drew in a big audience with the weekly tournaments he'd once fought in and now hosted. Not to mention the massive PVP battles.

"Look, this isn't anything new," Thorne said, rising from her chair and beginning to pace around the room. "I ran into stuff like this all the time as an agent. Being a representative of the Party, no one wants to talk to you. But sometimes you have to talk to them. So you go and find them. Calling someone is one thing, but a more personal touch tends to work wonders."

Kaiden frowned at her words. "You want to go find this guy in real life?"

Thorne burst out laughing, and for the second time in the past few minutes Kaiden found himself nursing a wounded ego.

"No, nothing like that," Thorne said. "Where's Maximus located? I'm saying we should go to their guild base. They can hang up a video call but they'll have a bit more trouble removing us in person. Or, in-game in person, I guess." She waved her hand. "Whatever you want to call it."

*Hmm. Well, I don't hate the idea.* There was some value in just cutting right to the heart of things. And besides, this meeting was too important to just let go.

"All right, I'm down," Kaiden said with a shrug.

"Agreed," Zelda said. "But let's grab a bunch of missions on the way. It'll be a bit of a flight over to Maximus' guild base. They're, what…" She checked a menu visible only to her. "Three systems away. We'll cover that distance quickly in a light cruiser like the *Veritas II*, but that doesn't mean we can't make the best use of our time." She rose from the table and turned toward the cockpit. "Recruz mentioned leveling up, anyway. If we show up stronger than we are now, maybe it'll buy us a bit more legitimacy. Probably won't, but we need the grinding anyway."

*Practical as always,* Kaiden thought. She was right, though.

"Sounds good," he said. "We'll check the major stations on the way, see what we can—"

"Captains!" Acton shouted from the cockpit. "We have something of a situation brewing here."

Kaiden frowned as he jumped from his seat and hurried toward the cockpit. Zelda beat him there.

"What's going on?" she asked.

"A Warden Corps ship just pulled up outside the station. It appears to be scanning the ships in the area."

"Looking for us?" Kaiden asked.

"If they aren't, they will be once they scan this ship." Acton strapped himself into his seat.

"Ah, crap," Thorne said, joining them at cockpit entrance. "I should have realized this sooner. I was tracking you pretty successfully when I was in the Corps. We need to change this ship's information. It'll take a black-market mod, but I'm sure we can make a pit stop. Won't be cheap, though."

"Yeah, we'll do that," Kaiden said. "But first we need to get out of here." He leaned down and peered through the windshield. Turen drones were still buzzing around the outside of the *Veritas II*, putting the finishing touches on the new hull armor.

"They almost done?" Kaiden asked.

"Moments away," Acton confirmed, looking down at a progress bar on his console.

"We might not have moments," Kaiden said, assessing the situation in front of them. At the entrance to the hangar a warden corvette was just passing through the force field that kept the air in and the void out.

A beam of light projected from the front of the corvette and fixated on the first of the landed ships in the hangar.

"Armor's done, Captains," Acton reported.

"Go, now," Thorne said, gesturing toward open space. "The corvette's in the middle of a scan. We need to be gone before it finishes."

The engines on the *Veritas II* roared to life, the entire hull shaking as they did. In a matter of seconds, the pilot had them in the air and headed out of the hangar.

"Faster," Kaiden said. "But not too fast. We don't want to look like we're running."

"No real way to hide that," Titus said. "They're going to notice us."

As if on cue, the corvette stopped scanning its original target and spun toward them.

"Gun it," Zelda said to the pilot. "Now! Go!"

The ship lurched forward and Kaiden was near thrown off his feet as the engines kicked up their thrust to max.

"We can't outrun a corvette," Thorne said, then leaned down next to the pilot. "Ram them on the way past."

"What?" Kaiden asked. "What do you mean? That'll just antagonize them."

"No, she's right." Zelda pointed toward the warden corvette. "Hit 'em!"

*Putting the new shields and armor to use sooner than expected, I guess.*

The pilot dutifully obeyed and swung them to the side. The

warden corvette seemed to recognize what was happening and tried to pull up.

It didn't make it.

Kaiden was thrown to the floor and rolled a pace away as the *Veritas II* slammed into the other ship, then rebounded off and into the hangar floor. The others fell as well, tumbling this way and that as the ship's shields flared outside and metal screamed against metal as they slid along the hangar floor.

Kaiden pulled himself to his feet in time to see the warden corvette in a similar state. And then it was gone as they blasted out of the hangar and into space.

**-15 Turen Geniocracy faction prestige for improper station departure.**

Kaiden read the message, then frowned.

"The turen didn't much care for that."

"Keep burning hard," Acton said, flipping through a status report on damage to the ship. "We've a head start on that corvette now. With any luck, it's too damaged to follow."

And it appeared that was the case. Acton pulled up a rear-facing camera and it showed the corvette following, but at a slow speed. One of its engines looked destroyed and the rest were belching smoke.

"I think we're in the clear," Kaiden said. At the same moment, the corvette opened fire. A barrage of laser fire flashed against the *Veritas II*'s shields but didn't make it through.

Something did, though.

The ship shook all at once, as if it'd been rammed. Acton flicked through exterior cameras until he found one showing the damage.

"Bad news," he said, a frown stretching across his face as he pointed to the video screen. It looked like something was embedded in their hull. A small ship, maybe? Or a torpedo? Honestly, it looked to Kaiden like a hybrid of the two.

"That's a boarding rocket," Thorne said, then cursed. "We've got company."

## Chapter Thirteen

"Just down here." Zelda led them in a sprint toward the rear of the *Veritas II*. "They've boarded through the cargo bay."

*That's close to where the mechanics normally work,* Kaiden realized.

"Braker!" he shouted as he pulled up a video call with the engineering bay. "Lock the door to the engineering bay and stay inside. Don't come out for any reason!"

"Got a ship needs fixin', I'm your man," Braker said with a nod.

"I think that's a yes?" Kaiden ended the video call and turned his attention to the situation brewing in front of them. Zelda led them around a corner to find some damaged part of the *Veritas II* was leaking acrid black smoke into the hallway.

*Well, I'm glad we just repaired this thing.*

"How many wardens should we expect?" Kaiden asked, scanning the hall for any sign of movement.

"From a boarding rocket that size?" Thorne said from beside Zelda. "Three, maybe four players. Not a lot of room in those things."

"Our turen marksmen and marines are on their way from the barracks," Acton reported through comms. "And I've got eyes on you from the bridge. If there's any way I can help in this fight, you let me know."

"Got it," Kaiden said, then nearly slammed into Zelda as she slid to a sudden stop.

"There's our guests," she said, then flicked her shield on.

She was right. There they were. Three of them in total. They stood in the hallway with the door to the cargo bay on one side and an airlock to nothing but space on the other. Kaiden focused on them and his visor brought up the specifics.

**Esme**
**Warden Skirmisher**
**Class: Power Warden**
**Faction: Warden Corps**
**Level: 39**

**Alvarez**
**Warden Skirmisher**
**Class: Blast Warden**
**Faction: Warden Corps**
**Level: 38**

**Clarissa**
**Warden Skirmisher**
**Class: Shield Warden**
**Faction: Warden Corps**
**Level: 39**

"A power warden, blast warden, and shield warden," Kaiden said, speaking through comms now so their uninvited guests wouldn't hear. "And all higher levels than us."

They moved into a tight formation, the shielder in front, the power warden at her side, and the blast warden, Alvarez, at the back and already firing off Improved Burst Arrows.

"What's the plan?" Titus asked, flicking his shield on and stepping in the way of the opening volley. The shots had been aimed at Kaiden but Titus stopped them short.

"The blaster's gonna stay back with the shielder," Kaiden said, predicting their strategy based on his knowledge of Warden

Corps fighting tactics. "And the power warden is going to rush us, try to keep us disorganized so the blaster can pick us off—"

Before he could finish, Esme charged, her massive hammer held high above her head. At the same time, Alvarez, the opposing blast warden, changed his target to Zelda and pulled the trigger.

Zelda ducked to the side, avoiding the attack but delayed from beginning her own, and Kaiden stepped toward the charging Esme, bracing for impact. He hadn't blocked any damage yet, though, so he had no charge and thus no access to his abilities. The wardens were designed as a reactive class, not meant to instigate fights.

*And yet, here we are.*

Esme closed the distance between them in no time. Kaiden raised his shield, but at the last moment, she turned off in favor of advancing on Zelda.

Titus stepped into her way and blocked her initial hammer strike before responding with one of his own. She let it hit, not even attempting to block in favor of attacking as much as possible.

"Power wardens gain charge from blocking attacks but also from dealing damage," Thorne said, rushing in to attack Esme from behind. "The more you let her wail on you, the stronger she's going to get."

Titus backpedaled, giving up ground as he tried to dodge the power warden's attacks. He was a shield warden, though, so his dexterity wasn't anything special, and his attempts to dodge the hammer strikes only lowered his defenses. Kaiden jumped forward to help him on instinct, but without charge his attacks weren't going to do much. Esme ignored him, focused on Titus for the moment. She'd built enough charge for an ability.

**Ability: Shield Break**
**Ignores armor, staggers the target, and deals 150% base damage.**

Kaiden's visor displayed limited information on the ability, as it did for all enemy attacks. Esme's hammer burst with energy then slammed into Titus' shield. The energy flashed forward, straight through his shield, and he was driven backward, a worrying chunk bashed from his health. Down to eighty-seven percent already – and Esme had only used one ability. With Titus staggered, Esme shrugged past Kaiden and his ineffectual attacks to turn back toward Zelda.

Thorne launched into the air, her hammer crackling with energy.

**Ability: Earth Shatter**
**You channel charge into your legs and leap into the air.**
**Upon landing, a shockwave bursts out from around you.**
**Opponents within 10 feet of you are knocked down.**
**Cost: 25 charge.**
**Cooldown: 1 minute.**

She slammed her weapon down as she landed and a shock-wave exploded outward, knocking Esme onto her back. Thorne took advantage of the moment to dart in and unleash well-aimed strikes at her opponent. They connected, but not for nearly the damage Kaiden would have liked to see. By the time Esme was back on her feet she'd only lost eleven percent of her health.

"I can keep her occupied," Thorne said, gritting through a barrage of damage as Esme lashed out. "But I'm not winning this fight. Not one on one."

The two power wardens danced back and forth, weapons swinging so fast as to be nothing more than vaguely hammer-shaped blurs. Thorne was taking the worst of the damage, though, which made sense considering she was several levels weaker than her opponent.

"Keep her off Zelda as long as you can," Kaiden said, then sprang into motion. *Range reigns supreme here. We need to take their blaster out of the fight.*

As if to hammer home the effectiveness of ranged classes, Alvarez spun from where he'd been slinging shots toward Zelda

— since Titus had been beaten away from covering her — and caught Kaiden in the shoulder with a Paralyzing Shot.

*Deals base damage, slows me by half for ten seconds,* he thought, then cursed but pushed on anyway. He sprinted toward Alvarez and the shield warden, Clarissa, but it was like his body was moving through tar; his legs were heavy and refused to move at their usual pace. He was a sitting duck.

Alvarez lined up another shot, an ability charging on the end of his hammer-gun.

"Oh, hell," Kaiden mumbled as his visor read out what was coming.

**Ability: Inferno Shot**
**Ignores some of the target's armor and deals a massive amount of damage to enemies and allies within range.**

"Got you covered!" Zelda shouted and Kaiden flinched as a Kinetic Grenade arced from over his shoulder toward Alvarez. Zelda must have been in Sniper Mode to be able to get such distance on her grenade, hoping to knock down the enemy blast warden before his ability could charge. Unfortunately, Clarissa stepped in front of it at the last moment and blocked most of the damage with her shield. Inferno Shot was ready to fire.

Then the boarding party burst into the fray, guns blazing to life and filling the corridor with a hail of screaming laser fire.

Clarissa raised her shield to block the shots but there were too many to stop. Her health flashed as the marines' attacks pecked away at it. Alvarez seemed caught off guard. He spun to aim his Inferno Shot at the marines, then seemed to think better of it and tried to spin back toward Kaiden. Too late, though. The attack finished charging and fired.

Kaiden threw himself to the side, mostly out of the path of the attack as a screaming explosion of damage poured past. His health bar flashed as the attack winged him —dealing significantly less damage than a direct hit would have. It mostly missed him, but several marines were not so lucky. Two were killed instantly as the Inferno Shot detonated.

**Marine Ally Slain!**
**Marine Ally Slain!**

Kaiden climbed to his feet as the slow effect from Paralyzing Shot wore off. He ducked behind his shield as Alvarez blasted an Improved Burst Arrow at him. It exploded against his shield in a flash of near-blinding light, but also filled his charge bar some. Enough, for the moment.

**Ability: Improved Blur**

Kaiden fired off the ability and two body doubles appeared beside him as he closed the remaining distance to Alvarez.

*It's time to turn the tide of this fight. We're gonna take 'em out like a house of cards. Knock out the base and the whole thing comes down.*

More laser blasts rained down at him, but they were inaccurate, the blast warden clearly unsure which Kaiden to shoot at. All the better; his heath was already down to sixty-five percent.

Kaiden side-stepped around the shielder, using his high dexterity stat to its fullest. It helped that his doppelgangers mimicked him, confusing his opponent as to which one was real. Kaiden raised his hammer and attacked Alvarez.

The blaster let loose an Improved Scatter Shot but it was aimed at one of the body doubles. Kaiden kept swinging, scoring three more hits. Alvarez's health flashed, but dropped far less than Kaiden would have liked.

Back in the midst of the fighting, Kaiden saw a burst of light as Esme fired off an ability. Thorne was flung up into the ceiling then tumbled back down to the floor with a resounding crash. Her health dropped by a good twenty percent. While she was down, Esme turned to the turen marksmen now firing on her and started swinging. They flew like bowling pins, launched this way and that, but dutifully still firing as she plunged into their ranks.

**Turen Marksman Ally Slain!**
**Turen Marksman Ally Slain!**

**Turen Marksman Ally Slain!**

Many more of them were going to die, Kaiden knew, but all they needed to do was buy time.

**Turen Marksmen Ally Slain!**

While Esme made a mess of the marksmen, Kaiden kept swinging at Alvarez. The shielder, Clarissa, tried to focus on covering him from the attacks, but the four remaining marines kept a steady stream of fire coming in and peppering them both, ticking away at their health.

**Ability: Improved Barrier**

The shielder popped the ability and a force field materialized around her and Alvarez, swallowing up the incoming fire. As it did, Kaiden found the full attention of both players turned toward him.

He dodged to the side as Alvarez let loose three rapid-fire shots, one at each body double and Kaiden. He moved quickly, but not quickly enough, and the attack caught on his shield, sparking as it hit. Alvarez spotted the hit and smirked, having identified which Kaiden was real.

"Titus! Zelda!" Kaiden shouted through comms, getting their attention through the hail of fire. "Hit Clarissa and Alvarez from behind!"

"On it!" Titus shouted back, then jumped into a charge. Zelda must have been forced out of Sniper Mode at some point because she followed him step for step, firing off abilities as she approached. The attacks landed on Clarissa's Improved Barrier and it shook under the assault.

Alvarez was still firing, though, and Kaiden backpedaled, weaving back and forth to avoid the continued barrage of fire that was starting to make mincemeat of his health bar. A moment later, though, the attacks stopped as Alvarez was forced to respond to Titus and Zelda's advance. The opposing blast warden charged up an Improved Kinetic Grenade and hurled it at them.

"Shield Link with Zelda!" Kaiden shouted and Titus smiled.

**Ability: Shield Link**
**Your charge is redirected to flow into a nearby ally. For a duration of 15 seconds, all charge you absorb is sent to a warden ally within 50 feet.**
**Cost: 30 charge.**
**Cooldown: 2 minutes.**

The grenade exploded and Titus's health dropped to seventy-two percent. Zelda took some of the splash damage as well, but she responded immediately and hit the Improved Barrier with another blast. Cracks were beginning to show in its surface now.

"It's better to give than receive," Zelda said.

**Ability: Lock On**
**You direct charge into your hammer-gun. For 5 seconds, as long as the last target you damaged is within your line of sight, your attacks will not miss. You cannot attack any other target. If you take damage this effect deactivates.**
**Cost: 30 charge.**
**Cooldown: 30 seconds.**

**Ability: Improved Warden's Bolt**
**You fire two bolts of lightning instead of one. Discharge bolts of lightning that jump to multiple targets within range of the impact target. Initial range 50 feet, jump range 10 feet. Deals +150% base damage, reducing by half with each successive jump.**
**Cost: 25 charge.**
**Cooldown: 30 seconds.**

Zelda locked on to Alvarez and unleashed her Improved Warden's Bolt at almost the same moment. Two bolts of lightning arced from the barrel of her hammer and into Clarissa's

Improved Barrier. What charge the shield warden might have had was depleted now as the damage from Zelda's attack forced the barrier to flicker, then disappear entirely. Its second ability triggered then and formed a protective shield around Clarissa. It absorbed the damage coming in from Zelda's Improved Warden's Bolt, but she wasn't the target of the attack. The bolt jumped to the only other enemy target within range: Alvarez. The blast warden cursed as the lightning electrocuted him with a savage hiss and his health dropped significantly. It'd already been around eighty-five percent from the few attacks that had connected, but now it was driven further down to sixty-nine percent.

*Blast wardens are always squishy once you get damage on them,* Kaiden thought, then put the second part of his plan into action. Titus and Zelda's push, combined with the concentrated fire from the marines, had been like a flurry of jabs. Not too damaging, but quick and designed to attract attention. Now that Alvarez and Clarissa were distracted, Kaiden loaded up for the heavy left hook that, with any luck, was going to be crippling.

**Ability: Lightspeed**
**Dangerous levels of charge are channeled into your leg implants, increasing movement speed by 200% for 10 seconds. You will take double damage if hit during Lightspeed.**
**Cost: 30 charge.**
**Cooldown: 1 minute.**

*Double damage if I get hit,* Kaiden thought, then smirked. *Good thing no one's looking at me.*

He exploded forward with so much speed it was almost hard to control. He came in swinging and used his momentum to hasten his attacks on Alvarez's back.

**Critical hit!**
**+50% damage (Headshot)**

**Critical hit!**
**+25% damage (Shattered Elbow)**

The already injured blast warden was damaged even further. His health dropped by another ten percent.

"Get ready, Titus!" Kaiden shouted.

"Ready for what?" the big man shouted back. He was able to lower his shield, since Alvarez had turned in response to Kaiden's flanking attack.

"I had you advance so you'd be close enough," Kaiden said, feinting in toward Alvarez. The blast warden backpedaled, trying to get outside of Kaiden's attack range – and that was his critical mistake.

"Close enough so you could grab and smash," Kaiden said, feeling a smile break across his face. He pointed with his hammer toward the blast warden who had just unknowingly left the cover provided by his shield warden teammate.

Titus got the idea instantly and struck out with Energy Grip. The crackling whip of energy lashed around the blast warden's leg, then dragged him across the floor and well out of the protection Clarissa had been providing.

Zelda focused her full attention to the blast warden and unleashed a string of attacks. Titus did the same, abandoning any attempt to protect Zelda in favor of landing several crushing blows on Alvarez. The blast warden was higher level than any of them, but that hardly made much difference when caught in the open and getting focus fired.

"No!" Clarissa shouted, then made to cover her teammate.

"Not today," Kaiden said and darted after the shielder.

**Ability: Shield Bash**
**The warden strikes out with their shield, dealing no damage but stunning the target for 2 seconds.**
**Cost: 15 charge.**
**Cooldown: 2 minutes.**

The stun caught Clarissa in the back and stopped her movement for two seconds – a critical two seconds in which Zelda and Titus continued their attack on Alvarez. Though nearly dead, he was returning fire as he beat a retreat toward the cover of his shielder. His health was low – twenty-two percent now – but high enough that there was a chance he'd make it back. At least, as long as Clarissa kept heading to meet him. Shield Bash's stun wore off and she made to do just that.

**Ability: Hamstring**
**Charge is redirected into your hammer. On your next successful critical attack this charge cripples your opponent. Their movement speed is reduced by 50% for 10 seconds.**
**Costs: 60 charge.**
**Cooldown: 2 minutes.**

Kaiden poured what was left of his charge into his new ability, then swung at the back of Clarissa's legs. The blow connected and she cried out, then stumbled forward. She tried to keep moving, but her movement speed was crippled and all at once she looked like she was trudging through molasses instead of down a hallway. Her limbs were slow and clumsy, as if they were numb.

Alvarez's eye went wide as he realized what was happening. He was close to Clarissa, but not close enough. Zelda detonated an Improved Kinetic Grenade at his back and combined with the still persistent fire from the marines, his health bar flashed and emptied to zero.

He collapsed like a bag of rocks, armor clanking against the metal floor as he went down.

**Blast Warden Alvarez assisted kill - 3,000 EXP gained!**

For a moment there was something approaching silence, but for the sounds of Thorne being smashed around the hall some distance away. Then Clarissa slammed a fist into the wall.

"Well, let's get on with it, then!" she snarled and advanced on Kaiden, still hamstrung but hammer raised anyway.

Zelda launched several attacks into her back and the shielder spun and raised her shield. She leaned into the assault, blocking most of the damage.

**Ability: Shield Link**

Kaiden's visor alerted him to Clarissa activating an ability.

*Shield Link? Alvarez is dead, so who's she...*

"Stop shooting!" Kaiden shouted. There were only two enemies left, which meant the only person Clarissa could be Shield Linking with was Esme. Kaiden turned his attention to the back of the hall in time to see Thorne launched through the air again. She landed, health at seven percent now, but threw herself into a roll and managed to make it most of the way to Zelda and Titus.

"Might be time for some backup," she grunted.

Zelda stepped past her and toward Esme, who launched into the air in a blur.

**Ability: Heroic Leap**

Esme landed in an explosive wave of damage. Zelda's health dropped to thirty-two percent. Esme, apparently, had gained a fair amount of charge from Clarissa's surprise Shield Link.

Titus rushed to get between her and Zelda, his shield raised.

**Ability: Improved Shield Break**
**Deals damage through armor and staggers the target.**

Kaiden sprinted forward, his visor reading out vague details on Esme's ability as he bypassed Clarissa and ducked under a wild attack from her. He left her in the dust, leaning on his dexterity to close the distance between himself and the fight brewing over the injured Thorne. Not fast enough, though.

Esme's Improved Shield Break connected with Titus' shield. The blow crushed a chunk of his health and staggered him backward. He tried to recover, but Esme had all the time she needed to get at Zelda.

**Ability: Improved Grip Like Iron**
**Grapples the target, roots them in place, and weakens their attack while grappled.**

**Ability: Improved Chained Fury**
**A series of attacks, each dealing more damage than the last.**

The power warden lunged forward with an outstretched hand that closed around Zelda's throat, then lifted her into the air.

"What the—" she began, then was cut off as Esme bashed her with a flurry of hammer strikes. Improved Chained Fury amplified the damage of each successive strike. Every attack did a bit more damage to Zelda than the last.

She managed to block the first few blows, but then her shield was overloaded and she was left entirely exposed. Her health fell to twenty-eight percent, then twenty-three.

Kaiden raised his hammer as he drew in behind Esme but then he toppled forward, health flashing as he faceplanted. The reason why became obvious as he turned to find Clarissa's Energy Grip wrapped around his ankle. She yanked hard and he slid back toward her.

He rolled over on to his back with a curse and charged an ability.

**Ability: Flash Bang**
**Discharge an intense light from your shield that blinds opponents within 10 feet for 5 seconds. Has a 3-second cast time.**
**Cost: 25 charge.**
**Cooldown: 5 minutes.**

Clarissa lashed out with a Shield Slam, trying to stun Kaiden. It worked, but Flash Bang fired off right as her ability did. She reeled back, covering her eyes while Kaiden froze, stunned for two seconds.

All the while, Esme's Improved Grip Like Iron held Zelda in place and her assault continued.

Seventeen percent. Ten percent. Zelda was just about done.

But Titus wasn't. He was back on his feet and lashing out with a Shield Slam. The attack broke Esme's hold and Zelda fell to the ground. Titus moved forward and pressed the assault. He got several good blows in before Esme climbed to her feet and retaliated.

**Ability: Gravity Sledge**
**Deals additional damage, launches the target on a successful hit.**

Energy surged into her hammer, then exploded as she swung it into Titus' chest. He was launched backward to slam into a wall, leaving Zelda on her own.

"Take her down!" Kaiden shouted, gesturing for the remaining turen marksmen to target Esme while he rolled away from a poorly aimed attack from Clarissa. There were only about four turen left though and Esme was still at thirty-one percent health. There was no way they could deal enough damage.

"Eye for an eye," Esme said and raised her hammer for a killing blow on Zelda.

*I need more charge!* Kaiden cursed his empty charge bar as he slipped away from Clarissa – she was far from the most pressing threat – and sprinted forward at a normal and painfully slow speed.

Esme's hammer crackled with energy as it swung downward. Zelda raised a hand as if to block it but there was no way she'd survive the attack.

The hammer came down and connected with a shockwave of force – except, it didn't hit Zelda. Thorne threw herself in the way at the last moment. Her health bar flashed, then drained to empty. She collapsed to the floor, dead.

**Party member killed!**

She'd saved Zelda from Esme's lethal blow, but sacrificed herself in the process. And she hadn't even hesitated. Kaiden stared for a moment, shocked at what he'd witnessed. Thorne hadn't had time to calculate the move, to play it as part of her plan. It'd all happened too quickly. She'd just... done it. Just thrown herself in the way and taken the hit.

*Just like a proper teammate would have done...*

But all for nothing. Kaiden cursed, still trying to close the distance. He couldn't get there in time.

**Ability: Last Rites (Passive)**
**When the warden reaches 0 health, Last Rites is triggered, allowing the warden 10 seconds to kill all opponents in a 50-foot radius of the point of death. Should they succeed, they will be given 1HP back. If not, they will die. Kills made during this time earn no EXP. No abilities can be used during Last Rites.**
**Cooldown: 6 hours.**

Thorne's power warden passive activated and she jumped up from the floor alive, but with not even a single percent of health coloring her HP bar.

"Not dead yet," she growled.

"But about to be," Esme retorted.

"On the contrary." Zelda leveled the barrel of her hammer-gun and fired.

**Ability: Paralyzing Shot**
**Fires an electric blast that confuses the electrical impulses in the target's muscles, deals base damage and slows targets movement by 50% for 10 seconds.**
**Cost: 30 charge.**
**Cooldown: 30 seconds.**

Esme's body spasmed as electricity surged through it and

Zelda backed out of range. Thorne lunged in with a renewed ferocity. She had no health, but for the next ten seconds, she also couldn't die.

"Titus, keep Clarissa off us!" Kaiden shouted, then finally reached the fight and started swinging.

The big man had advanced on the opposing shield warden. She was back where the battle had started, the cargo bay door on one side and the airlock to the void on the other. Titus squared off with her.

With no charge to speak of, Kaiden aimed several hammer strikes at the back of Esme's head.

That got the power warden's attention – and reduced her health to twenty-three percent.

She spun around with a hammer strike that Kaiden caught on his shield. His charge bar swelled, filling to thirty-five. He aimed another strike, and her reply came in the form of a sweeping blow that connected for critical damage. His health fell to thirty percent.

Thorne attacked Esme from behind with strike after strike. It was the best she could do considering she could use no abilities when Last Rites was active.

Zelda used Lock On, then fired an Improved Burst Arrow at Esme. The attack exploded against her, dealing damage and blinding her for three seconds.

Kaiden dumped what charge he had into one more ability.

**Ability: Enfeebling Strike**
**Loads charge into your hammer. On a successful hit, this charge floods into the target's nervous system, making them more susceptible to pain. Increases damage taken by target by 50% for 10 seconds.**
**Cost: 50 charge.**
**Cooldown: 2 minutes.**

Esme cried out as the attack landed, then again as the barrage from Thorne, Zelda, and Kaiden continued. Every one of their attacks was bolstered by Enfeebling Strike and Esme's health stood no chance against the onslaught. It fell to zero in just a few blows.

**Power Warden Esme assisted kill - 3,100 EXP gained!**

For a moment, Kaiden thought they were too late. Thorne's time was up – but no, Esme fell and Thorne stayed standing. She'd completed Last Rites – having killed the only enemy who'd been in range when it'd activated – and was rewarded with a measly one percent of health. Not much, maybe, but enough to keep her alive.

A moment later, though, Kaiden found himself staring down Esme once again as her own Last Rites activated. Luckily, the game's AI still seemed to count this as a kill for Thorne's own Last Rites. The ability must be considered an after-death resurrection ability, so the initial kill still applied.

"Get back!" Thorne shouted. "She's bound to the radius of the ability. Stay out of her range and we're fine."

"I got the other one covered," Titus called from across the hall, exchanging blows with the opposing shield warden. She was trying to make it to Esme, but Titus was the perfect person to keep her occupied.

Ten seconds passed in what felt like ten minutes, but with no abilities Esme's timer expired and she died again, collapsing to the floor and, this time, staying there.

"One left," Kaiden said, feeling the battle firmly in hand now as he faced the remaining warden. There was no way they could lose. But if any of them died, they'd still be out of the game for a week.

"How're we going to do this?" Titus asked, disengaging from where he'd been exchanging hammer strikes with Clarissa. At level thirty-nine, she was the strongest of those who'd boarded, and considering Kaiden had told everyone to stop hitting her in order to not fuel Shield Link, she was still comfortably in the orange on health. Sitting pretty at sixty percent.

All the same, she knew she was outnumbered. Seeming panicked, she backed up. The door to the cargo bay was on one side of her; on the other side, a pressure-sealed door led to an external airlock.

*We can work with that,* Kaiden thought.

"Titus, hit her with a Shield Charge!" he shouted.

**Ability: Improved Shield Charge**
**Charge at double your speed for 5 seconds. Direct impacts deal 100% of base damage.**
**Cost: 40 charge.**
**Cooldown: 2 minutes.**

Energy surged into Titus' legs, then engulfed him entirely. He shot forward in a blur and Clarissa just had enough time to raise her shield.

"Open the airlock, Acton!" Kaiden said.

"With pleasure."

The door hissed open just as Titus slammed into Clarissa. Kaiden saw her eyes widen, then she was thrown backward and out of the airlock and into space.

No assisted kill notification came in; her suit was pressurized and, like all warden suits, had its own short-term air supply. But they didn't need to kill her. This was close enough.

"Nice shot," Kaiden said, nodding toward Titus.

"Thanks for the layup," he said.

With the last of the boarders repelled, Kaiden let out a long breath, then slumped against the wall. Was it possible to feel physical exhaustion in a video game?

"Shall I have the pilot bring us around and finish off the last of our guests?" Acton asked through comms. "She'll be no match for our turrets."

"No," Zelda said. "It's more important we escape the corvette. Is it still following us?"

"We left it behind some time ago," Acton replied. "Ramming it worked out pretty well, all things considered."

Thorne flashed a smile at that.

"Looks like we don't make that bad of a team," she said, and at that moment, Kaiden couldn't say he disagreed.

## Chapter Fourteen

"You should eat," Thorne said, nodding to Kaiden's mostly untouched bowl of soup in between slurps from her own near-empty one. "You need to keep your energy up and your mind sharp."

"I don't know whether I should be more worried by the fact this soup-gel doesn't have an expiration date or the fact that it almost tastes edible," Kaiden said, slurping cautiously at his spoon.

"It's supposed to be a gel, really. You just squeeze it into your mouth. But seeing as we have a kitchen, I added a bit of salt, a little bit of broth, and heated it all up."

"To make a semi-soup, semi-gel abomination?" Kaiden said.

Thorne had pillaged a ton of the stuff from abandoned military reserves after the chaos of the Test. Each tube provided all the daily vitamins and nutrients a body needed. It was an extremely efficient way to eat. Furthermore, it was well documented that a hot meal was good for morale. Nutrients and a morale boost; what more could one ask for from food? Thorne frowned as her guests continued to make a fuss about the soup – particularly its taste, as if that was at all important.

"The good news is there's enough of this stuff in the cupboard to last us for years," Zelda said, only half paying attention to the conversation. She was on her handheld console, searching through the database as always.

Kaiden laughed. "That's also the bad news."

A looming shape filled up the entirety of the hallway as Titus emerged from the bathroom, drying his head with a towel.

"We complaining about the gel meals again? They're not so bad, eh?"

He tossed the damp towel on the back of one of the dining room chairs as he passed.

"Hey, hey!" Thorne snapped her fingers at it.

Titus groaned and rolled his eyes, but moved the towel to the heated drying rack.

"I know we live in a swamp bunker, but there's no reason it has to look like it," Thorne said, hoping if she repeated it enough one day the big man would stop needing to be reminded. Though they'd likely overthrow the Party – or be captured by them – before that ever happened. "The dehumidifier has enough trouble keeping this place dry without damp towels lying around and itching to get mildewy."

"Yes, *Mom*," Titus grumbled, then shuffled off to the kitchen to get his own portion of gel-soup.

Kaiden slurped another noisy mouthful, then checked his handheld console.

"Acton should still have the ship on course toward Maximus' guild base, but if we're online in the next thirty minutes we'll be able to pick up missions when he stops to refuel."

"I'll be ready," Thorne said, then raised her bowl to her lips and sucked down the remains of the gel-soup, broth and all. "Mmhmm," she said, trying to sound satisfied. "Invigorating."

Kaiden shuddered.

"Huh, this is ominous," Zelda said, pausing with her spoon halfway to her mouth. "'Operation Killswitch,'" she said, reading from the database. "'The latest attempt in the Party's ongoing struggle to leverage control over Nova Online.'"

"That sounds bad," Kaiden said.

Zelda set down her spoon and looked up at everyone.

"Bernstein's mentioned in here several times that the Party

has had its sights set on bringing Nova into its jurisdiction for some time. NextGen Games has always been too internationally and politically well positioned, though. Not to mention filthy rich."

"Nova has always been something of a thorn in the Party's side," Thorne agreed. "The creation of the warden program was meant to ease that pain point. And it has, but not entirely. As you've seen, wardens can only do so much. They're restricted to operating – mostly – within the limits of Nova. Within the limits of what NextGen says is okay."

"Something tells me that doesn't sit well with the Party," Titus said, dropping into a chair with a steaming bowl of soup.

Thorne shrugged. "Not in the slightest, but what can they do?"

"Operation Killswitch, apparently," Zelda said, but shook her head. "There's no more information on it, though. Just another dead link in the database." She sighed. "I really wish Bernstein had been able to finish this thing."

Thorne bit her tongue for a moment, then figured what the heck. *You won't know if you don't ask.*

"Can I look through the database?" She asked it simply, as if it wasn't anything special, but still the question hung in the air. She knew – or at least hoped – she'd been gaining trust with the trio, but it was slow going. They'd let her hear Bernstein's message, but aside from that, all her knowledge of the database came from them. She'd never gone through it on her own. Technically, Zelda was going to make a copy of it for Dawson, so Thorne knew she'd have a chance to look through it before delivering it for him to find. That felt deceitful, though. If she was going to make any meaningful progress here, she needed to be forthright.

"I know you still don't fully trust me," she said. "But I've worked for the Party for years."

"Exactly why we don't trust you," Titus said.

"Right, but it can also be an asset. How much information in there is missing pieces? How much of it might I be able to add to because of my time with the Party? Bernstein's seen everything from the outside. Combine that with my knowledge from the inside and we can have a more complete database." Thorne paused, then bit her lip.

*That's half the reason, at least.*

"And..." she said, then sucked in a breath. "And, I need to know the extent of the Party's crimes. The extent to which I've been complicit in them. How much have I unwittingly helped them? I've always served to help the people. Has anything I've accomplished ever done that, or has it all been to prop up a tyrannical oligarchy? How much of—"

"Yes," Kaiden said.

Thorne stopped. Frowned.

"All those reasons are good. Sensible," he said. "But the heart of the matter is, well..." He trailed off, then looked up with confidence in his gaze. "I trust you. *We* trust you."

"We do?" Titus asked, looking up from his soup with surprise. "News to me."

Kaiden shook his head.

"The circumstances are strange, I'll give you that. Thorne was our enemy. But things have changed. Just look at our last fight. Without her we would've been slaughtered. But Thorne fought her own past allies – and to great effect, as well. She took a massive beating keeping Esme distracted while we focused on their blast warden. That was a turning point in the fight."

"And she stopped what surely would have been a lethal blow on me," Zelda said, reluctant but nodding along.

"Without hesitation," Kaiden added. "There was no thought in it. No planning, no plotting. You just... did it," he said, looking right at Thorne now. "That was instinct."

"She knew she had Last Rites," Titus argued, arms firmly crossed.

"I don't think that changes anything," Kaiden said, unde-terred. "Look, we can't keep living in this limbo of suspicion. We're all a team, and we need to start working like one. Anything less means we're holding ourselves back, and if we're going to do this – if we're going to try to bring down the Party –

we can't hold anything back. We don't have time to doubt each other."

Thorne tried to hold back a smile.

*Don't gloat. Don't look too pleased,* she reminded herself. But this was exactly what she'd been thinking for so long now. Exactly what she'd wanted to say, but there was no way they would have accepted it from her. No, it had to come from someone else. That it was coming from Kaiden was all the better.

Titus still looked troubled at the idea.

"She worked for the Party, man," he said.

Kaiden nodded.

"And you for King Street. And Zelda for Bernstein. And me for... well, no one important, I guess. But the point is we're all on the same team now."

"If we let the past hold us back, we compromise the future," Zelda said suddenly and with a curt nod. She looked over to Thorne with a serious expression. "Bernstein would never have turned away a potential ally. But it's more than that. You've had every chance to betray us, and yet you haven't." She paused a long moment, then nodded again as if confirming something to herself.

"I trust you," she said finally, then slid the database across the table.

## Chapter Fifteen

"Buh bye," Titus said, his voice crackling and staticky as it came through comms. A moment later, Kaiden was forced to look away as a burst of fire from Titus' turret erased the last pirate fighter in a blossoming explosion of debris.

**Pirates killed: 40/40**

**Quest Complete: Purging the Pirate Problem**
**Reward: 8,000 EXP, 2,000 credits**

"Nice! The scenic route might take longer, but it's a lot more fun," Titus said.

"Not sure how much fun has to do with it," Kaiden said, turning off his turret and letting it whisk him back inside the *Veritas II.* "We have to keep hammering out these missions if we want to be high enough level to have any chance at taking Warden HQ." All the same, though, he had to admit their progress had been good. The quests were basic, maybe, but they paid in EXP and that was what counted. They'd each leveled once already to thirty-four and were on the verge of tipping into thirty-five. Thorne had leveled from the fight with the wardens, which had put her at thirty-five. Their recent grinding had her all the way up to thirty-six.

"This isn't a sight-seeing trip," Zelda said from the cockpit. "It's strategic. The major shipping lanes would be faster, but there's too much warden traffic on them. They've doubled, maybe even tripled the number of patrols. Us taking down that corvette didn't exactly go over well."

That was putting it mildly. Their faction prestige with the Warden Corps, which had already been a whopping negative 151, had dropped even further to negative 180. And then there were the broadcasts. The Warden Corps had been putting them out at least once a day since their failed attempt to board the *Veritas II*. Kaiden pulled up a screenshot of the latest one.

****Full System Alert! Full System Alert!****
**This is a Warden Corps All-Frequencies Broadcast. The Warden Corps is seeking the following fugitives currently believed to be in-game:**

**Player name: Kaiden**
**Player name: Zelda**
**Player name: Titus**
**Player name: Thorne**

**A bounty of 1,000,000 credits will be awarded to any player who provides information leading to the fugitives' capture. An additional bounty of 500,000 credits will be awarded to any player who engages or delays the fugitives until a warden is able to Shackle them.**

He'd been keeping track of the broadcasts with something approaching morbid fascination. The Corps had been steadily raising the bounty with each day that passed. *How long until we're worth ten million credits? One hundred million?*

"The corvette was just a drop in the bucket," Thorne said, appearing from the turret she'd been manning and joining Kaiden on the way back to the front of the ship. "If anything, it just pissed Moran off because they were close to having us and failed." She frowned a moment as if thinking an unpleasant thought. "He's gonna squeeze this game as tight as he can to stop us. He might not know what we're doing, but he'll know he needs to stop it. He's not going to just assume we're lying low and waiting for everything to blow over."

"All the more reason to be here, then," Zelda said.

Kaiden peered out a window as he passed, then nodded. The station wasn't listed in this system's list of registered facilities, but Thorne had assured them it was here and, considering they were on approach to it now, she'd been right.

Their scans had been unable to pick it up, and now that they were closer, Kaiden could see why. The station was thoroughly shielded. There were no landing lights visible from a distance; all the windows had been painted over to hide them, and likely the body of the station itself was entirely covered in signal-suppressing metals. Enough to hide the electromagnetic signal of their core and any excess heat it was venting.

Considering the system was officially listed as empty, there was no reason for players to come here. Nova's AI considered empty space boring, though, and in pursuit of engaging game-play it tended to fill it with random pirate spawns. Kaiden had made sure everyone always had one of the general "pirate purg-ing" quests active so they'd all been able to keep themselves occupied and grinding as they navigated through the allegedly empty space. Combined with the quests they'd been picking up from every station they stopped at to refuel, it'd made for an effective and consistent amount of grinding. And, considering this was the closest place to pick up the transponder they were after, it was kind of on the way.

"You're sure this transponder's going to work?" Kaiden asked, looking to Thorne who was walking in step beside him.

"Trust me, the amount of time I've spent trying to catch players using one of these things is absurd. We'd ID the crimi-nals' ship and go after them. Next thing you know, their transponder code has changed and they show up on scans as a completely different ship. All for the cost of a hundred thou-sand credits. It's honestly ridiculous. We've been telling NextGen these things are OP for years now, but they won't nerf the transponders. Probably just to annoy the Corps." She chuckled. "Seems like that's gonna work to our advantage now."

"Captains?" Acton said through comms. "We've hailed the station for landing clearance but there's no response."

"This place is hardly civilized enough to require landing clearance," Thorne said with a laugh. "Just pick an open pad and take us in."

～

**Location discovered: Blue Hex Station**
**Faction Alignment: None**

**Achievement Unlocked!**
**Finding the Unfindable - 300 EXP!**
**The legendary Blue Hex Station is a myth, of course. It certainly doesn't exist. But if it did, and if you found it, you'd get an achievement for doing so.**

Kaiden dismissed the achievement with a slight smile as they stepped off the *Veritas II*, then frowned as something else caught his attention.

"Uh, should we be worried about that? Or is flaming wreckage strewn across the landing pads just part of the aesthetic here?"

Thorne frowned at it for a moment, then shrugged.

"This is a PVP zone. You know how players can get sometimes. Probably just some bored kids rolled through here with nothing better to do."

"Acton, keep an active watch and let us know the moment you see anything amiss," Zelda said back to the ship through comms.

"Of course, Captain."

"Well, welcome to Blue Hex, anyway," Thorne said, stretching her arms out as they crossed the landing platform. Instead of a hangar, as larger, more traditional stations had, Blue

Hex had only exterior landing pads. Arrows painted on them led to an airlock that would, presumably, lead them into the station.

"Nice place," Kaiden said, careful to step around the burning debris of what had once been a shuttle.

"It can get... rowdy," Thorne said. "But nothing we can't handle at our current levels."

"Any chance we can pick up some missions here? I'm a pathetically small amount of EXP away from thirty-five," Titus said as they arrived in front of the airlock. Thorne waved her hand in front of it and it opened.

"The NPCs here will have missions. At least, I've heard they do. They would never speak to me when I visited previously. You know, me being a warden and all."

*That makes sense,* Kaiden thought. *Will they speak to her now that she's a free warden? If not, our prestige with Nassau's criminal underground might come in handy.*

The answer quickly became irrelevant, though, as the airlock cycled, then opened. The NPCs at Blue Hex weren't going to be speaking to anybody.

The lights inside the station were flickering, but even still, it was easy enough to see the space was littered with bodies.

**Lark Helling (NPC) **Deceased****
**Smuggler**
**Faction: Unaffiliated**
**Level: 12**

**Balthoz (NPC) **Deceased****
**Merchant**
**Faction: Unaffiliated**
**Level: 8**

**Inkernal (NPC) **Deceased****
**Merchant**
**Faction: Unaffiliated**
**Level: 15**

Name after name flashed in Kaiden's vision as he took in corpse after corpse. Seemed there were near forty dead NPCs strewn across all areas of the room.

"Shields up, hammers ready," he said without thinking as he prepared for an ambush.

Zelda slipped into the back of the group with a curse while Titus shook out his shoulders and scanned the room. Thorne advanced a cautious step, mouth set in an angry frown.

"Whichever 'bored kids' rolled through here certainly had a good time," Titus said.

"Shh," Kaiden said, then switched from proximity chat to comms so no one could listen in. "Whoever did this might still be here."

The station itself was cylindrical in shape, basically a big drum with solar panels extending from the top and bottom. It wasn't that big, though, and most of the space inside seemed to be taken up by the room they were currently in. It was a wide, oval-shaped space. Crates of cargo, ship hulls in the process of being stripped for parts, and various other clearly illicit items filled the space. The partially broken-down ship hulls gave Kaiden the most concern. Anyone could have been hiding in among their shadowy forms, waiting for the right moment to attack.

At the back of the room, he caught sight of an elevator bay sitting idle.

"You think it's like this on every level?" Titus asked.

"Doesn't matter," Thorne said, striding further into the room. "Whoever did this killed the NPCs – and recently. They'll respawn eventually, but in the meantime, the station can still serve its purpose." She pointed toward a terminal against the far wall. "That's where we buy our transponder."

"Cover her," Kaiden hissed, advancing slowly as he scanned every inch of the room.

*If I had charge, I could use Improved Enhanced Senses…*

But he didn't have any charge, so that was out of the question.

Thorne was nearly at the terminal before the voice spoke.

"Agent Thorne. It's good to see you," it said, echoing out from the darkness.

Kaiden's heart jumped in his chest as he spun toward what he thought was the source of the sound. Thorne, in contrast, shook her head and cursed.

"Werner. I should have expected as much. Things were far too pleasant without you around."

The voice – Werner, apparently – chuckled, and then a warden stepped into view.

**Werner08**
**Warden Captain**
**Class: Blast Warden**
**Faction: Warden Corps**
**Level: 20**

"Thorne," Kaiden said through comms. "Who is this guy?"

Thorne cursed in response. She seemed more annoyed than worried, though.

"You're a warden now all of a sudden? And a captain, no less?" Thorne asked. "Thought you were only focused on the real world?"

Werner shrugged.

"I'm focused where the Party needs me to be focused. Since you refused our offer and pulled your little disappearing act, that's been in this childish game."

"What offer did you refuse?" Zelda asked.

Thorne flicked a glance back over her shoulder.

"They wanted me to join their little cabal," she growled through proximity chat.

"Well now, that's not entirely true, is it?" Werner chuckled. "Some of us wanted you. I knew you'd never make the cut. Not made of the right stuff. No, you're more the sort to associate with scum like this, aren't you?"

Kaiden raised his shield as Werner's eyes fell on him.

"So, this is the famous Kaiden, is it? And the rest of the gang as well. Big man Titus! Quite the reformed gangster, I hear."

"Why haven't we offed this guy yet?" Titus growled. "He's only level twenty."

"And Zelda, too. The brains of the operation." He frowned. "Oh, uh, my apologies about your parents. But you know how it goes. Play with fire and you're likely to get burned."

"Go to hell," Zelda said then fired an Improved Burst Arrow. Werner didn't even move to block it. Instead, he just took the blow to the chest, his health bar flashing down to eighty percent.

"Why are you here?" Thorne growled. "You can't take us on, and if you had reinforcements we'd have picked up their ships on our scanners on the way in. You're alone. That's suicide."

"Why am I here?" Werner paused, seeming to consider the question. He was silent for several long seconds before finally shrugging. "Well, the Party wants me to find you. Wants me to retrieve that database of yours. So, I put my skills to work. As it happens, tracking someone down in Nova isn't that different from doing it in real life. The formula is strikingly similar. Know who the person is and what they want, and you can likely predict their next move. I know you, Thorne. Well enough, at least. Once that corvette spotted you a few systems over I knew you'd decide it was time to go dark. Try to throw us off your tail. The idea of a transponder isn't a bad one. It is unoriginal, though. I didn't know what station you'd turn up at, but it was a safe guess it'd be one that sold black market transponders. So, we spread out, paid visits to all of the stations." He looked around the station, at the dead NPCs, and smiled. "Got a few levels in the process and, well, it looks like I got lucky." He smiled wider. "I was very much hoping to run into you."

"You sure do like to hear yourself talk," Kaiden said. "But that doesn't change the fact that you're outnumbered and out-leveled."

"No, I'm afraid it doesn't."

"All you've done is kill a bunch of NPCs and buy yourself a one-week vacation out of game," Kaiden said, raising his hammer and advancing. From behind, Zelda fired again. Werner only smiled as it hit him in the chest and exploded in a spray of sparks. His health dropped to sixty-two percent.

"While a week's vacation does sound nice, I'm sure this meeting of ours has earned me more than that." He held up one finger. "For instance, I've confirmed you're after a transponder to hide your ship. Why do that if you weren't planning to spend more time in-game?" He flicked up another finger. "Secondly, based on your new levels, I've learned you've been grinding. Trying to get stronger for something. Further confirmation your plans involve Nova." He raised another finger. "And finally, I know you're moving from one end of the universe to another." He chuckled. "Oh, isn't this a fun game? You've given me the pieces of the puzzle and now I get to put them together."

*Man, this guy sure talks a lot. Long-winded if ever I've—*

Kaiden froze in place as the realization hit him.

"Thorne, buy that transponder, now!" He switched to comms. "Acton, prepare the ship for immediate departure. We need to leave."

"What's up, Kai?" Titus asked. "This dude's level twenty and there's four of us. He doesn't stand a chance."

"He's buying time. I'm sure he's already called for reinforcements. They're likely on the way now. We need to get that transponder and disappear." Kaiden switched back to proximity chat. "Enjoy your vacation, asshole." He raised his hammer.

Werner only smiled wider.

"You think this is my only account? You think the Party doesn't have people power-leveling accounts for all of us this very moment? You think—"

Kaiden brought his hammer down on the man's head. The blow cut him off and sent him stumbling backwards as his health dropped into the red. Another hammer strike and he was on his back, health nearly gone.

"Enjoy this, Kaiden Moore," he said. "The next time we meet, things won't be this easy."

Kaiden's only response was to swing his hammer one more time.

**Blast Warden Werner08 assisted kill - 1,000 EXP gained!**

Werner went limp and, finally, stopped talking.

"Got the transponder," Thorne said, stepping away from the console. "And good call sniffing out what he was doing."

Kaiden nodded as he walked back toward the airlock.

"We'll install the transponder in flight. If Werner sent out a call for backup, this place is about to be swarmed by wardens. Let's not be here when that happens."

"Oh, hey, look at that," Titus said as the airlock closed and began to cycle. "Killing that punk was just enough EXP. We leveled up after all."

## Chapter Sixteen

The planet had appeared in front of them some time ago as a glowing orange dot, impossibly far in the distance. By the second, though, it'd grown larger as they drew closer. Now, it was almost all they could see.

As it happened, the planet was a gas giant. And it wasn't orange, but a mix of reds, tans, and pinks, striped through the atmosphere in shifting, flowing belts of what Kaiden assumed were high altitude wind currents. A planet-wide jet stream of sorts, churning and mixing the various gases of the atmosphere together. In about a dozen spots, violent storms raged through the atmosphere, hurricane-looking pockets of swirling, angry red.

"Onwards and downwards, pilot," Acton said with a sharp nod.

**Location discovered: Kyraxis, Player-Controlled Planet**
**Faction Alignment: None**
**Resident Guild(s): Maximus**

"Just Maximus?" Kaiden asked, reading the message. "You mean to tell me this entire planet houses only one guild?" Player-controlled planets were common throughout Nova Online. Most were used as home bases for guild headquarters.

Purchasing land claims on one was a massive undertaking and required the accumulated resources of, usually, hundreds of players. But the demand to own a land claim and set up a town for one's guild was high; as such, most planets were over-crowded, with up to a hundred or more guilds calling them home. But Kyraxis had only one resident guild.

"They can't be *that* big," Kaiden said. "Big enough to own the entire planet. Right?"

"I'm not sure it's a matter of size so much as no one wants to be their neighbor," Zelda said. "Settle next to the largest PVP guild in-game and you shouldn't be surprised when they use you as training fodder."

"Huh, yeah. I guess that makes sense," Kaiden said with a nod. "Where are they, though?" He leaned closer to the hull window they were peering through, trying to catch a glimpse of any man-made structures below. "All I see are clouds." Even as he said it, the soupy, churning mix of gasses outside grew thicker. So thick he couldn't see further than a few feet beyond the window.

"They're down there," Acton said. "Should be visible any minute now."

The *Veritas II* shook as what must have been a particularly violent blast of wind broadsided the ship. The engines complained and the pilot feathered the afterburners to keep them on course.

"S.S. *Andronicus,* this is Maximus ATC. We have you on approach," a voice said from a speaker in the cockpit. Thorne grinned wide at the sound of the new name that she'd picked for the *Veritas II* – or, more precisely, had entered into the transponder before anyone could react. Apparently, she still found it hilarious. Zelda had had to explain it to them, but Kaiden didn't really see what was so funny about a reference to ancient literature.

"The name is *temporary,*" Zelda said to Thorne, but she only grinned wider.

"You're cleared for landing on visitor pad oh-three," the air traffic controller said.

"Very good. Landing presently," Acton said back, then directed the pilot toward what looked to Kaiden like more clouds. The ship's instruments had apparently picked up the pad, though, and as Kaiden watched, they eased downward.

A shape appeared in front and below them, then manifested itself into a landing pad. Flat, roughly rectangular, and with "03" lasered across it with high-visibility paint.

"Easy now. Easy..." Acton said, as the pilot worked the throttle to bring them in. Another savage burst of wind howled against the hull and the ship was driven sideways, slipping past the edge of the pad. A burst of power to the starboard maneuvering thrusters eased them back toward center, then the pilot dropped them down with a thud. Kaiden was jostled to the side as the full weight of the ship fell on its landing gear, then bobbed up and down as the suspension leveled out.

The wind still howled and whistled outside, but now that they were landed, it seemed unable to move the ship.

"Welcome to Kyraxis, *Andronicus*," the Maximus air traffic controller said. "Proceed to the visitor entrance for processing."

Maximus' guild base was in front of them – allegedly. The clouds were still thick as ever. Everything was a swirling fog of orange and tan as Kaiden strode across the pad with the others, struggling to catch a glimpse of the shadowy structure in front of them.

The pad was wide and flat. A bridge at one side led toward the hulking mass of some sort of building. And then, all at once, the clouds broke.

Sunlight poured in from above, and for a moment Kaiden could see everything around them.

A seemingly glass-domed building stood in front of them at the end of the bridge they were on. Except, it wasn't standing at all – it was floating. Or flying. Whatever was keeping it up, it wasn't the ground. Kaiden glanced down into an eternity of swirling gas and howling winds before remembering there was no ground. Not on Kyraxis. It was a gas giant, after all.

The clouds began to close in again and Kaiden snapped his attention back to the view in front of him, taking in as much detail as possible before everything was smothered again.

The bubble-like building in front was circular at its base and topped by a transparent dome. Inside, he could see smaller, squat buildings scattered throughout. Each structure looked to be modular, the same four smooth metal walls used to create a basic cube. In some places, larger buildings had been created by attaching several cubes together.

The clouds settled in and Kaiden glanced beyond the dome for a moment, straining to see more of the base. In the distance, he could just make out the silhouettes of more domes. They were connected by a latticework of sky bridges, their outsides reinforced with thick support columns. The bridges spanned between the domes, creating a web that stretched off into the distance. One particular dome caught Kaiden's eye. It was open on top, unlike the others. And inside there were explosions and flashes of light. An arena of sorts? With a fight going on inside?

A blast of wind hit the bridge and Kaiden stumbled to the side as the whole thing moved. Except, it wasn't just the bridge. The domed building in front of them moved as well. And the landing pad. And, as Kaiden watched, each bridge and domed building in the distance moved with them, one by one as the wind pushed through the interconnected web. Eventually, the entire base was drifting, driven by the harsh wind.

"This whole base is moving," Kaiden exclaimed.

"Free-drifting," Zelda said with a nod. "Pretty much the only way to exist in a place like this. No reason to waste resources fighting the winds. Instead, just let them carry you. It's not like you're going to run into anything in this atmosphere besides more wind."

"Yeah. It's a cool sight, but what are we going to say once we're in there?" Thorne asked, nodding toward the domed building waiting at the end of their bridge. "Let's not have a repeat of the conversations with Recruz, yeah?"

Kaiden set his eyes ahead and strode forward. "We'll say whatever we have to. Whatever it takes to get a meeting with PlayaSlaya." They'd all sent him friend requests on the off-chance he'd accept. He hadn't, of course.

A few more steps and the *Veritas II* had disappeared behind them. All Kaiden could see was the bridge beneath his feet and the domed building rising at the end of it.

Transparent doors made of the same material as the dome slid open as they approached. Kaiden led the way inside, then paused, taking in the surroundings. With a fully see-through ceiling the building had little need of artificial light – at least during the day. The light from the system's star, reflected and softened by the swirling clouds, lit up every inch of the space with a shining brilliance.

"Nicer digs than I expected from a PVP guild," Titus said.

"King Street's building isn't bad either," Zelda replied.

"Yeah, don't let the decor distract you," Thorne said as she followed them in. "This is all built on PVP spoils. Might look luxurious. Fragile, even. But the players here are anything but."

"This way," Kaiden said, leading them toward the interior building marked 'Processing.'

There was a doorway on the front of it, but no door, and as he stepped through it, he realized there was no ceiling either. The walls stood tall and strong, but where a ceiling should have been there was only open air. He stared through it and up to the dome a good two hundred feet above. It was almost as if each of the little buildings inside the dome was a glorified cubicle, partitioning space off for specific purposes without being fully cut off from the atmosphere of the rest of the dome.

"Crew of the *Andronicus,* right? Pumped to have you!" an excited voice said from behind the front desk.

**Halicar**
**Class: Cybernetic Knight**
**Faction: Maximus**
**Level: 55**

Kaiden read the information and looked the player over. He wore a black and red suit of power armor, similar to their own but for its color and mass. It was a bulky thing, reinforced in the chest and neck such that Halicar looked less a man and more a walking combat suit. Which, considering he was in a PVP guild, probably wasn't far off.

*Level fifty-five, huh? They're not playing around here, are they?*

"He's the highest-level player we've ever encountered," Kaiden said, speaking through comms so only his party would hear him.

"Private communication isn't allowed in the base," Halicar said, rising from his chair and leaning across the desk. "You have something to say, you can say it in proximity chat."

"Ah, sorry." Kaiden winced. "Didn't know."

"All good, all good," Halicar said with a wave. "You're new here. So, you've come to join up, yeah?"

"Actually, no." Kaiden focused on speaking confidently. He'd been uncertain when talking to Recruz, and everyone had seen how well that worked out. There was no room for indecision. Not here, not now.

"Ha, good one, dude," Halicar said, then pulled up a screen on the terminal at his desk. "Okay, so I see you're all pretty low level. You can't officially join until you hit fifty-five, but we can work with you if you're willing to put some effort in. Grind on your own, and when you get to fifty, you can fight in our arena." He gestured out of the dome, off toward where Kaiden had seen a fight happening as they'd walked in. Even through the clouds the explosive effects of abilities being fired off were visible in flashing bursts of light.

"A few wins in there will get you some rep, you know? And if you take down the whole tournament, you'll get to meet Playa-Slaya himself. Quite an honor," Halicar said. "Also, you're free wardens, which is good. Opens up some different combat combinations when we go into guild versus guild PVP." He looked up with a smile. "The higher-ups love that, too. Versatility, they always—"

"We're not trying to join," Kaiden said, cutting him off mid-sentence.

This time, Halicar stopped what he was doing, frowned, then shouted over his shoulder.

"Nassus! Need you for a sec."

Another player walked in. She wore black and red power armor similar to her partner's.

**Nassus**
**Class: Brawler**
**Faction: Maximus**
**Level: 55**

*Never seen that class before,* Kaiden thought. Though truly, they hadn't seen much of Nova Online outside of the Warden Corps. There hadn't exactly been time to freely explore since he'd started playing.

"Hey! Fresh meat," Nassus said, smiling wide as she saw them in front of the desk. "Whoo! Finally, someone lower on the totem pole than us who'll have to work this crap job." She paused. "Er, I mean, welcome! We're so happy you'd like to join."

"Said that's not why they're here." Halicar clearly ruined Nassus' good mood with that.

She looked at them, face all scrunched up in confusion.

"Then why the heck are you here?" She leaned down and pulled up a screen on the terminal. "You're not on the guest list. And you don't have an appointment." She stood straight. "So what gives?"

Kaiden swallowed hard and prayed his voice would sound half as confident as it did internally.

"We've come to speak to PlayaSlaya. We have information he'll want. And a proposition for him."

Silence then, as both members of Maximus stared, uncomprehending. Finally, Halicar shook his head, then laughed quietly.

"You don't understand how this works, do you? You think PlayaSlaya has time for people like you?"

Nassus laughed at that.

"Forget level fifty-five, forget the entrance requirements, these guys haven't even passed level forty." She shook her head as if in disbelief. "You're wasting our time."

"Not the only thing here I'm gonna waste," Titus growled.

Kaiden waved back at him.

*Stay calm,* he wanted to say. *I got this.*

He turned away from Titus and took a step forward, pressed both hands into the desk, and leaned forward until he was up in both of the players' faces.

*These guys respect confidence, right?*

"Why don't we let PlayaSlaya decide what's worth his time and what isn't?" Kaiden said, forcing his voice into his best impression of a growl.

Halicar smirked.

"How about nah?"

Kaiden shrugged and leaned back.

"When we go around you and he hears what we have to say, we'll be sure to mention it was you two who delayed us. Made things more difficult than they needed to be." He smirked back as he delivered the last line.

*What do you think about that, huh? Feeling big and strong now?*

Halicar and Nassus burst out laughing at near the exact same moment. Nassus bent over forward, catching herself on the desk to stop from collapsing.

Kaiden felt his face go hot. Were he out of game, he knew he'd be blushing uncontrollably.

"Threatened by a level thirty-whatever," Nassus said, whooping with laughter. "Man, no one told me today was gonna be this fun."

"Enough of this." Thorne stepped forward. Kaiden deflated a little as she did so. Clearly he wasn't as good at this as he needed to be.

"You two are just bottom-of-the-barrel desk jockeys," she said, a scowl stretched across her features. There was an intensity in her eyes as she spoke. "You don't have any power here. You just do what you're told when you're told to do it." She let that hang in the air a moment, then spoke again, her tone icy. "I'm telling you to get your superior. Someone here who actually matters."

Neither of them was laughing now. Apparently Thorne had struck a chord with them.

*These guys respect strength, confidence. But all their bluster is just fronting,* Kaiden realized. *Internally, they're paranoid that they're nowhere near as strong as those ranked more highly in the guild. That... makes sense.* Thorne apparently had some experience dealing with just these sorts of people.

"You want to go higher up the chain of command?" Nassus said. "Fine. Here we go." She waved to Halicar and he pulled up a video call on the terminal.

An unfamiliar voice answered and the hologram of a person appeared right after it.

"Nando here. How's it going, guys? You need something?"

"Yeah, we got some—" Halicar began to say then was cut off by a sharp elbow from Nassus.

"Butt dial, sir. Sorry about that."

"Ah, no worries then." The hologram of whoever Nando was disappeared.

Halicar gave his counterpart a confused look.

"That's not who I wanted you to call." She pressed a button on the terminal and another voice call started. An all-too-familiar voice answered this time.

"Sup?" Recruz said as his hologram resolved itself above the desk.

"Got some morons here that want a meeting with the commander," Nassus said. "We told them no, but they're persistent."

The ghostly image of Recruz turned around to face Thorne. Then his eyes moved to Kaiden and he frowned.

"You again? Seriously?" He shook his head.

"We're not going to accept no for an answer," Kaiden said, stepping forward and forcing himself to look confident. "I'm telling you right now, your commander wants to hear what we have to say."

Recruz looked back to the two at the desk.

"See them out," he said, hitching a thumb over his shoulder. "And don't call me about stupid stuff like this next time."

"Yes, sir," they said in unison.

Nassus ended the video call and then looked up, a smug expression on her face.

"I'm over this," Titus growled, then pushed past Kaiden and Thorne. "I'm over your attitudes. Over taking crap from you and your boss." He slammed his hand down on the desk. "If this were King Street, you'd have a little more respect."

Halicar seemed to flinch at the mention of Titus' old gang, but Nassus seemed unfazed.

"This ain't King Street," she said, smiling smugly once more. "Maybe everyone thinks you're the man there. Maybe they all think you're hot shit. But this is Nova, and in here, you're no one." Nassus stood up and leaned in close, voice dropping to a whisper. "Unless... you think you can prove otherwise?"

**Duel requested: Nassus (55) versus Titus (35).**

**Achievement Unlocked!**
**Walking the Walk – 100 EXP!**
**You, or one of your party, have instigated a duel! Congrats! Now you can finally back up all that smack talk. Or just get whooped. Let's see what happens.**

"Hold on, now," Kaiden warned, stepping up and resting a hand on the big man's shoulder. "This is an unwinnable fight, man. And if she kills you, you'll be out for a week. We can't afford to lose that much time."

Titus didn't respond, utterly silent as he stared directly into Nassus' eyes.

"Come on, big man," she taunted. "We're bored to death in here all day. Why don't you give us a little entertainment? Hell, I won't even use a weapon." She raised two empty hands and smirked.

"Don't do it, Titus," Zelda said. "She's baiting you."

"I know," he growled, long and low. "I know. And it's working."

**Duel accepted: Nassus (55) versus Titus (35).**

"Oh damn," Thorne cursed, then yanked Kaiden and Zelda back a step.

**Ability: Ambush**
**Launches at the target with incredible speed, deals additional damage on next hit.**

Nassus leapt over the desk in a burst of motion. Titus flicked his shield on and raised his hammer but she was already on him. Her promise not to use weapons rang empty as Kaiden realized her fists *were* her main weapon. They fell in a blurred frenzy, pounding on Titus' shield, then his armor. Even with his larger shield, he couldn't block everything as she darted left and right; he was just too slow. His health plummeted to forty percent before he managed to attack back. He led with Shield Slam, trying to get a stun on Nassus and stop her onslaught. The attack slammed into the ground and energy and dust exploded outward in a wave.

When it cleared, Nassus was gone.

Titus looked up in confusion, trying to figure out where she'd gone. Kaiden was doing the same when she dropped from the ceiling and brought both fists down on Titus' head, scoring a critical hit. His health flashed and he roared as he swung at her again and again to little avail.

Nassus ducked and dodged and darted side to side. Titus could barely keep up. Wherever he attacked he found only empty space, his opponent moving like she was an enhanced warden at near full speed.

*She's playing with him,* Kaiden realized, noticing that she'd stopped attacking back. Instead, she was dodging his attacks. Almost looked like she was waiting as long as possible before slipping out of the way. *She's enjoying this too much. She knows the way her class is built, and with their level difference, there's no way Titus can land a hit unless she lets him. The big man simply isn't used to fighting a seasoned player, especially not one on one. His class isn't built for it. Even without the level difference he would need a perfect strategy to bring her down. But he isn't even thinking right now.*

Titus finally got a hit with the area-of-effect damage from Shield of Rage. Nassus' health budged all of one percent.

"Oh, there ya go," Nassus said, laughing, then struck back with a side kick. Her boot burst into flame as it shot forward. An explosion like a Kinetic Grenade detonating filled the room as her attack connected.

**Ability: Dismiss**
**Deals additional damage and knockback on successful hit.**

*Why didn't he use Reflection?* Kaiden wondered. Then he realized: in a normal battle, Kaiden would have been helping with by sharing the data available via his visor, calling out all the big abilities and giving his allies the information they needed to plan their next move. Titus wasn't used to fighting alone.

The massive hit flung him into the wall, but didn't stop there. His health flashed frantically as momentum carried him through the thin wall and out into the middle of the dome, debris clattering down around him. His health fell to four percent, then held steady.

*He's still alive. It didn't kill him!*

A small victory, though, considering Nassus was still very much alive. She had Titus at her mercy, and since it was a duel, there was nothing anyone could do to step in. The game wouldn't allow it.

Titus growled as he climbed to his feet. His armor was scored around the ribs where Dismiss had hit, his shield was overloaded, and from the look in his eyes, he was definitely a bit dizzy.

"That all… you got?" he managed to stammer.

Nassus laughed at that.

"That's all you can take, big guy. Now get out of here before I send you on a weeklong vacation, yeah?"

Titus made to respond but Kaiden cut him off, stepping between him and Nassus before she changed her mind. Titus looked far from done, coasting on anger more than anything else. But the fight was unwinnable. Everyone knew it. Didn't mean the big man wanted to admit it, though.

"We're done here," Kaiden said, more to Titus than anyone else. "We're done."

"Come on," Thorne said through comms. "We'll find another way."

Titus grumbled some response but Kaiden wasn't listening, already dragging him out of the dome and back toward the *Veritas II* before Nassus could finish what she'd started.

## Chapter Seventeen

"Eighteen... nineteen... twenty." Titus groaned as he fought through the last push-up of the set. He'd been switching between different body weight exercises for over an hour now. Sweat ran from his forehead, splattered to the concrete floor below.

*Grinding in-game and out,* Thorne thought. *Though probably blowing off steam as well.* He was still angry about Maximus. Angry Nassus had baited him into such a stupid duel. Angry that he'd damn near gotten himself killed and hurt the whole damn team. Thorne had made sure he was aware of that. Titus had understood and apologized, but the anger was far from gone. Presently, he was working it out through physical exertion, but that didn't mean he was letting it go. No, if she was a gambler, she'd wager he was set on getting back at Maximus.

*As long as he keeps focused on the bigger picture and doesn't push himself too hard.* With how much everyone had been grinding in-game, and how little sleep they'd been getting because of it, it was important they all stayed as sharp as possible. Needed to keep clear minds.

*Probably I should take a bit of my own advice.*

She'd exhausted herself delivering a physical copy of the database to Dawson. Really, it'd been a simple task, taking the van back to the edge of the city then hiding the database and sending him a message with instructions on where to find it. Nonetheless, she'd been looking over her shoulder the whole time, and the exhaustion of that sort of paranoia didn't go away quickly. But she had to power through.

Zelda was a good example. An absolute workaholic. Between grinding, eating, and finding time to sleep, she used what little time she had left to scour Bernstein's database. It seemed her sole focus.

*There's a reason these three have gotten as far as they have,* Thorne reminded herself. *Zelda's knowledge. Kaiden's perseverance. Titus' strength and connections. And now, my knowledge of the Party,* she told herself. *It's enough to be a winning combination. I know it.*

"Crackdown's still on," Kaiden said from the far side of the room where he was slung across a chair and reading the news from his handheld console. "Curfew's stricter than ever and arrests are rising."

*Good news. Well, not because more arrests are good, but if the Party is tightening their grip, clamping down on freedoms, it means they're worried.*

"How are the people reacting?" Thorne asked. "If the Party's putting more pressure on them, they're doing us a favor. Add pressure to a closed system and it's only a matter of time before it explodes."

"Doesn't say. The only information's on what the Party's doing 'in the interest of preserving a safe and prosperous society.'"

"Makes sense," Thorne said with a nod. And it did. "Any attention the Party gives to dissidence only encourages more of it. They'll keep it quiet as long as possible."

"Or there's just no dissidence to report on," Titus said, pausing mid-crunch.

"There's always been dissidence," she said, glancing at him. "We were just good at covering it up."

Titus shrugged, then returned to his workout.

"Something else here," Kaiden said. "Sources from within NextGen Games leaked that there's some sort of spat going on between them and the Party?"

"Oh?" *Now that's interesting.*

Zelda perked up at that too, still reading something in the database, but turning an ear toward Kaiden nonetheless.

"An anonymous source, allegedly an employee of NextGen, claims that Party officials have been pressuring the company in ways that 'violate the sovereignty of NextGen digital properties, including our flagship game, Nova Online.'" Kaiden paused after reading the quote, then furrowed his brow. "What's that about?" But Thorne already knew the answer.

"Moran," she said. "He's always hated that NextGen has sole ownership over Nova. Not so much because he cares about the game, but because of what the ownership of it represents: weakness on the Party's part. Nova was – is – a thorn in their side. With the crackdown, the curfew, and who knows what else, it makes sense he'd push harder on Nova too."

"Especially considering he's searching for us in there," Zelda said, finally looking up from the database. "That run-in with – what was his name? Werner? That run-in with Werner seems evidence enough that Moran realizes we're hidden well away in the real world, at least for now. Doesn't mean he'll stop looking for us – we all know he'll do nothing of the sort – but probably he realizes his best chance of catching us – or more specifically, capturing the digital copy of the database – is in-game."

Thorne nodded at all of that.

"Exactly. Moran's gonna push harder and harder until he gets what he wants. A curfew, more arrests, pressure on NextGen to hand over authority of Nova – they're all part of the bigger plan. All designed to stop us." Thorne paused, then frowned. She'd realized all of this before now, but hadn't put it into so many words. Hadn't given voice to the thought. Now that she did, though, she knew there was something she'd missed.

"Werner mentioned having multiple accounts," she said, thinking on that.

"Said he had others power-leveling them for him," Kaiden said, nodding. "Honestly, it makes sense. If we had more time, I'd suggest we do the same."

Thorne leaned forward, resting her arms on her knees.

"That's just it, though. We don't have time. That's what concerns me." She looked around at all of them.

"I... don't follow," Kaiden said.

"We don't have any time to waste, right? So if you were trying to stop us, what would you do?"

Titus sat up from the floor, breathing heavy from working out, and shrugged.

"Waste our time. Delay us."

Thorne nodded. "And how best to do that?"

"Short of catching us in the real world," Zelda said slowly, "I'd try to kill us in-game. That buys a week at a time."

"Exactly. And they've tried and will continue to try. But what else can they do? What would delay us even more than killing us in-game?"

When no one responded, Thorne answered her own question.

"Taking our accounts, guys. Remember when we first logged in and all of our accounts were locked? That happens for two reasons: either NextGen bans you, or someone tries to break into your account."

"NextGen locked the accounts to protect them... " Kaiden said, eyes going wide as the realization hit him.

Thorne slapped her leg.

"Exactly! The Party was trying to force their way into our accounts. If they'd succeeded, they'd have been able to trade away the database."

"But they didn't get in," Zelda said, and from the look in her eyes, Thorne could see she was putting the pieces together now. "So now they're leaning on NextGen to give them access. That's what they're pressuring them over."

*Bingo.* Thorne nodded.

"That, or they're pressuring NextGen to just delete our accounts outright. That wouldn't get them the database, but it'd be game over for us. We're busting our rears sixteen hours a day to grind up to max level, but if we lost our accounts none of it would matter."

"No credits, no levels, no warden class." Kaiden shook his

head. "No *Veritas II* and no access to Braker, our NPC holding the database. We'd have to figure out a way to get all of that back before we could even consider our next move against the Party."

"I'd say that would slow us down a bit more than just killing us for a week," Thorne said, then cursed. "We were almost dead in the water and we didn't even realize it."

Zelda rose and headed over to her headset.

"There's no guarantee we're not." She picked it up and flicked the power switch. "If Moran's pushing for this, how long do you think NextGen can realistically hold out? They've always resisted the Party before, but have they ever been pushed this hard? If they're leaking things to the public then this is clearly something they're concerned about."

"NextGen's always held firm," Thorne said, thinking back to the dozens of times they and the Party had butted heads. "But you're right. The Party pressuring them and coming after our accounts is a ticking time bomb. And the worst part is, we don't know how long until it goes off. And if I know the Party, they'll be pushing in more ways than one."

"How else could they go about this?" Kaiden asked.

"No clue," Thorne said, shaking her head. "But believe me, they are."

"Bernstein did have that file on, what was it? 'Operation Kill-switch,'" Zelda said. "Just a mention of it, really, in the database. You think that's related?"

"Hard to say without more information on it," Thorne said. "If so, though, I'd hazard it's just one of a dozen plans they're pursuing. We can't counter them all – don't even know the full extent of them. No, our best bet is to get the database out before any of the Party's plans succeed. That's how we win. Simple as that."

"Huh." Kaiden laughed. "Yeah. Simple."

## Chapter Eighteen

**Welcome to Nova Online**

The text faded from view and Kaiden let out a long sigh of relief as he spawned into the game.

*Of course my account is still here.* But still, some small part of him had worried it wouldn't be. The Party had tried to break into his account before and failed. There was no reason to think they'd succeed if they tried again. Yet knowing his account had been targeted left him feeling exposed. And there was the remaining issue of the Party pressuring NextGen Games into... well, they weren't entirely sure what, but it was a safe guess it had to do with their accounts. Maybe with deleting them entirely.

But that hadn't happened yet. And if Kaiden was able to do anything about it, it never would.

The *Veritas II* was where they'd left it, in orbit above Kyraxis. The gaseous planet spun slowly beneath them. Towards its equator, a storm likely thousands of miles wide raged in a slow, swirling silence.

"I've never been so relieved to successfully log in," Zelda said, looking down at her character's hands as if they were new. "You don't appreciate what you have until you've lost it."

"Or nearly lost it," Thorne added.

"I knew the Party played dirty," Titus said, cracking his knuckles. "But there really is no low they won't stoop to, is there?"

Thorne shrugged.

"That's Moran for you. When he sets his mind to something, he becomes... singularly focused."

"Then we need to be just as singularly focused." Kaiden clapped his hands together. "Maximus are being a bunch of idiots and I'm not done with them yet. We can regroup and figure out a different approach to take with them, but in the meantime, I think we should chase a different lead."

"The free wardens?" Thorne suggested. "Their muscle might help us convince the idiots down there," she gestured toward Kyraxis, "to talk with us about something other than what level we are."

"Where do we find them?" Kaiden asked as he began pacing. "I mean, they don't have an established guild or anything, right? They're just a bunch of graduates from the program who still play."

Thorne nodded.

"That's true. But I know several of them. I can reach out. Arrange some meetings. Dawson might be able to help with that, too. Once he has the database. I told him where to find it, so he'll have that soon."

"We should wait on him, then. Wait until he has it before pursuing that option."

"Waiting isn't something we have time for, Kai." Zelda was on the terminal built in to the *Veritas II's* galley table. It looked like she was plotting a route.

"Maximus respects strength, right?" she said, still interfacing with the terminal. "Well, then we should show them strength. Bernstein pointed us in the direction of an ally he trusted. Or thought could be trusted." She gestured to the image of a planet on the terminal's screen. "Here."

"NC451," Kaiden said, reading the name. "Never heard of that planet."

"Probably because it's not a planet," Zelda said. "It's a moon, technically. But it's big enough to maintain an atmosphere. And it's owned by the potential powerful ally Bernstein recommended."

"Odditor," Thorne said with a knowing nod, then stepped up closer to the terminal. She leaned down to get a better view. "Never been to NC451, but I hear it's wild."

"Hold up. You said 'owned,'" Kaiden said, hung up on the word. "This guy *owns* a moon?"

Zelda smirked.

"I did say he could be a potentially powerful ally."

*Odditor...* Kaiden bit at his lip and tried to recall what else he'd heard about the player. *Dude's important, but kind of a hermit. Keeps a bunch of pet monsters, I think? And he runs some relevant factions?*

"Bernstein said he ran several factions, right? I can't remember how many."

Zelda shook her head.

"Bernstein didn't know for sure. And I didn't even know this guy was anything more than a weird streamer cashing in on people's bizarre tastes."

*Oh, right. The maze! That thing sounded awesome.*

"So, you think if we can get this guy on board with us, the combined strength of the factions he allegedly runs would be enough to convince Maximus to talk to us?" Kaiden asked.

"It's not a bad thought," Titus said with a shrug. "Though something tells me the only thing Maximus will respect is force."

"Odditor is a piece of Nova lore," Zelda said, stressing the last word. "The guy's been around since the beginning. If we can make an ally of him, there's a big chance we gain more than just the support of the factions he leads."

"She has a point there," Thorne said. "We're not particularly hurting for credits right now, but we will need a lot more than my stash to outfit an army. This guy's insanely rich, he's likely powerful too, and Bernstein thought there was a chance he could be trusted. Maybe even a chance he'd be sympathetic to our cause."

"And there's a chance if he does join us that Maximus will reconsider…" Kaiden pondered that a moment. "Apparently it takes allies to gain allies. Sort of like a line of dominos and we just need to knock down the first one."

Zelda raised her shoulders in a shrug.

"That's the theory, at least. And at present, I don't have a better one."

"What about 'The Syndicate?'" Titus said out of the blue. "Bernstein also mentioned them."

*Yeah, he did.* Something about them had resonated with Kaiden when he'd first heard of them. Something about their mystery, maybe.

"'The Syndicate' doesn't exist," Thorne said, fixing Titus with a firm gaze. "Odditor is a piece of Nova folklore, but 'The Syndicate' is just a collection of rumors and made-up stories."

"Probably," Kaiden added. "Probably just rumors."

Thorne scoffed at that.

"But I think Zelda's right," Kaiden continued. "We know Odditor actually exists. Whether he's as strong as Bernstein seemed to think, well, we'll see. But at the very least, we know where to find him. Everything else we can figure out once we meet him."

"Assuming we don't get the same treatment we did here," Titus said with a growl and cast a glance back toward Kyraxis.

*He's not letting that go anytime soon, is he?*

"So, it's settled, then?" Zelda looked up at them all. "We make for NC451 and Odditor. Find out if Bernstein's suspicions were correct and see if we can't win a major ally in the process?"

Thorne grunted her approval. Titus nodded.

Kaiden hesitated a moment, then nodded as well.

"Done." Zelda swiped at the terminal's screen and the route she'd plotted flew off to one side. "Acton," she said through comms. "I just sent up a course to a small moon."

"We received it, Captain."

"Great. It's a bit of a backwater, but that might just work in our favor. I know we have the new transponder, but let's do our best to avoid major space lanes on the way there, yeah? The

Warden Corps knows we're using a transponder, so there's a good chance they'll just be scanning every light cruiser they come across."

"Understood, ma'am."

The engines of the *Veritas II* fired to life, and outside the window, Kyraxis began to move slowly away.

"Well, there it is." Kaiden looked at everyone in the room with him. "Maximus didn't work out as planned, but it's gonna take more than that to stop us." He turned toward the bridge. Somewhere, far in front of them, NC451 waited.

"We should learn what we can about this Odditor guy. When does he stream? We could tune into one of those. Might help us learn what we'll be dealing with once we arrive."

Zelda shuddered at the mention of the stream.

"We could also not do that," she said. "There's a fair bit of information online. I'd rather read that.

"I don't know," Titus said, a smile pulling at his lips. "The obstacle course monster stream sounded kind of interesting."

*Finally!* Kaiden tried not to smile too much. *Someone agrees with me.*

"You have fun with that," Zelda said. "I'll stick to Bernstein's database and Novapedia."

"Thorne?" Kaiden asked, turning to her. "What d'ya say? You in?"

She looked to Zelda, hesitated, then back to Kaiden. Finally, she shrugged, then smiled.

"I mean, it counts as research, right?"

## Chapter Nineteen

*Almost there. Come on, you got this!* Kaiden watched from a too-close perspective as the camera followed the frantic player. Her breath was ragged, her stamina near expended from the ordeal, but she was close.

Kaiden could feel his own adrenaline pumping even though he wasn't actually the one running the labyrinth. The whole thing was being streamed from flying camera drones following HeleneSixer, the low-level player who'd somehow found her way into Odditor's Menagerie of Madness.

She'd stolen the flag – Kaiden could see it, strapped to her back and flapping in the wind – but now she needed to place it on the podium that was somewhere nearby. Normally that wouldn't have been so difficult. But then there was the ever-shifting labyrinth to consider. Oh, and the horde of grachnids she'd stolen the flag from.

Walls that looked to be some gruesome combination of machinery and organic material, complete with vein-like vines, rose around her. They whirred and whispered as they moved, sometimes rising higher, other times lowering to the ground enough to reveal a new path. They were player-made structures, which meant they worked differently than what the devs had put into the game. For one, they could move and change shape every so often.

Helene's breath came fast as she ran, then reared back, sliding on her heels to stop from tumbling into a seemingly bottomless pit that opened in front of her.

*Don't stop, jump!* Kaiden almost shouted aloud. But Helene couldn't hear him. She realized what she had to do, however, and launched herself across the pit. But she'd lost too much speed. She wasn't going to clear it.

Kaiden's view tilted sharply as Helene looked down to the pit below her – the pit she was falling into. Then she used an ability. Kaiden couldn't see what class she was but it must have been some sort of non-warden equivalent to an enhanced warden. A dexterity-based class. There was an explosion in the air beneath her and then she was tumbling forward. She flipped end over end, but the blast from the ability had launched her forward enough. She came down on the far side of the pit, dirt and sand flying as she rolled to a stop.

Safe.

"Hey... she's pretty good," a voice rang out, echoing through the labyrinth. Odditor's voice, Kaiden knew. He'd been commentating on the whole ordeal and switching the stream to whichever drone had the best view.

"You've, uh. Well, you've seen it for yourselves, folks. We have quite the competitor here," Odditor said. He had a strange manner of speaking. The flow of his sentences was broken, jumbled. He paused after certain words, or stammered a syllable or two, as if he was thinking about what to say next on the fly. And yet, he still sounded intelligent. Like he had so many thoughts flying around in his head that he had trouble picking which to say aloud.

"Take that, you big roach!" Helene shouted as she shook a fist at the grachnid that had been pursuing her. The massive insect-like alien was stuck at the edge of the bottomless pit, hissing and screeching, but unable to make the jump. She flipped it the bird.

"Well now. That was, that was just... uncalled for." Odditor said, disappointment in his voice.

*Focus on the labyrinth! You're almost there!* Kaiden wanted to shout at Helene. The walls and ground were still moving around her, but Odditor had switched the camera to the aerial view and Kaiden could see she wasn't far from the finish line. All she had to do was get to the exit of the maze and make it over one final jump.

"She's close. Look, look! She's close," Odditor said, excitement building in his voice. At the same time, it somehow didn't feel like he was excited for *her*, but for something else. "Oh, she might just have it…" His voice rang with an almost sing-song quality as he said the last line. Like someone dangling a toy in front of their cat, encouraging them to go for it, but ready to snatch it away at the last moment.

Helene was moving again, the brilliant red flag billowing in the wind as she sprinted around another corner, then slid under a closing archway. She came back up to her feet and then the exit was right in front of her. Twenty more paces to it.

*She's gonna make it!*

Something stirred in the ground in front of her, but Helene didn't see it. She was raising the flag, holding it high and sprinting toward the exit.

"We might have a winner today, everyone. Let's give it up for HeleneSixer, huh? She did so well!"

A burst of dust exploded from the ground and a grachnid hissed as it rose from its hidden burrow. Insectile legs closed around Helene. She had just enough time to scream before the grachnid squeezed her tight, locking her in a cage of limbs, and slid back beneath the earth like a trapdoor spider retreating into its hole.

A single puff of dust shot into the air as the door to the grachnid's burrow slipped shut. All that was left above ground was the lone red flag, lying in the dirt. Silence descended across the labyrinth. Even Odditor was quiet for a moment. Then, finally, he gave a little chuckle.

"Well, uh. There it is." The camera cut back to him, watching from his command center above the labyrinth. His character was older, with slicked-back gray hair, a thick-rimmed pair of glasses, and a salt-and-pepper colored beard of stubble.

He looked solemn as he spoke, but the corner of his lip was turned up ever so slightly, hinting at a smile. He shook his head.

"Helene, Helene. Oh, but you got so close! You almost had it!" The veneer of disappointment boiled away to be replaced by a knowing smirk. "But my menagerie is not so easily beaten, no, no." He clapped his hands next, holding them up in the air. "Everyone, a hand for today's competitors. They, uh, well. They tried."

"Kai! You're off target!" Zelda shouted through comms. "Kai!"

Kaiden pulled himself from the stream and back to the battle in front of him.

*Oh, crap. She's right.*

He'd been trying to multitask, watching Odditor's stream and battling the stolen light cruiser they were supposed to be crippling.

"Aim for the engines, Kai," Zelda said, frustration clear in her voice. Deserved frustration, if he was being honest with himself.

"Sorry, sorry. I've got it now."

He adjusted his crosshair and returned his barrage of fire to the enemy ship's engines. The shields were already down, so each shot dealt hull damage to the enemy vessel. After a few seconds of concentrated fire one of the engine cones exploded and spun off into space. A moment later a shot must have hit a fuel line as what remained of the engines went up in a burning explosion of rocket fuel.

**Quest Complete: Cripple the stolen cruiser**
**Reward: 7,000 EXP, 1,500 credits**

**Level 37 achieved!**
**Max health and stamina increased**
**+3 stat points**

**Ability unlocked: Matter Shift**

"Sloppy shooting, guys. But we did it, I guess," Zelda said through comms.

"Sorry," Kaiden said again. "Just zoned out a bit there. You can only take down so many enemy ships before it starts to get mind-numbing."

"Gotta stay focused," Zelda said. She was being diplomatic, he knew. Likely she was more aggravated than she was letting on. He knew how important it was that they keep leveling. But there were limits to how long one could focus. And besides, Odditor's stream had been a rush.

*I see why people like it.*

"That was a close one," Titus said, opening a private comm channel with Kaiden. A moment later he added Thorne to it too. "You guys saw that, right? She almost made it!"

"That burrowing grachnid at the end was kind of a dirty trick," Thorne said. She paused. "But it was pretty cool, too."

Kaiden was only half listening, though. He'd pulled up his character sheet and assigned his new stat points to dexterity.

### Character

*Name:*
**Kaiden**
*Race:*
**Human**
*Level:*
**37**
*Class:*
**Enhanced Warden**
**Attributes**

*Strength:*
**52 (+2)**
*Intelligence:*
**46**
*Endurance:*
**52**

*Perception:*
46
*Dexterity:*
132 (+2)
*Unassigned:*
0
Abilities
*Kickback*
*Shield Bash*
*Hammer Toss*
*Lightspeed*
*Improved Enhanced Senses*
*Riposte*
*Flash Bang*
*Improved Blur*
*Onslaught*
**Enfeebling Strike**

Slayer (passive)
Hamstring
*Matter Shift*

Perks
Turen Tinkering

Stat points assigned, his full attention could now be turned to the new ability he'd unlocked.

*Ooh buddy, this looks fun.*

**Ability: Matter Shift**
You glow with infused charge for one second, then teleport from your current location to another within 20 feet.
Cast time: 1 second.
Cost: 40 charge.
Cooldown: 2 minutes.

"Check this out, guys," Kaiden said to everyone as he screen-capped the ability and sent it to them. "Forty charge is a lot to use, but this is basically a free flank. Need me behind an enemy healer? No problem. As long as I have forty charge and one second of time, it's done."

"That could be very tactical when used correctly," Zelda said, no doubt reading through the ability. "But we have to make sure you don't overcommit and get cut off."

"Eh, I'll be fine. Combine this with Lightspeed or Kickback and no one's going to be able to keep up with me."

"I learned that one the hard way," Thorne chimed in.

*Oh, true that.* Kaiden thought back to when he'd squared off with her in the hangar of the *Anakoni.*

"It's all good," Thorne said with a laugh. "Considering how things have shaken out, it's a darn good thing you kicked my ass then."

Kaiden couldn't hold back a triumphant smile. He was glad he was in his turret and not face to face with her. He didn't want to gloat, but he had outplayed her that day.

The *Veritas II* shook as the pilot kicked the engines back up to full speed. The ship they'd crippled disappeared behind them. In theory, the security force that had assigned the quest to them was supposed to come and board it, then retake the vessel. Whether or not the game actually played that out, Kaiden wasn't sure. The ship was just as likely to despawn once they were out of range. He'd have liked to hang around to find out, but while they were grinding as much as possible, they were still doing their best to stay on course toward NC451. Had to be close by now, actually.

He was distracted as several screenshots popped up in his vision: everyone else's abilities.

"Check that," Titus said through comms. "Nothing flashy, but it's a solid upgrade."

**Ability: Improved Volt Field (passive, replaces Volt Field)**
**Send a current across your armor, causing 50% of base damage as electrical damage to all melee attackers.**
**Cost: 40% of total shield capacity. This ability is passive**

**when activated and is toggled on and off.**

*Nice!* The unimproved Volt Field had dealt thirty percent base damage at the cost of thirty percent of shield capacity. The improved version dealt twenty percent more damage for only ten percent more of shield capacity.

Zelda's new ability was next. Thankfully they all had pretty much the same amount of experience so leveling happened at around the same time. Thorne was on a completely different track, though. Judging from the lack of a screenshot, Kaiden figured she hadn't unlocked anything in their grinding so far. She had to be due soon, though.

He turned his attention to Zelda's screenshot.

**Ability: Improved Atmospheric Charge (replaces Atmospheric Charge)**
**Allows you access to an alternate source of charge, drawing energy from your surroundings at a rate of 7 charge every 1 second in combat.**

"I've been a bit starved on charge lately," she said. "Shield Linking with Titus has helped, but as we've faced stronger opponents I've needed to really unload attack after attack on them. Especially considering I'm the only respectable DPS in this group," she said, a taunting note to her voice.

"Hey now," Thorne fired back. "I have a very big hammer that has something to say about that."

"Pshh. That hammer isn't gonna help you if you can't get close enough to hit me."

"Alright, alright," Titus said. "We're preparing to storm Warden HQ, you know. There'll be plenty of enemies for both of you."

"We'll see who takes more down," Thorne said and from the confidence in her voice Kaiden could envision the smirk on her face.

"Captains," Acton's voice cut in. "If you're quite done, we've arrived."

## Chapter Twenty

"This is privately owned space. Access is restricted without special permission. Depart the area or you will be fired upon," a robotic voice said as Kaiden arrived at the cockpit. His turret was the forwardmost on the ship so he had a shorter walk than everyone else.

Looking out of the windshield, Kaiden could see the moon NC451 below them. From their current altitude it looked to be covered entirely in ocean, a deep, green-blue sea that covered all visible parts of the planetoid.

"This is privately owned space. Access is restricted without special permission. Depart the area or you will be fired upon." The message played again.

"Their orbital turrets just came online, Captain," Acton said. "We might not want to push our luck here."

*We're not getting turned away again. Not after that mess on Kyraxis.*

"Put me on," Kaiden said. A moment later a message appeared in his vision, confirming he was broadcasting down to the surface. "This is Kaiden, captain of the..." He paused. "SS *Andronicus*. We have information for Odditor. Information he'll want to hear."

Silence followed his words, broken only by the thumping of footsteps as Zelda and Thorne arrived behind him. Titus came last at a half jog.

"That might have done something... they're scanning us," Acton reported, then winced. "It's an advanced scan, though. Our transponder might not hold up to that."

"Why'd we get it, then?" Titus complained. "I thought it was supposed to keep us hidden?"

"From scans, yes. But advanced scanners have a chance of identifying it as a fake. Most players and factions don't bother to stock advanced scanners, though," Zelda said. "They're too expensive."

"We only have a few in the entire Warden Corps," Thorne added.

"This guy's got his own moon, advanced scanners, a zoo's worth of monsters..." Titus shook his head. "He's living large."

*And not taking any chances.* Kaiden cursed as the robotic message played again.

"This is privately owned space. Access is restricted without special permission. Depart the area or you will be fired upon. This your final warning."

"Turrets just locked on to us," Acton said. "Now would be a good time to brace yourselves."

*Darn it. Why can't anything just work out?*

"Get us ready to move," Kaiden said to the pilot.

"We'll pull back to a safe distance," Acton said with a nod.

"No." Kaiden leaned on the back of the pilot's seat and peered down toward NC451. "If they shoot, head for the surface. We need to get down there any way we can."

"Can we survive those turrets?" Zelda asked, concern in her voice.

"No." Acton left little room for uncertainty with his response. "A few hits and what's left of us won't be able to do anything but burn up in NC451's atmosphere."

"I'm not taking no for an answer," Kaiden said. "Not again. We have to—"

"SS *Andronicus*, huh?" a voice said through comms. It was deep and rough, with a somehow strained echo, as if unused to speaking. "Our scanners beg to differ."

*Shit.*

"Who is this?" Kaiden asked, peering down at the moon as if he could see the speaker down there.

"I speak for Odditor," the voice said. "And right now he'd like to know why you've shown up with a fake transponder. Are you trying to hide something from us? Bah. No matter. Our scans will answer that in a moment."

*Well, this is off to a great start. What option do I have now but the truth?*

"The transponder is to protect us from unwanted attention. We've had... some trouble getting here. I can understand why it seems suspicious to hide our identities, but we didn't mean anything dishonest by it. We're here to talk."

"SS *Veritas II*?" the voice said, then paused. A long moment later, it spoke again. "Odditor tells me that's a good name around here. You're cleared to land."

*Wait. What?*

Kaiden had been prepared to protest, to haggle their way down to the surface, but he hadn't expected this.

"Um, thanks?" he said, then shook himself. "I mean, thank you. We'll be down in a moment." He cut the broadcast to the surface and faced the others. "That went better than expected."

"They recognized the name *Veritas II*," Thorne said, then furrowed her brow. "Does that mean—"

"They know the ship," Zelda said with a nod. "Or they knew Bernstein. Either way, it's our ticket down there."

"Turrets are offline," Acton reported. "Looks like we're clear to head in. Captains?"

Kaiden gave a nod and the pilot eased them forward and down.

NC451, as it turned out, wasn't covered in ocean. As they approached the surface Kaiden could see more clearly. The uniform green color was the product of a moon-spanning jungle whose canopy was so thick the *Veritas II's* scanners couldn't penetrate it. Thankfully, a landing zone had been cleared and marked with beacons designed to guide them in.

Mist rose from the trees on all sides, swirling in the air and clinging to the ship's windows as thick droplets of water. And every mile or so, volcanic vents spewed a thick, heavy smoke up through the trees. The pilot guided them around one such vent as he brought them in to the landing pad.

The *Veritas II* touched down a few moments later. Kaiden gave Acton a nod before opening the side door and making his way down the ramp.

**Location discovered: NC451, player-owned moon**
**Faction Alignment: None**
**Resident Guild(s): None**

The message flashed the moment Kaiden's boot touched the landing pad. The rest of the group was just behind him, clanking down the ramp.

"So, uh, where are we supposed to go?" Titus asked, looking at the dense jungle surrounding the landing pad on all sides.

"That's a good question," Kaiden said.

The *Veritas II*'s lights clicked on and flooded the space in front of the ship with a blinding light. It reflected off of the billowing mist and Kaiden's visor auto-darkened to compensate for the glare.

"Our host says to follow the trail," Acton said from inside the ship.

Kaiden followed the path of the ship's lights and found a beaten dirt track beginning at the end of the landing pad.

"What? Was I supposed to bring my hiking boots for this?" Thorne asked, frowning at the path. "Why is the pad so far from Odditor's base?"

"You can ask him when we get there," Kaiden said, bounding toward the edge of the landing pad. "Come on, keep up."

The dirt squished underfoot as he stepped down into it. It was dense, and wet from the mist hanging in the air. All around the edges of the path jungle ferns leaned in close as if reaching out to grab ahold of him. Kaiden made it all of three steps before a howl burst from the foliage and a beast charged him.

Ramrunner
Level: 38
**Quick facts: Ramrunners are known for their poor sight and propensity for ambushing anything that surprises the—**

Kaiden's visor displayed information on the beast, but he was only halfway through reading it when the charging monster's head slammed into his stomach and launched him backward. His health bar flashed and dropped as he flew, then again as he slammed onto the landing pad and took fall damage.

"Ow." Kaiden pulled himself into a sitting position and took in the beast that had attacked him. It looked like a cross between a rhinoceros and a crocodile, with four legs, thick, scaly skin, and a long snout that ended with three upraised horns all in a line. The ramrunner stomped one massive foot on the ground, snorted, then turned toward the next nearest target.

"Come on, then, big boy," Titus growled and flicked his shield on. "Let's see what you got!"

A streak of light burst over Kaiden's shoulder as the *Veritas II* fired and the ramrunner exploded in a burst of flame and soil.

**Ramrunner assisted kill – 2,000 EXP gained!**

*Uh, sure. 'Assisted.' That's what I did.*
Kaiden looked back to see the *Veritas II's* front guns trained on the remains of the ramrunner. Through the windshield he could see Acton ready to fire again if necessary.

"Rather a rude way to greet guests," the first officer said, moving the guns side to side as he searched for more threats. As he did, Kaiden noticed something moving in the jungle.

"There!" he said, pointing at it with his hammer. It wasn't an animal, though, he realized as he looked closer.

"Is that... a camera?"

Thorne paced up to the trunk of the tree it was perched in.

"Sure is. Looks like it's on, too."

"Odditor," Zelda said. "He's watching us." She turned toward the path into the jungle. "How much do you want to bet there'll be more surprises waiting for us in there?"

"More surprises, and more cameras to record us fighting them. He could be streaming this," Kaiden said.

*Watching his streams is one thing, but I didn't expect to be in one anytime soon.*

"We're on one of his streams?" Titus asked. "That's awesome!" He banged his hammer against his shield and cheered. "Let's do it, then! We'll give you a show!"

"No, let's not give them a show," Zelda scolded. "If Odditor is streaming us then he's advertising our position to everyone watching. How long until the Warden Corps shows up?"

"Not long," Thorne said with a shake of her head.

"I've been informed that while the cameras are on, they are not streaming," Acton said from inside the ship. "Though I've also been informed that Odditor is looking forward to..." He paused. "'The show to come.' Apparently, there are more creatures awaiting you ahead. And in there, you're on your own."

Chapter Twenty-One

A frantic ripple of waves exploded out across the surface of Titus' Improved Barrier as another ramrunner slammed head-long into it.

Titus grunted and shook his head as if in pain.

"Shield is overloading. Can't take much more of this," he said.

Thorne darted forward from inside the barrier then swung a glowing hammer into the side of the ramrunner's head.

**Ability: Gravity Sledge**

The blow wasn't enough to launch such a large beast into the air, but it did spin it around and send it crashing to the ground.

Kaiden didn't waste any time, leaping from the protection of Titus' Improved Barrier to attack the downed beast.

**Critical hit!**
**+50% damage (Headshot)**

Considering the size of the beast's head and the fact that it was off its feet, it was pretty difficult to miss. He landed a third headshot, then a fourth before the ramrunner got its feet back under it. It shook its head side to side in a flailing attack and Kaiden dodged backward, then as soon as the danger was clear, lashed forward with another hammer strike.

**Critical hit!**
**+50% damage (Headshot)**

**Critical hit streak (x5)**

The ramrunner, its health in the yellow now, lunged toward Kaiden with a stomp attack, but he was already charging Matter Shift.

*Been wanting to try this out.*

**Ability: Matter Shift**
**You glow with infused charge for one second, then teleport from your current location to another within 20 feet.**
**Cast time: 1 second.**
**Cost: 40 charge.**
**Cooldown: 2 minutes.**

The ramrunner's leg, thick as a tree trunk, came stomping down right through Kaiden's insubstantial body. A moment later his vision flickered and then he reappeared at the spot he'd targeted behind his opponent.

*Yeah, this is awesome. I'm going to put this to very good use in future fights.*

The ramrunner seemed confused as to where he'd gone. It raised its foot and peered down to inspect the spot of ground it'd stomped.

Kaiden used the advantage of surprise to land a hammer strike on the back of his opponent's head.

**Critical hit!**
**+50% damage (Headshot)**

**Onslaught Mode activated.**

**Current movement speed and damage are doubled for 5 seconds.**

"Now we're talking!" Kaiden shouted. In addition to activating Onslaught Mode, each of his critical strikes had been regaining him charge thanks to the passive ability Slayer. He glanced down to confirm he'd enough to unleash a brutal combo.

**Ability: Enfeebling Strike**

Kaiden slammed his hammer into the ramrunner's rib cage. The thick hide hardly budged, but charge from the ability flowed into the monster and it growled in pain. Now, combined with the damage buff from Enfeebling Strike and Onslaught, each of his attacks would deal 250% damage. He laid into the beast.

The others were busy with their own fights. Titus' Improved Barrier was down and he was being beaten back beneath a barrage of ranged attacks from creatures called hominoids. Standing on far too-human legs, the hominoids looked to be some foul cross between man and ape. They jeered and howled from the tree tops and hurled down handfuls of some sort of seed that detonated in puffs of toxic powder on impact. Zelda had already chased off several groups of them as they'd fought their way down the trail. This bunch didn't seem likely to run, however. In the face of her attacks they stood firm, howling and tossing more and more toxic seed pods.

Titus Energy Gripped one down from a branch and lit into it with hammer strikes. Meanwhile, Zelda tossed an Improved Kinetic Grenade up into the canopy. It exploded in a plume of fire that left the treetops burning.

**Hominoid assisted kill – 1,500 EXP gained!**
**Hominoid assisted kill – 1,500 EXP gained!**
**Hominoid assisted kill – 1,500 EXP gained!**

"Ha! Take that!" she shouted as several corpses plummeted to the ground.

"Get out of there!" Thorne shouted, and as she did Kaiden realized the problem. The fire from the grenade had ignited the powder from the seed pods and the whole area was going up in a toxic inferno.

Zelda and Titus' health bars flashed rapidly as stacks of area-of-effect damage assaulted them.

*I'll help them in a minute. Gotta finish this up first.* Kaiden turned his full attention back to the ramrunner. It thrashed and stomped, swinging its massive head and the horns attached to it, but Kaiden was too fast with Onslaught Mode active. He danced and ducked around the beast's now slow-motion attacks, all the while lashing back with hammer strikes that each dished out large chunks of damage.

The ramrunner's health dropped into the red in the face of the barrage. The big beast cried out, then spun to retreat.

**Ability: Hammer Toss**

Kaiden's attack caught it in the back and drained what remained of its health.

**Ramrunner assisted kill - 2,000 EXP gained!**

The beast's feet went out from under it and it slammed to the ground, shaking the earth and nearby trees.

"Nice one," Thorne said, slapping him on the shoulder. "I hit level forty off that. Check this ability when you get a chance." She sent a screenshot to him but Kaiden didn't have time look at it.

"We should probably do something about that," he said, nodding toward the still-burning toxic cloud with Titus and Zelda trapped inside it. The hominoids had dropped out of the trees and surrounded it. Wherever Zelda and Titus moved to escape the inferno the hominoids cut them off, stacking up en masse and hurling more seed pods in to stoke the flames.

One of the bolder hominoids jumped right through the flames to attack Titus. The big man rammed into it, leading with his shield. His opponent was on fire, its fur aflame, but the shield kept it from burning Titus – up until the hominoid wrapped its arms around the edges of the shield and grabbed Titus in a sort of bear hug. The flames on its fur licked at his armor and Kaiden saw the big man's health tick down at an increased pace.

"My shield's building charge from the fire damage in front of me, but it's not blocking the damage coming in from the sides," Titus said through comms, sounding lost in thought for a moment, perhaps considering if the tradeoff was worthwhile.

"Forget about charge! Worry about your health," Zelda shouted, then blasted the hominoid off of Titus with an Improved Burst Arrow. She fired an Improved Scatter Shot next that caught several of the other hominoids, but only one died. The rest stood firm, daring her to try and push toward them.

Time wasn't on her side, though. Her health was down to fifty-three percent and dropping by the second. Titus was beside her at fifty-eight percent himself.

"We have to get them out of there!" Kaiden shouted.

"Ooh, actually, this is perfect," Thorne said and strode toward the chaos.

"How is this perfect?" Kaiden shook his head. "Never mind. Just focus on the hominoids. If we can make a hole in their formation Zelda and Titus will be able to get out of the fire."

"I've got this," Thorne said.

**Ability: Earth Shatter**

She leapt into the air…

… straight into the cloud of flame. Kaiden felt his brow furrow as he watched. She landed with an explosive boom and a shockwave that swept out and stunned several of the nearby hominoids.

"Great, now there's three of us trapped in here," Zelda said.

Thorne smirked.

"On the contrary…"

Ability: Improved Instigated Fury
The fervor of battle sweeps over you. For the next 8 seconds, each time you take damage, your base attack increases by 15%.
Cost: 20 charge.
Cooldown: 1 minute.

Kaiden's visor showed him the specifics as she activated her ability.

Inside the toxic, flaming cloud, Thorne was taking constant damage. Enough to kill her if she stayed long enough, but from the looks of things, she wasn't going to be there very long. With every second she took area-of-effect damage from the cloud, her base attack power increased by fifteen percent.

She charged the nearest hominoid. Its companions rushed to its side, but that only seemed to embolden Thorne. She brought her hammer down on it and drained a good third of its health.

The flaming cloud continued to chip away at her health bar as the hominoids attacked, howling as they flung themselves at her and struck with arms thick as Kaiden's thighs.

Thorne's health bar flashed constantly, but all of that damage converted right back into increased attack power. She swung her hammer relentlessly, giving as good as she got.

Hominoid assisted kill – 1,500 EXP gained!

And then giving better than she got.

Hominoid assisted kill – 1,500 EXP gained!
Hominoid assisted kill – 1,500 EXP gained!

And finally, giving so much the hominoids started to panic. Every swing of her hammer dropped her target to half health or less. And that was just with basic attacks. When Thorne used Hammer Sweep, a simple area-of-effect ability that damaged all targets in front of her within five feet, three homi-noids dropped dead. Experience poured in from all of the assisted kills and Kaiden smiled as another notification joined the rush.

**Level 38 achieved!**
**Max health and stamina increased**
**+3 stat points**

Those that remained of the hominoids shrieked, then panicked. With arms flailing and eyes wide, they turned and ran. Thorne used Heroic Leap and landed on one of the fleeing enemies. It died instantly.

Her health was down to thirty-five percent, but it hardly mattered. The fight was over. The few surviving hominoids disappeared into the jungle and Zelda and Titus hurried from the inferno.

"Holy crap," Kaiden said, unable to stop himself from laughing at what he'd just seen. "That's... an inventive way to use that ability. But I can't knock it. Talk about stacking damage!"

"That. Was. Awesome!" Titus slapped Thorne so hard on the back that she stumbled forward. When she turned, he already had both hands in the air for a double high five. "I mean, we totally had things under control, but still. That was sick!"

She smirked as she gave him a firm high five, then flicked her buckler-like shield off. Even Zelda was forced to give a shrug and a nod.

"It was clever."

"Saw the opportunity and went for it, I guess," Thorne said.

"So, the lesson we learned is that the next time we need to deal a bunch of damage quickly we just have to set Thorne on fire," Kaiden said, smirking at her still-smoking armor as he pulled up his character sheet to give it a quick once-over and assign his stat points.

### Character

*Name:*

Kaiden
*Race:*
Human
*Level:*
**38**
*Class:*
**Enhanced Warden**
**Attributes**

*Strength:*
**53 (+2)**
*Intelligence:*
**47**
*Endurance:*
**53**
*Perception:*
**47**
*Dexterity:*
**136 (+2)**
*Unassigned:*
**0**
**Abilities**
*Kickback*
*Shield Bash*
*Hammer Toss*
*Lightspeed*
*Improved Enhanced Senses*
*Riposte*
*Flash Bang*
*Improved Blur*
*Onslaught*
**Enfeebling Strike**

Slayer (passive)
Hamstring
*Matter Shift*

## Perks
## Turen Tinkering

"Well, now. That was certainly a spectacle," said a voice Kaiden didn't recognize. Except he *did* recognize it, he realized as he closed his character sheet. It was the voice he'd heard in the cockpit of the *Veritas II*. The voice that had claimed to speak for Odditor.

He turned to find a bulky figure emerging through the smoke from the flames. It stood eight feet tall, at least, and was exceptionally hairy.

*A massive hominoid!* But it wasn't. Not exactly.

While it was massive, ape-shaped, and hairy, the figure also had undeniably turen features: slits for nostrils, wide, intelligent eyes, and arms that, while they were packed with thick muscle like the hominoids' had been, were also elongated like those of a turen. Kaiden focused on the figure and his visor did its thing.

**Whenstone**
**Class: Medic**
**Modified Species: 'Turenoid'**
**Faction: The Menagerie**
**Level: 60**
**Quick facts: Max-level medics who have invested in the Genetic Modification specialty may complete a class-specific legendary quest to evolve into a 'modified species,' which is created by mixing two of several predetermined species. Doing so gives the player 80% of the strengths and 100% of the weaknesses of both species.**

"Nice to meet you in person," Whenstone said to the gawking faces in front of him. "I work for Odditor." He gestured up to the cameras that had been watching them all along the trail. "He appreciates the show you've put on. So, if you'll follow me, he might care to speak with you."

## Chapter Twenty-Two

*Turenoid?* Thorne observed Whenstone from behind. *That's a combination that makes a lot of sense. Strength from the hominoids, intelligence from the turen. Plus all the normal skills of a max-level medic.*

They followed the turenoid along what was left of the path, cameras watching them every step of the way. Creatures stirred in the jungle on both sides, but even the boldest of them were sent running with the slightest growl from Whenstone. Not that she could blame them. He was level sixty and, given this was a PVP zone, wouldn't have much trouble crushing all of them at once, if he wanted to.

*Medics aren't designed for offensive combat, but still. It probably wouldn't matter, not with that level disparity.*

"And here we are," Whenstone said, gesturing forward as his deep, strained voice spoke the words.

Thorne followed the gesture up to where, just ahead, the path ended. Where it did, the jungle opened up around it. A small patch of grass led to a metal platform. As she looked closer she realized the platform was actually an old freight elevator, but attached to a large ramp that led up and up to...

"The Madhouse," Whenstone said, looking up at it as well. And what a sight it was.

The structure had to have been forty stories tall, at least, and appeared to be mostly in the shape of a large ring. *Hollow in the center?* Thorne couldn't tell from their current spot. The sides of the building – base? Complex? Town? It could have been any of them from its size – were covered in creeper vines and moss and a whole mess of other green foliage growing out of every nook and cranny. Thorne found herself reminded of their humble swamp bunker in the real world, except this structure, in comparison, stretched all the way up to the low-hanging, rain-heavy clouds above.

"Odditor lives there?" Kaiden asked as Whenstone led them all on to the elevator. Somewhere in the distance, something massive roared – a sound that shook the very air itself and seemed to reverberate through the ground – and Kaiden turned toward it, concern in his eyes. Thorne couldn't blame him.

Whenstone, however, merely chuckled.

"The longer you're here, the more you'll find the inhabitants of this moon are quite... diverse. But pay them no mind for now. They know to stay well away from The Madhouse." He waved his hand at a sensor on the elevator. It beeped and then the whole platform began to move, sliding up along the ramp with a groan of well-used metal.

"We came here to see Odditor," Thorne said, turning her attention from the vast jungle around them and meeting Whenstone's eyes.

"It's critical that we speak with him," Zelda said.

"Odditor will determine what's critical and what isn't," Whenstone said. "For now, you should be grateful he allowed you to land. That's more than most unannounced visitors are offered."

"Why *did* you let us land?" Thorne asked. The question had been bothering her. It'd seemed like Odditor had recognized the *Veritas II*, Bernstein's old ship.

*Does that mean he knew Bernstein?* The database implied some connection, but wasn't specific.

"You were allowed to land because Odditor said so," Whenstone said. "It's not my place to speculate as to his motives." With that, he fell silent, seemingly lost in staring out at the world falling away beneath them.

*This guy takes his roleplay seriously, huh?*

The elevator had carried them halfway up the side of the building now, and far above the canopy. Their view of the jungle moon stretched all the way to the misty horizon. Thorne found herself distracted by its beauty, lost in the rolling waves of the wind in the treetops.

With a long groan, the elevator came to a stop and Thorne found they'd arrived at an opening in the outside of the Madhouse. A steady stream of animal sounds poured out from within – growls and chirps, howls and barks – but they were twisted and distorted as they echoed down the metal hallway, deformed into a cacophony of sound like some discordant chorus of nightmares.

Whenstone stepped off the platform, then waved them after him.

"If you'd like to know why Odditor let you land, perhaps it's best you ask him yourself?"

With that, he strode into the hallway.

Everyone else hesitated.

"This is what we came here for," Zelda said. "So what are we waiting for?" She stepped off the elevator and jogged to catch up with Whenstone.

*Gotta admire her dedication.*

Thorne swallowed any doubt the monstrous noises had created and followed after Zelda. Titus and Kaiden were right behind, though a glimmer of blue light revealed Titus had flicked his shield on.

"This is straight spooky," he said as they continued down the hallway and the overcast, gray light from outside was replaced with dull metallic tones and the dim yellow lights that lined the floor and led them onward.

The monstrous chorus grew louder with each step as Whenstone took them toward whatever was responsible for the noise.

"Odditor is this way?" Kaiden asked from behind, his voice unsure.

Whenstone's only response was to wave them on, then disappear around the corner. Thorne hurried after him, not wanting to get left behind in the darkness. It was silly, she knew, to be afraid of a game, but sometimes Nova felt so real it was easy to forget you were even playing it.

Zelda turned the corner first, then skidded to a stop. Thorne nearly bowled her over, but managed to slip to the side with only minor contact.

"What was that about?" she asked, looking at Zelda. But she didn't reply. Instead, her eyes were wide and her mouth open as she stared at... something.

Thorne followed her eyes to the thing she was looking at. Except it wasn't just one thing; it was a dozen. No, more. Two dozen, at least.

Beasts, monsters, gigantic insects, and things Thorne had no way to describe all stared back at them. Some mewled, others howled. Some seemed itching to strike, claws as long as Thorne was tall and twitching in anticipation. Some hissed and reared back, fangs and venom glands threatening a quick death. Everywhere Thorne looked there were eyes looking back at her. Some reptilian, others mammalian, and still more she couldn't classify.

The only mercy was that they were all in cages.

"Odditor's Menagerie of Madness," Whenstone said, walking confidently down the middle of the hall and gesturing out to the cages stacked three high on all sides. "He's rather fond of it. It has taken an extremely long time to collect."

"These things are really high level," Kaiden whispered. "My visor's reading none of them below forty. Most above fifty." As he spoke, he stepped closer to Titus, who raised his still-active shield into a ready position.

"Have no fear," Whenstone said, then frowned. "Well, fear is healthy, and many of these majestic creatures are efficient predators. Fearsome to face in a fight. But they can't harm you now. Not as long as Odditor decides to keep them in their cages."

"'Decides to?'" Thorne asked. "Are you implying he might uncage them?"

Whenstone shrugged.

"It's not for me to speculate. Come, now. Odditor is waiting." And with that he continued down the hallway.

The cages and beasts and echoing growls continued as they progressed deeper into Odditor's base. From what Thorne could see as they walked, her initial assumption about the place had been correct. It was a big ring. The hallway they were in followed a curve so gentle it seemed unending. At every intersection, they passed hallways which allowed views down into the center of Odditor's Madhouse.

It was a view Thorne recognized all too well from the streams she'd watched. At the center of the massive building was the whole structure's focus and purpose: the labyrinth. At present, it appeared dormant. The walls stood unmoving. No grachnids screeched from within. And no player ran for their life, desperately trying to outwit, outlast, or simply outplay whatever monstrous challenge awaited. But all of that could change, Thorne knew. *Would* change during the next stream. Hopefully not sooner.

Watching through a stream, the whole deal made for good entertainment. Now, walking through the very halls so many others had trodden before perishing in the labyrinth, Thorne was starting to reconsider that opinion.

The menagerie was mostly behind them now, though. Instead, the cages were replaced with... museum exhibits? Thorne did a double-take. Instead of monsters behind the glass there were now life-sized figures, unmoving and posed in various ways. Some looked to be in combat. Others accomplished seemingly random feats such as repairing a ship or scaling a mountain.

"What are these?" Thorne asked, squinting in the low light to get a better view.

Whenstone gestured, and lights clicked on inside the displays.

"Oh. Oh, wow." She felt her breath catch in her throat.

With proper illumination, she could make out exactly what the displays were: players, dressed in their finest gear and posed in scenes of battle or great triumph. All of them, though, were dead. Or more specifically, retired. It was easy enough to tell from the empty, still darkness in their eyes.

"These are all trophies," Zelda said. "And they're authentic? Not recreations?"

"Everything Odditor owns is authentic," Whenstone said as if insulted by the suggestion.

"I'm sorry," Kaiden said, seemingly confused. "I don't understand. Are these not just manikins?"

Zelda pointed to the nearest one.

"Trophies are deactivated accounts, normally from players of some acclaim. Top-level PVPers will sometimes put their accounts on the line in exclusive tournaments. It's seen as the ultimate form of PVP. To lose is akin to permadeath. Whoever beats you gains your account."

"Like racing for pink slips," Titus said.

Thorne nodded along, then jumped in herself.

"PVP isn't the only source, though. Players who've achieved notable firsts – like exploring a new system or completing a new legendary-tier dungeon – can sometimes gain enough acclaim to make their accounts valuable. When they retire, or just really need some real-world money, they can deactivate their accounts and sell them to become trophies. Considering the most famous of accounts sell for hundreds of millions of credits, and even less famous ones can be in the tens of millions, well, that's a nice chunk of real-world cash once you convert it."

Titus whistled low as she finished.

"Sounds like easy money to me."

"Not even close," Thorne said with a laugh. "There aren't that many accounts worthy of becoming trophies." She gestured to the dozen or so lining the hallway around them. "This selection here has to amount to, what, ten percent of all existing trophies in the game? I forget how many there were valued at over ten million at last count, but it wasn't that many."

"How does he have this many?" Kaiden asked. "He can't possibly own all of these."

Whenstone let out a low laugh at that.

"The rules of what can and can't be owned change when you're as powerful as Odditor. Excess is not a word in his vocabulary."

Even from a pace away, Thorne heard Kaiden swallow hard at that.

"No reason for nerves," she said to him, switching over to group comms so Whenstone wouldn't hear. "The more powerful he is, the more it'll benefit us when we convince him to join our side."

"Or the more likely he is to just brush us off as a waste of his time," Titus said.

"That's... not going to happen," Kaiden said finally. "Not again. I won't let it."

*That's the spirit,* Thorne wanted to say, but she was distracted as the seemingly unending hallway came to an abrupt end. Whenstone turned to face them in front of an unexceptional looking door.

"Odditor is ready for you. It goes without saying that, should you treat him with less than the honor he is owed, it will not end well. For you." With that happy message, he made a gesture with his hand and the door behind him slid open.

## Chapter Twenty-Three

The room was barren but for three things: a holotable at the center, a wall-sized window looking down to the labyrinth, and Odditor. Everything else was, well, nothing. Empty floor space, barren walls. A strange choice of decor, but Kaiden wasn't interested in any of it. There was one person he'd come to see.

**Odditor**
**Class: Medic**
**Faction: Unaffiliated**
**Level: 60**

"Oh, they made it!" Odditor turned from where he'd been leaning over the holotable. What looked to be a schematic of the labyrinth was projected above it, but he turned it off with a snap of his fingers. "It's always a bit of..." He trailed off as if searching for the right word. "A bit of a surprise when visitors make it this far. The menagerie is just so hungry," he said with a knowing nod.

Zelda frowned. "You mean those cages weren't secure?"

"Absolutely."

"Absolutely they weren't secure? Or absolutely they were?"

Odditor gave a firm nod.

"Yes."

Zelda frowned all the more and moved a pace away from the door.

"Odditor, uh, sir," Kaiden said, waving and stepping forward. "We came because—"

"Ooh, look at you!" Odditor placed his hands on his hips and strode forward with an excited smile. "An enhanced warden? How unique! You must be... heh... you must..." He trailed off again with a chuckle, the rest of whatever he'd been planning to say still hanging in the air.

*I must be what?* Kaiden had genuinely no idea what the man had been getting at. *Bernstein did say he was eccentric...*

"Enhanced wardens," Odditor said, shaking a finger at him. "Tsk-tsk. You're slippery. All those jumps and dodges." He leaned to one side then the other in what Kaiden assumed was supposed to be an imitation of said acrobatics. "Oh, and that one thing, uh, that thing you do where there's multiple of you." He waved his fingers as if doing a magic trick, then chuckled. "Oh, that drives the menagerie insane." He clapped a hand down on Kaiden's shoulder. "They get *so* angry. Why, the last one, when they caught him..."

"I... uh... must've missed that stream." Kaiden stumbled over his words, unsure how to respond.

*Focus, darn it!* He forced himself to remember why they'd come.

"We're big fans of your stream."

"We are?" Zelda asked.

"But we came for a different reason. We think you knew a friend of ours, someone very important. Fred Bernstein."

Odditor bit his lip and scrunched up his face.

"Bernstein... Bernstein..." He snapped his fingers as if trying to remember. "Didn't he...? Wasn't...? Oh, yes! He's the one that left the... thing. The, uh..."

"The dreadnought, sir," Whenstone said.

"Yes, that big ship!" Odditor turned to Kaiden with a whisper. "A real pain to store, if you know what I mean. What was it called? The *Very...* something. Heh. Ha." He gave an awkward laugh. "The *Very Big*, should... should have been called that."

"The *Veritas?*" Zelda asked, sounding as if she didn't believe it.

"Ayy! That's the... that's the one!" Odditor said pointing at her. "And your ship, your little thing, it had a similar name. I thought it sounded familiar. That's why I had my turrets not kill you."

"Bernstein loaned you the *Veritas?* Loaned you his dreadnought?"

"Loaned, surrendered, lost in an attempt to beat my labyrinth." Odditor waved his hand as if they were all pretty much the same thing.

Kaiden shot Zelda a look, then switched to group comms.

"Bernstein tried to run the labyrinth? Why would he have done that?"

"Maybe he was trying to get closer to Odditor?" Zelda replied with a nod toward the strange man. "If he bet his dreadnought on it then it was clearly important to him."

"Hey, hey! Uh, Whenstone? Whenstone!"

Odditor was snapping toward the turenoid.

"Their mouths, their mouths are moving but, but I don't hear anything." Odditor pointed at them. "Am I, am I going deaf? I don't understand."

"They're talking through private comms," Whenstone said matter-of-factly. "Which is rude."

"Oh. Oh, yes. Of course." Odditor breathed a fake sigh of relief. Or a real one. Kaiden honestly couldn't tell. "Don't, don't scare me like that," he said, looking to Kaiden as he clapped a hand over his chest.

*This is the guy who's supposed to control a dozen or more factions? The guy Bernstein thought would make a powerful ally? He's... well, probably crazy. Or, at the least, just really, really odd.*

"Look," Zelda said, easing past Kaiden and moving to stand in front of Odditor. "We came because Bernstein wanted us to. We need to talk about the Party."

Odditor perked up at that.

"The party, right, yes." He nodded. "For whom?"

"What? Who... no." Zelda shook her head. "Not a party. *The Party.*"

"Oh, right. That Party. The one with, with all the tyrannizing and the arresting and..." He flicked his hand as if tossing away the thought. "And all that." He turned toward Whenstone and lowered his voice. "Not a fun bunch, this Party."

"I am aware, sir."

"Clearly you know what they've done," Zelda said. "Outside of this, outside of Nova. When your stream is over, when the menagerie is all fed and you log off and go back to the real world, you go back to them." She was gaining momentum as she spoke. "Back to the world they've created. Or destroyed, more like. That's why we've come here. To fix what they've broken."

"Fixing, fixing, always fixing." Odditor tossed his head from one side to the other each time he said the word. "Bernstein was also set on, on fixing things. That's why he came to me."

"So you know, then? You know about..." Zelda paused, seeming uncertain for a moment, then pushed ahead. "About the database? About all the evidence Bernstein gathered? Enough to bring down the Party?"

"Know about it? Know about it?" Odditor turned to Whenstone, chuckling as he gestured at Zelda. "She thinks I don't know about the database." He produced an item from his inventory. "This Bernstein fella loaned me a piece of it."

*Excuse me, what?*

Kaiden had to stop himself from lurching forward and taking the item as soon as he saw it. It was a little padlock, just like the one they'd had when solving the cipher to open Bernstein's database.

"It's locked, of course. Tricky little thing." He pulled at it with his fingers as if that would magically make it open. "So, it's useless. A clever, a clever move on his part. But still, it's one of a kind, so, you know... that gives it value."

"He gave that to you?" Zelda asked, and Kaiden could hear the anger in her voice.

"Gave, loaned," Odditor said, shrugging. "Used as his collateral in order to run the labyrinth. The specifics aren't, aren't important."

"Bernstein risked part of his database to run the labyrinth?" Kaiden asked through comms. "Why? And how? Don't we have all of the database?"

"It could be a copy, couldn't it?" Titus asked. "I know it'd take forever to upload a full copy into Nova, but Bernstein could have just uploaded a bit of it."

"No," Zelda said. "Remember all those blank folders we keep finding in the database? All those broken links?" She frowned. "This is why they exist. Bernstein used a part of the database as his ante. But he encrypted it, too. So even though he lost it, Odditor hasn't been able to open it."

"We have to get it," Kaiden said.

"Yup, yup, you see? You see? There they go again," Odditor said, pulling Kaiden's attention back. "No manners, no manners at all."

"Sorry," Kaiden said, switching back to proximity chat.

*Gotta stop doing that.*

"Why did Bernstein want to finish your labyrinth so badly?" Zelda asked. "First he risked his dreadnought to do it, then part of his database. Why?"

"Fixing, fixing, fixing," Odditor said, head moving side to side again. "Bernstein wanted to talk about fixing things, about ruining the Party. For some reason he thought... I could help."

"Can you?" Zelda asked.

Odditor smiled. A sly smile that built slowly across his features.

"Bernstein seemed to think so, wouldn't you, wouldn't you agree? He was convinced, he was. Enough to stake his *Very... very whatever* on it. And then a piece of his database after he failed the first time."

"You can help us," Zelda said. "You can do the right thing and fix the real world."

"Can. Can?" Odditor seemed to ponder the word. His eyes focused on a space in the air in front of him as if the manifestation of the word was there. He swatted it away with an errant hand. "Tons of people can do things. That's not in doubt. Heh." He chuckled as if that were a funny thought. "No, no. The real question you should ask is 'Will they?'" The smile fell away from his features. "And, particularly, will I?"

*He wants something from us.*

"What do you want?" Kaiden asked. "What will it take for you to help us?"

Odditor smiled again and his eyes flicked to the side.

Kaiden felt his brow scrunch.

"Huh?"

Odditor flicked his eyes to the side again.

"The... window?" Kaiden turned toward it.

"No, not the window!" Odditor exclaimed. "The labyrinth, of course. The labyrinth. I was, was being dramatic." He shook his head. "Don't you... don't you..." He sighed. "If you want my help, want me to risk everything I've built with my own two... er, digital... hands in order to fix what's broken, then what you have to do is simple. Complete my labyrinth."

*The labyrinth we've seen everyone fail? The player-made labyrinth you built that responds to your every command? That kills players so consistently you stream it on a weekly basis? Sure, bud. Like we'll rise to that bait.*

"I'll do it."

*What?*

Kaiden looked over to see Zelda staring down Odditor.

"I'll do it," she said again. "Release your menagerie, or prepare the maze – whatever you have to do – then let me in there so I can win and we can stop wasting time on whatever game this is you're playing."

Odditor smiled.

"Brave, brave." He nodded, then looked to Whenstone. "She's a brave one, isn't, isn't she?"

"Very brave, sir."

"What are you doing?" Kaiden hissed, turning to Zelda and using group comms. Rude or not, it didn't matter. She was about to get herself killed. "No one survives the labyrinth. Even Bernstein failed it – twice!"

"He makes a darn good point," Titus said, nodding in agreement. "This is pretty much suicide."

"I know," Zelda said, and there was no fear in her eyes. "But Bernstein thought Odditor was a powerful enough potential ally that he had to try. And we've seen the trophies. There's no doubt how rich this guy is. We still don't know how many factions he runs, but you don't accrue the kind of money he has from just grinding missions and running a popular stream." She shook her head, as if she'd momentarily doubted her decision but pushed the thought away. "If we want to win him as an ally, we have to play by his rules. If this is what he wants, then so be it."

Kaiden wanted to argue more – losing Zelda would be a major blow. Could they afford having her on a seven-day respawn timer? – but Odditor cut into the conversation.

"Kids these days, just so horribly... rude," Odditor was saying to Whenstone. "Really, I should feed them all to the menagerie. Do you think, do you think they'd like that? The menagerie, I mean. They can be picky eaters on occasion."

Zelda cleared her throat and Odditor and Whenstone turned to look at her.

"Oh, oh, so you're done conspiring now? Ready... uh, to talk to me?" He waved his hand. "It's okay if you need more time. You all just continue your little pow-wow. I'm fine. I'll find my own entertainment." The tone of his voice said the exact opposite was true. "Be real entertaining just to feed you lot to the menagerie," he grumbled, then looked shocked. "Oh, oops. Sorry. That just slipped right out."

"If I complete your labyrinth, you'll talk with us about what Bernstein wanted? About fixing what's wrong with the world?" Zelda asked.

"Well, I don't, I don't know about all that." He chuckled toward Whenstone and lowered his voice a bit. "There's far too much wrong with the world for me to fix. Rude children among it."

"Of course, sir."

Odditor turned back to Zelda.

"But... I might be convinced to help you bring down the Party. If, uh, if you have a viable way of doing it, that is. I don't throw my support behind just anyone, you know."

*And there it is,* Kaiden thought, feeling his breath catch in his throat at the words. *Bring down the Party.* Was there really a chance they could convince Odditor to help them do it? If not, why else had they come here?

"We want you as an ally," Zelda said.

"I think you mean you *need* me as an ally," Odditor corrected.

Zelda hesitated, then relented with a nod.

"Yes."

"Well, all right then!" Odditor near shouted, clapping his hands together and smiling wide. "Let's ante up! Tell you what," he said, leaning in close and whispering. "I'm feeling particularly generous today. Maybe I like you, kid. So in addition to my potential support of your... ambitions, I'll offer up this fragment of the database Bernstein loaned me. Now that, that's a good deal." He smiled. "And what will be your ante?"

Zelda frowned at that.

"Bernstein put up his dreadnought," Odditor continued, "then, when he wanted another crack at it, part of his... special... little... database." He emphasized the last three words. "So, then. What can you offer as ante?"

Zelda hesitated and Kaiden didn't blame her.

*What do we have as ante? Some credits? But that won't work. The dude's filthy rich. Our ship? I guess he could complete his Veritas collection, but what's a light cruiser to someone who already has a dreadnought? So... what, then?*

Kaiden was at a complete loss, and judging by everyone's expressions as he looked around, they were too.

"The best ante I have is—"

"No, that will never do," Odditor said, cutting Zelda off. "I'll accept one thing and one, uh, thing only," he said, sounding as casual as could be. "The rest of the database. And not encrypted this time."

Zelda hesitated a long moment. Long enough that Kaiden almost thought she was crazy enough to accept. He was just opening his mouth to protest when she finally responded.

Her shoulders slumped. She sighed.

"I can't make that deal."

## Chapter Twenty-Four

"We'll find another way," Thorne said. "You did the right thing."

She reached out for Zelda's shoulder but was brushed off as the blast warden hurried up the ramp into the *Veritas II*.

*She doesn't want consolation. She wants progress,* Kaiden knew.

She hadn't accepted Odditor's demands, because of course she hadn't. How could she? How could any of them? The database was their only leverage. Without it they had nothing, or would have to waste a year trying to upload an offline copy in whatever clever, careful way Bernstein had. Like that was actually an option. There was one copy of the database in Nova and they were going to use it in the All-Frequencies Broadcast. That was the plan, and if Odditor wasn't willing to help, then screw him.

*We'll find another way.*

Zelda wasn't speaking to anyone, but Kaiden knew how she felt. Could imagine the weight bearing down on her, because he was feeling the same himself. But she wasn't one to mope.

*She gets angry and then she channels that into a redoubled effort to make the plan work.* It was the right attitude to have. That driven, unbeatable spirit that viewed setbacks only as reasons to work even harder. *Which is exactly what I'm going to do.*

He hurried past the others and into the *Veritas II*, then pulled a hard turn toward the cockpit. The weight of their failure, and, more specifically, his, drove him forward. His boots thunked against the bulkhead harder than they normally would and the sound echoed out around him.

*We've come up short at everything we've tried so far, but I'm not accepting that. That's not good enough.*

"Captain," Acton said with a small nod, then grimaced. "It would appear things went less than satisfactorily."

"Doesn't matter," Kaiden said. "Set a course for Boyd City."

"Sir?"

"We're going to pay a visit to an old friend."

"Very good, sir." Acton turned to speak with the pilot, then strapped himself into his seat. Moments later, the *Veritas II's* engines fired up.

"Care to tell the rest of us where we're going?" Thorne asked, waiting for Kaiden in the main compartment with hands on her hips. Titus was beside her and Zelda as well, though she was staring out the nearest window, still fuming.

"Maximus got us nowhere," he said. "They won't do anything but laugh at us."

"Yeah, I recall," Titus growled.

"And Odditor is being unreasonable."

Thorne crossed her arms.

"So what are you thinking to do about it?"

"Bernstein gave us leads for potential allies. Two of those are dead ends right now, so I'm exploring a different option."

From her seat by the window Zelda looked over at him, frowning. Then her brow relaxed as she seemed to figure out what he was thinking. Kaiden saw this, gave her a nod.

*It's our next best chance.*

"Thorne's not going to like it," Zelda said.

"I'm not going to like what?" She looked between them, waiting for an answer, then stopped abruptly. Realization dawned on her face and she laughed in disbelief.

"Really, Kaiden? Really? I already told you—"

"The Syndicate doesn't exist. Yeah, I remember."

"So why do you want to waste our time on this? Chasing rumors instead of coming up with something real?"

"Because Maximus was a dead end. Because Odditor's crazy. Because I have a feeling about this one, and because we've tried everything else." His voice was coming out angrier than he would have preferred, but damn it, he was fed up with dead ends. They needed to make real progress.

He forced the anger from his words as he continued.

"It's time we thought for ourselves instead of blindly following what we've been told to do. Bernstein suggested potential allies but they haven't worked out. Maybe that's on him, maybe that's on us, but it doesn't matter. The end result has been the same. So, I say it's time we make our own way."

"Hell yes!" Titus said, striding forward and loading up for a big high five. "That's what I'm talking about, man!"

Thorne frowned all the more, shaking her head slightly.

"I guess there're some mistakes you have to make on your own. But fine, whatever. You want to waste time chasing rumors, then go for it. In the meantime, I'll be working on an actual, actionable plan. A concrete way forward."

"Why Boyd City, though?" Titus asked. "Why do you think The Syndicate's there?"

"Aside from it being a hub of piracy and criminal activity? Because we have an old friend there," Kaiden said, calling the NPC to mind.

"Marty," Zelda said, rising from her seat, excitement in her eyes now. Not the excitement that said she thought his plan might work, but just enough that maybe, maybe she was entertaining the idea. Saw some value in it.

"At this point, he owes me," Kaiden said. "I fought in his arena and sold him our loot from the freighter raid at a disgustingly discounted rate."

"Excuse me?" Thorne asked. "You did what for this man? Who even is he?"

"Uh, yeah..." *Forgot she didn't know about all that.*

"It's a long story," Kaiden said. "We'll catch you up on the way there, but Marty's almost a friend at this point, I guess. At the very least, he's been reliable."

"And you think he has information on some supposedly extremely secretive criminal organization that pulls the strings behind the scenes all across the universe? This Marty must be a pretty notable criminal."

Titus gave an enthusiastic nod.

"He runs a theatre."

Thorne cocked an eyebrow at that, seeming to have no idea what to make of it.

"Marty's a good thought," Zelda said, the excitement in her eyes changed now. It'd gone from raw potential to focused energy. She was driven now, deep in thought and speaking as ideas occurred to her. "There's a chance he'll know something about The Syndicate. At the very least, he might be able to tell us it's all fake."

"There's also a chance it's real and I can convince him to tell me about it." Kaiden pulled up his character sheet for a moment. "After all, my status with Nassau's criminal underground is 'favored.' Combine that with a negative one hundred and eighty points of prestige with the Warden Corps and I bet I've a fair bit of influence in the back alleys of Boyd City."

"It's a start," Zelda said with a nod. "But I don't want to put all of our eggs in one basket. Even if The Syndicate does exist, I'm worried Marty's not enough of a big shot to know much about them."

Kaiden frowned at that.

"You and Titus should go to Boyd City. Take the *Borrelly*. Even with our fake transponder the *Veritas II* will likely draw too much attention. There's no reason to risk getting ID'd and having everyone know we're flying as the *Andronicus* now." Zelda spoke faster as she gained confidence. "Thorne and I will take the *Veritas II* and head to a less populated spot. To Jonduu, the ice planet with the turen archival facility on it."

"Right!" Kaiden said, a smile building as the memories came back to him. They'd gone there looking for information on Jax's guild. Wow. It felt so long ago now. That'd been, what? Their first week in-game? So much had changed since then.

Kaiden let the smile spill across his features.

So much had changed, and if they had any say in it, so much more was still going to change.

## Chapter Twenty-Five

"Marty Macmara!" Kaiden said, smirking and stretching his arms wide as he led Titus into Nassau's 'finest theatre.' "I see the old place is looking dreadful as ever."

"Excuse me, sirs," the lean-framed and sharp-featured Marty retorted, offense plastered across his face. "How dare you visit my respected establishment unannounced and spewing insults! There's no finer theatre on this planet."

"There are no other theatres on this planet," Kaiden said.

Marty adjusted his worn-out suit and smiled.

"It would seem my point stands, then."

The same overdone red cushions and stained loungers decorated the lobby of the theatre. The holograms on the wall flicked between ads for two different shows, and Kaiden was pretty sure they were the same two shows as every other time he'd visited. Something was off, though. It took him a moment to realize exactly what.

Lou, Marty's ever-present sidekick, was, apparently, no longer ever-present.

"Where's Lou?" Kaiden asked.

"My esteemed associate is off on official theatre business," Marty said, as unspecific as ever. "So, tell me: why have you come, old friend? Looking to reprise your starring role in my production?"

*Pretty sure I'm far too high-level to fight in your arena now,* Kaiden wanted to say. But that wasn't how things were done here. Marty was all double meanings and veiled intentions. A bit of a tiring game to play, but things always seemed to go smoother when he played along with the NPC.

"Actually, no. I think my acting days are behind me."

"Shame, shame," Marty said, shaking his head. "The crowds would love to watch your triumphant return. So, then." He leaned on his scarred and chipped counter and lowered his voice. "What can I do for my favorite warden?"

"We've come for information," Titus said bluntly. "About an organization called 'The Syndicate.'"

Marty slid back off the counter to stand up straight.

"I am no mere peddler of rumors and heresy, sir. I am a purveyor of the arts! Of stories to make one weep, or cheer. If rumors are what you're looking for, might I suggest any one of our esteemed drinking houses? They're always happy to perpetuate nonsense, or so I hear. I abstain, personally."

"Err... let me handle him," Kaiden said to Titus through comms. "He has a particular way of doing things."

"Yeah, this one's all you, dude," Titus said with no small amount of relief.

Marty still appeared annoyed when Kaiden turned back to him.

"Marty, Marty, my apologies for my friend. He's not a fan of... the fine arts. A bit out of place in a theatre, if you know what I mean."

"That much is painfully clear," Marty said. "This is a palace of art! An institution beyond repute. I cannot have passersby off the street wandering in and..." He shuddered. "And speaking plainly."

"Of course you can't. I completely understand," Kaiden said, trying to look sympathetic. *Do NPCs pick up on such things? Or is the success of my request going to depend solely on my prestige with the criminal underground and my past work with Marty? Eh. Can't hurt to play the part, right?*

"If it's all the same, though," Kaiden said, leaning on the

counter and lowering his voice. "My friend's question still stands. You see, we find ourselves in something of a difficult position."

"I'm sure I don't know what you mean."

*All right, come on now. I'm no good at this game.* Kaiden held back his sigh and forced an understanding smile.

"Marty, we're what you might call in between productions. You see, our last show was a smash hit. Wildly popular. Maybe even too popular, because now the pressure's on for a follow-up. I'm sure you've been in a similar situation yourself."

"Too many times to count."

"Ah, so you understand what it's like, then? You see, we know what we want to do next, and we're sure audiences are going to love it. The problem is, though, we need some help to make it happen. We have the actors, the story, but what we need are producers. We need the support of some real big shots behind the scenes."

Marty seemed not to like the sound of that; he pinched his mouth, as if tasting something sour.

"Look here, Kaiden. We've done some good work together, there's no denying that. But if you've come to my quaint theatre looking for 'big shots,' I'm afraid you've come to the wrong place."

"There's no need to be humble, Marty." Kaiden rapped his knuckles on the wood counter. "This is the finest theatre on all of Nassau. I know the performances put on here aren't massive, but there's no denying they attract attention. And with how long you've been successful, I can't imagine you haven't made certain contacts. Or, at the least, that you've heard a thing or two. I think you might know something about the... producers we need." Kaiden gave a wink. "Which is to say the Syn—"

"Okay, okay." Marty waved his hands. "I'll thank you not to use their name." He shook his head, seemingly troubled by the conversation. "You and I have a history as temporary partners. A history that's benefitted us both. But what you're asking about, it goes way beyond my little piece of dirt. These *producers* aren't the sort of people you want to go asking about. If they see potential in you, they'll contact you. That's how it goes."

*So The Syndicate does exist?* Kaiden shot a glance over his shoulder. Titus met it, then gave a little thumbs up.

*This is progress. But we need more.* Kaiden turned back to Marty.

"They'll reach out if they want us. Okay. That's good to know, but is there anything else you can tell us? Any stories you might have heard about them? Anything that might help us catch their eye?" Kaiden looked him dead in the face and did his best to look sincere. "We really want our next production to be a success."

"These producers have a lot of people vying for their attention, you have to understand. And, the critics – oh, the critics are always after them."

*Critics? Does he mean the Warden Corps? Or the Party?*

"These producers aren't the sort to bother with a humble operator like myself. They're the real upper echelon of the... performing arts. Private box seats sorts. When they give their blessing to a production, it succeeds. Simple as that."

"Thank you, Marty." Kaiden reached across the counter to pat the man on the shoulder. "I can feel our impending success already." He switched to comms and shot a glance back at Titus. "We really need to get in contact with these guys. They could be exactly the ally we need."

"You're right, Kai. But I've known people like this. They're not just going to help us out of the goodness of their hearts. We need to make it worth their time. They need to be able to gain something from it. That's the only way things happened on King Street, and I doubt it's any different here."

"You're saying we need to make bringing down the Party profitable?"

"Yeah, probably. If we want The Syndicate to work with us."

"Well, we did that once, in a way, with King Street," Kaiden said. "Maybe we could do it again here?"

"King Street only manages to operate because the Party doesn't crack down on them. These Syndicate guys sound like they operate in spite of the Party. Hell, it almost sounds like they're running the show in Nova. I don't think it's going to be easy to convince people like that."

"You're probably right." Kaiden shook his head. "But we gotta try. We'll figure something out. We always do." He faced Marty again. "I can't thank you enough. You've done good here today. Really made a difference."

"What I've done is put my neck on the line talking about things it's better I shouldn't," he said. "But I have a soft spot for my star. Still keeping hope alive that he might return for another performance, perhaps."

"I don't—"

The door hissed open.

"Take them alive!" A shout burst into the room and Kaiden flung himself to the side. At almost the same moment, a Burst Arrow whipped over his shoulder and exploded just above Marty. The NPC was thrown to the side, his health bar flashing and dropping well into the red.

"Get out of here!" Kaiden shouted at him. "And keep your head down!"

Marty didn't hesitate, crawling behind the counter then sprinting out of a side door. Once he was clear, Kaiden spun around and activated his shield. Too slow, though. Another Burst Arrow exploded into his chest, dropping his health down to eighty-eight percent.

*Twelve percent damage from one attack?* Kaiden swallowed hard at that as he worked his way over toward Titus and raised his eyes to their attackers.

The first of them was all too familiar. In looks, at least, if not in level.

**Werner10**
**Warden Captain**
**Class: Blast Warden**
**Faction: Warden Corps**
**Level: 53**

## Chapter Twenty-Six

"Jonduu, huh?" Thorne said as the pilot set their ship down deep inside the icy cave. The turen ships that had escorted them in hovered for a moment, then turned to depart, heading back toward the frozen surface of the planet.

"Been a long time since my last visit," Thorne continued. "Though I never had a reception quite like this."

In front of the ship, a gathering of turen was forming, the aliens dressed in flowing robes so light and soft they almost seemed to float in the relatively low gravity of the planet.

"They, uh, didn't do that the last time I was here either," Zelda said, looking at them quizzically for a moment before shaking her head and making for the ramp out of the *Veritas II*.

They'd deactivated their transponder on the way in, flying under the ship's true name so as not to arouse any thought of deception. Zelda and the others' prestige with the turen was through the roof, so even though they were all wanted fugitives, Thorne had been confident the locals wouldn't turn them in. Better, then, to be honest about their ship. The turen were notoriously intolerant of 'mistruths,' as they called them. Lies, really, but anything factually incorrect was just as bad. A transponder broadcasting a fake ship name would be a double affront to their sensibilities – inaccurate and deceitful.

"Honored friend Zelda, you are welcome on Jonduu," the foremost of the turen greeting party said.

"Thank you. It's a pleasure to be back?" Zelda said, seeming taken aback, but adjusting quickly. "We've come seeking knowledge and would like permission to use your archival facility to attain it."

"The council of Jonduu has declared our archives open to all who seek to better themselves through knowledge."

"Yup," Zelda said, nodding. "That's... exactly what we're here for."

"I'm not sure we're technically planning to better ourselves by learning about some all-powerful criminal organization," Thorne said through private comms. "Particularly one that doesn't exist."

"We're... better preparing ourselves to resist the Party. So, you could say our overarching goal is to change the world for the better?" Zelda replied, seeming to think it up as she went along. "That's close enough to bettering ourselves, yeah?"

The turen crowd had parted now, revealing a path through the cavernous space of ice and snow toward one of their smooth, rounded buildings.

The foremost of the turen gestured toward it with a graceful sweep of her hand.

"You are familiar with the archive, Zelda. It is at your disposal. We do not know your friend, however." The lead turen seemed to squint at Thorne a moment. "If you vouch for the goodness of her intentions and the purity of her mind then she may accompany you. But know that any action of hers will reflect on you, as well."

"I don't know," Zelda said through comms and threw a smirk at Thorne. "Can you be trusted? You gonna break something in that archive and get us both thrown out?"

"Oh, you know me. Walking disaster," Thorne laughed back. "Tell 'em I'm pure of mind, or whatever. I'm with you, after all, so I can't be that bad, right?"

"Yeah, just an outlaw terrorist wanted by every member of

the party," Zelda said with a chuckle, then switched back to proximity chat. "Thorne's with me. She's all right."

The lead turen looked confused at that, like it hadn't made any sense.

"I fail to see how her wellbeing is relevant in this matter," she said.

Zelda muttered at that, then tried again with only a bit of a mocking tone.

"Thorne is pure of mind and has only good intentions. I hereby vouch for her."

"So it is." The lead turen nodded, then looked to another in the group. "Elistar, I will ask you to assist our guests."

"I will do so."

Thorne squinted at Elistar. For the most part, he looked similar to those around him. Slits for nostrils, four eyes, and a tall, slender frame. He did look a bit... bookish, though. Given, one could describe just about all of the turen as bookish, what with their gentle demeanors, slow, measured speech, and apparent disdain for any physical activity. Still, though, even for a bookish alien race, Elistar looked slightly more bookish than the rest.

"Welcome back, Zelda," Elistar said as the rest of the turen group seemed to melt away, walking off back to whatever they'd been doing, each step so gentle it seemed they were almost floating. The snow was hardly disturbed in the wake of their passing.

"You may remember me from your last visit. I am Elistar, an archive secretary. It will be my task to assist you in your search for the duration of your stay here."

"Elistar, right," Zelda said, nodding. "You helped us last time we were here. Good to see you again. How's it hanging?"

"I do not know what the 'it' you are asking about refers to."

"I meant, how are you?"

"My bodily functions are operating within acceptable ranges."

*Nice ice-breaker, guy. I bet you're a blast at parties.* Thorne shook away her sarcasm and tried to look friendly as she stepped forward and gave a little wave.

"Captain Thorne of the Warden Corps—er, well, former captain. Now, I don't know. Just Thorne, I guess."

"Don't get him started on rank," Zelda said through comms, but it was too late.

"Rank supposes an alleged categorical hierarchy based on merit, yet our research has found it to be largely corrupted by wealth, societal status, and nepotism. As such, we have deemed it superficial and do not recognize it as an effective system for titles."

"Oh, uh. I see..." Thorne said, at a loss for how to respond. "Cool?"

Elistar seemed unfazed.

"This way, please," he said, turning and heading toward the archive.

"Actually, you might be able to help us," Zelda said, jogging to catch up with him. Her steps were heavy and labored through the snow, leaving it churned and tossed in her wake. In comparison, Elistar's passing seemed no more than a gentle breeze.

"I intend to help you, as discussed prior."

"We appreciate that," Zelda said. "But you know the archives, right? Spent your life studying them?"

"My knowledge of the archives is vast and my memory is precise, yes."

"Are you familiar with the rumors about a vast criminal organization some refer to as "The Syndicate?" Thorne asked.

Elistar stopped walking. His eyes went out of focus a moment. Thinking, maybe? Then he blinked, all four eyes at once, and spoke as if reciting a passage from memory.

"No such organization as 'The Syndicate' is known to exist within the boundaries of the universe," he said, speaking with confidence, or as close as a turen could get to such an emotion.

"Ha! Told you!" Thorne said to Zelda though comms. "Bunch of rumors. It's just like I said, this whole thing—"

"'The Syndicate,' is however..."

Thorne stopped mid-sentence as the turen continued speaking.

"Among a list of known monikers used to erroneously refer to an entirely different organization. But this knowledge is restricted. Only the wisest of our people may have access to it."

"Elistar," Zelda said, leaning in close. "I think you may have heard about some of our recent exploits involving the dark turen?"

*Forcing a prestige check,* Thorne realized. *Nice.*

Elistar was still for a moment. He blinked, then nodded.

*Prestige check passed.*

"Of course, as you have been such a great friend to our people, you are welcome to this knowledge," Elistar said, focusing on Zelda. "Your friend does not hold such status, however. Thorne may not be present while I disclose this information."

"Oh, sure, sure," Zelda said, nodding along. "Though you should know the first thing I'll do when I leave will be to relay all of the information to Thorne." Zelda shrugged. "So, really, it'd just be inefficient not to tell her now."

Clearly that had an effect on the turen. The muscles in his face twitched as he took in her words. Finally, he grimaced – or as close as a turen got to grimacing – and sighed.

"Once the information has been relayed to you it is yours to do with as you please. I cannot stop you from telling Thorne. I also cannot tolerate inefficiency." Another turen grimace. "Okay, then. I will make an exception on this occasion."

Zelda smirked at that. Thorne almost gave her a high-five, but right in front of Elistar that just seemed rude.

The turen looked at them both, two eyes on each of them. "As I was saying, 'The Syndicate' is among a list of known monikers used to erroneously refer to an entirely different organization. An organization whose knowledge, influence, and ability to reshape the universe to its very will requires us to hold it in high regard. The name of this organization and its members is itself a secret known only to the most educated. Criminals think they are The Syndicate. This is a misnomer. The grachnids think they are the holy broodmothers, and worship them as the *ssghrützeeen.*" Elistar opened his mouth wide and did an honestly impressive impression of a grachnid's screech.

"This is also a misnomer. The Ship Builders, a particularly ancient and somewhat wise race, think they are the original builders themselves, and call them—"

"Get to the point," Thorne said, anger building. "Who is this all-powerful organization you want us to believe exists?"

Elistar focused all four eyes on her and... smirked? Was that a smirk? Turen didn't smirk. They hardly ever showed emotion. And yet, the narrow slit of his mouth seemed upturned ever so slightly at the edges.

"They are akin to the very creators of this universe," he said. "They are the Pansophists."

## Chapter Twenty-Seven

"Werner? That's the guy from Blue Hex Station," Titus said through comms as he eyed up their surprise visitors. There were three in total, Werner10 in the middle and two level fifty wardens flanking him. They stood blocking the exit from Marty's theatre.

"I thought you killed this guy?" Titus asked, staring down Werner10.

"That was Werner08," Kaiden said, cursing and checking the man's info again.

**Werner10**
**Warden Captain**
**Class: Blast Warden**
**Faction: Warden Corps**
**Level: 53**

"This is Werner again, but he must be on one of those alternate accounts he mentioned. And a considerably stronger one, no less."

"Where's the rest of the gang?" Werner10 asked. He fired another blast. Titus stepped into its path and caught it on his shield. The attack exploded against him, scorching the floor and setting one of Marty's loungers alight. Titus' shield flickered for a moment, then held firm.

*His shield is almost overloaded just from blocking one attack. Not good.*

"We can't win this fight, Titus," Kaiden said, then tried to dodge as Werner10's two companions – both level fifty power wardens – charged. He caught the first hammer strike on his shield and his charge bar spiked rapidly, filling to forty percent. The other power warden's blow caught him in the side and dropped his health bar to seventy-eight percent.

Kaiden swung back with a hammer strike, but it was more about buying time than dealing damage. The power warden didn't even bother to block it and just attacked again.

"Power wardens gain charge with each attack," Titus shouted through comms.

*That's right. I knew that.*

Kaiden backpedaled, trying to keep distance between him and his opponents while searching for an escape route. They were too close on him, though, hammers swinging constantly. He blocked what he could, but there was no stopping the onslaught. His shield overloaded after two more blows and shut off.

This was bad.

"Remember, no kills. Shackle them," Werner10 commanded.

"Cover me for a minute," Kaiden shouted, mind reeling as he tried to piece together a plan. He could just activate Lightspeed and escape, but that would mean abandoning Titus, and that wasn't an option.

"How?" Titus shouted back from where he was hunkered down beneath an Improved Barrier as Werner10 unloaded on him. Explosions rocked the room and most of the furniture was on fire now.

"Excuse me for a moment," Kaiden said to the power wardens in front of him, then activated an ability.

**Ability: Matter Shift**

It took a second to charge, but then swirling energy

surrounded him, and the power wardens' next attacks missed completely because he was no longer there. Kaiden's vision went dark, then flashed back to life as he reappeared behind Titus. The safety of the barrier protected Kaiden now too, which was helpful because his health already down to forty-eight percent.

"What's the plan?" Titus growled, teeth gritted against Werner10's sustained fire. Worse, the power wardens had spotted Kaiden and launched into the air with Heroic Leap.

"Just buy me three seconds," Kaiden shouted.

Three seconds seemed to be asking a lot, though, as both power wardens landed their Heroic Leaps and a wave of area-of-effect damage lashed out with two hundred percent base damage buff. Titus' barrier, the ground beneath them, and the walls on both sides all shattered. What was left of poor Marty's flaming furniture was thrown about the room in the shockwave.

"Gah," Titus grunted, turning to face the power wardens, who were already rearing back to strike again. "I can't hold them back!"

"No need!" Kaiden's ability was done charging.

## Ability: Flash Bang

Blinding light exploded from Kaiden's shield and the two power wardens cried out, hands going to their eyes.

"To the shuttle!" Kaiden shouted.

"You're not going anywhere, kid," Werner10 said, then raised his hammer-gun. Instead of firing, though, he paused for a moment.

*He has a high-level account, but someone else leveled it for him. He doesn't know his abilities well yet, so he's reading the description,* Kaiden realized. Titus capitalized on the hesitation.

## Ability: Energy Grip

A coil of energy lashed around the blast warden's leg.

"Wha—?"

Titus yanked and Werner was sent flying across the room to

Titus' feet. The man scrambled to stand up while simultaneously trying to aim his hammer-gun.

**Ability: Improved Shield Charge**

Energy surged around Titus' legs and shield, then he burst forward in an explosion of speed and brute force. Werner10 just had time to yelp before he was driven back into the wall, then through it and into the street.

*Ha!* Kaiden darted past the power wardens and out through the newly made hole in the wall.

Titus' Improved Shield Charge lasted long enough to crush Werner10 into the wall of the building on the opposite side of the street. Kaiden wasn't content with that, though. He darted forward and fired off a Hamstring. The attack caught Werner10 before he could recover from the crater Titus had left him in.

"Now go! Back to the *Borrelly!*" Kaiden shouted, turning to run. Titus followed, right behind him.

"You can't run from this!" Werner10 shouted, then stopped abruptly.

*Just figured out what Hamstring does*, Kaiden thought. *As it happens, we can run from this just fine. It's you who can't chase. Not with any speed, at least.*

"That'll slow them, but I don't think we're going to lose them so easily," Titus said, turning down a side alley. Even as he did, the sounds of the power wardens in pursuit reached Kaiden's ears.

"Get to the shuttle. It's our best chance."

## Chapter Twenty-Eight

*A secret organization so powerful it can reshape the reality of the universe?* Thorne thought, replaying Elistar's words. *They'd have to be... what? Special NPCs created by the developers? Or maybe developers themselves playing Nova? No, they don't do that. So... what, then? High-level players? Could any player be powerful enough that the NPC factions create lore about them?*

"You called them the Pan... Pan... what?" Thorne asked, still trying to make sense of it all.

"The Pansophists," Elistar repeated. Then, when that failed to clear much up, he blew a jet of air out of his nostrils and turned back toward the archive. "Follow me this way. I will show you."

"You ever heard of these guys?" Thorne asked Zelda through comms as they both followed the bookish turen.

"Bernstein's database only referred to 'The Syndicate.' Beyond that, I've never heard another name used, which isn't surprising considering these guys are – apparently – extremely secretive. And powerful," Zelda replied. "But we know that NPC factions were coded with their own beliefs as to their creation. Could the turen, the grachnids, and the others be confusing this 'Syndicate' with their creation beliefs?"

"Or maybe they're just dumping their useless lore on us?"

Thorne fired back. "We could be wanting this to be the answer so bad that we're forcing it to be, when in reality it's nothing more than lore."

"I mean, it'd be a good way to hide your activities, wouldn't it?" Zelda asked. "If everyone thinks your organization is either useless lore or doesn't exist, why would anyone come looking for you?"

*Well, she has a point there. But who's so powerful even the turen look up to them?* There were few races, if any, that the turen didn't consider to be lesser civilizations.

"The Pansophists are a collection of higher beings. Life forms that have, through the knowledge they have collected, transcended beyond mortal bodies. They are akin to what you humans would call gods. Omnipotent. Ever-enduring. They are what all turen aspire to become. Some postulate they were turen once, and evidence points to this being the most likely conclusion."

*Ah, there's the usual superiority complex.*

"If these... gods are so secretive, so almighty, how do you know they exist?" Thorne asked. *Still not sure I'm buying this whole thing.*

"Evidence of the Pansophists' existence is rarely direct or apparent. Instead, it persists and is made certain through various interconnected events which may, to those not educated enough to understand, appear unrelated," Elistar lectured. He paused as they reached their destination. A light on the front of the building flashed, blinding bright, and when it clicked off, they were inside the archive.

The room was dark, and somehow seemed larger than it should be considering the exterior dimensions of the building. It was hard to make out anything with certainty in the low light. In front of her, Thorne found several rows of bookshelves stretching off into the darkness. Faintly glowing blue pinpoints of light rested on the shelves where books otherwise would have. There must have been millions of them, row after row, shelf after shelf stretching into eternity.

*Compensating for something?* Thorne chuckled to herself. *No one needs an infinitely large library to store data. My handheld console has enough memory to hold all of this.*

"Observe," Elistar said and waved toward an empty spot on the floor. As he did, a hidden hatch slid open and a brilliant light projected into the air above. Pixels swam and spun in the air, a formless swirl of unfocused light.

"Long have we sought knowledge of the Pansophists. In our unending studies of everything there is to be known, we could not help but to find hints and traces of them. The more we looked, the more we found." Elistar snapped a finger and the formless pixels resolved into an image. It was a panorama in space; a bunch of ruined stations – why were there so many in one place? – and debris floating slowly through the dark, illuminated only by the faint light of some distant sun. But as Thorne looked closer, she realized they weren't the wrecks of space stations, just the wrecks of really, really big ships. Dreadnoughts.

"This is the 'Fields of Ruin,' as they have been named," Elistar said. "Or, more correctly, it is the remains of what is now known as the Titanomachia – the largest battle in the history of the known universe."

*Largest battle in the history of Nova Online, right*, Thorne thought, translating the NPC's description into human terms. *Something like seventy-five dreadnoughts were destroyed that day, along with who knows how many smaller ships.*

"Everyone knows that Titanomachia was a territorial dispute between coalitions of the largest human factions. The battle began long after the war had gone cold and it appeared both sides were ready to negotiate. A maintenance oversight by the faction that controlled sector V-R5RV allowed it to become contested. V-R5RV was a critical sector in the conflict, and losing it would mean losing the war. All at once, the full force that both sides could muster flocked to the sector. In a matter of hours, thousands of ships were destroyed, including seventy-five of the – at the time – two hundred dreadnought-class ships in the universe. In a war that appeared to be ending, suddenly thousands of ships were destroyed and billions of rounds of ammunition were fired."

"That's what happens when the two biggest coalitions of guilds in-game go to war," Thorne said with a shrug. "What's your point?"

"That the maintenance oversight that caused Titanomachia was not a coincidence." Elistar snapped his fingers again and the view changed to a scrolling list of documents. Receipts for the purchase of various in-game businesses?

"Shortly before Titanomachia, a suspicious number of real estate transactions occurred in which very rich, very anonymous individuals purchased dozens of ship and weapon manufacturers, as well as ammunition suppliers. The very same companies that were preparing for a steep reduction in profits as the war ended but, as a result of Titanomachia, saw profits rise exorbitantly."

"Okay, so some big-time investors got lucky? It happens," Thorne said, unconvinced.

*Since when do the turen believe in conspiracy theories?*

"Luck had nothing to do with it. We are always scanning and studying various sectors. Shortly before Titanomachia, our scanners picked up an unknown team of private soldiers infiltrating sector V-R5RV. During this infiltration, they caused the maintenance issue which allowed Titanomachia to occur. Our probing revealed this team was hired by a corporation that owed allegiance to neither side of the war. Instead, sources indicate they were owned by one of the very same anonymous individuals who had just before bought up numerous ship and weapon manufacturers."

"So, you're saying the Pansophists orchestrated the whole thing? You're saying they created the situation in order to profit off of it?"

"I am not saying it; the facts are," Elistar said and snapped his fingers. The projection changed again, this time to show a group of non-uniformed soldiers moving through the halls of a space station. The one at the heart of sector V-R5RV, Thorne didn't doubt. She turned to Zelda and shook her head. "Conspiracy theories aren't evidence. And why would turen 'gods' interfere in something like this? Doesn't sound very god-like."

"It is one of our greatest aims to uncover why the Pansophists do what they do. But they are wise, mysterious. We do our best to identify the signs of their presence and link them together. Titanomachia is but one of the numerous times we've seen the Pansophists not only profit off of unique situations, but act such that they seem to know these situations were going to occur before they actually do. Such knowledge, such ability to shape reality to one's own desires, cannot be the work of mortals."

"I can see how an NPC would think that," Thorne said. Elistar frowned at her words, seeming not to understand.

"Oops," Thorne said, switching to private comms. "Didn't mean to upset Elistar's world view by hinting his entire existence occurs inside a game."

"You know, a thought just hit me," Zelda said through comms. "The turen call these guys the 'Pansophists,' but war profiteering? Anonymously buying companies then manipulating the market to your advantage? That doesn't sound like the acts of gods. That sounds like the acts of—"

"Criminals," Thorne said, hating that the idea made sense to her.

Zelda nodded.

"But more than criminals. These Pansophists, or 'The Syndicate' – call them what you will – sound a lot like players to me. A lot like a group of high-level players who've come together to act in their own best interests. I mean, that's what guilds are, after all, right? But what if you dream bigger? What happens if you take the strongest, richest, most powerful players in Nova and put them all in one room? Imagine the sort of things a collective like that would have the influence to cause?"

*It... makes sense. But come on, how could something like that stay secret?*

"If something like this existed, surely we'd know about it,"

Thorne said through comms. "How does something like this stay quiet?"

"When everyone in it has more to gain by keeping it that way." Zelda looked back to Elistar. "If we wanted to find the Pansophists, how would we go about it?"

"Hah. Heh. Hah." Elistar made a croaking noise and his head rocked back and forth.

*Is that supposed to be... laughter?*

"One does not 'locate the Pansophists,'" he said once the croaking stopped. "How would one locate the gods? We are but mortals. They are so much more."

*I'm really starting to doubt that.*

"It's a good question, though," Thorne said through comms. "If we want to locate an organization of all the most powerful people in the game, maybe we should start with..."

"Start with what?" Zelda asked.

"Hold on," Thorne said. A message had just appeared in her vision.


**DM from: Kaiden**
**"Ambushed at Marty's! High level players, can't win fight. Trying to get to shuttle."**


"Kaiden and Titus are in trouble," she said, screenshotting the DM and sending it to Zelda. "We need to leave. Now."

"Acton! Get the ship ready! We're leaving in a hurry!" Zelda said, immediately patching them into a comms channel with the ship. She didn't hesitate, just turned for the door. Or rather, the teleportation-light thing the turen used instead of doors. She waved a hand, the light flashed, and then she was gone.

Elistar seemed confused by their sudden urgency.

"Is some—"

"No time. Gotta run," Thorne said. "Thanks for everything. Have a good one!"

"I do not know what the 'one' you are referring to is!" he shouted back, but Thorne waved and the light flashed all around her and then she was outside, a few paces behind Zelda.

"We'll never get there in time," Zelda said. "We're a full system away from Boyd City."

"You're right," Thorne fired back. "But I know someone who can."

## Chapter Twenty-Nine

"It's going to take a moment to start up the shuttle. We don't have time for that! Assuming we make it that far," Titus said as they ran through the trash-strewn streets of Boyd City.

**Ally targeted by ranged attack.**

"Incoming!" Kaiden shouted as Improved Enhanced Senses dinged in his ear and told him Titus was about to be hit.

The big man cursed and ducked as another Improved Burst Arrow from their pursuers exploded beside him, nipping at his health. He had his shield held behind him as best he could, but it was at an awkward angle and Werner was proving a darn good shot. The fact that the whole fight was happening during the course of their mad dash to escape wasn't helping anything.

Titus' Improved Shield Charge and Kaiden's Hamstring had given them a head start on Werner, but now it was dwindling. The only boon was that the power wardens that had been with him had disappeared. Fallen behind, maybe? Kaiden didn't have time to worry about it because what Titus had said earlier had been right. Shuttles and other vehicles always took a short time to power up – a mechanic that was supposed to discourage starting fights then retreating to your ship.

"We can make the starport," Kaiden said, focusing on the

path ahead of them. It wasn't more than a hundred paces out now. "But once we get inside, we need a plan. Need to distract Werner long enough to—"

**Targeted by ranged attack.**

*This guy's relentless!*

Kaiden turned hard to the right, trying to throw off Werner's aim, then vaulted over a bench. A good attempt, maybe, but it wasn't enough. A Warden's Bolt exploded through the bench, spraying burning splinters and electric arcs in all directions. Several slammed into Kaiden's back and dropped his health to twenty-two percent.

Kaiden shook off the damage and tried to focus on running. From the alleys, buildings, and side streets all around, NPCs were starting to gather. Noticing the fight, it seemed. They didn't look concerned, though. Instead, they looked... excited. They were gathering in a crowd along the sides of the street and a few of them were already jeering and cheering at the battle.

*Okay, yeah. I'm sure it's real entertaining for you to watch us run for our lives.*

"We need a way to delay Werner long enough to get the shuttle online. How's your charge looking? What are we working with?"

"Thirty percent," Titus shouted back. "Not much, but I can get off at least one ability."

**Ally targeted by ranged attack.**

"He's targeting you again!"

Titus growled, then spun just in time to catch the attack on his shield and activate an ability of his own.

**Ability: Reflection**
**Reflects 20% of damage absorbed by the warden's shield**
**back against the attacker for 10 seconds.**
**Cost: 20 charge.**

**Cooldown: 2 minutes.**

*Good thinking.* Kaiden glanced over his shoulder to watch as the Improved Burst Arrow that'd been targeting Titus exploded against his shield. Twenty percent of its damage reflected back at Werner. It rebounded as half-formed, smaller, and seemingly unstable versions of the original Burst Arrow. Didn't look too impressive, really, but twenty percent of the damage from a level fifty-three player's attack was nothing to scoff at.

Werner might as well have scoffed at it, though. He didn't even try to dodge it; just put his head down and pushed right through the blast. His health bar dropped to eighty-two percent, but he was closer to them now.

"Titus, keep moving! We have to reach the starport!" Kaiden shouted, but the big man had already returned to his sprint. The crowd parted as he moved through it with impressive speed. No doubt none of them were looking to get in the way of that much directed momentum.

There was another ding in Kaiden's ear.

**Targeted by ranged attack.**

*Werner really needs to learn the concept of focusing his fire. Switching between Titus and me is hardly the most effective strategy. Which is a good thing for us, actually.*

Improved Enhanced Senses ran out and shut off, but Kaiden's visor flashed text across his vision and he was just able read it before an attack slammed into him.

**Ability: Improved Paralyzing Shot**

*Oh. Oh no.*

His health bar dropped down to eleven percent, but the wasn't the worst of it. Energy crackled all over his body. His sprint slowed to a jog, then a stumbling walk. He was tilted forward, urging himself to move, but every movement felt slow, like he was drunk, or worse, catching some lag. But he wasn't.

The 'paralyzing' part of Improved Paralyzing Shot was kicking in, reducing his speed by... some amount. He'd only seen Zelda's Paralyzing Shot – the unimproved version – but even that slowed targets by fifty percent for ten seconds.

*Running from this fight just got a whole lot more difficult.*

And with his health so low, one more attack was likely to finish him off.

*Okay, okay. So I just can't get hit. That's priority number one.* Kaiden used the charge he had remaining to keep himself alive.

**Ability: Improved Blur**

His charge began to deplete – five units for every second the ability was active – and his body began to vibrate and fall out of focus. In moments, he was vibrating side to side, jittering, almost. And then a body double stepped out from him. And another. Two in total, and both of them vibrating and shaking and jerking around just the same as he was. Three targets, each as hard to hit as the next, and only one of them real.

Several 'Oohs' and 'Ahhs' trickled out from the crowd at the sight.

*If he can't hit me, he can't kill me.*

**Ability: Lock On**

**Werner10 has locked on to you.**

*Uh-oh.* Zelda had the ability, he knew, but he couldn't recall its full description. He tried to use his visor to pull up specifics on the ability, but as usual, it would only give a vague description of enemy abilities.

**Locks on to a target so attacks will not miss. Deactivates if target is out of sight or when damage is taken.**

*Okay. This is officially a problem. A very big problem.*

"Keep going, Titus. Get to the *Borrelly* and get out of here!"

"What?" the big man shouted back, but Kaiden wasn't listening. An idea had just occurred to him.

*Lock On can't hit me if Werner can't see me, right?*

It was worth a shot. Kaiden looked to both sides and quickly dismissed that as an option. He was a good three or four paces from any sort of cover, and with the paralysis still slowing him, he'd have no chance.

"Tough luck, kid," Werner10 said, then began charging what was sure to be a lethal shot. Looked like an Improved Kinetic Grenade.

*Except...* Kaiden felt his eyes go wide. *Damage! Lock On 'deactivates if target is out of sight or* when damage is taken.'

Kaiden canceled his Improved Blur and stopped vibrating. His body doubles disappeared, leaving him exposed, but his charge bar also stopped draining.

*Twenty-three charge left. Just enough.*


## Ability: Hammer Toss

Kaiden lunged forward and threw his hammer with everything in him. Not that it helped any – the game determined how hard his throw was based on his stats – but still, he willed it forward.

The hammer flew through the air and caught Werner10 before he'd finished charging his attack. It did negligible damage, but achieved the intended effect.


## Werner10's lock has been broken.

"Ha! Yes!" Kaiden pumped a fist in celebration. A few of the crowd cheered with him. Then Kaiden realized something.

*Ah. Crap.*

Werner10 wasn't locked on anymore, but that didn't mean he couldn't shoot. And he'd had to turn off Improved Blur to have enough charge for Hammer Toss. He'd been so focused on breaking Lock On that he'd forgotten the rest of the fight was still happening.

Werner smiled, raised his hammer-gun, and fired.

Kaiden closed his eyes and sighed.

The Improved Kinetic Grenade exploded with a deafening boom and Kaiden waited for the message telling him he'd been defeated.

But it didn't come.

"C'mon, Kai. You didn't think I'd leave you here?"

Kaiden opened his eyes to find Titus in front of him, his shield raised and flickering.

"No! You should have kept going. At least one of us would have survived."

Werner10 fired a follow-up Improved Burst Arrow. The attack overloaded Titus' shield. The thin, transparent barrier of energy that'd been protecting them flickered once more, then disappeared.

"Nowhere to run, and nowhere to hide," Werner10 said.

*He's level fifty-three. Even if we closed the gap on him, our attacks just flat out aren't strong enough to bring him down. We can't make up for a level gap this big.*

Werner advanced, his hammer-gun lowered.

*Preparing to Shackle us, no doubt.*

Werner smiled as he approached. "I'd say you put up a good fight, but being honest, you didn't. Not that it matters. All this will be irrelevant once Killswitch comes online and—"

Something big and gray came hurtling down from above. The crowd screamed and parted as engines roared and the vehicle spun around and slammed into Werner with a loud thud. He was launched backward, tossed down the street. His health bar went wild as he landed, took fall damage, and rolled into the side of a building. His HP had taken a massive hit, but he wasn't dead.

It was only then Kaiden could make sense of what happened. He looked up to the thing that had hit Werner. It was a shuttle. But not just any shuttle. The *Borrelly*.

"Hold on boys, we're doing a fast extraction here," a familiar voice said, broadcasting through proximity chat.

"Is that... Ellenton?" Titus asked.

*It is!*

"Where did you come from—oh god, what are you doing?"

The shuttle was faced away from them, its rear loading ramp down, but the whole thing was backing up at speed – right toward them, the lip of the ramp scraping along the ground and shooting sparks everywhere.

"Fast extraction," Ellenton said. "I already told you."

Kaiden tried to dive out of the way but then the ramp was beneath his feet. Nova's physics freaked out for a moment, jerking this way and that as he and Titus were swept off the surface of the street and slid tumbling into the *Borrelly's* internal gravity grid.

"Ha! Perfect shot!" Ellenton called from the cockpit. "Now hold on. We're getting out of here." The ramp rose behind them, whirring mechanically as it closed and sealed them inside the shuttle.

"I'm thoroughly confused," Kaiden said as they rocketed upward, the shuttle groaning from the strain of the engines pushing at full force.

"Last place I logged off was in here," Ellenton said. "The game saved my spawn point. So when Thorne sent me a message in the real world about ten minutes ago saying y'all were in trouble, well, I guess you got lucky you brought me with you. Intentionally or not." She gestured to the open space of the shuttle's main compartment. "Dawson's here too, or he will be once he logs back in. He wanted to help too, but he wasn't near his pod when Thorne called."

Kaiden staggered toward the cockpit, then finally walked in a straight line and at a reasonable speed as the effects of Improved Paralyzing Shot wore off.

"Thank you," he said, mind still reeling from everything that had just happened.

"I didn't even know you could scoop someone up like that," Titus said, still staring back at the now-closed ramp. "Is the game even meant to handle that?"

"Uhhh... not really," Ellenton said. "But it works most of the time. I've only killed a couple players doing it."

"We're not out of this yet," Kaiden said, then pointed out of the cockpit window. Two shuttles were approaching. Warden shuttles, from the looks of them.

"Now who's that?" Ellenton asked, leaning forward and squinting.

"Werner's friends," Kaiden said, remembering the power wardens who had disappeared during the chase on foot. "They must have gone to get their ships to head us off."

"Let's take 'em out!" Titus growled, then paused, a look of confusion spreading across his face. "Oh, right. I keep forgetting this thing isn't the *Veritas II*. It doesn't have turrets."

"The *Veritas II*?" Ellenton asked, looking excited at the mention of their light cruiser.

"We'll explain later," Kaiden said. "Let's deal with those shuttles first!"

"Oh, them? They're no problem. They're wardens," she said. "They won't fire ship-sized weapons in an urban area like this."

**Shield Integrity: 96%**
**Shield Integrity: 90%**
**Shield Integrity: 85%**

The whole of the *Borrelly* rocked and jumped as a hail of laser fire slammed into them. Many of the shots missed, though, and exploded against the surrounding buildings and streets. The NPCs down below who'd been watching for sport earlier ran for cover now, and Kaiden swore he saw a few of them go up in puffs of flame.

"These guys are a different sort of warden," Titus said.

"Yeah," Ellenton said with a growl. "An insult to the name, mostly. Getting real tired of Moran and his personal goons." She slammed the throttle forward as she said the last part and Kaiden found himself clutching at the walls of the cockpit.

The *Borrelly's* engines groaned and the hull shook, but Ellenton knew what she was doing. The pilot they had on the *Veritas II*, Sias, was a good NPC pilot. Ellenton, however, was no NPC.

The other two shuttles continued firing, streams of lasers

pouring out, but Ellenton dodged and strafed, always staying ahead of their fire. Kaiden found himself transfixed. He'd forgotten what it was like to fly with her. Terrifying, for starters. But also exhilarating. A masterpiece to behold.

"Wardens are supposed to avoid collateral damage, you morons," Ellenton said as she hit the afterburners and the shuttle's engines went into overdrive. The two attacking shuttles followed as they climbed out from among the buildings of Boyd City.

They continued to climb through the clouds, rising into an orange-pink world as the sunset appeared over the distant horizon. If this was a retreat, though, it wasn't working. The pursuing shuttles were fighting to keep up, but managing it.

Flame erupted against the windshield of the *Borrelly* as it broke through the atmosphere of the planet. The engines were increasingly released from the pull of gravity and now, with no wind resistance, the shuttle's engines were given free rein.

Ellenton checked to make sure the pursuers were still behind, then smirked and flipped a switch on the dash.

**Decoupled mode activated.**

A shudder went through the *Borrelly*. Looking out of the window, Kaiden noticed the engines of the shuttle, which were usually locked in tandem, always moving the same direction at the same time, were no longer doing anything of the sort. Instead, they appeared to be moving independently, adjusting ever so slightly to keep the ship moving in the direction Ellenton desired.

Then, all at once, she pulled hard on the sticks and the *Borrelly* spun around to face the oncoming shuttles. Normally, spinning like that would have pointed the main engines backwards, causing the ship to do a 'flip and burn' and slow down. Whatever decoupled mode had done, they weren't slowing down. Instead, they were facing backward toward their pursuers, but maintaining the same velocity as when they'd been facing forward.

"It's a spaceship, but everyone tries to fly like they're in a plane. There's so much more possible if you're willing to get creative," Ellenton said, opening up with the *Borrelly's* guns and targeting the right-most shuttle first. Its shields flashed to life beneath the attack, and whereas the shots the shuttles had fired earlier were mostly off target, Ellenton's were all on the mark.

Both opposing shuttles returned fire, but only for a moment. The right-most shuttle's shields went down, then its cockpit was ruptured a moment later as the *Borrelly's* fire tore into it. The shuttle slowed, the pilot most certainly dead, and was out of the chase in moments.

"One down," Ellenton said, face firm with concentration. "One to go."

**Shield Integrity: 81%**
**Shield Integrity: 75%**

The other shuttle was still firing, but it seemed Ellenton had a plan for that too.

**Decoupled mode deactivated.**

Kaiden was thrown full off his feet as the engines snapped around back to their usual position and the afterburners kicked in. The *Borrelly* groaned like it was going to tear itself apart under the strain of stopping so suddenly. The pursuing shuttle wasn't able to adjust quick enough and ended up shooting past them.

Ellenton let off the afterburners and spun around, now behind the last remaining enemy.

The shuttle didn't hang around to find out how that would end. Instead, its afterburners flared to life as it rocketed away as fast as possible.

"Good decision," Ellenton said, raising her fingers from the weapons' trigger and smirking.

"Hell yeah!" Titus shouted, pumping a fist in the air, and Kaiden couldn't blame him. Found himself cheering right along.

After the groans and blasts and roaring engines of the ship-to-ship fight, suddenly everything seemed too quiet. Kaiden's pulse was still pounding in his ears, but the fight was done.

Ellenton watched the retreating opponent to make sure they weren't going to circle back around, then laughed.

"Come back when you know what you're doing."

## Chapter Thirty

Returning to the *Veritas II* had never felt so good. Aside from its thick hull, protective shielding, and guns big enough to deter most attackers, it also had a medbay. A medbay that Kaiden and Titus were putting to very good use after the beating they'd received in Boyd City.

"Note to self: buy stimpacks. We've been so busy we haven't picked any up since I don't know when. Could have cost us back there," Titus said, raising a hand and staring at it as white light flooded around him.

The medbay had come equipped with two healing stations, which were a sort of bed that could fold up automatically to become chairs. Wrapped around each bed – and their occupants – was a series of smooth, metal rings, the underside of which was equipped with an array of sensors and lights and who knew what else. Kaiden certainly didn't. Whatever the tech was, it did its job.

The rings were glowing and humming now, bathing Kaiden and Titus in soft white light that scanned back and forth over their bodies. With each second he spent under the light, Kaiden watched his health replenish. Normally, health in Nova recovered slowly over time when out of combat, or could be regenerated via a stimpack or a medic. The medbay was a mid-to-late-game unlock that provided any ship of adequate ability to serve as something of a mobile clinic. No one had used the medbay yet, but now, wrapped in its healing embrace, Kaiden was thankful Zelda'd had the foresight to acquire the upgrade back when they'd been on Bernstein's scavenger hunt.

Kaiden was distracted as a big notification appeared in his vision.

**Full System Alert! Full System Alert!**
This is a Warden Corps All-Frequencies Broadcast. The Warden Corps is seeking the following fugitives currently believed to be in-game:

Player name: Kaiden
Player name: Zelda
Player name: Titus
Player name: Thorne

A bounty of 1,500,000 credits will be awarded to any player who provides information leading to the fugitives' capture. An additional bounty of 700,000 credits will be awarded to any player who engages or delays the fugitives until a warden is able to Shackle them.

"Another one," he said, seeing everyone else's eyes go distant as they read the broadcast. "Apparently Werner isn't happy about our escape."

"So he was back, and on a different account? And a much stronger one, from the sound of it," Thorne said. She cleared the top of a table, pushing the various medical supplies off to one side, then sat down on it, her expression a mixture of pondering and worried.

"Werner can't stand Nova. For the short time I worked with him, he made it very clear the real world is the only place worth bothering with. If he's in-game, it's because he was ordered to be, and that's telling."

"Telling how?" Kaiden asked, trying to meet her eye but

having to duck away as the white light scanned up his face and blinded him for a moment.

"It means the Party, and Moran specifically, are seriously concerned. They're redirecting real-world resources into Nova. Pulling Werner off the streets? Forcing people to power-level accounts for him and the rest of Moran's thugs?" She shook her head. "They're feeling the heat. Can't find us in the real world—"

"Shoutout to trusty ol' swamp bunker," Titus added. "You're mildewy and smell a bit weird, but you're doing a great job keeping us alive."

"–so they're focusing all of their attention on Nova," Thorne finished, smiling a bit at Titus' spur-of-the-moment ode to the swamp bunker.

"Careful," Zelda said, giving Titus a look. "The less Ellenton knows of where we are, the better."

"Look at this ship!" Ellenton slammed into the other side of the medbay window. It looked in from the hallway where she'd been running back and forth, scouring every inch of the *Veritas II*. "This thing is incredible!" Her expression was one of unbridled joy, eyes wide and smile wider, though maybe that was just the way she was pressing her face up against the glass. "How did you keep this thing to yourselves all this time? I mean, the *Borrelly's* my baby and always will be, but this ship is freaking *magnificent*."

Kaiden began to reply, but she'd already peeled her face off the window and disappeared out of sight toward the engine room.

"That's more like it," Titus said as a pleasant ding sounded and the rings around his med station opened and retracted. "Good as new." He stood and stretched.

Kaiden's own station dinged as well. He confirmed his health was back to one hundred percent, then stood and shook his arms out. Being in a game meant his body didn't actually feel tired or sore, but his mind expected it to, and some mannerisms were hard to forget.

"Now that that's done, back to the matter at hand," Thorne

said, drawing everyone's attention back to her. "Werner being in-game means the Party is feeling the heat. They want to get that database back ASAP."

"And Marty confirmed The Syndicate exists," Kaiden said. "The turen told you guys pretty much the same, just labeled with a different name."

"The Pansophists," Zelda said with a nod.

"I like your theory, though." Kaiden began to pace. Always helped him think better. "The Syndicate, or the Pansophists, or whatever, have to be a group of players, right? I mean, it just makes sense. It's… how'd you put it, Thorne?"

"Like a big, secret guild of players," she said. "Just taken to the next level. A guild where you have to be powerful just to join. Lead a guild of your own, or own a solar system. You know, *real* power. Well, real fake power. But real power in-game."

"There's no difference," Zelda said. "Real power, fake power? It doesn't matter. Every advantage we can gain in-game gets us one step closer to the All-Frequencies Broadcast System which, coupled with Bernstein's in-game database, can bring down the Party. That's real power. Some may say being important in Nova doesn't mean anything in the real world, but right now, it might just mean everything." She looked around the room. "We need allies. Powerful allies, so we can make a real difference in the world."

*It's a good point. Maybe in the past Nova was just a game, but now? Well, now it just might overthrow a government. Might make a better world for everyone.*

"We need allies…" Kaiden said, working his way through things as he spoke. "But Maximus is a dead end. Odditor has unreasonable demands. And The Syndicate, well, we don't even know where to find them." He stopped pacing abruptly. "But what if we already found one of them?"

Thorne made a show of looking around dramatically.

"It's not any one of us, so unless you're accusing Acton of secretly being part of some shadowy, might-not-actually-exist organization of gods, who are you talking about?"

"PlayaSlaya," Kaiden said. "Leader of the biggest PVP guild

in-game. Everyone knows his name and he's one of the strongest players in Nova."

"Things didn't exactly go so well the last time we tried this route," Thorne said. "I mean, Titus almost got…"

Kaiden cringed, preparing for Titus' anger at the memory.

"Maximus turned us away because they're a bunch of PVP-obsessed punks," Titus said, and there was no anger in his voice. Or, at least, far less than Kaiden had suspected. If anything, the big man sounded like he was thinking through a plan. "But they also turned us away because we were too low-level, right?"

"Being max level is important for PVP," Thorne said with a shrug.

"We don't need max level," Titus said, the beginnings of a smirk pulling at his lips. "We just need level fifty."

"Why's that?"

"Those punks we met on Kyraxis, they said Maximus run PVP tournaments, right?" Titus was full on smiling now. "I've been thinking about this since. Didn't think it was the right time – we were going to meet Odditor, then look into The Syndicate – but now, well, no better time than the present. If we hit level fifty, we can all enter in Maximus' PVP tournament."

"Okay…" Thorne said, apparently still not following.

"If one of us can win that tournament, we'll have earned a meeting, or at least a conversation with PlayaSlaya. And if we think there's even the slightest chance that he's in The Syndicate – assuming it does exist – then we need to talk to him."

"You sure this isn't about getting back at those jerks?" Zelda asked.

"Never said it wasn't," Titus said and cracked his knuckles. A moment later, he shrugged. "But two birds with one stone, yeah? Whether The Syndicate does or doesn't exist, we still want PlayaSlaya on our side."

"Can't say I fault the logic," Kaiden said, mulling over Titus' point. Sure, he likely wanted to go back and kick Nassus' ass, but there was more to it than that. Nothing they learned about The Syndicate had changed the fact that they needed PlayaSlaya as an ally if they were going to take on Warden HQ. Uncovering

The Syndicate could help them if they managed it, but so would completing Odditor's labyrinth and winning his support. And so would finding themselves a massive army. And unlimited funds. And a dozen other things. Kaiden shook his head at the monumental tasks ahead of them.

"We might be trying to do too much at once," he said to the group. "There's a ton of stuff we have to accomplish before we go after Warden HQ. The simple fact of the matter is that we want PlayaSlaya or Odditor by our side. Preferably both. What else we might need we still don't know, but those two we're set on. So, let's focus on them." He looked to Titus. "I like the tournament idea. That's a surefire way to PlayaSlaya if we can win."

"Maximus' tournament makes sense," Zelda said, hand on her chin, clearly thinking it over. She nodded. "That... that might be something. Maybe we can get a one-on-one with PlayaSlaya. Tell him about the database, feel him out as an ally. But you're forgetting something, Kai." She looked right at him. "Odditor demanded ante. The only way we were going to get a crack at his labyrinth was if we staked the database to do it. That's not a risk we can take."

"That's what he said, but there must be something else he would want. Something of value we can stake. Hell, we'll fake the database if we need to. Well, probably that's not the best way to kick off a relationship with a potential ally, but what I'm trying to say is, other people run his labyrinth. They obviously stake things less valuable than Bernstein's database. There have to be things Odditor is willing to accept as ante instead of the database. We just have to find out what."

"I don't think..." Zelda paused. "Well, maybe?" She shook her head as if shaking off the thought. "I'm not sold on that being the case."

"But it is possible, right?" Kaiden said, waving his hand for her to agree.

*Come on, think creative here. Be a bit adventurous.*

She sighed.

"It's possible. Sure."

"Then let's at least think on it. See if we can't come up with something Odditor would accept. And, in the meantime," he turned to Titus. "We can take down Maximus' tournament."

"It's not a bad plan," Thorne said, nodding to herself. "A bit crazy, and a bit of a stretch in a few – okay, *a lot* – of places. But... there might be something to this."

Kaiden smiled at that. Smiled because maybe everything wasn't set in stone, maybe nothing was certain, but what did that matter? If in the past they'd only reached for things that were certain, they'd never have made it this far.

"Sometimes it just takes a little faith, guys," Kaiden said. "And maybe a little luck. But we can make this work."

"A little faith, a little luck, and a whole lot of grinding," Zelda said. "If we're going to hit level fifty, which we have to in order to even qualify for Maximus' tournament."

"Actually," Thorne said, her voice unsure at first. "I've been thinking about that. I need ten levels to hit fifty. You all are at level thirty-eight, so you need twelve. That's a fair few, but not all that much. I... I might have a solution."

"Oh?" Kaiden perked up at that. "But I was just about to give a pep talk about how we needed to start dedicating like twenty hours a day to mindless grinding. About how it was going to be hell, but we were going to pull together and fight through!" He shrugged. "It was going to be very rousing."

His humor was apparently lost on Thorne. Or she was too distracted to notice it. She was looking off into space, mouth slightly open. Finally, she nodded to herself.

"This might just work."

## Chapter Thirty-One

**Location Discovered: Langrangia**
**Faction: None**

"Uh, are those orbital turrets going to be a problem?" Kaiden asked, pulling his eyes from the planet below them and to the massive Warden Corps turrets. Even as he asked, they must have picked up the *Borrelly* on their scanners. They came to life all at once, massive guns turning to lock on to the ship.

*Remind me why we came here in the shuttle and not the* Veritas II?

"Open a channel with them?" Thorne asked. Ellenton did so and Thorne leaned forward, peering out of the windshield of the *Borrelly* and toward the nearest turret. "Time to get to work," she said, speaking slowly and enunciating clearly into the microphone.

"Access granted," a robotic voice said through comms, and all at once, the turrets deactivated.

"That was… easy," Kaiden said, marveling at the sheer size of the closest turret as Ellenton guided them past and down into the planet's atmosphere.

"Only a handful of wardens know that password. Once those turrets activated, we had five seconds before they blew us to shrapnel. Must've told command a hundred times that we needed to change the password on the turrets at least monthly." Thorne shrugged. "Guess I'm glad they didn't listen to me. Still, let's keep our signature as small as possible." She looked to Ellenton. "Cut power to everything but emergency systems. Only use as much thrust as necessary, too. No reason to spike our infrared."

"Woman, I know what I'm about," Ellenton shot back, sounding only half joking. "But it looks like your suspicion was correct," she added as they broke through the cloudy skies of the planet and eased down toward what looked to be a barren surface. "I'm picking up at least a hundred player signatures down there."

Thorne smirked at that.

"Hold up," Kaiden said, not believing what he was hearing. "Can we backtrack a bit? Why does this planet – home to nothing but a backwater Warden Corps outpost – have an orbital defense system? More importantly, why are there 'hundreds of players' down there?" He peered down to the rapidly approaching surface. It was totally empty.

"Land at the emergency exit," Thorne said, pointing to the bottom of a small impact crater. It was surrounded on all sides by more of the same barren landscape. It might have been molten once, but now it was solidified and desolate. The was no movement, no ships, not even a single mob.

Ellenton huffed by way of response, but eased the shuttle gently on to the surface then cut the engines the moment they were down.

"Excuse me," Zelda said, pushing into the cockpit. "What are we doing here? You still haven't explained anything."

Kaiden stepped next to her and nodded. "Seriously. Where are we and why are we here?"

Thorne looked at them both with a touch of confusion in her eyes.

"Sometimes I forget how short a time you spent as wardens. You'd have learned about this place if you'd stayed longer, but circumstances being what they were..." She waved away the thought. "Anyway, no time to waste. Follow me and I'll explain on the way in."

"The way in to where?" Titus asked from where he was standing by the now-open rear ramp. "There's nothing here."

"Oh, you just don't know where to look," Thorne said, patting him on the shoulder as she passed, then strode down the ramp.

Kaiden followed her at a jog.

"Talk to me, Thorne. Where are we?"

*For all intents and purposes, it looks like we're in the middle of nowhere. We didn't even land next to the warden outpost on the planet.*

Thorne pointed ahead and Kaiden found himself staring up at the wall of the impact crater, rising several hundred paces into the sky. Except there was something at the base of the wall. It was covered in a layer of ashen dust, but still, it reflected a bit of light.

"Langrangia is just a nowhere backwater," Thorne said as she approached the metal wall. But no, not a wall. A door. "Or that's what the Warden Corps wants everyone to believe." She stretched out and touched the tip of her hammer to the door with quiet *dink*. Light poured out from a pinhole on the door and scanned her hammer. It went over it once, top to bottom, then once more, and switched off. There was a hiss of compressed air, then a puff of ash, and the door opened.

"When we found Werner on that station, he mentioned the Warden Corps was power-leveling accounts, right?" Thorne asked, peering into the dark hallway beyond the door. "He shouldn't have said that."

"What does that have to do with anything?" Kaiden asked.

"Because this is where they're doing it." Thorne stepped into the hallway then waved them after her. "Follow me and keep close."

"Wait a minute," Zelda said, refusing to step past the door. "You mean to tell me those hundred player signatures Ellenton saw were *all wardens?*"

*Oh, shit.* Kaiden stopped mid-step, standing in the doorway next to Zelda but going no further.

"They sure were," Thorne said. "But they're busy power-leveling, like I said. With any luck we're going to slip past them unnoticed."

"And do what?" Kaiden asked.

Thorne nodded at him.

"Take another step. Just one more."

He hesitated – what was she on about? – but stepped forward and into the hallway.

**Location Discovered: The Grinder**
**Faction: Warden Corps**

"What the hell is 'The Grinder?'" he asked, reading the name aloud.

"The Grinder is the Warden Corps' power-leveling facility," Thorne explained. "And it's how we're going to get the levels we need to enter Maximus' tournament." She walked further down the hallway, forcing them to follow.

"The Warden Corps has a power-leveling facility?" Kaiden asked, taking in his surroundings as he followed Thorne. The hallway was unremarkable, rough-hewn walls cut from the natural black stone of the planet. Ahead, though, Kaiden thought he could see an intersection with another hallway, and that one better lit.

"This Grinder's only supposed to be used on special occasions," Thorne said through comms. "Mainly because of how many resources it takes to maintain it." A door appeared, jutting out of the rock wall on their right. Thorne pointed at it but kept walking.

Kaiden looked toward the door. It was much the same as the one they'd entered through except there was a display on its front.

"Room Status: Unoccupied?" Zelda read aloud.

"Means there's nothing in it," Thorne replied, pointing to the green glow of its display.

"Thanks. Really cleared that up."

"Like I was saying," Thorne continued. "It takes a lot to maintain this place because, well, we have to stock it." She pointed toward another door, this one on their left. It too had a display, and a realization dawned on Kaiden as he read it.

**Room status: Unoccupied.**
**Mob status: 30/30 Voidspawn, Level: 15**

"Voidspawn?" Kaiden felt his jaw drop. "Wait. The Corps is stocking this place with voidspawn?"

"Not just voidspawn," Thorne said as she reached the intersection and paused to peer around the corner. Once she'd confirmed the hallway was empty, she gestured for Kaiden to look down it.

More doors. Hundreds of them, lining the walls of the hallway as far as he could see. Displays on them read out the status of each room, what was inside it, and how many.

"Voidspawn. Grachnids. Dark Turen. Baboulian Manhunters. Pretty much any mob of use ends up here," Thorne said. "Of course, it's a major pain in the ass to transport them all here. Total grunt work – you three are lucky you got out before you ended up on collection detail," she said with a smirk.

"How big is this place?" Zelda asked, her eyes wide as she took in the seemingly endless number of doors lining the hallway.

"Big enough that I'm confident we can slip into a room or two without being noticed. Plus it's even fuller than I thought it would be. I've never seen so many stocked rooms. This place was empty last time I checked," Thorne said. "And once we're inside, the room status will show 'occupied,' so no one's going to bother us. We'll be free to grind away on all the mobs in the room." She nodded down the hall to two doors whose displays were red, in stark contrast with hundreds that were green.

"This is something of a disused area," Thorne explained. "Overflow storage, essentially. There's much more closer to the heart of the facility. Hopefully here we can go unseen for a while."

"I'm seeing different levels of mobs listed on each door?" Titus said, poking a head around the corner and squinting.

"They're all organized by level. That way, when you kill all the mobs in one room, you can move right to the next. It's grinding at its most efficient. Or, well, it is for those who get to use it. The mobs don't respawn – once they're killed, more have to be captured and brought here. The grunts who stock this place hate it. Do you know how hard it is to capture mobs, get them onto a ship, and bring them here?"

"If the Warden Corps has had this place all along, why not use it? Why isn't every warden power-leveled here?" Kaiden asked, his mind reeling at the possibilities of such a place.

"Well, for one thing, power-levelling even a single warden takes massive resources. Usually only high-ranking Party officers reassigned from real-world to Nova detail would get access. Getting one player to max represents months of collection duty for junior wardens. These mobs don't respawn, after all. This is all manual. So, levelling more than the occasional officer is hugely inefficient. You would have to reassign hundreds of patrolling wardens from their usual duties just to keep it running."

Thorne paused, looking back at him, her expression pained. "Second, it defeats the purpose of the program. The warden program's primary goal is to rehabilitate prisoners. Turns out spending hundreds of hours grinding in an isolated room on a backwater planet really doesn't do a stellar job of preparing convicts to reenter society." She shook her head. "Of course, now that Moran's on his power trip and dying to find us, I figured he'd be using this place. It doesn't really matter that having a hundred wardens in here will deplete the stocked mobs faster than grunts can replenish them. Or that huge areas of Nova are probably going unprotected as he reassigns good, honest wardens to mob pick-up for his power-levelling cronies. Moran knows he's on the clock to find us. I doubt the long-term viability of this facility – or its effectiveness in rehabilitating convicts – is his top priority. When Werner said the Corps was power-leveling, it clicked instantly that this would be where they were doing it."

"There's no way we go unnoticed here, though," Kaiden said. "I mean, there's a *hundred* wardens here."

"We can make this work," Titus said. Kaiden looked over and found a hunger in the big man's eyes. And a determination. "Back in the day, when I was preparing for a fight, I'd cut everything else out. Train like it was life or death." He didn't need to say more for Kaiden to remember that the sort of boxing Titus had fought had very often been life or death.

"I'd work out all day then study everything I could about my opponent by night. Complete and utter obsession." He looked out at the hallways around them. "Kinda like what this place is."

"Pretty much the idea," Thorne said with a nod. "And it's risky being here, sure. But as long as we're careful moving from room to room, we should be fine. The whole of the Warden Corps is looking for us, right? Well, something tells me the last place they're going to look is here. I mean, who in their right minds would try to hide so close to their enemies?"

"Yeah, who in their right mind would do tha—" Kaiden stopped as a *thunk* echoed out through the hallway. One of the nearby doors opened and a group of five or six wardens piled out.

Thorne grabbed Kaiden's shoulder and yanked him back around the corner, then jammed him into a crevice in the carved-out stone wall before finding one for herself. Zelda and Titus did the same with differing levels of success, particularly for the big man.

"Whew," one of the nearby wardens said through proximity chat. "Gonna need a shower in the real world after that one. That was tense!"

The wardens passed through the intersection and kept going, heading down an offshoot hallway.

"You ain't kidding," another voice agreed as they passed. "This virtual reality gaming stuff is pretty impressive, actually. Tell you what, it's a far better job than pushing papers all day up at the state house. Kinda wish we'd been reassigned here sooner."

The voices dwindled as the wardens walked further away

down the hallway. Soon only the distant thunking of their boots was audible and then even that faded.

"Thorne," Zelda hissed. She was talking through group comms so she didn't need to be quiet. but considering the circumstances, Kaiden hardly blamed her. "This is crazy."

"Yeah, we're totally going to get caught," Kaiden said.

"Crazy," Zelda said again. "But just crazy enough to work."

"Oh, hell yes," Titus said. "I'm tired of flying all across the galaxy just to shoot down a few pirates for weak EXP. It's time we did some true training." He stepped away from the wall and looked toward the closest door.

**Room status: Unoccupied.**
**Mob status: 30/30 Voidspawn **Elite**, Level: 20**

"Not that one," Thorne said, directing his attention away from it. "Those voidspawn are too low-level. They're Elites, so they'll be worth more EXP, but still not the sort of EXP we need." She gestured toward a door further down.

**Room status: Unoccupied.**
**Mob status: 20/20 Cryo-mummies **Huntsman** Level: 38**

"Eh, actually, those have the Huntsman tag so they're only going to focus on the highest-level player. I'd rather not go in there just so they can zerg me," Thorne replied.

"Fair enough. That one, then?" Kaiden asked, pointing to a door several more paces down the hallway – in the direction the power-leveling wardens had gone just a few moments ago, too, Kaiden noticed.

"Unoccupied. Twenty out of twenty Grachnids. Level forty. Yeah," Thorne said striding toward it. "This'll do nicely." She touched her hand to the door's display and there was a heavy *thunk* as it unlocked.

"In we go," she said, giving a half bow. "Last one in be sure to lock the door behind you. We don't want any of these buggers getting out to roam the halls."

Chapter Thirty-Two

"Bring him down!" Zelda shouted, retreating from the gobber in front of her. A good decision, considering she was down to five percent health and the furious gobber was level forty-six. Kaiden hadn't even realized gobbers could spawn at such a high level. The dozen they'd already killed in this room proved they did.

"I got it," Kaiden said and darted forward, using the final seconds of Lightspeed. He moved so fast the room around him was a blur – not that it mattered. He'd stopped paying attention to the different rooms hours ago. They all looked the same on the inside: poorly lit, with rocky walls and ceilings, and countless numbers of mobs snarling in the half-light. Really, the mobs were the only difference from one room to the next. Hominoids two rooms ago, grachnids after that, and now gobbers.

Kaiden activated Hamstring as he reached the gobber, then slammed his hammer into the back of its knee. The creature cried out – something between a squeal and a growl – but kept chasing Zelda. The reduction to its movement speed let her slip away, though, and she fired an Improved Burst Arrow into its chest from a safe distance.

The gobber squealed again as its health dropped into the red. Kaiden swung his hammer for a finishing blow but found only empty air.

**Ability: Energy Grip**

Kaiden read the notification on his visor just as Titus let out a grunt.

"This one's mine."

Kaiden looked over to see the gobber at the big man's feet, an energy lasso wrapped around its leg. Titus swung his hammer down once, twice, and the gobber's health fell to zero.

**Gobber assisted kill – 3,200 EXP gained!**

"Incoming!" Thorne shouted from across the room. "Heads up!"

Kaiden glanced over in time to see the last gobber sprinting toward her. From across the room, Zelda hit it between the shoulder blades with a Warden's Bolt. At just about the same moment, Thorne pumped charge into her hammer and swung hard.

**Ability: Gravity Sledge**

The bundle of fur and claws and anger was launched through the air. It slammed into the ceiling, then thudded back down to the floor, dead.

**Gobber assisted kill – 3,200 EXP gained!**

"That should just about do it…" Kaiden said and then sure enough, the notification popped up on his screen.

**Level 42 achieved!**
**Max health and stamina increased**
**+3 stat points**

*Nice!* Kaiden breathed a sigh of relief as his health was restored to full, but mainly he was relieved for Zelda's sake. He'd been down to thirty percent health but she'd been on the verge of death.

*Should've brought more stimpacks with us,* he thought as he checked his character sheet.

**Character**

*Name:*
Kaiden
*Race:*
Human
*Level:*
42
*Class:*
Enhanced Warden
**Attributes**

*Strength:*
57 (+2)
*Intelligence:*
51
*Endurance:*
57
*Perception:*
51
*Dexterity:*
152 (+2)
*Unassigned:*
0
**Abilities**
*Kickback*
*Shield Bash*
*Hammer Toss*
*Lightspeed*
*Improved Enhanced Senses*
*Riposte*
*Flash Bang*

*Improved Blur*
*Onslaught*
Enfeebling Strike

Slayer (passive)
Hamstring
*Matter Shift*
Distortion Field

**Perks**
Turen Tinkering

Kaiden closed his character sheet. Zelda's health bar was back to full and she was shaking off the remains of gobber fur and spit clinging to her armor.

"Nasty little things, aren't they?" Thorne said, pacing across the space. "Looks like you all got your next levels, though?"

Kaiden nodded. Thorne had earned hers earlier in the fight. Thankfully, she hadn't taken too much damage finishing off the gobbers; her health sat at a comfortable eighty-eight percent.

"I could get into this," Titus said, catching his breath. Despite his good mood, there was a seriousness to his face. "Feels like some quality time hitting the bag, as my old coach would say. Always prepping for that next fight."

Kaiden didn't have to guess what fight Titus was thinking about. The big man wasn't over the beatdown he'd received at the hands of Maximus, and Kaiden had a sneaking suspicion he wouldn't be until the score had been evened.

"This is good training, maybe," Kaiden said. "But is anyone else's head a bit fuzzy? Like, senses dulled just a bit?"

"That's mental exhaustion you're feeling," Thorne said. "Grinding at this rate really isn't possible anywhere else in Nova. Real-time combat is taxing on the nervous system. It'll wear you down. There are medical bays scattered throughout, but they can't help with the mental exhaustion."

"We can sleep when we're dead," Titus said with a grunt.

"He's got a point there. We don't have time to take a break,"

Kaiden said and followed him. "Every moment we're here is dangerous. The sooner we get done here, the better."

"Fair enough," Thorne said with a nod. "Well, go on. Send the screenshots."

*Screenshots? Oh, right.* They'd leveled up not long ago, and forty-one had unlocked a new ability. He'd seen the message flash across his vision but it'd quickly been forgotten in the fighting.

*Maybe I'm more tired than I realize. We have a lot more to go, though, even if we are making good time.*

Still feeling like he was out of breath, Kaiden pulled up the details of his new ability and took a screenshot of it. He fired the shot off to the group then took a moment to focus on the new ability.


**Ability: Distortion Field**
**A field of energy surrounds you. You and all allies within 15 feet get a 25% increase to dodge chance. (Does not affect chances of dodging area-of-effect damage.)**
**Cost: 10 charge per second for a max of 10 seconds.**
**Cooldown: 2 minutes.**


*So, it can cost up to one hundred charge if I use it for the full duration, which is a lot. But it basically gives Blur to all allies near me. Not bad. Not bad at all.*

Blur was a powerful ability on its own, but being able to give it to himself and all allies around him? That was even better. *Just gotta make sure we don't try dodging any area-of-effect attacks with this. Excluding those, though, this seems a great way to keep everyone alive longer in a fight, or cover us in the event of a retreat.*

"Distortion Field looks handy," Zelda said, looking over to Kaiden.

"Yeah it does," he agreed. "Can't wait to put it to use. But what about everyone else? What'd you all pick up?" he asked, then turned his attention to the screenshots they'd sent him. He started with Titus'.

**Ability: Intransigence (passive)**
**Your defensive expertise makes you an immovable oppo-**
**nent. You are immune to knockback abilities, and damage to**
**allies within 10 feet is reduced by 10%. Does not stack**
**when multiple shield wardens are present.**

Kaiden's mind flashed back to when they'd pirated the freighter for the King Street boys. The cybernetic knight they'd fought in the process – what had his name been? – had thrown Titus around like a toy with his powerful attacks. Not anymore. Even abilities like Thorne's Gravity Sledge wouldn't break through this passive.

*If Titus wants to stay somewhere, he's going to. Bodes well for keeping our defensive formations together. And there's a damage resistance buff to nearby allies. Basically, this makes Titus even more of a beachhead to rally around in combat. I dig it.*

"Intransigence," Kaiden said, looking at Titus out of the corner of his eye. "As if you weren't already stubborn enough."

"Heh." The big man chuckled. "Seems the game's encouraging me. I'm gonna take that as a sign I'm going in the right direction."

The next new ability was Zelda's.

**Ability: In My Sights (passive)**
**As long as you are locked on to a target, all allies deal +25%**
**damage to the target.**

*Ah, this partners up with Lock On.* He pulled up a tab on the ability to re-familiarize himself with it.

**Ability: Lock On**
**You direct charge into your hammer-gun. For 5 seconds, as**
**long as the last target you damaged is within your line of**
**sight, your attacks will not miss. You cannot attack any**
**other target. If you take damage this effect deactivates.**
**Cost: 30 charge.**
**Cooldown: 30 seconds.**

*Nice! So, Lock On will lock her on to a target, then the new passive, In My Sights, will let each of us deal additional damage to that target for up to five seconds.* A pretty convenient way to focus important targets. Pick off an opposing medic or blast warden in order to swing a battle in their favor. *More combos. They're each very powerful, but we'll need to coordinate to make the most of them.*

So, that was it for new abilities for the moment. Thorne was above them in level by a bit so she hadn't unlocked anything new just yet.

"Well, what are we waiting for?" Titus asked, looking around at the remains of their last fight. "This room's clear, on to the next one. What is that, five down now? Six?"

"Something like that," Kaiden said as he moved toward the door that led back out into the hallway. This was always the most dangerous part. Once they were in a room, they were fine, but switching between them always ran the hazard of being spotted.

"The guys in the next room over are still fighting," Zelda said, pressing her ear to the wall. "Sounds like they're in the thick of it, too."

"Good." Thorne nodded at that. "Let's move while they're busy."

Kaiden sucked in a deep breath. This whole plan was insane, but he had to admit it'd been working. Normally, when they fought mobs, they were in limited numbers; or worse, killing enough of them would level him above the mobs. Once that happened, killing them didn't make much sense. The EXP gained was too little. The Grinder had sidestepped that problem entirely, though.

Kaiden flipped the lock on the door and it snapped open. He peered out cautiously. No one in the hallway.

*Good.*

"The next several rooms are all level forty-five or six. Easy to get to, but…"

"Too low-level," Zelda said. She joined him, peeking into the hallway as well. "There," she nodded. "I can see a few level fifty rooms just beyond that next intersection."

"Big level jump," Titus said. "I dig it."

"We'll have to be careful, but I think it's worth it," Kaiden said. "The sooner we hit level fifty, the sooner we can get out of here."

"He's right," Thorne said. "No reason to tempt fate."

"Level fifty it is." Kaiden sucked down another deep breath, checked the hallway was still clear, then stepped out of the room.

*Stand up straight. Look casual. No one knows who you are unless they get close enough to read your name. Play it cool,* he told himself. But there was no one else in the hallway.

He heard the others join him as he set a brisk pace down the hall. The lights above cast the space in a constant yellow glow. It reflected off minerals in the stone walls in a thousand little pinpoints. The wall was punctuated every twenty or so steps by another door. Kaiden couldn't help but read their displays as he passed.

**Room status: Unoccupied.**
**Mob status: 0/0 Voidspawn, Level: 45**

Looked like someone had already cleared that room out. Maybe it'd been them? Honestly, Kaiden couldn't remember. All of the rooms they'd been in were blurring together.

**Room status: Occupied.**
**Mob status: 15/15 Ramrunners **Huntsman**, Level: 30**

The sounds of abilities firing off echoed out of that one, paired with the shouts and exclamations of a team of wardens coordinating their attacks. Kaiden winced and picked up the pace as he passed the door.

*They're busy in there, though. We're fine. We're fine.*

He paused again as he reached the intersection. To either side, more doors and rooms stretched into the distance. Down the right-side route, though, Kaiden could see a change in the layout of the base. The hall ended in some sort of larger room. A barracks or something, from the looks of it.

"Don't wanna head that way," Thorne hissed as she stepped past him and continued toward their next room.

"Come on, Kai," Zelda said, nudging his shoulder as she followed Thorne through the intersection.

"Right, right." Kaiden shook off the trance that had come over him. The mental exhaustion was really messing with him now. It mixed with the constant worry of being discovered to create what he could only think of as a significant real-life debuff. His status in-game was fine, but his mind in real life was tired. He shook the feeling off – *no time to be off my game* – and followed the others to the far side of the intersection.

"Yo! Hold up a second!"

A voice called out from down by the barracks. Kaiden near jumped out of his armor from the shock of it. It took all the concentration he had to force his body to keep walking at a steady pace as if he hadn't heard the shout. It was three painfully long steps before he was out of the intersection and back into the hall.

"Go, go, go!" Thorne hissed, breaking into a run toward the next room. She pulled up short at the last moment, then ducked into a different room.

**Room status: Unoccupied.**
**Mob status: 0/0 Weirdlings, Level: 10**

"This one's empty," Titus said as he ducked in.

"If they come after us, we don't want to be pinched between them and a room full of mobs," Thorne explained.

"Yeah, uh, bad news about that," Kaiden said, stealing one last look back out into the hall. The warden who'd shouted was approaching at a jog. Kaiden snapped the door shut.

"Where'd you go?" The warden's voice trickled through the door, still approaching in the hallway. "Shift's up, guys. We're swapping out."

"This guy's not gonna pass us," Kaiden said, ear to the door and listening as the jogging footsteps drew closer and closer.

"All right, time's up," Zelda said. "We'll take this guy out and make a run for the *Borrelly*."

Thorne cursed at that.

"Thought we'd get more levels out of this," she sighed. "Ellenton, have the shuttle ready."

"Something happening?" Ellenton's voice came back through comms after a short delay.

"No time," Kaiden said, then raised his hammer as the door opened.

**Hendell**
**Warden Sergeant**
**Class: Blast Warden**
**Faction: Warden Corps**
**Level: 48**

"Gah!" Kaiden shouted as he jumped forward and brought his hammer down on Hendell. The man was too startled to react and the blow landed for a headshot and a critical hit.

Before Hendell could recover from the attack, Kaiden was swinging again and Thorne was on him. The warden's health bar drained as three more blows landed. An Improved Burst Arrow zipped over Kaiden's shoulder then exploded against the already overwhelmed warden's chest in a shower of sparks.

Hendell was a blast warden, caught off-guard and already in close quarters with his attackers. He might've been higher level than them but it hardly mattered. All the same, winning this fight didn't earn them anything, Kaiden knew. Hendell finally had his shield on and was leveling his hammer-gun to retaliate, but there wasn't any attack he could throw at them that was more damaging than what he'd already done: called for help. Kaiden hadn't heard him, but he'd seen the man's mouth move. He'd used a private comm channel to call for backup.

*It was a good plan, but the gig's up. Time to get the hell out of here.*

Hendell fired an Improved Scatter Shot into Thorne's chest

that set her health bar to flashing as a chunk of HP fell away. Thorne responded with a Gravity Sledge that slammed him into the far wall, denting it outward. Zelda blasted again. Kaiden darted in and landed two crits. And then Titus was there, fighting like a man possessed. The focus in his eyes was intense as he unloaded attack after attack on the warden. Hendell's health plummeted into the red before he could get back to his feet. His knees extended, pushing him upright, then his health dropped to zero and he collapsed right back down.

**Blast Warden Hendell assisted kill – 5,000 EXP gained!**

Kaiden paid no mind to the notification, sprinting into the hallway instead. It was a long run back to the emergency exit. Clearing rooms had led them further and further into the base. It was only then that he realized exactly how far in they'd come.

"We can make it," he growled, pushing himself to run as fast as he could. "We can make it."

Chapter Thirty-Three

"We can't make it." Kaiden slid to a halt and cursed.

The hallway in front of him was filled with wardens. A group of four were the closest, but further behind them he could see a group of six. Then there was shouting behind him and Kaiden turned to see a door had opened in the distance. Another group was pouring out. At least seven players, maybe more. And all this was only the wardens that had been close by. Considering the alarm now blaring through the entirety of the base, Kaiden had no doubt all hundred or so wardens would be on them before long.

"We'll go down fighting," Titus said, raising his shield and setting his feet. "Get as much EXP as we can before we do."

"Don't fight them in the open," Zelda said, grabbing Titus and pulling him toward the door to an empty room. "We'll create a chokepoint. Make their numbers less relevant."

"It won't be enough," Thorne shouted. "We need to make a run for it."

"Who's able to run through that?" Zelda asked, pointing toward the oncoming wall of wardens. The blast wardens among their ranks opened fire and Kaiden ducked into the room with everyone else as lasers exploded all around them.

"Titus, Kaiden. Hold the door with me," Thorne said, taking

up position just inside it. "Zelda, dish out all of the damage you can from the rear."

Kaiden moved into position beside Titus, but his mind was reeling.

*We can't hold out forever. Hell, we won't be able to hold out for more than a few minutes, if we even make it that long.*

"This isn't going to work!" Kaiden said.

"You got a better plan?" Thorne snarled back. "Cause I'm trying to find one and coming up awfully empty." She lashed out with a hammer strike as the first of the wardens arrived in the doorway.

**Erick Day02**
**Warden Captain**
**Class: Power Warden**
**Faction: Warden Corps**
**Level: 48**

Titus stepped up and smashed his shield into the power warden, holding him in the doorway. Erick Day02 slammed his massive hammer into it and set its surface to shaking, then attacked again, and again, trying to beat him back and make way for more wardens to rush into the room, but Titus held his ground. Might've even gained a step, actually. All the while, his Improved Volt Field nipped back, sparking and biting at Erick's health.

**Ability: Rallying Cry**
**All party members within 50 feet gain a 20% boost to base stats for 30 seconds.**
**Cost: 20 charge.**

Titus used the surge of charge pouring into him from blocking the attacks to fire off the ability. Glowing light swarmed around Thorne then Kaiden as the stat buff kicked into effect. Kaiden lashed out with another hammer strike. It hit for a couple percent of damage – mainly thanks to the buff from Titus. Kaiden wanted to activate an ability but he didn't have any charge yet. The power warden was just focusing on Titus. Thorne had been building charge with each hammer strike thanks to her passives, though, and she used it to pair Rallying Cry's buff with an ability of her own.

**Ability: Improved Chained Fury**
**Your combat prowess allows you to chain attacks together. For the next 5 seconds, each attack deals an additional 20% damage for every successful attack before it.**

With her damage boosted through the roof, Thorne set in, swinging again and again at Erick, bashing his health away with each hit. The other wardens were arriving now, though. They stacked up behind the lead power warden, each jostling and pushing to get into the action. The doorway was jammed, though. Between Erick trying to get in, Titus trying to keep him out, and Thorne and Kaiden swinging away every chance they got, there just wasn't any more room. Didn't stop the blast wardens, though.

**Ability: Improved Warden's Bolt**
**You fire two bolts of lightning instead of one. Discharge bolts of lightning that jump to multiple targets within range of the impact target. Initial range 50 feet, jump range 10 feet. Deals +150% base damage, reducing by half with each successive jump.**

Zelda's attack flew over Kaiden's head, and from the size of it, he could tell Zelda had fired it from Sniper Mode. The Improved Warden's Bolt arced into the crowd, where it went crazy, zapping from one opponent to the next and chewing away at their health. Not a moment later, though, the same attack was fired back at Zelda. It detonated and Kaiden found himself swimming in electricity as the ability tore into him and the others. His health dropped to ninety-two percent.

*I wasn't built for this,* Kaiden thought, growling as more attacks poured in. Improved Burst Arrows and Improved Scatter Shots from the blast wardens, Hammer Tosses from the power wardens – he blocked what he could, his shield wavering under the assault, and lashed out at Erick whenever there was an opening. On the upside, all the attacks meant Kaiden finally had charge. On the downside, he couldn't ignore his health bar, flashing near constantly now and dropping rapidly.

*Seventy percent. Sixty-eight. I'm not a shielder. And even less a power warden...*

"We need a plan," Zelda shouted between blasts of her hammer-gun. "A way out. Something!"

"Let 'em come," Titus growled, teeth gritted against the assault on his shield. He was fighting with a focus Kaiden hadn't seen before. Had a look in his eye like each of the wardens out there had personally insulted him and he'd come for payback. There was an opening between Erick's attacks and Titus fired off a Shield Slam, stunning his opponent. He followed with Shield of Rage and a burst of energy rushed from his shield, dealing damage to Erick and the wardens right behind him.

The stun wore off and Erick came back swinging hard, but Titus was ready.

**Ability: Reflection**
**Reflects 20% of damage absorbed by the warden's shield back against the attacker for 10 seconds.**

"Let the bastards come," Titus growled again.

"These are just the wardens that were closest to us," Thorne said, then paused to land a blow on Erick. "But there are certainly higher-level wardens here. Their wing is just further away. You can bet they're on their w—"

"Gah!" Erick was in the red now, but he wasn't giving up. He shouted a battle cry as he reared back his hammer.

**Ability: Gravity Sledge**

He swung the attack into Titus' shield and Kaiden prepared

for the big man to launch backwards and the rest of the wardens to come rushing in. Erick's hammer exploded with energy as it connected, but Titus absorbed the attack. He gritted his teeth and held his ground.

"Intransigence. Bad luck for you," Titus said with a snarl, then struck back with a flurry of hammer strikes to Erick's head and shoulders.

**Power Warden Erick Day02 assisted kill - 4,800 EXP gained!**

Erick went down, and for the briefest of moments before Last Rites triggered, there was a gap. Kaiden's view filled with names as his visor scanned the enemies in the hallway.

**Manzer**
**Warden Sergeant**
**Class: Shield Warden**
**Faction: Warden Corps**
**Level: 47**

**Tomson**
**Warden Sergeant**
**Class: Power Warden**
**Faction: Warden Corps**
**Level: 47**

**QuertyBoy01**
**Warden Captain**
**Class: Blast Warden**
**Faction: Warden Corps**
**Level: 49**

Too many names to read. Still more filled his view.

**Frankie04, Enhanced Warden**

**Panzerpants, Power Warden**

**Werner06, Blast Warden**

**HaroldMay, Shield Warden**

Even in that brief moment, another group of wardens arrived and still more names filled his view. There was even a Werner account, removing any doubt that this was where his alternate accounts were being levelled for him.

*We can't fight this. There's no way we can take them all.*

"Traitor scum!" A power warden named Tomson came in swinging. Titus blocked the first flurry of attacks, then activated Shield Link with its target set to Zelda.

"Appreciated," she shouted from behind, then let loose a renewed barrage of attacks.

Two Improved Kinetic Grenades flew in from the hallway and Kaiden ducked as they detonated, blasting damage through the room. His health flashed wildly at the hit. Titus absorbed the damage, his large health pool built for the task, and even Thorne seemed mostly okay. They were each floating at around seventy percent health. But Kaiden didn't have stats meant for tanking damage like them. Neither did Zelda. Even a couple of paces removed from the fighting her health was taking a beating. Down to sixty-two percent.

But it didn't matter. None of it did, he thought as Zelda flung a grenade, bouncing it off of the wall so it angled around the corner and exploded out of sight among the wardens.

*We can't win this fight,* Kaiden thought. *It's purely a numbers game. All we're doing right now is delaying. And I'm no use just bludgeoning away at whoever steps into the doorway. That's not what my class is built for.*

*Hold up.* He paused at that, stopping his attack mid-strike as a thought exploded in his mind.

"I'm not built for this sort of fight," he said through comms.

"We need you anyway!" Thorne shouted back. "Keep fighting!"

"I will," Kaiden said and began charging Flash Bang. "But not like this. You said these doors lock, right?" he asked Thorne.

"Even if we managed to get it closed, they'd just unlock it. That won't do us any good," she grunted between swings of her massive hammer.

"Not why I was asking," Kaiden said as a plan came together in his mind. A stupid plan, maybe. And one that was as like to get them killed as it was their enemies. But there wasn't time for doubt now.

**Ability: Flash Bang**

The attack burst outward, searing the assembled wardens' eyes.

"Hold the door as long as you can," Kaiden shouted, then lowered his shield.

"What are you doing?" Zelda shouted back.

"Something stupid, probably." Kaiden eyed one of the few spots in the hallway not already filled with wardens.

**Ability: Matter Shift**

Kaiden rematerialized outside the room and behind the crowd of wardens. Between his Flash Bang and their focus on Titus and Thorne, no one noticed him – a perfect chance to score some critical hits from behind. But why think so small? No; he had bigger plans.

**Ability: Lightspeed**

Kaiden dumped just about half of his remaining charge into the ability, then burst into motion toward his target: not a warden, but a door.

*Last one in, be sure to lock the door behind you. We don't want any of these buggers getting out to roam the halls,* he remembered Thorne warning when they'd first arrived at the facility. He slid to a stop in front of the door he'd picked out.

**Room status: Unoccupied.**

**Mob status: 20/20 Voidspawn **Huntsman**, Level: 40**

*Creatures with Huntsman status attack the highest-level enemies in the vicinity first,* he thought, smiling. *I never thought being lower level than our enemies would be a good thing.*

He tapped his hand to the door and it unlocked.

Kaiden paused in front of the open door so the horde of voidspawn inside noticed him. They hissed and chirped, then rushed forward in a surge of flesh and slime and fangs.

"Dinner time, boys!" he shouted. The voidspawn burst into the hallway in a tumble of fury and hunger. Kaiden shot away at the last moment, Lightspeed carrying him at a blistering speed toward the next door. The voidspawn paused a moment, then turned toward their highest-level opponents in the vicinity: the crowd of wardens. A great echoing hiss tore through the hallway as they charged the unsuspecting players.

But Kaiden wasn't done there. He continued on. The next room had mobs with no particular status. The one after that was full of elites. Then, finally, he found what he was looking for.

**Room status: Unoccupied.**
**Mob status: 30/30 Grachnids **Huntsman**, Level: 35**

"What's a party without some grachnids?" He unlocked that door too and continued on.

**Room status: Unoccupied.**
**Mob status: 20/20 Cryo-mummies **Huntsman**, Level: 45**

"You'll do." Another door unlocked, then on to the next; a room full of gobbers, but Kaiden wasn't discriminating when it came to the chaos he was sowing. He let them get close enough that they were in aggro range of the wardens.

"Plenty of things to smash and bite that way!" he said, pointing toward them, then sprinted out of the gobbers' range, leaving them to attack the unsuspecting wardens.

"Just need a few more rooms," he muttered as Lightspeed

ticked down its final seconds. He rushed forward, unlocking every door in reach.

He released a pack of hominoids, then a second batch of grachnids after that. He followed those with a pride of Baboulian Manhunters and then even a swarm of weirdlings, all with the Huntsman status.

Screams and shouts echoed through the hall as Lightspeed wore off and Kaiden jogged to a stop. He couldn't help the smile spreading across his face as he turned to find what had once been a crowd of wardens now reduced to a savage melee.

It was utter chaos. Abilities fired off in all directions. Improved Kinetic Grenades exploded against the walls and ceiling. Gravity Sledges sent voidspawn flying like pieces of slime-covered debris. But for every five or six mobs that died, Kaiden saw another warden go down. They'd been unprepared and attacked from behind. More wardens were pouring in from the other side of the fight – lower levels than the other wardens, but still high enough that the mobs would ignore Kaiden and the others, or so it looked like. The monsters welcomed the new combatants with glee as they bit and tore and slashed at anything within reach.

"You there! Stop!"

*Shit.* Another group of wardens approaching. His visor read out their details and he cursed again. There were five of them, and each was level fifty-five or above. Almost max level.

*The high-level wardens Thorne was worried about. They're finally here.* Were there enough mobs to take down five almost max-level players? No way to know, but facing them on his own wasn't going to get him anywhere. Kaiden began to backpedal, retreating toward the melee, when he spotted an unopened door.

**Room status: Unoccupied.**
**Mob status: 30/30 Ramrunners **Huntsman**, Level: 45**

*One last addition to the fun, then.*
Kaiden gave the approaching wardens a little wave.
"Welcome to the party," he said, then unlocked the door.

## Chapter Thirty-Four

"You're crazy! And brilliant!" Zelda shouted through comms as Kaiden rejoined the melee.

"A lot of the former, less of the latter," he said as he ducked under a whipping tentacle from a nearby voidspawn. It was beating down a warden, but its wayward blows threatened to strike anyone in the vicinity. The rest of the melee looked pretty much the same – a chaos of flailing voidspawn tentacles, slashing grachnid legs, slobbering gobbers, and more that Kaiden didn't even have time to process.

He made his way through it, ducking and dodging and trying not to draw too much attention as he made for the door where he could still see Titus' shield glowing bright. A beacon of light amid the insanity. Thankfully, he was still one of the lowest level wardens in the room, which meant none of the mobs were targeting him. All the same, Kaiden had Improved Blur active.

"Get back here," Titus called through comms. "Most of the heat's off us now, thanks to you."

"With pleasure," Kaiden said, whipping his shield up just in time to block the crackling electricity of an Improved Warden's Bolt lashing out at everything around it. It tore at his health anyway, dropping him to fifty-two percent. In the chaos of the melee there was just too much damage flying around to avoid being hit, even with Improved Blur active. Matter Shift was still on cooldown, but there was another option. Kaiden pulled out the Matter Insubstantiator he'd looted from the Dark Turen forever ago and activated it.

**Warden Matter Insubstantiator**
**Rarity: Rare**
**Durability: 100%**
**+2% movement speed**
**+2% dodge chance**
***Special ability: Once per day, you may activate this item to become insubstantial for 2 seconds. During this time, no attack can hit you and damage cannot be dealt.**

He broke into a sprint as his character became semi-transparent. A group of wardens had gathered into some semblance of a formation and stood between him and Titus.

*No matter,* he thought, chuckling at the pun as he ran straight through them like a ghost through a wall.

The two seconds expired and Improved Blur timed out as well. Kaiden was still a few paces from Titus. The big man was waving him in as Kaiden sprinted as hard as he could. Something hit him in the back, dropping his health to forty-seven percent. A glob of acid missed a nearby warden and splashed on to Kaiden's hip, and his armor sizzled as his health dropped another five percent.

*Almost there.*

The last obstacle was a blast warden, leveling his hammer-gun at Kaiden. He raised his shield and the attack exploded against it, making its surface waver. Kaiden rushed forward before the blaster could attack again. He landed a hammer strike on the warden's head then slipped past him. Titus lowered his shield for a moment and Kaiden darted into the room.

*Safe! Little health left, but safe! At least for the moment.* He'd brought stimpacks with him, as had the others, and they'd managed to keep him alive so far. They were all used up now, but they'd done their job. Had been enough of an advantage over the wardens who didn't have any; most would have come thinking they could rely on the medbays.

Kaiden let out a heavy breath as Titus and Thorne stepped back up to the door. His relief was cut short a moment later, however, as he realized how low on health they were. Thorne was down to ten percent, and Titus fifteen. They'd taken a beating while he'd been gone. No doubt they had used all of their stimpacks, too.

"We might still die here," Thorne said, swinging her hammer at any mob or warden that dared get close to the doorway. "But at least we're taking all of these bastards with us, yeah?"

"We have to stay here," Kaiden said. "Use the room as cover. The Huntsman mobs are going after the highest-level targets in the area. Thankfully, that's not us. If we can avoid taking much more damage until the fighting dies down, maybe there's a chance we can fight our way out past the survivors."

"That's a long shot," Thorne said. "I don't think—" Her eyes went wide, and a split second later, Kaiden saw why. Her health bar was replenishing. It filled all the way back up to one hundred percent.

"I... I leveled up," she said, shock in her eyes. "Why did I get assisted kill credit for..."

Even as she spoke, Kaiden noticed a message had appeared in his vision. It'd been there a moment but he hadn't paid attention to it until now.

**Blast Warden QuertyBoy01 assisted kill - 5,000 EXP gained!**

Kaiden stared at the notification a moment. He'd done damage to a blast warden on the way in, sure, but he hadn't killed him. Kaiden peered through Titus' shield and saw Querty-Boy01 face down on the ground. A group of hominoids was attacking his corpse.

"I dealt damage to him..." Kaiden said as the realization hit him. "And then the mobs finished him off! But I still get assist credit on the kill!"

"*We* get assisted kill credit," Thorne said, excitement filling her voice. "And experience!"

**Power Warden Tomson assisted kill - 4,700 EXP gained!**

"Tomson…" Kaiden said.

"Was the power warden we fought in the doorway," Titus said. "He must've just died."

The full impact of what was happening began to settle on Kaiden. He felt his eyes go wide, felt the breath catch in his throat.

"Guys…" he said. "This is our way out."

"Hit every warden you can!" Zelda shouted. "Get damage on them all, and when they die, we get assist credit." Even before she finished speaking she began firing into the hallway; an Improved Scatter Shot that winged several wardens, then an Improved Warden's Bolt that zapped even more.

**Shield Warden Manzer assisted kill – 4,700 EXP gained!**

Titus' health blossomed back to full as he leveled up from the experience. At the same time, a notification appeared in Kaiden's vision.

**Level 43 achieved!**
**Max health and stamina increased**
**+3 stat points**

"Level up!" Zelda shouted, also back to full health.

"This… this is good." Thorne turned toward the melee beyond Titus' shield. "It's open season, everyone. Hit every warden you can, just once, then move to the next."

"One second," Kaiden said. "I have a gift before we leave."

**Ability: Distortion Field**
**A field of energy surrounds you and nearby allies. You and all allies within fifteen feet get a 25% increase to dodge**

chance. **Does not affect chances of area of effects to hit you or your allies.**

"Oh hell yeah," Thorne said, then raised her hammer and plunged into the chaos.

Titus followed her, bellowing a battle cry.

Kaiden adjusted his grip on his hammer, then gave Zelda a nod.

"Full health, abilities coming off of cooldown, and a horde of mobs that might as well not know we're here." He smiled. "Let's go make some trouble."

The chaos of the melee was dying down. Most of the mobs had been killed and even more of the wardens. It'd been a fight, even with the chaos giving them an advantage, but they'd all made it through. Kaiden had taken several hard hits as blast wardens had managed to steal a moment to fire at him, and there'd been one particularly rough bit where an exceptionally persistent power warden had managed to stay right on him, but the constant leveling from the EXP they were gaining meant his health had restored fully every few minutes. Altogether, they'd each leveled four more times, meaning he was up to forty-seven. Every time a new level was achieved his health had topped off back at one hundred percent – a fact he was sure his opponents would have found annoying, were they not too busy being swarmed by Huntsman mobs.

The assisted kill notifications had been coming in at such a steady pace Kaiden hadn't been able to keep up.

**Shield Warden HaroldMay assisted kill – 4,700 EXP gained!**
**Power Warden Panzerpants assisted kill – 4,700 EXP gained!**
**Enhanced Warden Frankie04 assisted kill – 4,700 EXP gained!**
**Blast Warden Werner06 assisted kill – 4,400 EXP gained!**
**Shield Warden Tomatillo assisted kill – 4,400 EXP gained!**

**Power Warden HammerRammer assisted kill – 4,400 EXP gained!**

So many names; it was just about all Kaiden could do to see the battleground in front of him. The sides of his vision were flooded with notifications. Assisted kills. Level ups. New abilities. On and on.

As more enemies died, Kaiden leveled up more, closing the level gap between him and the other wardens. It risked drawing the attention of the Huntsman mobs, he knew, but the good thing about having his enemies fighting his other enemies – the wardens fighting the mobs – was that they were killing each other off. Still, how many more were there throughout the base? He didn't really care to find out.

The fight immediately in front of them had boiled down to just a few scattered remnants now.

"Well, if I were a betting man, I'd say the mobs just about have this one in the bag," Titus said, pointing to the last group of wardens: four in total and surrounded on all sides by Huntsman mobs. A few steps away, Zelda was in Sniper Mode. She lobbed an Improved Kinetic Grenade into the remains of the fight to make sure she and the rest of the group would get assisted credit when the wardens finally died.

"Moran's gonna have an aneurysm when he learns about this," Thorne said, then laughed. "Kaiden, thank you for this." She spread her arms out wide. "For all of this." There was an edge to her voice. Excitement, it sounded like. But also something more. Vengeance, maybe? Kaiden couldn't blame her. He was feeling it himself. The Party was power-leveling accounts with this place, grinding out an army as quickly as possible, but in one fell stroke, he'd put an end to that. For a week, at least.

"Seriously, though. This was insane, Kai." Titus slapped him on the shoulder so hard he wouldn't have been surprised if a point of health had ticked away.

"Things, uh…" Kaiden smirked. "Turned out better than expected."

"You can say that again."

"Let's not let our guards down just yet," Zelda warned, cautious as always. "We're almost in the clear. It's time we got out of here before something goes wrong."

"She's right," Thorne agreed. "The surviving wardens will have called for help. Probably some time ago, really. Reinforcements will be on their way to the planet. We should get back to the shuttle. Get scarce."

"For sure," Kaiden said, but he didn't move. He found himself morbidly interested in who was going to come out victorious.

The last of the hominoids died with a screech, but it took one of the wardens with it.

**Shield Warden HammyTheManny assisted kill – 4,400 EXP gained!**

"Three wardens left," Kaiden said.

"We should leave, Kai." Zelda was still in Sniper Mode. She raised her hammer-gun toward the final few combatants.

"Yeah, I guess you're right. But we gotta loot this place first. Look at all this!" He spread his arms wide, taking in countless weapons and suits of armor scattered across the battlefield. "There's a fortune lying around for the taking, not to mention higher level gear. Couldn't hurt to bring some of that to the tournament."

"Still a few levels before we can join the tournament," Titus grunted. "Forty-seven isn't fifty."

"It's close enough," Thorne said. "No reason to push our luck here. After all—"

A burst of light filled the hallway and Kaiden recoiled as Zelda blasted an Inferno Shot at what was left of the remaining wardens and mobs. Combined with the damage buff from Sniper Mode it hit with enough power to obliterate everything in front of it.

Three more player assisted kill notifications came in along with eight mobs, and then finally, for a moment at least, there was silence.

A notification flashed into Kaiden's vision.

**Achievement Unlocked!**
**You Have Become Death - 20,000 EXP!**
**You broke the record for kills or assisted kills in a single battle! Congratulations, you murder-happy psychopath. Unique Title Awarded: Destroyer of Worlds**

**Level 48 achieved!**
**Max health and stamina increased**
**+3 stat points**

**Ability unlocked: Lethal Precision**

"A world first, eh?" Titus nodded, his face bent into an expression that seemed to say 'not bad, not bad.'

Kaiden found himself stunned into silence. He read the achievement again, then once more for good measure. Slowly, a smile bloomed on his face. So much of what they'd done with their time in Nova had been because they *had* to do it, and technically, this wasn't any different. But for the first time in a while, Kaiden felt the joy of taking pride in what he'd done. Were circumstances not what they were, he would've been dying to achieve something as noteworthy as a world first. Compared to the grand scheme of what they were trying to do – to take down the Party – it wasn't much. But for the moment, it made him happy.

"All right, all right. Enough celebration," Thorne said. "Let's loot and get out of here. We're on the clock. One hundred and two Party employees just logged out, no doubt pissed off and looking for vengeance. This place is going to be swarmed very soon."

"We'll make this quick," Kaiden assured her as he began looting. Dead mobs were piled everywhere, and among them, wardens. Dozens and dozens of them.

**DimReaper **Deceased****

**Power Warden**
**Faction: Warden Corps**
**Level: 47**


**LorenThyme **Deceased****
**Shield Warden**
**Faction: Warden Corps**
**Level: 48**


On and on, corpse after corpse. All of them had been real players, but not true players, Kaiden knew. Most of them were Party employees who'd been ordered to power-level accounts. Not that it mattered now. They were out of game for a week. Could come back on new accounts, no doubt, but that'd start them all over at level one.

"Here." Kaiden stepped up to the corpse of what had been a level fifty blast warden. "This'll do," he said as a 'loot corpse?' prompt appeared.

Unsurprisingly, the corpse didn't have many items on it. No need to when it'd spent all of its time in-game stuck in the Grinder. It did have two things that drew Kaiden's attention, though: its armor and weapon.

He focused on the armor first. The armor Kaiden was wearing now – and had been wearing since the battle against the grachnids on Zeross – was sleek and matte gray, with tubing flowing over its frame like tendons attached to muscles. In contrast, this armor was a whole different beast. There were no tubes around it, no joints between pieces. There weren't even pieces to it. The whole thing was slim, sleek, and looked like it was completely made out of one solid piece of metal. Like a second skin, really. Some areas – particularly around the chest, thighs, and neck – were thicker. Reinforced, no doubt. Looking closer, Kaiden noticed there was small lines flowing through the otherwise matte-gray metal skin. Almost like veins. They flowed out from the chest of the suit and down the arms, across the torso toward the legs, and to every other extremity.

*For carrying charge,* he realized. Their current armor had tubing to do that, but this new set – this almost max-level warden armor – had miniaturized that technology and integrated it even more holistically into the suit.

*I wonder how that affects the charge capacity?*

**Warden Bombardier Power Suit**
**Rarity: Rare**
**Durability: 55%**
**+5% charge gained from Atmospheric Charge**
**+5% AOE damage resistance**
**+15% melee damage resistance**
**+30% charge capacity**
**Stimulant Cooling Slots: 3**

*Based on these stats, this thing's made for a blast warden. No surprise, considering it was on the corpse of a blast warden.* Kaiden smirked to himself. *Zelda's going to love this.*

He looted the armor set and the corpse on the ground was suddenly wearing only a thin undersuit. *Gotta love game logic,* he thought with a chuckle, then turned his attention to the corpse's weapon.

**Warden Hammer-Rifle, Heavy Hitter Edition**
**Rarity: Rare**
**Durability: 85%**
**+15% damage to ranged targets within twenty feet**
**+5% damage on attacks that target a single enemy**
**Your first critical hit of each combat deals double damage to its target.**

*Is this better than Zelda's current weapon? It's once-daily ability to make an attack hit three targets is pretty useful. Probably best to let Zelda decide.*

Kaiden snapped a screenshot of the armor and weapon and sent it to the group.

"Oh dang," Titus said. "That makes what we're wearing now look like scrap."

"Yes *please!*" Zelda said through comms a moment later.

"Just found a set for you, Titus," Thorne said. "'Warden Guardian Power Suit.' Same thirty percent increase in charge capacity, some damage resistance, but mainly it buffs your shield. On first equip it lets you pick a type of damage to reduce by thirty percent until you die."

"Don't even play. You're serious?" The big man hurried over to her, then looted the armor set immediately.

*Gotta find armor for myself, too.* Titus' exclamations over his new armor continued as Kaiden turned his attention to the rest of the corpses, searching for an enhanced warden among them.

**Harrolde02 **Deceased****
**Shield Warden**
**Faction: Warden Corps**
**Level: 48**

*Titus is already covered.*
Kaiden looted the armor and hammer anyway. Could probably be sold for a nice profit. There was a limit to how much each of them could carry in their inventory, but as long as they looted what they wanted first, then they could use the rest of their inventory spots to just loot valuable gear.

**Daudilus05 **Deceased****
**Power Warden**
**Faction: Warden Corps**
**Level: 52**

"There's one for you," Kaiden said, pointing Thorne toward the corpse. He took a quick glance at the armor's stats before moving on.

**Warden Berserker Power Suit**
**Rarity: Rare**
**Durability: 62%**
**+15% ranged attack damage resistance**

+5% AOE damage resistance
+5% melee damage resistance
+5% stun resistance
+30% charge capacity
**Stimulant Cooling Slots: 3**

*Not bad, not bad at all. Stun resistance is cool, too. Haven't seen that before. Makes sense, though. Power wardens are all about attack. Stuns can throw a big wrench in that plan.*

The armor, though, like all of the others Kaiden saw, was damaged and had a lowered durability. No doubt from the lethal fight they all had just been involved in.

*We'll need to repair any of these we want to keep.*

"Think I found the only enhanced warden armor in the room," Thorne laughed, then waved to Kaiden. He rushed over, tripping on corpses of wardens and mobs alike in his haste.

*Jeez. Really thought there wasn't going to be any.* The idea of being stuck with low-level armor while everyone else got upgrades wasn't exactly a pleasant one.

**Warden Blitzer Power Suit**
**Rarity: Rare**
**Durability: 81%**
+8% dodge chance on ranged attacks
+8% dodge chance on melee attacks
+10% chance of critical hits when attacking from behind
+30% charge capacity
**Stimulant Cooling Slots: 3**

*All right, all right,* Kaiden thought, looking over the stats. *We can work with this. Good boosts to dodge chance, but most importantly, a thirty percent increase to my charge. That'll be a big one. Means my shield can take more hits before overloading and I can attack back with more abilities.*

"There's a weapon, too," Thorne said. She was right.

**Chrono Sledge**

**Rarity: Rare**
**Durability: 95%**
**+5% damage dealt on critical hits**
**+5% damage when attacking from behind**
**On critical hit, target is target is slowed by 30% for 2**
**seconds (does not stack).**

*Whoa. Hello there!* Kaiden thought, looting the hammer as quickly as he could. Looking closer at it, he could see it had small, ornate designs carved into its grip. They looked to be... hourglasses?

*Oh. Chrono Sledge. Chrono as in time. And it slows opponents on crits. A bit on the nose, but it makes sense.*

The handle looked to be made out of some kind of metal, but it'd been roughened to provide a better grip. Wires ran along the hammer's length, seeming to flow from the little ornate hour-glasses and up to the heavy metal head.

"Mean-looking thing," Thorne said, admiring it as well.

"Hate to break up the party, y'all, but we're running out of time," Ellenton said through comms. "Get back here. It's time to skedaddle."

# Chapter Thirty-Five

*Back to Kyraxis, then,* Kaiden thought, leaning against one of the *Veritas II's* man-sized windows and watching the digital stars of Nova pass beyond. *Back to Kyraxis, but this time, we're prepared.*

Nothing gave him more confidence in that than his new level. Fifty, now. Grinding out ten levels might've taken a special – and life-threatening – trip to the Grinder, but after that, earning two more was a cakewalk. They'd stopped off at a turen station where they'd sold the loot they weren't keeping, then picked up missions that kept them moving in the general direction of Kyraxis. From there, all there was to do was knock the missions out one after the other – a feat made all the easier thanks to Titus' new-found drive.

The big man had been more focused than ever since the Grinder, studying his new abilities and putting them to use in just about every way he could. Partly because the whole Maximus tournament plan was his, probably, but there was more to it than that; a score to settle, and Titus had been preparing for it like a boxer ready to fight for the title.

*Level fifty,* Kaiden thought, then chuckled. He couldn't deny it felt good. He felt powerful. Felt strong. Felt like the Party had better watch its ass, because he was coming for them.

It helped that he and the rest of the team had so many new abilities backing them up. Kaiden pulled up the screenshots to go over them one more time. Titus had been studying virtually non-stop and, being honest, Kaiden figured he could take a note from the big man's playbook.

The screenshots of the new abilities appeared in his vision, but Kaiden disregarded them for a moment to open his character sheet. *Better to start with the changes there.* And a lot had changed, mainly his stats.

**Character**

*Name:*
Kaiden
*Race:*
Human
*Level:*
50
*Class:*
Enhanced Warden
Attributes

*Strength:*
65 (+2)
*Intelligence:*
59
*Endurance:*
65
*Perception:*
59
*Dexterity:*
164 (+2)
*Unassigned:*
0
Abilities
*Kickback*
*Shield Bash*
*Hammer Toss*
*Shackle*

*Lightspeed*
*Improved Enhanced Senses*
*Improved Riposte*
*Flash Bang*
*Improved Blur*
*Onslaught*
*Enfeebling Strike*
*Slayer*
*Hamstring*
*Matter Shift*
*Distortion Field*
*Intangible Defense*
*Lethal Precision*

**Perks**
**Turen Tinkering**

*Everything in there's shot through the roof.* Each of his attributes had risen by nineteen points since level thirty-eight, except for dexterity. Thanks to the level-ups and the three unassigned points that came with each level – which he always put into dex – the stat had jumped all the way to one hundred sixty-four.

The implications of this weren't lost on Kaiden. Many of his abilities relied on dexterity. All of them would be more effective now. It'd seem like a big jump, but that was just because he'd jumped up to fifty so quickly.

The other thing that caught his eye about his new and improved character sheet was the addition of two new abilities. He'd seen Distortion Field when he'd earned it in the Grinder. The others, though, he hadn't looked closely enough at.

*Time to change that.*

He focused on the ability he'd gotten for level forty-four.

**Ability: Intangible Defense (passive)**
Charge pours into your body, causing you to vibrate at such speeds that you become semi-intangible. When combat begins, the first damage you take is reduced by 100%, after

which this ability deactivates. If no damage is taken during the following 3 minutes, this ability reactivates.

*Now this one is something special. This can be a total game changer. Basically, I get to blank the first attack that hits me every time I go into combat. Then, if I can avoid taking damage for three minutes, I can blank another attack. Three minutes is a long time, but relying on dexterity means I'm hard to hit, and I have my shield to block attacks. So, three minutes will be tough, no doubt. But it can be done. Just gotta be smart.*

The downside to being a warden was that one needed to block attacks on their shield to build charge and use abilities. It was a fine line, though, blocking attacks versus taking damage from them. A line Kaiden was all too familiar with walking, though. And all the same, increased survivability was a plus. He didn't have the defenses of Titus or the ranged prowess of Zelda, which meant staying alive in combat was more of a challenge. With Intangible Defense, though, things had just gotten that much – well, not easier, but at least interesting.

Last up was the ability he'd received for level forty-eight.

Ability: Lethal Precision
Your knowledge of the enemy increases the chance of you and your allies landing critical attacks. For a duration of 15 seconds, all attacks from you or your allies (within 50 feet) gain a +20% chance of becoming critical attacks. Improved Enhanced Senses must be active
Cost: 80 charge.
Cooldown: 5 minutes.

*So, it's like giving my allies a bit of my ability to dish out critical hits. They won't get the same bonuses from them that I do, but a critical hit, at the least, deals more damage than a regular one.*

Increased Enhanced Senses needed to be active first, but that only cost ten charge to activate. *Really, this ability costs ninety charge, then. But still, if timed correctly before Zelda unleashes a flurry of attacks, or Thorne charges in all buffed up, this could change the tone of an entire fight.*

Two new abilities, then, and both of them good. It seemed like at these higher levels the game was directing him to be less of a solo player and focus more on helping the group. Instead of abilities improving what he could do, they improved what his group could do. Apparently, group combat was key at the higher levels. He'd sampled a bit of that in PVP encounters so far, but that had truly been only a taste.

On to everyone else's abilities, then. He needed to memorize them as well, particularly if combos were going to be important going forward.

Kaiden looked back to the screenshots he'd pulled up, then started with Titus'. That was the natural place to start, considering the insane ability the big man had picked up at level fifty.

*This is endgame-type stuff,* Kaiden thought as he looked it over again. *Feels like the ultimate ability for a shielder.*

**Ability: Saving Grace**
**You expend a massive amount of charge to save yourself or an ally from death. If a target within 100 feet has been reduced to 0% health in the last 5 seconds, they return to 50% health instead, with 10 charge.**
**Cost: All of your remaining charge and 50% of max health if targeting an ally. If targeting yourself, all of your charge but no health and you resurrect with only 5% health and 10 charge.**
**Cooldown: 6 hours.**

*This is a rez, plain and simple. I mean, Titus would have to pay half of his max health to use it, but this... this is huge. He can save himself or someone else from dying. From losing a week out of game.* Kaiden had read through the ability several times since Titus first unlocked it. There hadn't been a chance to use it yet – which was a good thing, he supposed – but still, it was hard to believe the big man had been gifted such a powerful ability.

*Though he does risk killing himself to do it,* Kaiden realized. *'Fifty percent of max health.' That means if Titus is below fifty-one percent health, he can't use the ability. And even if not, it could leave him so weak the next stiff breeze would kill him.*

"Titus!" Kaiden called, then remembered he was the only one still in-game. The others were logged off, getting some much-needed sleep. Something he needed, too. But he had a bit more studying to do first.

It wouldn't be good practice to rely on Saving Grace to make their strategies work, but having it in their back pocket was not something Kaiden was displeased about. They could take bigger risks, could afford to make a mistake here or there. Considering the path ahead, he was pretty sure they'd be making a mistake or two. Having a 'get out of jail free' card was exactly what they needed.

He forced his thoughts from Saving Grace in order to look at the next ability Titus had unlocked.

**Ability: Karmic Reprisal**
**Your shield glows brightly, infused with charge. You may expend X% of max charge to reduce damage from a single attack by that percentage. Additionally, your next attack deals base damage plus additional damage equal to the amount this ability negated.**
**Cooldown: 3 minutes.**

*Big counter attack potential on this one. Never hurts to blank an enemy's biggest attack, then smack them back with bonus damage, eh? It's almost similar to my Intangible Defense in how it can suck up an attack. Just more intentional and with a bigger upside, I suppose.*

Kaiden lost himself for several moments as he imagined all the ways Karmic Reprisal could be used to throw an opponent's damage back at them, each of them increasingly more fun and wilder than the last.

*A blast warden in Sniper Mode could fire an Inferno Shot, I could warn Titus it's coming, and he could blank it, then attack back for how much damage?* His head spun at the thought. *Let's just say 'a lot.'*

So, that was Titus' abilities. Saving Grace and Karmic

Reprisal. Not to mention Intransigence, which Titus had already been putting to excellent use.

Next up, Zelda's abilities. The first was upgrade on a pre-existing one.

## Ability: Improved Paralyzing Shot
**Fires an electric blast that confuses the electrical impulses in the target's muscles, deals 110% base damage, and slows target's movement by 60% for 10 seconds.**
**Cost: 40 charge.**
**Cooldown: 1 minute.**

*I've seen this before.* Kaiden thought for a moment, then remembered where. *Werner! He used this on me back in Boyd City. A pretty effective ability to handicap my speed. If – or more likely, when – we fight more wardens, I'm going to need to watch out for this one. On the other hand, if we ever run into an enemy enhanced warden, we know what to hit 'em with.*

On to Zelda's second ability, then; the one she'd unlocked at level forty-eight.

## Ability: Execution
**Your sharpshooter prowess allows you to finish off wounded opponents with ease. If your target's health is below 10%, your next attack will deal 200% of base damage.**
**Cost: 15 charge.**
**Cooldown: 1 second.**

*Remind me not to drop to less than ten percent health in front of a blast warden,* Kaiden thought to himself. *This will finish anyone off quickly. Especially with a cooldown time of one second. The devs made this ability to be spammable.*

Fifteen charge wasn't nothing, but it certainly wasn't a lot. Plus, when targeting a wounded opponent, Zelda would be able to pair Execution with a big attack – say, Improved Kinetic Grenade – to deal massive amounts of damage. *Stacking abilities, comboing with allies... things are going to get real crazy soon.* It was making Kaiden tired just thinking about it. Or maybe that was the result of the craziness that had taken place in the Grinder and the days prior. Either way, a yawn worked its way out of him. Yawning and exhaustion didn't exist in Nova – they hadn't been programmed as a feature or a status state – but the tiredness of his mind in the real world must have been extreme. He could feel the beginnings of it all the way through his headset and into Nova.

*Two more quick abilities,* he told himself. *Then off for a break and some sleep.*

Thorne had already been level forty when going into the Grinder, so she'd just unlocked her level forty-four and level forty-eight abilities. Of the warden classes, Kaiden was least familiar with the power warden variant, but he planned to learn. Studying Thorne's abilities was a good first step. She was part of the group now, wasn't she? However their relationship had begun, they were all on the same team now.


**Ability: Debilitating Blow**
**You channel charge into your hammer. Your next attack deals 120% base damage and staggers the target. Target's base attack power is reduced by 50% for the next 5 seconds.**
**Cost: 50 charge.**
**Cooldown: 1 minute.**


*Stagger...* Kaiden thought on the keyword for a minute. He'd seen players staggered before, but never looked up the exact definition in the game. He did so now, digging through a few menus before finding the in-game mechanics guide, then reading the definition to himself.

*'Staggering an opponent can be achieved through dealing particularly powerful blows. A staggered character will be knocked a half-step backward and the next attack on them will ignore armor.'* Okay, so it's like a *mini-knockback paired with a mini-shield break. But Debilitating Blow tacks on the additional clause that the target's attack power is reduced by half for five seconds. That's pretty mean.*

So, all in all, a fine ability. Worked out well for a power

warden, actually. The more Kaiden thought about it, the more it made sense. The class excelled when up in their opponent's face. Lowering an opponent's attack power and mini-stunning them was a good advantage. Good enough that Kaiden shuddered at the thought of staring down a power warden in close quarters.

*Thank goodness for Kickback and Matter Shift,* he thought, calling to mind his best escape abilities.

Thorne's last ability was called 'Embolden.' Kaiden pulled it up and gave it a once-over.

**Ability: Embolden**
**An aura of rage surrounds you. For the next 5 seconds, you and all allies within 20 feet deal double damage on melee attacks, but take 50% more damage.**
**Cost: 80 charge.**
**Cooldown: 5 minutes.**

*Ooh, bit of a risky one here. Thorne and all of us near her would deal double damage but also take more damage. Fair, but dangerous. This'll be useful if we don't plan on getting hit, but not exactly something to break out when you're in the thick of the fighting.*

Probably there was a way to use Embolden to a greater effect that he was missing at the moment. Based on his exhaustion, that would make sense.

*I'll think more clearly after some sleep. It's a long flight to Kyraxis anyway, and we'll need to be ready once we get there. It'll be time to put these new abilities to the test.*

A smile crept on to his face at that thought, and Kaiden's vision went black as he clicked the logout button.

# Chapter Thirty-Six

Titus cracked his knuckles, but was otherwise silent as he led them across the bridge and back toward Maximus' visitor entrance. Clouds billowed past them on all sides, but the building loomed ahead, its transparent dome a beacon of light in the shade-filled gloom.

"All right," Kaiden said, shouting to Titus but also speaking to the rest of the group around him. "We need to be strategic about this. Each of us is going to be fighting alone, so we need to make sure our strategies account for that. Thorne, you'll have to, well, attack. That's usual, I suppose. But Zelda, you're going to want to keep your distance. Don't let your opponen—"

"We know how to play our classes, Kai," Zelda said, cutting him off.

"I just think we should be prepared. We got a lot of new abilities very quickly and haven't had as much chance as I'd like to practice with them. And what happens if we get paired against each other? We have to figure that out, too. I mean, one of us will have to beat the other. How do we decide who?"

"You're getting ahead of yourself," Thorne said. "Let's get into the tournament first, then we can focus on crushing our opponents, winning fame and glory, and finally, convincing PlayaSlaya to hear us out."

*Fine, fine.*

Titus entered the domed building and Kaiden broke into a jog to catch up.

"How's it hanging, punks?" Titus was saying as Kaiden slid into the room. Halicar and Nassus were at the counter as they'd been last time and from the looks on their faces, they weren't particularly happy to see Titus, or any of the group, back so soon.

"What have y'all been up to? Bit of grinding? Bit of PVP?" Titus asked, leaning an elbow on the counter. "Oh, but you're still level fifty-five, just like the last time I saw you. Huh." He paused at that, as if confused, then nodded. "That's cool, that's cool. You know, I've been doing some grinding myself. PVPed a few players. Earned a bit of EXP. Nothing major, just a bit here and there."

"How did...?" Halicar looked utterly perplexed now. He'd noticed Titus' new level, no doubt. He looked at Nassus beside him. "Have you ever seen someone level that fast?"

Her lack of response seemed answer enough.

"I'm a hard worker," Titus said. He flattened one hand on the counter and leaned over it. "Now, about this tournament you run." He gestured out through the dome, toward where the arena was, though it was currently hidden by clouds. "I want in."

"Hits level fifty and all of a sudden he thinks he's hot shit," Nassus finally said, her voice more a growl than anything. Still, there was uneasiness in it. She'd been caught off guard.

"Tournament's scheduled for later today. I'm going to fight in it. Sign me up," Titus said.

"You qualify for the *lower* division," Halicar said, working the controls of his console but looking none too happy about it. "Players level fifty to fifty-five. There's a spot open."

"Perfect."

Halicar tapped the console's screen a few more times, then looked up with a smirk. Quite a quick change of expression from how he'd looked prior.

"Done, big shot. You're all signed up. Tournament starts in two hours. Be at the arena for your pairing." Halicar's smirk boiled into a smile. "Of course, you're aware this tournament is to the death. There's no holding back."

"I'm counting on it." Titus hiked a thumb over his shoulder. "And so are they."

"Sign us up too," Kaiden said, stepping up beside Titus.

*The more of us compete, the better a chance we have of winning and getting a shot at speaking with PlayaSlaya. Might as well stack the odds as much in our favor as possible.*

"Yeah, uh, no can do." Halicar said with a hint of smugness to his tone.

"Come again?" Kaiden frowned. "The tournament's still two hours away. You just said sign-ups were open."

"Sign-ups *were* open, bro." Halicar was full-on smiling now. "But big shot here took the last spot. Tournament's all full." He looked up, feigning earnestness. "But if you'd like, I'd be happy to sign you up for next week's tournament."

*Next week? We don't have time for that!*

"Next week's too long to wait. We don't have that kind of time," Zelda said from back where she was standing beside Thorne.

"Sorry, hun." Halicar shrugged. "Tournament's full. Nothing I can do about that. Although..."

Kaiden looked back from Zelda as Halicar trailed off. *Although what?*

"Ah, yes. There is one spot left!" Halicar smiled again, and Kaiden had the distinct impression that wasn't a good thing. "Though I can't give it to you."

"What? Why not?" Thorne stormed forward. "Do your damn job and sign us up. Me, specifically." She switched over to private comms. "No offense, guys. But I'm level fifty-one. Gives me the best chance of winning this thing."

Kaiden wanted to grumble at that, but he knew she was right.

"Fair enough," he said.

"So sorry, but I don't think I can give out this spot," Halicar said, thoroughly enjoying his power trip. "But I'll tell you what. Let me check with my manager." He made a dramatic show of turning in his seat, then looked up to Nassus standing beside him.

"Hey, manager. You know that spot that was reserved? Any chance I could give it up so one of these fools can embarrass themselves for our amusement?"

Nassus grinned.

"Well, that does sound tempting. I'd love to watch these overconfident noobs learn what real PVP is about." She acted like she was considering it, but Kaiden was sure her mind had already been made up. This was just some game they were playing.

"I'm afraid, though, that the spot in question *has* been reserved. And by a VIP, no less. I can't overrule that." She shrugged. "As much as I'd like to help you all, there's really nothing I can do."

Halicar looked back to them.

"Guess big shot's going to be on his own, then. That's fine. I'll settle for watching him get humiliated."

"This is crap," Zelda said through private comms. "We were supposed to have four shots at winning the tournament, not one."

"It's fine," Titus said.

"No, it's really not. This is statistically even worse than before."

There was no denying that. Though previously the worst-case scenario had involved all of them losing, which would have locked them out of game for a week straight. At least now only Titus would be locked out. But still, they'd be no closer to getting PlayaSlaya's attention.

"Well, I suppose if one of you *really* wanted to compete, the big man could give up his spot," Halicar said, staring dead at Titus. "If he'd be so generous, that is."

"I'm the highest level here," Thorne said through private comms. "And I have the most fighting experience in-game. It should be me."

"Normally, I'd agree with you," Titus said. "But I'm gonna ask you to trust me on this one." Titus looked at each of them in turn and Kaiden met his eyes when they got to him. The big man didn't look the same as he always had. No, he'd changed. Kaiden recognized the look he was seeing now. He'd seen it before, when Titus had pitched the plan to grind high enough to enter the tournament. Then again when they were in the grinder. It was a look that met fear and doubt and impossibility head-on and laughed in their faces. It wasn't overconfidence. It wasn't foolishness. It was the product of sheer determination. Of earned confidence matched with the real-world experience of getting the job done. In that moment, Titus was so focused it was almost frightening.

*Is this how he used to look before stepping into the boxing ring?*

"If you want me to give the spot to Thorne, I'll understand. Going off of levels, she makes the most sense. I can't deny that. But this is a one-on-one tournament. It's basically digital boxing. I don't like to get into it, but this used to be my thing. And I was *good at it*." He shook out his shoulders and rolled his neck. "I haven't forgotten as much of it as I make it seem, either."

Thorne grumbled an unintelligible reply, then shook her head.

"You've got the grit for it, I'll give you that. At the core of any good PVP player there's always grit."

"I need to do this," Titus said. "Not because Nassus embarrassed me in a duel. It was stupid of me to even accept that. I let my emotions get the better of me and I paid the price for it. But this isn't about that. This is about proving something to myself. About proving I deserve to be on this team." He looked around at them once more, one at a time. "Each of you has picked this team up and put it on your back at some point. Proven your worth."

"You don't need to prove anything to us," Kaiden said.

"No. I need to prove it to myself." Titus sucked in a deep breath, then let it out slowly. "I'm focused. I'm ready. I got this," he said. "Trust me?"

"You got this, big guy," Kaiden said. Zelda nodded in agreement.

"Kick some ass," she said, a smile pulling at her lips.

"Thorne?" Titus asked last. "You're okay with this?"

She chewed her lip for a moment.

"Honestly? I think I'd do better in there. But that's the lone wolf in me thinking. That's the Thorne that worked for the Party and couldn't trust anyone but herself. I don't want to be that person anymore." She ran a hand through her hair, then nodded. "You got this, Titus. Go kick some ass."

## Chapter Thirty-Seven

"All right, big man," Kaiden said, patting Titus on the shoulder. "You're on next. You ready?"

"Itching for it," he grunted back. His eyes were trained forward, down the narrow tunnel to the blinding light of the arena. Other competitors waited around them, double checking weapons or equipping armor as the first fight of the day wrapped up. Explosions and crashes left the tunnel shaking back and forth as the fight drew to what sounded like a dramatic conclusion.

Kaiden found himself suddenly glad it wasn't him that was about to step into the ring for a fight to the death.

*There are other ways I can help, though.* He turned his eyes to the player standing just across from them. The player the officials had made it clear Titus was paired with.

**Ham Slamwich**
**Class: Cybernetic Knight**
**Faction: Maximus**
**Level: 50**

She was a cybernetic knight, as most of the Maximus guild members seemed to be. Evidently, that class was well-suited for PVP combat. In her hands she held a massive two-handed axe.

Combined with her lighter armor, she painted quite the picture of an all-attack class. She'd been glancing over at Titus for the last minute and making what Kaiden assumed were supposed to be intimidating faces.

"First opponent's a cyber knight," Kaiden relayed to Titus. "We've fought them before. Basically the civilian version of a power warden. High-damage attacks, poor defense."

"Right, right." Titus nodded along, taking in all of the info. He looked at his opponent. There was no malice in it, though. No intimidation. It was purely analytical. Studying and making a game plan.

"She's probably going to have decent mobility, and you can expect her to try to toss you around with moves like Thorne's Gravity Sledge."

"She'll hit hard," he said with a nod. "But my larger health pool will help even that out."

"You'll just need to squeeze every point of damage you can out of your attacks," Kaiden said. "Gonna need to punch a bit above your weight class."

"Heh. I think I can make that work."

From the end of the tunnel came a deafening boom, and then silence. The fight was over.

"Next fighters!" an official called.

"You got this," Kaiden said and gave Titus one final slap on the back.

The space for fighting was a circular patch of what looked to be some sort of Astroturf about forty feet in diameter. The remains of past fights – too much broken armor, destroyed robots, and sagging stone and rebar walls to be just from the today's fighting – were scattered around the space. There was enough debris to make the field of combat interesting. All around the perimeter transparent force fields hovered. Presumably, they'd stop any attacks from leaving the arena, but were mostly invisible until something hit them. Beyond the force fields, the bleachers wrapped around the arena, raised slightly so everyone had a good view of the carnage to come.

From where Kaiden, Zelda, and Thorne were watching in the first row they had a good view of the competitors; Titus on the side closer to them and the cyber knight on the opposite.

"Good day to bash each other to death, isn't it?" Titus' opponent said with all too much cheer in her tone. Her voice was amplified for the audience due to some unseen tech in the arena.

Titus' only reply was to grunt.

Kaiden wanted to give him some words of encouragement, but per tournament rules, the big man had been forced to leave their party temporarily. No communicating with him via comms, then. It was going to have to be old-fashioned shouting or nothing.

"And we're back!" an announcer's voice blasted through the stadium. "You all ready for the second fight of the day?" The announcer paused a moment to allow for applause before continuing. There wasn't much. The majority of the stands were filled with Maximus guild members in red and black armor. They cheered the loudest and the longest at the prospect of another fight. Initially, Kaiden had been worried they'd sell Titus – and everyone else – out to the Warden Corps., but assurances had been made by the tournament organizers. Maximus didn't cooperate with the Corps. or the Party, period. It was said Maximus' members were loyal to a fault. Seemed that was going to be put to the test now.

"All right, all right. You know the rules," the announcer said. "This will be a one-on-one contest. Stimpacks can't be used, and the fight ends when one of you dies and stays dead. Combatants ready?"

Titus drew his hammer in response.

Across from him, Ham Slamwich laughed and hefted her own two-handed axe.

"Begin!" the announcer's voice boomed across the arena and the crowd burst into a cheering roar.

"Woo! Let's go, Titus!" Kaiden shouted, trying to sound encouraging.

"You got this, big guy!" Thorne joined in. "No holding back!"

Titus eased back into a fighting stance and flicked his shield on. Its energy field glowed a bright blue as he positioned it in front of him.

His opponent shook out her shoulders and smiled. "Never killed a warden before. This should be fun!"

Titus opened his mouth to respond but Slamwich was already in the air, a puff of dirt flying up from the arena floor as she launched upward.

**Ability: Meteoric Launch**
**Player launches into the air. Landing deals AoE damage and next attack deals additional damage.**

Kaiden read the limited info his visor gave him on the attack, then looked back just in time to see Slamwich come crashing down. She swung her axe as she landed and Titus caught it directly on his shield. The energy field flickered, but absorbed the hit, giving Titus charge. At the same time, crackling electricity lashed out from Titus' armor to nip at Slamwich's shoulder.

*Improved Volt Field*, Kaiden knew.

Her health bar took a small hit, but she didn't seem to notice, still continuing forward with a series of heavy, hard swings aimed at Titus' head.

He backpedaled, blocking the attacks he could but unable to stop them all. His own health took something of a beating, dropping down to eighty-four percent, but for every attack Slamwich threw at him, Improved Volt Field zapped her back for fifty percent of Titus' base damage. He wasn't a DPS class, so that wasn't much, but it was something.

"And it's a merciless onslaught from Slam to kick things off!" the announcer said, a bit of excitement creeping into his voice now that the fight was on. "Titus is on the back foot already."

"Is he, though?" Kaiden asked quietly. "He's defending, but that's what's his class does best. And he's been getting damage in without even attacking." Titus was down to eighty-four percent health, lower than his opponent's ninety percent, but he hadn't even attacked yet.

"It's a strategic start," Thorne said with a nod. "He's using his opponent's attacks to hit her back while he builds charge."

Even as Thorne spoke, Titus retaliated, leading with a Shield Slam – which dealt area-of-effect damage and briefly stunned Slamwich – then following with a Shield of Rage. His shield burned brightly then shot out a burst of energy that caught his stunned opponent dead in the chest for one hundred and fifty percent base damage.

The stun wore off and Slamwich restarted her attack.

**Ability: Melt**
**A powerful strike that bypasses armor and shields.**

The blade of her axe lit up, glowing a fierce red. Several globs of what looked to be molten metal trailed behind it as she swung at Titus with a rising strike. He blocked with his shield, but the axe passed through it as if it wasn't there and cut directly into his health bar.

"Ooh, that looked like it hurt!" the announced shouted.

"What was that?" Zelda cried out as Titus' health flashed and dropped by a good ten percent. Down to seventy-four percent now.

"Melt bypasses armor and shields," Kaiden said, cringing as he relayed what his visor had told him.

Improved Volt Field had thrown back some of the damage, but Slam was still at eighty-three percent while Titus was down to seventy-four. Spurred on by the success of Melt, Slamwich pushed her attack, following with several more basic swings of her axe.

Titus blocked them and his shield began to flicker – too full of charge, Kaiden knew. It was near to overloading and turning off. Titus seemed to recognize it as well. He popped off another quick Shield of Rage and then a Hammer Smash.

**Ability: Hammer Smash**

**The warden pounds the ground with their hammer, dealing base damage to enemies in a 5-foot radius.**

Area-of-effect damage was fairly insignificant against a single attacker, but if Titus didn't want his shield to overload he needed to keep using abilities and burning off excess charge. Slam's health dropped to seventy-nine percent, but that was still a good bit above Titus'.

*She's not even trying to block his attacks,* Kaiden realized. *She thinks she can hit hard enough to just out-DPS him. And she might be right.*

The fight had been moving around the arena, mostly backwards as Titus had given ground under Slam's assault. The combatants were right up on the edge now, and as Titus swung his hammer around for an attack, it clipped the invisible wall encircling the arena. The thing flared to life in a spray of sparks and an arc of electricity lashed out. Titus shook violently for a moment as it zapped him and his health dropped another four percent.

"The wall's electrified!" Kaiden said, hearing the dread in his voice. "That's not good."

Slam seemed to think otherwise. Her axe began to light up a fiery red again, except this time, the heart of the weapon was glowing, not just the blade.

**Ability: Concussive Strike**
**A forceful strike that travels along the ground for a short distance, dealing direct and knockback damage to any enemy in its path.**

"Enjoy the wall, warden boy," Slam taunted, then drove her axe into the ground. The attack exploded forward, energy shooting in a blazing trail toward Titus. However, without Kaiden's visor Titus had no way of knowing the details of the incoming attack. He leaned into it.

His health bar flashed as Concussive Strike bashed into him, but he wasn't knocked back.

"Loving this new passive," Titus said, looking up at his opponent.

"What's this?" the announcer asked, seemingly puzzled. A few audience members leaned forward, their interest growing.

Slam also seemed confused by the ineffectiveness of her attack. She didn't get to think on it long, however, as Titus lunged forward.

**Ability: Shield Slam**
**The warden slams their shield into the ground, stunning enemies in a 5ft radius for 2 seconds.**

Titus jammed his shield into the ground in front of her and a blast emanated outward. It swept over Slam, dealing no damage, but locking her in place with its stun effect.

"My turn," Titus said. He took the chance to circle around behind her before popping his next ability.

**Ability: Improved Shield Charge**

Rooted in place thanks to Shield Slam, Slamwich had no chance to dodge as energy surged around Titus' legs and he burst forward. Her health drained to seventy-three percent as Titus charged into her back, but the initial damage was the least of her worries. Titus kept her on the front of his shield as he continued the charge – forcing her face-first into the wall he'd just accidentally touched moments before. It sparked to life again as Titus drove her straight into it with an audible boom.

"That's gonna hurt!" the announcer shouted, and the Maximus guild members in the audience jeered, apparently not happy with the development. Slam cried out, electricity flowing through her. The wall drained her health by the second, dealing far more damage than Titus could. Tank classes weren't built for that, after all. Nonetheless, Titus had filled up his charge bar from tanking the onslaught earlier and was far from done.

"Rule number one of fighting a warden," Titus said. "Try not to give them charge."

**Ability: Rallying Cry**
**All party members within 50 feet gain a 20% boost to base stats for 30 seconds.**

Titus had no party members, but the ability affected him well enough. The increase to his base damage became apparent as he swung hammer strike after hammer strike at Slam. Each one hit hard, taking chunks out of her health. The wall helped as well, still spraying sparks as it electrocuted her. Her health plummeted. By the time she was able to regain her senses and pull herself off the wall she was down to thirty-seven percent health.

"Ha! There you go, big guy!" Kaiden cheered. He'd taken a definitive lead in the damage race with his wall trick. Now all he had to do was finish strong. Keep trading damage for damage.

"You're tough, I'll give you that," Slamwich snarled. "But not tough enough!"

**Ability: Fiery End**
**A high-damage attack. On a successful hit, the target is set on fire.**

Slam wound up for a big swing, axe head spitting embers like a fire threatening to burst to life, but Titus seemed unfazed.

*This is about the time that I would dodge away,* Kaiden thought.

Titus scored another hammer strike, then Slam's massive axe burst full-on into a roaring inferno. "Been a fun fight, but it's time to end it," she said and swung the flaming axe.

"I agree," Titus said.

**Ability: Reflection**
**Reflects 20% of damage absorbed by the warden's shield back against the attacker for 10 seconds.**

He raised his shield and blocked Fiery End. Flames exploded outward, charring and burning the turf around, but most of the damage never reached Titus. His shield tanked it, then began to waver and shake, clearly on the verge of overloading from

Slamwich's powerful attack. The flames from the attack caught on Titus' armor and began eating away at it, dealing burning damage each second.

Reflection bounced twenty percent of the damage back at Slam and set her health bar to flashing. Improved Volt Field zapped her for half of Titus' base damage and her life total settled at twenty-nine percent.

The exchange left Titus' health in the red, all the way down to forty-five percent, and it was dropping by the second thanks to the flames. Still, Slam had a lot of work to do to make up the disparity from being thrown into the wall. Titus' shield was near overloaded. She recognized that and charged in again.

But Titus knew what he was doing.

**Ability: Improved Barrier**
**You stand still and become the epicenter of a large barrier to defend your allies, increasing in size depending on how much charge you use. During this time your shield does not absorb additional charge. 10% of all damage blocked during this time converts into a protective force-field around you once ability ends. Unable to use if your shield is already overloaded.**

He fired off the ability and the barrier swelled around him. He kept pumping charge into it until it was big enough to encompass him and Slamwich. And then, all at once, he canceled the ability and the barrier fell away.

*He's dumping charge!* Kaiden realized. *Using any ability he can to burn off charge and keep his shield from overloading. Nice!*

Slamwich huffed at that, pausing for a moment to take in the situation. She was facing a shield warden with a still-active shield and all the charge he could want. Sure, Titus was on fire – the flames had eaten away at him, dropping his health to thirty-nine percent – but Slamwich was even lower on health.

"Guess it's just a damage race then, eh?" Titus said, then lashed out with a hammer strike. The blow connected, knocking three percent off of Slamwich's health

She took that hit, then two more, health down to nineteen percent, before she used Meteoric Launch again – this time to retreat. She launched into the air and did her best to put distance between herself and Titus.

All the while, the flames on him chewed through his armor.

*She's trying to let the damage over time finish him off,* Kaiden realized.

Titus was down to thirty-three percent. He wasn't waiting around for Slamwich's plan to play out, though. She landed from the Meteoric Launch to find an energy lasso wrapping around her torso. Titus yanked and she was dragged back to him.

She clambered to her feet and lashed out with her axe. Titus simply stepped into the attack. Slamwich seemed taken aback as he tanked the damage, then wrapped her in a bear hug.

"Wait, what's this?" the announcer said, also taken aback by the strategy. Kaiden didn't blame him – right up until he remembered their earlier fight on Odditor's planet. Particularly the part where a flaming hominoid had wrapped Titus in a similar hug.

The still-burning flames from Slamwich's earlier Fiery End spread from Titus' armor back to their creator. Both players took damage from the fire, but with Titus holding such a large health lead – twenty-seven to nineteen, now – time was against Slamwich.

"Damn it," she said with a frown as the flames snapped and spat. She heaved Titus off, clearly having the higher strength stat, and slashed with her axe, but Titus attacked as well. They traded blows back and forth, cutting chunks from each other's health. Titus' lead was too big, though, and as a tank he could take more hits than his DPS-based opponent.

"Hey, good fight. Though in future you might want to remember that shield wardens are one of the highest HP classes in the game," Titus said with a calm, almost friendly tone, then landed a hammer strike on Slamwich's head that wiped out the rest of her health. Her eyes rolled up and she crumpled to the ground.

There was silence for a moment, everyone seeming to try and process exactly what had happened.

"And there it is, folks! A surprise turnaround!"

"Yeah!" Kaiden shouted, jumping to his feet and cheering. Zelda and Thorne did the same, but they were the only ones in the arena to do so. The Maximus guild members who'd been watching broke out in a flurry of boos and shouted insults.

Titus ignored it all, though, instead slapping at the flames still nipping at his armor.

"Uh, a little help here?" he called, looking around. "Fight's over, right? Someone have a bucket of water or something?"

## Chapter Thirty-Eight

"Titus, dude! That was awesome!" Kaiden said, sprinting forward. The big man was sitting in the shelter of one of the arena's entrance tunnels, having been ushered out of the arena as the next fighters had been led in. The next fight was already underway, cheers and blasts of light evident in the background.

Titus looked up as Kaiden approached. There was an intensity in his eyes, fierce and single-minded. Like he was still in the fight, and was measuring Kaiden up and figuring out how to take him down.

"You okay, big guy?"

Titus blinked and the look was gone.

"Kai," he said with a nod and a small smile. "Got her pretty good, didn't I?"

"You totally baited her in, then used her own attacks – not to mention the environment – against her," Kaiden agreed, replaying every moment of the fight.

"Had to get creative," Titus said with a shrug. "Shielders don't deal that much damage."

"Well, you dealt enough to advance. I'd say that's plenty."

"You're back on after this fight," a voice said. A medic, Kaiden saw as the man approached. He looked to be in a hurry and wasn't paying full attention to either of them.

"Here, heal up. Then when they call for you, don't waste any time."

He popped an ability and the air around Titus began to glow green. Particles formed and rushed toward him. They globbed onto his armor like some sort of plasma, and everywhere they touched, damage began to repair itself.

"That's the stuff," Titus said, leaning back and sighing. A moment later he looked at Kaiden. "Dude, we need a healer in the group."

"Don't I know it. We have the medbay on the *Verit*–" He stopped, hesitating to use the ship's real name in public. "On the *Andronicus*, but that doesn't really help us in combat."

"Next time we get arrested and sent to jail, remind me to find a friend to play healer before we decide to break out, yeah?"

Kaiden chuckled at that.

"Yeah, sounds good."

A particularly loud explosion from the ongoing fight caught Kaiden's attention and he looked toward the arena for a moment, then pulled himself back to Titus.

"They wouldn't let us all come down and see you, so Zelda and Thorne sent me ahead. Gave me some advice to pass along for the next fight."

"Is it 'don't die?'"

"Well, we'd have hoped that part was obvious." Kaiden punched him in the shoulder. "No, but seriously. Your last opponent didn't seem familiar with the shield warden class. That's why you were able to bait her in like that. We don't think you're going to get so lucky next time. Zelda says if your opponent wasn't watching, their friends definitely were." Kaiden looked back to the entrance to the tunnel where Thorne and Zelda were waiting, just on the other side of two security guards.

"I know, I know," he said with a nod. "It's like boxing. You can't always go in with the same strategy. People catch on."

"Keep things fresh. Exactly. And Thorne said, well..." Kaiden paused. "Thorne just said to beat the crap out of whoever it is you face next."

Titus laughed at that. A good, long belly laugh, and Kaiden

couldn't help but smile. He hadn't found Thorne's advice particularly helpful, but maybe now it made sense. Titus wasn't new to Nova, and even outside the game he knew how to fight. He didn't need everyone clogging his mind with their worries and plans before the next round. What he needed was to be relaxed and focused. Probably Thorne understood that. Probably this had been her way of conveying it.

Another explosion from the arena and the announcer shouted excitedly. Apparently, the fight was drawing to a close.

"Beat the crap out of my opponent?" Titus said, still chuckling as he turned his attention to his now-repaired armor and replenished health.

"Okay, enough chit chat. Mind on the next fight," Kaiden said, looking over to Titus' next opponent. "What the heck is a 'gravity slinger?'" he asked as his visor gave him info on the challenger.

**Supermassive**
**Class: Gravity Slinger**
**Faction: Unaffiliated**
**Level: 52**

**Quick Facts: Gravity slingers specialize in the manipulation of gravity to create powerful ranged attacks. But don't let that fool you; their melee attacks, though few, can be used to devastating ends.**

The man was dressed in a suit of power armor made of... well, it looked to be rocks. Except, he wasn't exactly wearing them, and they weren't formed into any cohesive suit. The rocks, all different shapes and sizes, floated in the air, inches away from his body but close enough that they'd likely block incoming attacks. There weren't enough to cover all of him, only his chest really. But they seemed to slip around him, bobbing ever so slightly as they rotated around in a slow circle as if flowing in some sort of invisible current.

*He's manipulating gravity to keep the rocks there, I guess? Must be an ability. So how does he fight? My visor seemed to suggest ranged attacks, but there was some mention of melee attacks as well?*

"I don't know much about this class," Kaiden confessed as he relayed the info from his visor.

"Sounds like I want to stay away from his melee attacks. Fight him like he's a ranged class, I guess?"

"That'd be my guess, but that armor of his is strange. It looks heavier than I'd expect from any ranged class. I don't know what to tell you here. This might take some feeling out."

"And that's the fight, folks!" the announcer's voice echoed through the tunnel.

The officials gestured and Supermassive moved toward the arena.

"I'll figure it out," Titus said, then followed his opponent.

"What's this guy gonna do? Throw rocks at Titus?" Thorne asked. The idea seemed laughable right up until the fight began.

"And we're off!" the announcer shouted.

Supermassive charged forward with a sound like a tidal wave of stones clattering and tumbling over one another. A sprinting avalanche.

Titus raised his hammer to strike, then seemed to think better of it. He retreated, but Supermassive was far faster. Titus was forced to duck behind his shield as the attack came in.

*So much for avoiding his melee attack,* Kaiden thought, wincing as his visor read out the gravity slinger's opening attack.

**Ability: Mass x Acceleration**
**A high-damage melee attack that deals damage based on the user's level and dexterity.**

Supermassive punched forward with a fist, but as Kaiden saw, it wasn't just his fist. The previously invisible currents around the gravity slinger briefly became visible as faintly glowing lines spinning around him. *Spinning, or orbiting?* Kaiden thought. Then, all at once, the lines changed direction, swarming toward Supermassive's reared fist. The rocks followed and in the blink of an eye his fist was coated in them – the hand of a stone giant punching forward at Titus.

The blow slammed into his shield and a shockwave exploded outward from the impact. Dust and dirt and even several loose stones were blasted away, flying through the air. Gale-force winds swept over Titus, and were it not for Intransigence, Kaiden had no doubt the big man would have been launched directly into the electrified wall behind him. He held firm, though. Unfortunately, his shield didn't. It flickered once and went out.

"Overloaded? From a single blow?" Zelda asked, shock plastered across her face.

"That's not good…" Thorne added unhelpfully. "This guy's gotta be a glass cannon if he can hit like that."

Titus was still standing, though. Given, his health had taken a beating; even through the shield it'd dropped to seventy-two percent.

"That attack dealt twenty-eight percent damage *through* his shield!" Kaiden shouted, not believing what he was seeing. "That's insane! That would one-hit kill if unblocked."

"He'd better not get hit by it again, then," Thorne said. "It has to be a once-per-combat ability, or at least have a ridiculously long cooldown, right?"

Improved Volt Field had dealt damage to Supermassive because he'd attacked with a melee attack, and as Kaiden looked, he realized it'd dealt far more damage than it normally did. That, or gravity slingers had far less health than most classes. He was already down to ninety percent.

*Titus can whoop this guy if he can land a few hits.*

"Whoa, look at that," Zelda said, pointing toward Supermassive. The arm he'd punched with was hanging limp at his side in what appeared to be some sort of visual cooldown cue. Titus must have spotted it as well. He lunged forward and pressed the attack.

The upside to an overloaded shield – if there ever was one –

was a full charge bar. All of Titus' abilities were theoretically open to him. The problem was, any that required a shield couldn't be used, which, for a shield warden, happened to be most of them. Nonetheless, the charge was enough to start dealing some damage back. Titus used Rallying Cry then lashed out with several hammer strikes. The first of the strikes connected and tore a whopping twenty-six percent of Supermassive's health away.

The gravity slinger retreated, and fast. As he did, the rocks that had been around his fist returned to their original orbit around his torso.

Titus tried to keep pace with Supermassive, swinging wildly. A blow connected solidly with his opponent's shoulder. The orbiting rock armor absorbed the hit, but as Kaiden looked closer, he could see the spot that had been hit was damaged. The rock there had a spiderweb of cracks running through it. Titus swung again and Supermassive sidestepped so the blow landed on a different piece of armor. That one cracked as well.

"Hit the same spot!" Kaiden shouted, but his voice was lost among the crowd as others jeered at Titus' seeming success. The big man was quick on the uptake, though. He'd noticed the damage to his opponent's armor and his next attack landed in the same spot as the first.

This time, the rock there shattered completely, falling away in a rain of pebbles, and Supermassive's health bar flashed and dropped to sixty-four percent.

"Gah!" he cried, then scowled.

**Ability: Conservation of Mass (passive)**
**Broken armor lashes out at the attacker, then begins reforming.**

*Like Volt Field,* Kaiden thought as the ability activated. A rain of shards of shattered rock armor flew up from the ground and at Titus' face. They clinked off his helmet, dealing only one percent damage but clearly obscuring his vision for a moment. He grunted and swatted at them. The pebbles were flung away, then turned and rushed back toward Supermassive. They returned to the place they'd originally been above his shoulder, but instead of forming into a solid rock again, they remained as dozens of little pieces.

The pebbles' distraction had been enough for Supermassive to slip out of Titus' range, and thanks to what Kaiden imagined was a pretty high dexterity stat, he wasn't having much trouble staying there. Titus trudged after him, hammer swinging non-stop, but Supermassive was just a step quicker. As long as there was room to move, he could stay out of reach. The arm he'd used to punch with earlier was still hanging limp. Apparently Mass x Acceleration had quite a cooldown on it, which made sense considering how powerful it was.

**Ability: Kinetic Velocity**
**A ranged attack that deals moderate damage.**

Supermassive slung his still-functioning left arm at Titus and a chunk of rock split away and hurtled forward. Titus leaned to the side but was too slow to avoid the blow. It caught him in the chest plate and shattered with a thud so forceful Kaiden could feel it in his own chest. Titus' health dropped to sixty-three percent. The now broken pieces of rock flew back to Supermassive's arm and remained there as another cloud of pebbles.

Supermassive shifted his armor and the pebbles moved away, then were replaced with a fresh piece of rock armor. Then he used Kinetic Velocity again.

"He's sacrificing armor for damage!" Kaiden realized.

With no shield, Titus had no option but to try to dodge the attack. His low dexterity made that a grim prospect, and sure enough, the blow struck again.

*Down to fifty-three percent health.*

"That Volt Field ability of yours is annoying," Supermassive said. "It only hits back on melee attacks, though, and the good news for me is I have plenty of range." He smiled, then attacked again with another Kinetic Velocity.

*Titus can't take this beating forever. He needs to get in close and hit back. Put some of that charge to use!*

Now in the red at forty-four percent health, Titus seemed to have the same idea. His shield came off cooldown and flicked back on. Titus wasn't focused on it, though.

"You have plenty of ranged attacks?" he growled and reared back his hammer. "Then I guess I need to keep you close."

**Ability: Energy Grip**

Titus struck forward and a lasso of energy burst from his hammer and wrapped around Supermassive's leg. Titus pulled and his opponent was yanked toward him and dragged along the ground.

"No more running now," Titus said then attacked with several hammer strikes. Rallying Cry's effect had worn off but the big man was aiming for the exposed spots where Supermassive's rock armor was already shattered. The first blow was glancing and didn't deal full damage, the second missed, but the third connected full-on. All told, Supermassive lost thirty-four percent heath. The gravity slinger was squishy, and his rock armor was becoming less and less effective as he used more of it for Kinetic Velocity.

Supermassive climbed to his feet, health now reduced to thirty-one percent. Roughly even, considering Titus was at forty-four percent himself.

**Ability: Shattered Shot**
**Sacrifices a small amount of armor to distract the opponent.**

Kaiden's visor read out details of the attack as a small piece of Supermassive's armor broke free. Just like before with Conservation of Mass, the floating pebbles swarmed Titus' face. They dealt another three percent damage and bought a much-needed moment for the gravity slinger to retreat outside of Titus' reach. His right arm was still limp – apparently Mass x

Acceleration had a *very* long cooldown – and his armor was shattered in several areas.

"Based on how he's fighting, and how much damage Titus is dealing with each attack, this guy is like a ranged class with one really powerful melee attack," Zelda said, analytical as always. But it seemed like she was right. As Supermassive and Titus continued their fight, the former constantly retreated, buying time to continue spamming his Kinetic Velocity ranged attack.

Titus went for another Energy Grip, but Supermassive dodged it this time – relying on his high dexterity stat, no doubt. Still, there was only so much arena to dance around in, and as Kaiden now noticed, Titus had been intentionally chasing his opponent into a corner.

"Nowhere to run now," he said, closing in on his slippery opponent.

"On the contrary," Supermassive said.

**Ability: Render Inert**
**Uses armor to immobilize an opponent.**

Several rocks pulled away from his armor and flew toward Titus. They were low, though; off target. Or—no, they were right on target, Kaiden realized as they slammed into Titus' feet and piled up around them. The big man tried to step forward but his feet were rooted to the ground. Supermassive took advantage of the moment to slip by just out of reach and get himself back into the openness of the center of the arena. Once there, he loaded up for another attack.

**Nothing Wasted**
**Deals damage based on percentage of broken armor.**

Titus raised his shield to block the attack as all of the pebbles orbiting Supermassive launched forward in a piercing lance of debris.

The attack washed against Titus' shield, but no damage got through.

"There we go!" Kaiden cheered. Several others in the audience booed.

The root effect from Render Inert wore off – the rocks at Titus' feet flying up to rejoin Supermassive's armor – and Titus was free.

He lowered his shield and smirked.

"With my shield back, I can do this all day."

"Guess it's time to end this, then."

**Ability: Gravity Well**
**A crowd-control ability that creates a strong gravity field around an object within forty feet.**

Kaiden's vision fed him information on the ability and he felt himself frown, not understanding what was happening. Why use a crowd-control ability on just one opponent?

A moment later, though, Kaiden swallowed hard as he realized what was happening.

A lightless pinpoint of black void had appeared directly above Titus' head, so close it was almost touching him. Immediately, dust and dirt began to rise into the air. It rushed toward the dot, then gathered around it in a violent swirl. It wasn't another second before heavier debris began to inch in closer. The orb grew and seemingly strengthened. As it did, the larger debris stopped sliding along the ground and launched into the air instead. Titus was lifted as well, legs kicking as the ability held him aloft. Supermassive wasn't trying to move Titus around the arena; he was trying to move the arena to Titus.

Titus' eyes went wide, then he curled into a ball as a chunk of broken wall the size of his torso nearly decapitated him. It missed by an inch or so, but from all around the arena, debris was zooming in now. Only Supermassive seemed unaffected by the ability.

Titus wasn't done, though.

**Ability: Improved Barrier**
**You stand still and become the epicenter of a large barrier to**

defend your allies, increasing in size depending on how much charge you use. During this time your shield does not absorb additional charge. 10% of all damage blocked during this time converts into a protective force-field around you once ability ends. Unable to use if your shield is already overloaded.

**Cooldown: 10 minutes.**

Titus made a small barrier this time, just big enough to protect himself. *Conserving charge, probably.*

Energy glowed around him, inches away from his body, and the flying debris slammed into it. Where it hit, the barrier flashed, but held steady. An entire stone wall smashed into the barrier, then a trail of rebar, and next some shattered armor from a contestant who'd been defeated earlier. All of it slammed into Titus' Improved Barrier. But the barrier held, and after several seconds, Gravity Well ended and the debris – and Titus – all collapsed to the ground.

The big man rose and dusted himself off.

"You almost had me there."

Titus ended Improved Barrier and a small personal force field formed around him. *It has health equal to ten percent of the damage the barrier blocked,* Kaiden thought, recalling the secondary clause on the ability.

Supermassive growled in response to Titus' advance. At the same time, light bloomed around his right arm and it came back to life, hanging limp no longer. He looked down at it, then smiled up at Titus.

*Mass x Acceleration is off cooldown!*

Supermassive attacked with renewed intensity, hurling stones with Kinetic Velocity and pausing only to dodge Titus' attempted Energy Grip every time it came off cooldown.

"He's trying to overload Titus' shield again," Kaiden said, watching the assault. "Trying to open the door for a lethal Mass x Acceleration attack."

The crowd was cheering now, sensing the end was near. Titus was hard to see in the middle of a cloud of dirt and dust as he blocked a seemingly endless barrage of hurled stones. His personal force field went down, but his shield was holding. It was going to overload sooner or later, though.

Apparently, sooner was the answer. After one last attack, the shield flicked off.

"I thought it'd last longer than that," Thorne said, frowning. "It should have—"

But Supermassive saw it and knew the kill was near. Mass x Acceleration had dealt twenty-eight percent damage *through* Titus' shield earlier. How much was it going to do when he didn't have a shield at all? Kaiden didn't have an answer beyond 'too much.'

**Ability: Mass x Acceleration**

Supermassive lunged forward, his right arm reared back. The rocks around his body – those that hadn't been destroyed in Titus' attacks – rushed to form up around his fist.

Titus backed up, then looked side to side as if searching for some way to escape. But his dexterity stat was undoubtedly far lower than his opponent's and speed wasn't exactly the forte of shield wardens. There was nowhere to run.

Supermassive was two strides away now, committed to the attack. Committed to ending the duel. He closed the remaining distance and threw his punch.

Titus spun to face him, staring down his death, and... smiled? If Supermassive noticed it, he didn't react. Couldn't. He had already thrown his punch and in the blink of an eye it would obliterate Titus.

Blue light flashed to life as Titus turned his shield back on.

The realization hit Kaiden all at once. The shield hadn't been overloaded; Titus had just turned it off. He'd baited his opponent into this attack!

Titus had just enough time to fire off an ability before Mass x Acceleration hit him.

**Ability: Karmic Reprisal**

**Your shield glows brightly, infused with charge. You may expend X% of max charge to reduce damage from a single attack by that percentage. Additionally, your next attack deals base damage plus additional damage equal to the amount this ability negated.**
**Cooldown: 3 minutes.**

Supermassive's punch slammed into Titus' shield. Another shockwave exploded outwards and Titus' shield overloaded, but this time he only took a few percent damage.

*He must have poured enough charge into Karmic Reprisal to reduce the attack by a massive amount. Which means…*

Improved Volt Field lashed out at Supermassive, biting at him for a chunk of damage, but that wasn't really relevant – not when Titus followed up with a hammer strike. A hammer strike with its attack power boosted by all of the damage that had just been absorbed through Karmic Reprisal.

Supermassive had just enough time to curse before Titus' hammer slammed into his chest with enough force to fling him clear across the arena. His armor shattered all at once and pebbles flew everywhere. His health reduced to zero and he was dead before he even took the fall damage from his landing.

In the wake of the attack, Titus rested his hammer across his shoulder as if it were a baseball bat and smiled.

"Karma's a bitch."

## Chapter Thirty-Nine

"That one was just showing off," Kaiden said, smirking as he approached Titus. Judging from the glowing gobs of goop healing him, the medic had already been by.

"Turns out hitting a shield warden is a good way to get hit back," Titus said with a smirk. He was riding high on the last victory. *And why shouldn't he be?*

"Good job, though. Really." Kaiden sat down on the bench next to the big guy. "You're tearing it up out there. Really top-notch stuff."

"Careful now, all this praise is going to go to my head." He said it jokingly, but Kaiden could see there was a grain of truth to it. Titus shook his head and looked toward the end of the tunnel, where the sounds of the latest ongoing fight were strangely quiet.

"So, who's next?" Kaiden asked, trying to refocus on the task at hand. "Who's going to get sent on vacation in your final fight?" He looked around for a competitor but there was no one there. They were alone in the tunnel but for the medic and a few officials who were gathered up at the entrance to the arena, chatting animatedly while watching the fight.

"My next opponent hasn't been determined," Titus said and nodded toward the arena.

"Oh, right." Of course it hadn't been decided. The next fight was the final, so of course the last semi-final had to be going on now.

"All right, well, that's unhelpful. I wanted to get a look at them, see what class you'd be up against."

Titus shrugged.

"I'll figure it out on the fly. Sometimes it's good to know going into the fight, but you can't always expect to know who or what you'll be up against."

Kaiden leaned toward the exit of the tunnel, listening to the sounds of the fight. Those prior had been boisterous, booming affairs. In comparison, the current one was positively silent.

"That's strange," Kaiden said, trying to catch a glimpse of the fighters between the gaggle of officials.

All at once, the crowd cheered and the announcer went wild.

"Sounds like I have an opponent," Titus said, looking toward the clamor.

"Ladies and gentlemen..." the announcer said, letting his booming voice echo around the stadium and building tension for several long moments, "...welcome to the final fight!" Cheers burst out at his words and the entire stadium rose into a roar of applause and shouted excitement.

"This is it," Kaiden said, struggling to sit still in his seat. Sitting on the sidelines and watching Titus do all the hard work was just about the toughest thing he'd done. It wasn't in his nature to let someone else carry the weight for him. Probably that was something he needed to work on. He trusted Titus, and being part of a team meant sharing responsibility.

"Titus' got this," he said aloud, trying to reassure himself as much as anyone.

"Yes, he does," Zelda said, no hint of doubt in her voice.

"Our first competitor is something of a new face around these parts," the announcer said and already the boos had started. Most of the audience seemed to be made up of Maximus guild members. Some fans had broken ranks, though, and their cheering was audible above the tidal wave of boos.

Titus responded to the boos and lackluster cheers with a confident smile as he stepped out of the tunnel and into the arena. He held both arms out wide and let the hate pour down on him. Almost like he was reveling in it. Letting it psych him up.

"All right, all right," the announcer said, easing the audience to something approaching quiet. "Save your breath, because you're going to need it for our next combatant. You know her, you love her, and she's the reigning champion seven weeks in a row now!" Even more cheers, so loud the whole stadium shook as if there was an earthquake happening – not that earthquakes were a common occurrence in a city floating in the upper atmosphere of a gas giant.

"Everyone, give a loud and proud welcome to your champion!"

A figure stepped into the arena opposite Titus, and Kaiden focused on her. His visor pulled up her details.

**Nassus**
**Class: Brawler**
**Faction: Maximus**
**Level: 55**

*Nassus? Nassus!* Kaiden could instantly call her to mind. She'd been the one in charge at the visitor desk they'd always had to pass through on their visits to the planet. Suddenly it made sense why she'd taken so much apparent pleasure in letting only Titus sign up for the tournament. Hers was the last spot that'd been reserved. And now, the bad blood between her and Titus was finally about to be worked out.

"She's five levels above him," Zelda said. "Oh crap. This is bad."

"You... might have a point," Thorne said, then nodded. "Titus is a good fighter and he knows what he's doing in there, but some disadvantages just can't be overcome."

"No," Kaiden said, confidence filling his voice as he recalled the look of driven concentration he'd seen on Titus' face in between fights. The man was locked in. Focused on the goal. He'd seemed a different person entirely. "He's got this." Something had changed in Titus when he'd lost the first duel against Nassus. Changed, or maybe reawakened. He'd been a man on a mission since. From his absolute dedication to grinding to the way he'd been studying his abilities and creative ways they could be used, he'd been preparing for this. There was no way he'd known he'd be paired against Nassus herself, but Kaiden had no doubt Titus was more than pleased with the situation now. In the duel, he'd let his emotions get the better of him. But not this time. This time, he was ready, and he had the levels and combat expertise to back it up.

"Combatants, ready yourselves," the announcer's voice boomed.

"Well hello there, noob," Nassus said. It was hard to hear her through the resounding shouts and cheers in the stadium, but sitting in the front row, Kaiden was just close enough. "I've been wanting this fight for a while now. So glad you decided to come back to get your ass whooped."

"I'll be sure to beat you quickly," Titus said, his face all steely confidence. "I know you have to hurry back to your job at the front desk. Important work to be done, and all."

Nassus flushed at that, then spat to one side. "I'm going to enjoy this."

"Strange, to enjoy losing. But whatever you're into."

"And... begin!" The announcer's voice boomed through the arena and the fight was on.

Kaiden hadn't properly seen the brawler class in combat before, and as he thought about it, he realized none of them had. Sure, there'd been the duel against Titus, but that hadn't been a fight so much as a beatdown. It did give Titus some inkling of what to expect from his opponent, though, and Kaiden took some solace in that. He used his visor to pull up what information it'd give him on the brawler class.

**Quick Facts: Brawlers are a combination of rogue and berserker. They excel at one-on-one combat, using evasion to ambush enemies, debuffs to restrict movement, and combo attacks to inflict increasingly severe damage.**

As Kaiden read, Nassus walked forward calmly, hands open and carrying nothing. Not a weapon, not a shield. The only thing on her was what looked to be a light layer of mesh armor around her torso. Two lengths of chain were also coiled around her. Memories of the duel came back to Kaiden, however, and he didn't need to be reminded of just how effective Nassus' fists had been.

"Off to a slow start, but don't let that fool you," the announcer said. "These two are deadly combatants."

Chains rattling, Nassus strolled at a leisurely pace, advancing on Titus as he settled into a fighting stance.

"You see, a mindless opponent would just charge in and start attacking. Relying on alpha strike damage to push through your defenses and hoping that, since shielders don't hit hard, they'll be able to kill you before you can kill them." She raised an open palm and stared at it as if she were bored. "But I'm not a mindless opponent. I know you specialize in reflection abilities."

Titus shuffled his feet impatiently, seemingly itching to get to the actual fighting. Nassus only appeared interested in delaying, though.

"So maybe I should focus on trying to overload your shield? Like your last opponent? You can't reflect damage if you don't have a shield. But then, you'd be expecting me to do that, wouldn't you?"

"Enough chit-chat." Titus stomped forward, feigning a charge.

Nassus hardly reacted but to smile.

"No, you see, both of your past opponents tried to go aggressive, but both strategies meant going through your shield. You're a shield warden. Your shield is your strong point. But if it doesn't get hit, it can't build charge and you can't fight back." She smirked. "Which is why I'm not going to go through your shield, I'm going to go around it." As soon as she delivered the last word, she activated an ability.

"And here we go!" the announcer shouted, the excitement in his voice carrying through the stadium and pouring energy into the audience.

**Ability: Ambush**
**Increases speed. The next attack will deal additional damage and stagger the target.**

Nassus' feet carried her forward so fast she was hardly more than a blur. Titus leaned forward with his shield but she didn't attack it. Instead, she pulled a hard right-turn, slipped around behind him, then attacked.

*She's like an enhanced warden!* Kaiden thought, marveling at her speed. *Just more offensively oriented.*

**Ability: Frenzied Barrage**
**A series of quick attacks, each more damaging than the last.**

Nassus' fists flared to life, glowing with energy then punching forward, proving the ability to be accurately named as a frenzy of blows fell against Titus' back. His health bar flashed as each blow landed, taking worryingly large chunks out of his life total. Somewhere around five percent with each hit.

"Ooh, that has got to hurt! I don't care who you are." The announcer seemed positively giddy with excitement.

Titus spun around quickly, getting his shield in front of him, but even still he'd taken twenty percent damage. Improved Volt Field had slapped his opponent back for a bit, lowering Nassus' health by a measly four percent.

As soon as Titus had his shield facing the attacks, she pulled back, peeling off and using the remainder of the speed boost from Ambush to put a few strides of distance between them.

"Titus didn't catch a single blow on his shield," Kaiden worried aloud. "He didn't gain any charge at all."

"Charge-starving," Thorne said with a knowing nod. "Makes

sense. In group combat it's not really possible, but when facing down a single warden... well, it's a difficult strategy, but if executed correctly, the warden will never have a chance."

"One more reason to play blast warden," Zelda said. "We generate our own charge... not that that's going to help Titus." She frowned down toward the arena. "He's going to have to block something."

"Even then, he's going to be extremely limited on charge." Kaiden frowned at the prospect. Wardens hadn't been built for one-on-one combat, he knew. Especially not shield wardens. A frightening proposition when considered against the fact that the brawler class had literally been described as a one-on-one specialist.

"This is clearly a very tactical fight we're witnessing, folks. But is that any surprise coming from our champion? Show her what you think of that!"

The audience roared in response to the announcer, several jumping to their feet and pumping fists in the air. It was safe to say Titus did not have home field advantage.

"Level fifty," Nassus said, her taunting tone clear even if her voice was barely audible over the roar of the crowd. "That's far too low level to have any hope of winning this thing. You had to know that coming in, right?" She shrugged. "It won't make beating you any less satisfying, though."

Titus moved to close the distance between them as she spoke, but she mirrored each of his steps, staying just out of his melee range.

"You're not gonna beat me by running all day."

She smirked at that.

"Fair enough."

She lunged toward him, then when he raised his shield, side-stepped away. Titus turned to follow, keeping his shield faced toward her and no doubt hoping to catch an attack on it. They spun in almost a complete circle, Nassus leading and Titus fighting to keep up. He was just quick enough, just able to keep enough of his shield between them. Until Nassus changed tactics.

She sprung forward and planted a foot against the sloped surface of one of the collapsed walls littered across the arena.

**Ability: Launch**
**High dexterity launches the user high into the air.**

A spiderweb of cracks shot through the wall beneath her foot, then she exploded upwards in a graceful arc.

"Look at her go!" the announcer said, awe clear in his voice. "Now that's a jump!"

Nassus slipped into a backflip, then landed directly behind Titus.

**Ability: Mano A Mano**
**A 'trap and scrap' ability, Mano A Mano locks the user and one target together for a short time.**

The chains around Nassus' back unwound, then shot forward and wrapped around Titus' torso, linking the two of them together with only a half stride between them. The brawler wasted no time, then, unleashing another Frenzied Barrage and landing three solid hits.

"Oh, the big guy's in trouble now!" The announcer made it sound like Titus was doomed. All things considered, he might be right. Titus was far from in a good spot.

Titus growled, spun around, and pulled his shield up. Nassus danced to the side, fists at the ready as she looked for an opening. They spun in another circle, the chains between them keeping them close.

Titus struck forward with a hammer strike. Nassus shrugged it off – only taking three percent damage – and punched back. Titus was ready, and made to block with his shield. Nassus directed the punch wide at the last moment, avoiding hitting Titus' shield and giving him charge.

Clearly annoyed, Titus roared and attacked again. Nassus ducked under it, caught Titus in the ribs with a punch, then made to back away. Mano A Mano kept them bound, though, and Nassus couldn't get further than a half stride from Titus if she wanted. She threw a punch instead and Titus made to block it. It was a feint, though. She pulled it, then came in from the opposite side with a hook. Titus tried to lean away from the attack but it connected with his jaw and dropped his health to fifty-five percent.

In the wake of the blow, Titus stumbled backwards. Still connected by the chains, Nassus was dragged with him for a few steps. The big man's brow creased as he noticed that, but then the ability ended and Nassus was free.

*Forty-nine percent to ninety-three percent health. That's a heck of a disparity,* Kaiden thought, not liking Titus' prospects after the opening minute or so of the fight.

"You going to run all day?" Titus snarled. "Come on, you've got me where you want me. Charge-starved and down on health."

Nassus opened her mouth to respond but Titus lunged, bringing his hammer down on her head. Even with his low dex stat he managed to score the critical hit, then another normal hit before she danced out of range. Her health was down to eighty-six percent and Titus had his shield at the ready, no doubt hoping she'd attack it.

She didn't, keeping her distance instead.

"You hit hard," Titus said, shaking his shoulders out but making sure to keep himself behind his shield. "But you're so afraid to commit to an attack I don't think it matters. You must have really beaten some pushover opponents to make it this far if this is how you fight."

"Will that make you a pushover too, once I put you down?"

"Why don't you come over here and find out?"

Titus stomped forward and this time Nassus flinched back, keeping her distance. *Is she actually worried about this fight?*

Instead of following his opponent, Titus shrugged, then turned and sprinted in the opposite direction.

"Where you going, big man?" Nassus shouted at his back, then fired off an ability.

**Ability: Chain Lash**
**A ranged attack that deals low damage.**

Nassus swung an arm forward. The chains on her back followed it, whipping after Titus, but he was apparently out of range. The attack slashed into the ground, kicking up a puff of dust. An "Ooh!" broke out from the crowd at the ferocity of the attack and its near miss.

"If he can't go to her, he's going to make her come to him, I guess?" Thorne said, but there was no certainty in her voice.

Nassus seemed similarly confused, but she followed at a jog, wary of any surprise attacks. Titus didn't seem to be planning anything of the sort, though. Instead he ran right up to the wall and planted his shield into it. Electricity snarled and zapped, hitting his shield mostly, but plenty of bolts arced into him as well. Titus growled as damage poured into him from the lashing, crackling storm. His armor began to smoke and sizzle and his health was chewed away.

"What the hell?" Kaiden shot to his feet in shock. "What is he doing?"

"Well, that's probably not a winning strategy..." the announcer commented. "This is... well, this is certainly a first."

The wall spat and crackled as electricity poured into Titus. More of it poured into his shield, though.

"He's using the damage to charge his shield!" Kaiden shouted, the tactic suddenly making sense.

As if on cue, Titus peeled off from the wall and turned to face Nassus. His health had dropped by two percent, then six, then twelve, before he finally pulled away. He'd sacrificed a decent chunk of health, but that was only a small portion of what it would have been had he not blocked most of the wall's damage with his shield. The shield must have absorbed triple that, maybe more.

Titus held a hand out to Nassus then made a "come at me" gesture.

"You're real good at attacking when I can't fight back. But let's see how you good you are when I'm fully charged."

# Chapter Forty

"I'm not entirely sure what just happened, but I think he used the wall to power himself up. That really is a first, folks. This fight might not be over just yet!" The announcer rambled on, seeming to figure out what was happening as he was describing it. Titus was unfazed, however, already launching into an attack.

"Get over here!"

**Ability: Energy Grip**

He wrapped a coil of energy around Nassus' leg, then dragged her over to him. As she slid to a stop, he put his newly gained charge to immediate use.

**Ability: Rallying Cry**
**Ability: Hammer Smash**
**Ability: Shield of Rage**

He rapid-fired the three abilities, and the last two dealt out damage before Nassus was even back on her feet. But get up she did, and made to put distance between them again.

**Ability: Shield Slam**

Titus slammed his shield into the ground and caught her with the stun. She froze in place and Titus set to work landing headshot after headshot with his hammer strikes. Fewer hit than Kaiden would have liked, but Titus didn't have the dex of an enhanced warden.

Titus struck over and over again, his blows coordinated and quick, landing like they'd come from an expert. Considering Titus' real-world experience, that might not have been far from the truth.

The ferocity of the barrage caught Nassus off guard. She looked shaken, her eyes wild and frantic as she dropped to sixty-one percent health. The stun wore off and she scampered away, chest heaving as she fought to collect herself.

"Ouch! I don't think our champion feels too good after that one." The audience hissed and booed at that, but there was no denying Titus had struck some relevant blows.

Nassus' frantic expression calmed a bit, but her eyes were still wild.

"Not feeling so great?" Titus asked.

She growled, then opened her mouth to respond, just as a rope of energy curled around her waist. Titus had seized that moment to strike, the verbal jab he'd delivered nothing more than a distraction.

Titus dragged Nassus right back to continue his assault. This time, she seemed to panic, and instead of retreating, once she was on her feet she attacked without thinking, lashing out with Frenzied Barrage. The opening strikes connected – and Improved Volt Field slapped back a few percent of damage – before Titus abandoned his attack in favor of blocking with his shield. He caught the last two punches of Frenzied Barrage on it and then a wallop of a blow as Nassus activated a new ability with panic in her eyes.

**Ability: Pyroclastic Pulverization**
**A high-damage attack with knockback and damage over**
**time that bypasses armor.**

She raised both fists, interlocked above her head, then slammed them down. Titus activated Reflection at the last moment, then took the brunt of the attack. The ground beneath him collapsed inward a bit, as if an explosive amount of force has passed through him and into it. That wasn't all, though. Something molten and hissing was flowing from Nassus' fists. Magma, Kaiden realized as the oozing inferno poured around the edges of Titus' shield and down onto his head and shoulders.

He growled and backed away, health bar flashing as he fought to wipe the magma from his helmet's visor. Reflection had thrown twenty percent of the damage from Nassus' ability back at her, but it only worked on damage absorbed by a shield. The damage over time from the magma was only hurting Titus.

There was a moment of calm as Titus and Nassus both seemed to recover from the flurry. For the most part, Titus had come out on top. Well, he'd taken a ton of damage – was down to thirty-four percent health now – but he'd also dealt a good bit in return. Nassus was also low with forty-five percent health remaining. Still, Kaiden knew, it was more than a comfy enough lead to clinch a victory. The odds were not in Titus' favor. Though, blocking Nassus' last flurry had definitely given him more charge, so at the very least he could continue attacking without having to throw himself into an electrified wall again.

Nassus took in the scene around her and a look of disappointment crept onto her face.

"You're a tricky punk, I'll give you that," she said, but even from the stands Kaiden could hear the uncertainty in her voice. She seemed disappointed Titus had shaken her with his taunts and sudden attacks. Disappointed that she'd panicked and played into his strategy by attacking his shield.

*All that considered, maybe there's a chance for Titus to pull out a win?*

"Come on, big guy, you got this!" Kaiden shouted, pumping a fist in the air and cheering him on. Thorne and Zelda rose as well to join him. And, to Kaiden's amazement, a few others did as well. Previously, most of the cheering had been for Nassus, but it looked like Titus' clever use of the electrified wall had won some more of the audience over to his side. They joined in now, their voices echoing through the stadium loudly enough that the big man looked up for a moment and smiled. Nassus, on the other hand, let a massive frown stretch across her features. A look of hurt betrayal rose in her features then boiled over into a scowl. The audience had turned on her, or at least, enough of it to mess with her confidence. The scowl broke, and for a moment, Kaiden saw fear in her face.

"Imagining what it'll feel like when you lose to me?" Titus asked, pressing a verbal advance. "Spoiler alert: not good."

Nassus swallowed hard, then tried to steel herself. Her supporters in the audience chose that moment to make themselves heard. Their shouts and cheers fought against Titus' newfound fans, then slowly drowned them out.

The Maximus fans cheered as loud as they could, chanting their champion's name over and over in a rapid rhythm.

"Nassus! Nassus! Nassus!"

That seemed to steady her a bit, but even Kaiden could see her confidence was gone.

"Nassus! Nassus! Nassus!"

"Kick his assus!" someone shouted from a few rows back.

"That's right! Let your champion hear you!" the announcer egged the audience on.

But even as the cheers rose louder and louder, Nassus seemed to shake more and more.

*She's afraid of letting them down,* Kaiden realized.

Titus couldn't have cared less about the audience. He'd chosen his strategy and played it well. His opponent was off her mental game. He charged, coming in fast and swinging the whole way. He and Nassus exchanged blows back and forth, trading hit points for hit points. She was higher level, so each of her hits did more damage. Still, her blows were wild and many of them missed. Titus was taking the brunt of the damage, but his focus was laser sharp. He'd been here before, just not in Nova – in the real world. His health ticked away but he kept attacking. More of his blows landed than Nassus' and he caught several of hers on his shield. By the time his opponent noticed she wasn't doing as much damage as she wanted the disparity between their health totals had largely evened out. Titus was down to twenty percent but Nassus wasn't far behind, sitting at twenty-eight percent.

Nassus backed away from the engagement, trying to figure out where she'd gone wrong. Titus didn't give her much time to think.

He turned and ran.

Nassus' eyes lit up at the sight of her foe retreating and she couldn't resist pursuing. She struck out with a Chain Lash, then followed it with Mano A Mano. Her chains shot forward and caught Titus, then dragged her up behind him. She tore into his exposed back with a series of blows.

Then, all at once, Titus looked over his shoulder and smiled.

"Don't let go," he said. "Oh, that's right, you can't."

## Ability: Shield Charge

Titus shot forward, energy pouring into his legs and blasting him across the arena. Nassus was dragged with him, still attacking his back. A moment later, though, she realized what was happening and tried to disengage, but Mano A Mano kept them locked together.

Titus Shield Charged directly into the electrical wall. Sparks flew as both he and Nassus were electrified. Their health dropped in rapid bursts – roughly four percent per second – and thanks to Mano A Mano, and Titus' unwillingness to move, neither was able to pull away from the wall.

Titus dropped to ten percent health. Nassus to twenty-four.

Then Titus to six, Nassus to twenty.

"He's going to die!" Zelda said.

And then a thought hit Kaiden and he broke out into a smile.

"He is going to die, but I think that's part of the plan."

"What?" Zelda asked, but Thorne was smirking now. She'd figured it out too.

Titus dropped to two percent health and Nassus to sixteen. And then, a second later, another burst of electricity flowed through them both. Nassus' health was shocked down to twelve percent, and Titus down to zero. His health bar was entirely empty. He collapsed to the ground, dead.

Nassus pulled herself off the wall to massive cheers from the audience. The look on her face said she was thoroughly confused, but she had, apparently, won. The crowd went wild. And then an ability activated. The one Kaiden had been expecting.

**Ability: Saving Grace**
**If a target within 100 feet has been reduced to 0% health in the last 5 seconds, they return to 50% health instead and are given 10 charge.**
**Cost: All of your remaining charge and 50% of max health if targeting an ally. If targeting yourself, all of your charge but no health and you resurrect with only 5% health and 10 charge.**
**Cooldown: 6 hours**

Energy flared around Titus' corpse and then he was lifted into the air, as if scooped up by the hand of some invisible giant. The force turned him upright, and as his feet settled back to the ground, he opened his eyes. His health bar flashed, then filled back to five percent.

The crowd stopped cheering at the sight. Nassus noticed the change and turned around just in time for Titus' Energy Grip to catch around her waist. He pulled hard and she was thrown toward him.

At the last moment, though, he stepped aside and she flew right into the electrified wall. Her health took a four percent hit. She seemed to react on instinct – startled by the sudden reversal – and struck out at Titus with a Chain Lash. He blocked it on his shield as the wall shocked Nassus down to eight percent, but she wasn't held in place by Mano A Mano this time, so she was free to move off of the wall. Or, at least, she was until Titus attacked.

**Ability: Shield Slam**

Titus lunged forward and slammed his shield into the ground at the edge of the wall. The stun washed over Nassus and froze her in place for two seconds. Sparks flew and the wall did its work.

Four percent health left.

Zero percent health left.

Nassus' eyes rolled up into her head, then she collapsed forward stiff as a board and faceplanted into the charred soil of the arena.

Stunned silence followed.

## Chapter Forty-One

"Titus!" Kaiden hissed again, elbowing the big man excitedly. "You did it, man! You freakin' did it!"

He'd been healed by the medic directly after the match, then they'd all been whisked off for their reward: a meeting with PlayaSlaya. They were surrounded by Maximus guild members now and being led up a sloping ramp on the exterior of the stadium. A handrail was all that separated the ramp from the billowing clouds of the planet's atmosphere, and as they rose higher up the side of the stadium, more of Maximus' guild base was visible. Clusters upon clusters of floating domes, all linked together by skybridges and swaying into the horizon.

The guild members flanking them were trying to look focused, but even distracted with his excitement Kaiden couldn't fail to notice them sneaking glances at Titus. They were impressed. Everyone was. What he'd done shouldn't have been possible, but he'd done it. With strategy and ferocity and a brilliance that'd caught everyone by surprise.

Considering the present company, it didn't seem in good form to jump up and down shouting about Titus' win, but still, Kaiden could hardly contain himself.

"Dude! You did it!" he said again, grabbing him by the shoulders and giving him a shake.

"I did, didn't I?" Titus said, smirking and letting himself be shaken.

"You did it!"

"I did it!"

"You—"

"Yes, yes, we know. *He did it*," Zelda said, stepping between them. "Titus, you kicked ass and it was awesome. We're all immensely proud of you. But can we please focus on what comes next?"

"She's right," Thorne said from a pace behind. "That win is going to go viral. Biggest upset Maximus has seen in a long time. It was excellent. But none of this means anything if we can't..." She switched to private comms. "Can't convince PlayaSlaya to help us. We need to divulge enough information about the database to convince him to support us, that our plan to attack Warden HQ is viable, but not so much information that we'd be screwed if he sells us out to the Party."

"There's no way to do this without taking a risk," Kaiden said, swallowing his excitement and instead focusing on the bitter taste accompanying the thought of what was to come. "None of us know this guy, so we're going to have to feel him out on the fly. But our plan is solid, and thanks to Titus, we look like we know what we're doing. We'll convince him to work with us. And we have the sample file Zelda uploaded, after all."

"We're here," the lead Maximus guild member said as the ramp came to an end at the very top of the stadium. A private skybox had been set up, complete with plush chairs, a buffet – not that you actually needed to eat or drink in Nova – and an assortment of magnifying lenses to better show the action happening down in the arena below. Draped across one of the chairs as if he hadn't a care in the world was a player in full heavy armor. He had blond hair, though it was tinged with green as if it'd been recently dyed, and he'd foregone a helmet in favor of a flat-brimmed baseball cap worn backwards. Kaiden focused on him, though he already had a good guess who it was.

**PlayaSlaya**

**Class: Cybernetic Knight**
**Faction: Maximus (leader)**
**Level: 60**

"Yo! The man of the hour," PlayaSlaya said with a casual nod. "That was an ass-kicking if ever I've seen one." He slapped his thigh and laughed. "Ooh man, I'm not gonna let Nassus live that one down. She's been killing it down there for weeks, but there's always a bigger fish. Even if their level doesn't show it." He rose and strode over to Titus, then reached out for a bro hug. Titus seemed to react on instinct and clasped hands, then went in for the one-armed hug.

"That's what's up," PlayaSlaya said as he pulled away. "Titus, right?"

The big man nodded.

"That was a hell of a show, Titus. We'll need to get you some more levels, obviously, but once you're ready, man, I can't wait to get you into the mix. Can't wait to have a go myself," he said, looking the big man up and down with a smirk. He shook his head. "That could be a fun fight."

"With all due respect," Titus said, careful with his words, "I don't want to join Maximus. You guys are... cool... and all, but I'm a bit busy right now."

"Busy?" PlayaSlaya frowned as if the word was new to him. "Dude, you won the tournament! The lower branch, admittedly – the real fights start in the level fifty-six to sixty tourny – but still. Since you're a champion, I can offer you immediate membership in Maximus *and* an officer position. That's huge, man. What are you busy with that's better than that?"

*All right, here's your chance, big guy,* Kaiden thought. Honestly, he wanted to step up himself and handle this. But it was Titus who'd won the tournament and earned this meeting. PlayaSlaya had come to meet with Titus, not his friends who'd tagged along and watched the whole tournament from the sidelines. *It's fine. Titus has got this. He knows what to do. We just have to be careful about how much we say. This is a delicate topic, so we'll introduce it slowly. Don't want to just blurt out our plan to take down—*

"I've been busy tracking down a database of government crimes and plan on using it to topple the Party," Titus said simply.

*Ah. Uh. Well, that's one way to do it.*

A stunned silence followed in which a series of emotions played out across PlayaSlaya's face. He frowned at first, then his eyes narrowed with suspicion only to be replaced a second later by what looked to be shocked disbelief. Then, a frown again.

He waved dismissively at his guards.

"Get gone."

And they did, moving without hesitation and disappearing back down the ramp so that only Kaiden, Titus, Zelda, and Thorne were left atop the stadium with the guild leader.

And one other. Kaiden hadn't noticed him at first; had taken him for just a guard. He was a dour-looking guy, with black hair and a pale face set in what seemed a perpetually sad expression. Kaiden's visor pulled up information on him.

**Nando**
**Class: Brawler**
**Faction: Maximus**
**Level: 60**

Considering he was still there, he must have been important to the guild. The number two in charge, maybe?

As Kaiden considered what in the hell to do next, and everyone stood in a stunned silence, one of the massive, billowy clouds that eternally circled Kyraxis' atmosphere swept over them. For a moment the whole of the world was foggy and dark, then it passed and the sun beamed down once again, fierce and bright.

"Care to elaborate on that statement?" Nando finally asked, breaking the silence with a voice full of doubt. "Or were you just going for shock value? Trying to make an impressive entrance?"

"Kai?" Titus said, nodding back to him. "You're better at this than me. Take it from here?"

*Oh, gee. Thanks, dude. Drop a bomb and let me come in and clean up the mess.*

Kaiden took a deep breath and stepped forward.

"What's up, Playa?" he said and extended a hand in a rough imitation of the bro hug Titus had been greeted with.

PlayaSlaya frowned at him and didn't move. Nando coughed, directing attention to him.

"Uh, yeah." Kaiden dropped his hand back to his side and stood up straight. "So, here's the thing…"

At this point, what was there to hold back? He started with the backstory on the database, then moved on to examples of the information it contained. He finished off that bit by trading the sample file Zelda had uploaded – just a taste of some of the more damning files – then transitioned into what they'd been doing, the attack on the grinder, and what they were planning to do next.

"And that's why…" Kaiden hesitated before going further. *If I tell this guy our plan and he sells us out to the Party, we'll be dead in the water. But we need his support.*

"And that's why we're going after Warden HQ. If we can get to the All-Frequencies Broadcast System, we can share this database with everyone in the game. We can expose the Party's crimes to the masses."

"Nando," PlayaSlaya said after Kaiden finished. "You hearing this shit?"

"I am. Not sure I'm believing it, though," the apparent second-in-command of the guild said, still eyeing them with suspicion. "You have the database on you, right now?" he asked.

PlayaSlaya nodded at the question, as if asking it as well. His expression had been the same throughout Kaiden's entire explanation: a mix of amusement and disbelief. As if the thought of the idea was good fun but too good to be true.

"Of course not. This is a PVP zone," Zelda said. "We're not that dumb."

Nando nodded at that.

"The sample file we traded to you was just a sliver of the database," Kaiden said, looking first at Nando then Playa. "A few small files we were able to upload into the game without the censors catching on. Getting the whole database in would take forever – something Bernstein luckily already did. We have multiple copies offline and the all-important one in-game. That's why the Party is after us – in the real world and here."

"Not to mention the bit where we offed like a hundred wardens at once," Titus said with a smirk.

"Hell yeah you did!" PlayaSlaya reached out for a fist bump and Titus obliged him.

Neither PlayaSlaya nor Nando had believed the bit about what had happened at the Grinder until Kaiden had screen-capped the assisted kill notifications from his combat log and shown them.

"You're what this crackdown is all about, then?" Nando asked. "In real life, I mean? That whole thing is because you have the database?"

"Afraid so," Thorne said with a shrug.

Nando looked at PlayaSlaya, his expression suddenly stern.

"You know I have no love for the Party, but the repercussions of getting involved with this would be immense." He crossed his arms and turned back to Kaiden. "It would be a wise course of action to pretend we never spoke of this."

"You don't get it," Kaiden said. "There's too much at stake here to hide. Too much has already been sacrificed."

"I can't control the choices you've made to get to this point. All I can control is the choices we make going forward." Nando let the words hang in the air with no small amount of finality.

"I hear you. I hear you." PlayaSlaya nodded toward his second in command. "But let me just clear one thing up." He looked to Kaiden now. "If the Party catches you, it's over. You're done." He laughed. "No one will ever hear from you again."

*Not exactly a thought I like to laugh about...*

"They're not going to catch us," Zelda said, her tone deadly serious. "We have more work to do and we're determined to see it through."

PlayaSlaya whistled low, then let out another laugh. "Final-ly!" he clapped his hands together, then fist-pumped and half shouted, half laughed into the sky. "Where have you four been all this time?"

Kaiden frowned at that.

*Did I miss something?*

"I thought Titus here was something special. Ballsy enough to take on incredible odds and strong enough to come out on top. But I was wrong." PlayaSlaya smiled. "It's not just Titus, it's all of you! Three escaped prisoners and a turncoat warden captain, taking on the whole of the Party! Now that's insane." He clapped his hands together. "It's fresh. It's exciting." He smiled wide. "I love it."

*Oh. Oh?* Kaiden's thought struggled to catch up with Playa-Slaya's logic.

"You love it?" he asked.

"How could I not?" He pounded a fist against his chest and nodded emphatically, then turned to Nando.

"I told you, man! I told you there was more to do in this game! More than quests and PVP. *This* is our next great challenge. This is gonna break the stagnation that's taken over this place. Our next big win, and this one's gonna be so big it'll put Maximus' name in the history books."

"Speak carefully here," Nando said, doubt all too clear in his voice. "If this goes south, it could be the end of Maximus. Sane minds would say there's no way anyone could do this. Believe me, I more than anyone would like to see the Party brought to justice, but it's just not possible. Worse, it's foolish."

PlayaSlaya only smiled wider.

"And there was no way lowly level fifty Titus would kick Nassus' ass, was there? But he did it anyway." He shook his head. "No, we're doing this. This is too fun to pass up. I'm sick of sitting here beating on the same chumps day after day. But this? This is what I play for."

"You're in charge and you know I support you, but—" Nando began but Playa cut him off.

"It's done," he said, then faced Kaiden again. "All right, man, we're in." He opened his arms wide.

Nando sighed, then regained his composure.

"So be it."

"You're in? Just like that?" Kaiden fought not to frown.

*Why does this feel too easy?*

"Hell yes we are!" PlayaSlaya looked like he could barely contain his excitement. Was bursting at the seams with it. "You're going to take a shot at Warden HQ. There's no way we're missing out on that. Look, guys. I've done everything this game has to offer. I've slain bosses twice my level, I hold the record for the deepest run into the endless waves of voidspawn, and I've beaten every opponent who's challenged me in a one-on-one." PlayaSlaya shook his head at that, almost as if the thought made him sad. "Do you know what that feels like? Do you know what it's like to be so good nothing's a challenge anymore?" His features fell into a deep frown and there was no denying the sadness in his eyes. Pain, almost. "It sucks, man. It sucks bad. Then you four show up offering something new. And an in-game first, no less?" He chuckled at that. "No, no, no. There's no way I'm passing that up."

"You understand the repercussions of this, right?" Thorne asked, doubt in her voice. "Attacking a warden in-game isn't a big deal in the real world, but when it's alongside us – when you involve yourselves with this whole database debacle – you'll be bringing heat down on your heads. Real heat. The Party could come looking for you in the real world. Could show up at your front door."

*He's on board with the plan. Don't chase him away now!* Kaiden wanted to say. But he found he agreed with Thorne. As much as they needed the allies, anyone joining them needed to understand the stakes. Lives had already been ruined and no doubt more would be before the whole thing was over.

PlayaSlaya waved Thorne's words away as if they were no concern at all.

"You don't understand us at all if you think we'll miss a chance to raid Warden HQ. That asteroid's been taunting us forever. A PVP zone but one no one has raided it before? It's long past time we changed that."

"And also the part where you help bring down a tyrannical regime and build a better world," Zelda added.

"Yeah, yeah. That part too. Whatever."

"If we're... *doing* this, they'll want to know," Nando said to Playa, who nodded.

"Sure, sure."

Nando's eyes went distant a moment. Navigating some menu, no doubt.

"What's he doing?" Zelda asked, stepping forward, then turned to face Nando directly. "What are you doing?"

"It's all cool," PlayaSlaya said. "Hey, so, uh, this has been fun, but I gotta run." He nodded over his shoulder, down to the arena where three or four players were gathering, swinging their weapons and checking armor as if readying for a fight. "Gotta keep my skills sharp, you know?" PlayaSlaya said, then walked to the end of skybox.

"Nando, handle the specifics," he said, the leaned backwards and fell out of sight.

"What the—?" Kaiden rushed to the edge of the skybox in time to see PlayaSlaya using some sort of ability to negate the fall damage. He crashed down into the arena like a meteor, then rose and strode into the center of the players waiting for him.

"That was, uh, quite an exit," Kaiden said.

"That's Playa for ya," Nando said, drawing Kaiden's attention back to the skybox. The second in command inhaled a deep breath, then shook his head and pinched the bridge of his nose. "How many different VPNs could I possibly run my connection through before logging into Nova?" he asked, mainly to himself, it seemed.

"I understand this is a lot," Kaiden said, trying to be sympathetic. Sometimes he forgot that not everyone had spent the last few months as a sworn enemy of the Party. For many, the Party appeared to be doing a fine job, though the increasing severity of the crackdown had to be straining that goodwill.

"It's no easy thing to turn against a group as powerful as the Party. But it's the right thing," Kaiden said. "Sometimes, that means it's even harder to do."

Nando turned his eyes to Kaiden.

"I don't know your situation, Kaiden, but not everyone has so little to lose as you apparently do. I have a family to consider. Children to raise. If I get involved in this and it goes south, the Party could turn up at my front door." He scowled at the thought. "I've seen that story before. Already lived what it's like to lose a father for his political involvement." There was a sadness in his voice as he spoke. A sadness that struck Kaiden as utterly, painfully honest.

"Playa's only here because he has too much money and not enough responsibility in the real world. And I'm only here because he pays well for me to handle the details of running this place. But this plan you've proposed? It's more than a game. There are real risks. Real consequences."

"I understand that," Kaiden said, not fighting the somberness in his tone. And why should he? It was true. "A friend of ours, Bernstein, was killed for opposing the Party. Zelda's parents were arrested. And a good man, Merrick, gave his life to save ours. He detonated charges to cover our escape. Buried himself under hundreds of tons of concrete and rubble so we could live to fight another day. Could live to have a shot at making a differ-ence." Kaiden looked Nando straight in the eyes. "There are real consequences here. Real stakes. But they're worth it. If we succeed, no one else is going to be killed for believing something different than their government. No one else is going to lose a father because of his political beliefs."

*Where did all that come from?* Kaiden wondered as he finished speaking. He hadn't planned to say it, but it'd just... happened. Had just spilled out. And yet, looking back at it, he knew it was true. Knew it was honest. It was what they were fighting for.

Nando seemed to recognize that as well. His stare lingered on Kaiden a long moment, too much going on in those eyes of his for Kaiden to figure out. Whatever the man was thinking, though, a moment later he nodded sharply.

"Maybe you do understand the stakes."

## Chapter Forty-Two

They hadn't been on the *Veritas II* for long – couldn't have been more than an hour – when the call rang in.

"Nando? What's up?" Kaiden answered it and an image of the man materialized in the air in front him. Zelda looked up from where she'd been reading, then waved over Thorne and Titus.

"PlayaSlaya already committed us. You know we're in," Nando said. This time, there was less dread in his voice. Maybe even a bit of hope? "He's confident we can do this alone, but if we're going to do this, I say we're going to need all the help we can get."

*Well, finally someone's speaking sense.*

"What did you have in mind?" Kaiden asked, liking what he was hearing.

"Some… friends of mine have a message for you. I'm passing it along now."

**Message from [anonymous sender] received. Open?**

Kaiden felt his brow furrow.

"What is this, Nando?"

"Just open it. I'll meet you there," he said, then ended the call.

"Okay, that was weird, right?" Kaiden said, looking around to the others. "Anyone else think that was weird?"

"Open the message," Zelda said, leaning forward in her seat.

Kaiden selected 'open' and several lines of text appeared in his vision. He projected them in front of him so everyone could read them.

**Message from [anonymous sender]**

**Kaiden, Zelda, Titus, and Thorne,**

**I've heard you four are an ambitious bunch. The organization I represent is very interested in ambitious players. Especially those clever enough to achieve a world first and daring enough to attempt the impossible. We'd like to meet. Tomorrow.**

Attached to the bottom of the message was a link with some coordinates.

"Okay, now things are officially very weird," Kaiden said as he re-read the message.

"Where do these coordinates go?" Titus asked, but Zelda already had a galactic map up and was searching them.

"Here," she said, pointing to a nondescript planet. "Aqukinho."

"But there's nothing there. Just an area of the game waiting for future DLC," Thorne said with a shrug.

Kaiden looked closer at the spot designated by the coordinates. She was right. It was just a patch of ocean. No land around for miles.

"I mean, we have to go anyway, right?" Kaiden said.

"Could be a trap," Thorne said. "That area is a PVP zone."

"I don't know," Kaiden said. "It doesn't feel like a trap."

"What good trap would?" Titus asked.

*Fair point.*

"I don't think Nando would set us up, though. I mean, I know we just met the guy, but... I don't know. I felt like we had a connection. I think he might be more like us than he knows."

"I'm not risking the database on an imagined connection," Thorne said. "If we go, we leave the database on the *Veritas II*. We'll take the *Borrelly* down to the planet and hightail it at the first sign of trouble."

"'The organization I represent,'" Zelda said, reading aloud from the message. "What do you think that means?"

"I think it means whoever these guys are, they don't want to give us their name," Thorne said. "Not a good way to start a relationship."

"Wait," Kaiden said as he understood what Zelda was asking. "You don't think…?"

"I don't know anyone else melodramatic enough to talk about themselves like that," Zelda said.

Realization dawned in Thorne's eyes. "The Syndicate?"

Titus perked up at that. "No shit?"

Zelda shook her head. "There's only one way to be sure, right?"

"All right, all right," Titus said as he pulled his VR headset off. "Let me get this straight. First, I kicked that tournament's ass. Then I impressed PlayaSlaya so much he wanted me to be a guild officer. *Then* Nando liked our plan so much he passed it along to The Syndicate, and now we have a meeting with them tomorrow?" The big man leaned back in his chair, crossed his arms, and smiled wide. "All in a day's work, I guess."

"This is insane." Kaiden placed his own headset on the table and then held his head in his shaking hands. He still couldn't believe it. Everything was happening so quickly now. Three days ago it'd felt like they didn't have a chance in the world, and now? They were meeting The Syndicate *tomorrow*. Probably.

His breath shook in his chest and he felt dizzy.

*We can really do this. We can really take down the Party.*

It was almost as if some part of him hadn't actually believed it was possible. Despite all of their efforts, all of his efforts, it was like some deep part of him had still been in denial. Had been, but was no longer. Now... well. Now they were going to take on the world, and for the first time, it looked like they might have an actual chance at winning.

"All right, let's not get ahead of ourselves," Thorne said, bringing everyone back down to Earth. "If this even is a meeting with The Syndicate, that doesn't mean they're immediately on board. We still have to convince them of the plan. But we can figure that out in a bit. First of all, everyone needs fluids and food." She headed over to the kitchen and began switching on appliances. As they warmed up, she tossed a water bottle to each of them.

"I don't even know how long we were in-game there, but it's a sure thing we're all dehydrated. Not to mention exhausted. If we're going to convince The Syndicate tomorrow, we'll need to be fed and rested."

Kaiden took a long drink and realized just how parched he'd been. His throat was dry and swollen. Hurt a bit as he swallowed, but the water was doing its work. He was feeling better by the moment. Food would be good, too. It was easy to ignore the body's needs in-game, but now that he was out, he could feel the hunger inside of him. How long had it been since he'd eaten last? Fourteen hours? More?

*We've been busy*, he told himself. *Busy, and making progress.*

He took another long drink of water and leaned back to take in their surroundings, the small bunker they'd been calling home. He'd been in Nova so long he'd almost forgotten they were living here. Hiding out in a swamp while a savage crackdown searched for them back in the city. It was easy to forget, honestly. They'd been so busy in-game and he'd been so focused on the goal. Thorne was right, though. They couldn't allow the game to be their only focus. They still needed to eat, drink, and sleep. And probably shower, too, if he could make time for it. It was suggested to never spend more than a few hours a day in VR but they'd been putting every waking moment into the game.

"Guys," Zelda said from where she'd been coiling her headset cable into a tidy pile on the table. "I don't want to speak for anyone else, but I'm pretty sure Bernstein would be proud of us." She hesitated a moment, then nodded. "We're finishing his work. Finishing the work he dedicated his life to. The work that the Party killed him for. And I don't want to get ahead of myself, but it feels like we're finally making progress. Real progress."

Kaiden nodded at that, thoughts of where they'd started and how far they'd come welling up inside of him. It'd all begun less than a year ago – half that, even – and still it felt almost longer than everything else in his life. Probably that was just because the warden program, the hunt for Bernstein's database, and now their struggle to topple the Party, had consumed his every waking moment since it'd all begun. But for the first time, there was an end in sight. A victorious end.

"He would be proud," Kaiden said, looking over to her. "Proud of how far we've come. And how far we're going to go. We're going to make this happen."

"All right, enough sappy crap," Titus said, playfully pushing Kaiden as he strode toward the kitchen. "Let's get some dinner. Then we can get back to talking about how much ass I kicked in that tournament."

Chapter Forty-Three

**Location Discovered: Aqukinho**
**Faction Alignment: None**
**Resident Guilds: None**

"This is... it?" Kaiden asked, standing at the open rear door of the *Borrelly*. As far as he could see, the planet was entirely ocean. And the scans had confirmed it: there was no land here. No continents, no islands, nothing. Just water and wind across the surface of the entire planet.

A crashing wave reached up and broke against the bottom of the shuttle, spraying him in a fine salty mist as Thorne and Titus joined him at the rear door. Zelda came last.

"This is the meeting place, but there's nothing here. Nowhere on this entire planet. It's just empty space. One of the dozens of procedurally generated planets they have in-game waiting for content."

"It'd be a fine place for an ambush," Thorne said, eyeing the skies.

"I've got the engines primed to go if so," Ellenton said through comms from the cockpit. "If anything unexpected shows up I'm ready to bolt."

"How about that?" Kaiden asked, pointing to where the

surface of the ocean had suddenly begun to boil. "Is that unexpected enough?"

"Oh, come on," Titus said with a low laugh. "Now they're just being dramatic."

"Who is?" Kaiden began to ask, then paused. He'd just noticed the ocean wasn't boiling, it was bubbling. And as he watched more, something began to emerge. The bubbling water was mostly white foam, but then it darkened as a shape neared the surface. A metal shell made of interlocking plates. There were no windows in it, or anything to indicate what it was. Water rushed off its smooth sides as it broke the surface then bobbed in place.

"Is that some sort of ship?" Kaiden asked, trying to focus on it with his visor but getting no results. Even as he wondered, though, the metal plates at the top of the shell retracted, sliding back and into each other to reveal a hollow interior with two figures standing on it. PlayaSlaya and Nando.

"'Sup?" PlayaSlaya said with a casual nod.

"Let's go," Nando said, waving them over. "You don't want to be late."

"Where are we going?" Kaiden asked as Ellenton eased the shuttle down, coming in slow seeing as she was flying backwards in order to line it up so they could step off the ramp and onto the platform.

"Down, dude. Duh," PlayaSlaya said. "Come on, we don't have all day."

Zelda took a small jump and landed on the deck of the platform with a thud that reverberated through the metal.

"This thing's like a space elevator," she said, bending down to get a closer look at it. "Except it's in the ocean. So... a sea elevator?"

"Pretty much," Nando said.

Kaiden went next and the others followed until it was just Ellenton left on the *Borrelly*.

"I'll be waiting here in case you need a quick evac," she said. "Never much cared for water anyway. Swimming's bad enough, but that?" She paused, and Kaiden could imagine her shudder. "No thanks."

"Hit it, Nando," PlayaSlaya said and the second in command flipped a switch on a panel off to one side of the platform. The metal plates extended back into place, shooting out over the top of one another and extending to close completely around them with a series of clanking bangs. A whirring sounded from somewhere below them and then they lurched downward. As they did, video screens on the inside of the metal plates flashed to life. They took a moment to get focused, then all at once, Kaiden could see the *Borrelly* and the sky, and the water around them. They were moving down, though, and the view was quickly lost as they sank below the surface and the ocean swallowed them.

Once fully underwater, the platform picked up speed and the light began to darken, diffused more and more by the deepening water around them. The result was a strange blue half-light that transitioned to green, then to an ever-darkening black. Kaiden kept his eyes peeled for any signs of wildlife around them – only partially out of worry at the thought of what might happen to them if the shell were breached at such a depth – but nothing seemed to be nearby. Only more and more water. And then the light was gone and it was black all around them.

"Well," Thorne said, the first to break the silence. "This explains why we never found Syndicate HQ. Scans can't penetrate this deep, and there's no surface infrastructure here to give anything away." She paused a moment, then looked to PlayaSlaya. "It's gotta be a pain to get people in and out of here, though. You can fit, what? Eight people in here at once?"

"There's other elevators," PlayaSlaya began to say but Nando quieted him with a hiss.

"Ah, right. We're not supposed to talk about the base."

"We've agreed to help you raid Warden HQ," Nando said. "But as far as our friends go, today is just a meeting of general interest. Feeling you all out. They don't know you and they certainly don't trust you, so don't ask any prying questions."

"We were invited here," Kaiden said. "Surely that means The

Syndicate – er, your 'friends' – have more than a passing interest in what we're trying to do?"

Before Nando could answer, a groan moaned out through the platform, no doubt the contraption battling against the increasingly intense pressure of the depths they were traveling through.

"It'll be fine," Nando said, waving away the noise, then returning to Kaiden's question. "Being invited here means you have their attention. But if you want their help, you're going to need to capture their curiosity. You'll have five minutes."

"Five minutes?" Zelda frowned at that. "We're going to need to be convincing."

"This isn't a group presentation for extra credit," PlayaSlaya said. "None of that 'teamwork makes the dream work' crap. Pick your best speaker and pitch your idea. From what I've seen, that'd probably be Thorne, but she was a well-known warden captain, so probably not too well-liked around here. Nah, I'd send Zelda, maybe Kaiden. But it's not my choice."

*Zelda's probably a good choice*, Kaiden thought, while simultaneously swallowing hard at the thought of the entire group's hopes resting on his oratory skills. He'd never been much of a public speaker sort – or any type of speaker, for that matter. No, probably it was better to let Zelda handle this one. Right?

The elevator groaned to a stop and a door in front of them hissed open to reveal a long corridor. The floor was metal with a cross-hatched grating and the walls curved up into a smooth, transparent dome. The water outside was visible, or would have been if there'd been any light at whatever insane depth they were at.

PlayaSlaya strode off the elevator and waved them after him.

"Welcome to, well... let's not use any names, huh? If The Syndicate throws you out on your asses, the less you know, the better." As he led them forward, water dripped from above in infrequent streams.

"Should we be worried about that?" Zelda asked, nodding up to one of them.

Neither PlayaSlaya nor Nando replied. Instead, they continued down the corridor at a brisk pace.

"Okay, we need to figure this thing out," Thorne said, speaking to Kaiden and the others. "Who's going up there to pitch our case?"

"Zelda," Kaiden said.

"Kaiden," Zelda said.

They both paused for a moment, looking at one another with confusion.

"You're way smarter and you've been the driving force behind this thing since the beginning," Kaiden said. How did she not see that? "It should be you up there."

"I'd only piss them off. Say something I shouldn't." She shook her head. "My habit of being blunt doesn't always translate well to winning sympathy."

*Well, she has a point there.*

"Besides," she continued, "you're obviously the leader here."

Thorne and Titus nodded at that, but Kaiden balked.

"You're kidding, right?" He choked back a laugh. "The leader? I don't even know what I'm doing half the time. Flying by the seat of my pants." How could they think he was the leader? At best he was the one who'd brought everyone together, but even that hadn't really been planned.

"Nah, you're pretty much the boss man, dude," Titus said simply.

"What?"

Thorne nodded in agreement.

"Even when I was with the Warden Corps, they pegged you as the party lead. Had you on a fast track for promotion. You're a natural leader."

"I don't even know what I'm doing half of the time!" Kaiden reiterated, exasperated.

Zelda clapped a hand down on his shoulder.

"And that's okay. You don't have to have it all figured out. None of us do, if we're being honest. But you're the one who brought this whole group together in the first place. You trusted Titus when I wanted to do anything but. You trusted me when you had no reason to. Hell, you even brought Thorne into the fold."

*No I didn't!*

"I mean, it was me that found you," Thorne said. "But yeah, after I joined and everyone was suspicious of me, it was you, Kaiden, who gave me a chance. Helped ease me into the dynamic."

"I didn't try to do any of this!"

Thorne chuckled. "Like I said, a natural leader."

"Ay, rookies," PlayaSlaya said from in front. "We're here, and they're ready for you. Send your speaker up."

All eyes turned to Kaiden. His mind was still reeling.

"You got this," Titus said and punched him in the shoulder.

## Chapter Forty-Four

"Any, uh, last-minute tips?" Kaiden asked, fighting the panic building in his chest.

He stood in the antechamber. The door in front of him undoubtedly led to the meeting room of The Syndicate. He could picture it already – expensive decorations that illustrated the group's wealth, intimidating bodyguards looming over the shoulder of each of the members, and probably some sort of bizarre execution method – a shark pit or something – if he displeased them. Or maybe that was just tropes from old mobster and spy movies getting the better of him. Either way, he could picture what he was about to walk in to, and it didn't take much imagination beyond that to see how out of place he was going to look in the middle of it all.

"Any tips?" Kaiden asked again. PlayaSlaya had slipped off to join the meeting – or maybe to fight something, it was hard to tell with him. Either way, it'd left just Kaiden and Nando in the antechamber. The others had been forced to remain in the corridor.

"Don't BS anything. These guys'll sniff it out in an instant," Nando said with a shrug.

*Okay, cool. Thanks. That helps so much.*

Kaiden swallowed hard and focused again on what he was going to say. *The Party is a clear and present danger. The crackdown in the real world is evidence enough of that. But we can do something about it. We can make a stand. Light the spark. Ignite the fire that will burn down the old order, and from the ashes, a better world will be born.* Or was that too dramatic? Did people actually say things like that? Or maybe...

Kaiden took a deep breath to calm the shaking in his hands. Sometimes Nova Online was too realistic.

"You got this," he said to himself. "You got this." *Look calm. Look confident.* He pictured The Syndicate again – all wealth and propriety and calculated wisdom – and tried to mimic what he imagined that looked like. *Gotta look the part.*

"You're on, and the clock's running," Nando said as the door in front of them slid into the floor with a hiss. "And hey. Good luck, yeah?"

A blast of noise so loud it near knocked Kaiden over poured out. He frowned, but Nando was pushing him forward already.

"Ridiculous! That's the most absurd thing I've ever heard!" someone was yelling.

"Your mother's the most absurd thing I've ever heard!" someone else yelled back and the room was filled with a chorus of "ooohs" as if that comeback hadn't been dead since long before Kaiden's lifetime. Another retort was shouted back and then a dozen different parties joined in, all shouting in favor of or against, well, whatever it was they were... debating? *More of a shouting fest than a debate,* Kaiden thought, his senses still reeling. *This is The Syndicate?*

He couldn't see who was yelling – couldn't see anyone, for that matter – on account of the fact that the room didn't have anyone in it.

It was a cavernous space full of massive pipes that vented steam up toward the ceiling. Condensation covered everything such that Kaiden began to wonder exactly how watertight the whole place really was. In between the pipes and in every crevice and cranny visible, semi-opaque glass had been installed, creating what appeared to be small private booths. At least fifty of them, tucked into every corner and available spot and each reflecting back an image of Kaiden as he stared at them. The sounds of the 'debate' emanated from the front of all of these booths, from speakers there, no doubt. The glass was just translucent enough that shadowy forms could be seen behind it, but there was nowhere near a clear enough view to make out any sort of detail. The most Kaiden could tell was that every booth was occupied, and, at the moment, all of those occupants were seemingly shouting.

Kaiden worked his way to the center of the room, unsure if he was supposed to do something. He half raised a hand, as if to wave, then thought better of it.

"Ahem," Kaiden tried, but he couldn't even hear himself over the noise.

"Hello!" he shouted next to no avail, then waved both arms above him. "Hello!"

"Enough!" an echoing voice boomed across the space. Deep and gravelly, it resounded through the room so loud the pipes vibrated with it and Kaiden could have sworn he felt it in the floor beneath his feet. The shouting began to die down. Some voices kept going, but with no one responding to them, they soon fell to silence.

"The next item on the agenda is a pitch from..." The voice paused. Kaiden felt like he recognized it. *Why does it sound familiar?* It was deep and rough such that each word seemed a struggle to speak.

"...from player name: Kaiden, former warden and now outlaw. He comes before us representing a group of free wardens. The Warden Corps has added each of them to the most-wanted list."

*Thanks for the excellent introduction,* Kaiden thought with no lack of sarcasm. *Off to a good start. Though The Syndicate are mostly criminals, right? Or see themselves as beyond the law, at least? Maybe being outlaws earns us some cred?* He wasn't sure and there wasn't time to think on it. The clock was running, as Nando had said. Five minutes to convince them. That was all.

He sucked down a deep breath, and began.

"Thank you for your time," he said, leading with his best attempt to sound official and respectable. "It's a pleasure to be here, and I think the plan I bring before you today is one that is going to change the—"

"Get on with it!" someone shouted and a chorus of agreement followed from a few other booths.

Kaiden bit back a curse.

*Okay. Fine, then.*

"I represent a powerful group of free wardens who have inside knowledge of the Party. This knowledge, combined with our skills, has made us a pain in the rear for the Party and the Warden Corps. They're after us with everything they've got. That's why I've come to this..." He hesitated a moment. *Screw it. I'm all in already.* "This *esteemed* organization."

Someone laughed at that but Kaiden continued as if he hadn't heard it.

*Come on, build some steam. You gotta wrap them up in this. Sell them on it.*

"For too long, the injustices of the Party have run rampant and unchecked. For too long, those in power have done whatever they want to whoever they want and faced zero consequences for it. That ends today – or it can, with your help."

*Good, good. Now keep it going.*

"You see, my friends—er, the group I represent has taken possession of a database chronicling all of the Party's injustices as well as the full scope of its corruption. The Party fears this database so much that they're willing to kill to get it back – and have several times already. I'm here today to ask for your help because with it we can reshape the world."

*Nice one. Dramatic. All right, now let's ramp it up. Really sell it to 'em!*

"It's a rare day when the power to completely remake the world falls into your lap. Some would say an impossible day, but I'm telling you right now, that day is today. In this moment, you have that power. Or you can, if you ally with me. The group I represent has formulated a plan that, with the help of this database, will do no less than bring an abrupt and final end to the tyranny of the Party. And you can be a part of it. You can make history."

He was hitting his stride now, could feel the momentum building. Maybe he was cut out for this leader stuff after all.

"This is the chance of a lifetime. A chance to change the course of history. To correct a generation of injustice. Gentlemen, I'm talking about doing no less than reshaping society as a whole. This wouldn't just be a service to every person who's ever felt the sting of the Party's cruelty; no. This would be a service to the entire world. Ally with us, lend us the strength of your forces in Nova, and together we'll end the Party once and for all. Together, we'll unite and bring about a better future for all of humanity."

Silence followed his words, and in that silence, Kaiden allowed himself a small smile.

*Not bad for having such short notice. Not bad at all.*

The silence continued for another long moment until the speaker in front of one of the booths echoed out into the room.

"I have a question."

Kaiden turned toward the booth and focused on the opaque glass, making it seem as if he could see who he was speaking with. He couldn't see them, but they could see him. He tried to look at where he figured their eyes would be.

"Please," he said with a small nod. "Ask away."

"Yeah, that plan of yours sounds good and all. Grandiose and dramatic and all that. But what's in it for us?"

*What's... what's in it for you?*

Kaiden tried to formulate a response but the words caught in his throat.

"What's in it for you?" he finally managed.

"Yeah, exactly."

*I covered this, didn't I?*

"Together," Kaiden said, speaking a bit slower, "we'll bring down the Party and make a better world for everyone."

"Yeah, no. I got that. But like, monetarily, and in Nova, what's in it for us?"

Kaiden opened his mouth to respond but found himself at a loss.

"Well, uh..." There wasn't any monetary profit in the plan,

but he suddenly had a strong feeling that wasn't going to be an acceptable answer.

"Without the Party, the Warden Corps would falter," another booth said. "If we position ourselves correctly, there's something to be gained from that."

"But enough to justify the effort?" another booth questioned.

"And to openly defy the Party?" More voices were joining in now, throwing questions back and forth amongst each other, then arguing their merits. Questions of investment, of expenditures and profits.

"Excuse me," Kaiden said, but no one was listening to him now. "Listen to me!" he shouted above the noise. That got their attention. "This isn't about profit," he said, appalled by the thought. "This has been my life for too long now. A life of being on the run, of making sacrifices, of doing everything I can just to keep myself and my friends alive. We haven't done any of this for money or personal gain. We've done it because it's the right thing to do. Because people are suffering – people we care about and people we don't even know. Because the Party is a corrupt oligarchy and someone needs to do something about it." He stood up tall, puffed his chest out. "I'm that someone. I'm going to do something about it, and I'm asking for your help."

Silence, for a long moment. And then someone coughed.

"Uh, yeah. I've got better things to do than this. Hard pass." A general chorus of agreement followed and Kaiden's hope came apart at the seams.

## Chapter Forty-Five

"Well, that went freaking great," Kaiden said and punched the bulkhead of the *Borrelly* as he walked up the rear ramp.

"Hey, hey, hey! Be nice to my girl," Ellenton shouted from the front. "Else I'll dump you back into the water."

"Sorry," Kaiden said, shaking his head. "It's just that…"

*That I failed miserably? That I was laughed out of there? That they shoved us all on to an elevator and ejected us back to the surface so fast it near killed us?*

"Shit!" he shouted. "That was our chance. That was everything we've been fighting for. And I blew it. Again. First with Odditor, now with The Syndicate." He laughed bitterly. "Damn it. The Party couldn't do a better job stopping us than I have. I've ruined every chance we've had. At this point, your best chance at succeeding probably involves just locking me in a closet or something so I can't do any more damage," he said, looking at the others as they boarded behind him, sopping wet from where their elevator had sprung a leak.

"Don't be so hard on yourself, man," Titus said. "You win some, you lose some."

"No, Titus. This wasn't a fight we could lose. You all put your trust in me and I screwed it up. It's simple as that."

"If you couldn't do it then this wasn't a fight we could win," Zelda said. "None of us could have. We didn't know what The

Syndicate was like. We were totally unprepared for them. You took a good approach, appealing to their humanity like that. We just got screwed because they apparently don't have any humanity."

"All right, calm down, everyone," Thorne said as she walked up the ramp. "This isn't the end of the world. A setback, sure. But PlayaSlaya's still with us. That's something."

"Are we sure?" Kaiden asked as the ramp whirred closed, sealing them all in the shuttle. Ellenton eased the throttle up and carried them up toward the atmosphere. "After that display, I wouldn't be surprised if he decided to back out. Hell, the rest of The Syndicate would probably laugh him out of the group if he teamed up with us."

"It's not about that," Zelda said, her face serious but contemplative. "PlayaSlaya lives for PVP combat, right? For the next big thrill? Well, we're promising to give him the fight of a lifetime by raiding Warden HQ. He wants that too badly to back out. I don't know how far we can trust him, but we can trust that he wants something we can give him."

"She's right," Thorne said with a nod and sat down beside Kaiden.

"I told everyone about the database and about our plan to use it to bring the Party down, though," Kaiden said, cursing his idiocy. "How long until that gets out? How long until the Party gets wind of it and starts to prepare? They don't know what we're trying to do with the database, but now it's only a matter of time before they find out. We've lost the element of surprise."

"No. Not yet." Titus leaned against the wall and rubbed his chin. "But we are on a timer now. We can still catch the Party by surprise at Warden HQ. We just have to move quick. We should talk with PlayaSlaya. See how soon he can have Maximus ready to launch an assault."

"It doesn't change anything," Kaiden said. "Maximus is big, but not big enough to take on the Warden Corps and guarantee a victory. We've only got one chance at the AFBS. This plan is too important to risk on a gamble. When we hit Warden HQ, we have to do it with overwhelming numbers." He clenched a fist and cursed. "You guys put your trust in me and I blew it. I'm sorry. I screwed up. I wasn't good enough."

"Cut that shit out," Titus said and punched him in the shoulder. Hard enough that it wasn't playful. "I don't want any of that defeatist bullshit. I'm not out of this fight until I stop breathing. We're far from done." He looked over to Thorne. "How about you?"

"Till the last," she confirmed with a nod.

"Ellenton?" he asked next.

"I know you're just asking for dramatic effect but of course I'm in to the end. And Dawson, too. Not to mention all the free wardens he's been recruiting. I think you'll be surprised how many out there share our cause."

"And Zelda?" Titus turned to her.

"Stupid question. Of course." She nodded, but she sounded distant. As if she was distracted by something.

"Great," the big man said, then looked back to Kaiden. "Everyone else is still dedicated to this, dude. So stop moping. We lost this battle. So what? We're not done. Are you?"

Kaiden sucked in a deep breath.

*He's right.*

"I misjudged The Syndicate," Kaiden said, trying to puzzle out where he'd gone wrong, and how he could avoid it in the future. "They value their accounts more than they care about the injustices of the Party."

"Hold up," Zelda said all of a sudden. "Say that again?"

"I misjudged The Syndicate...?"

"And 'they value their accounts more than they care about the injustices of the Party.'" She said the words like there was some deeper meaning there. Kaiden certainly hadn't meant any.

Zelda suddenly shot to her feet.

"What?" Kaiden asked, looking up at her.

"Ellenton, can you reach the *Veritas II?* Tell them to set course for NC451 and be ready to go the moment we dock."

"On it," she said from the cockpit.

"NC451?" Kaiden asked. "That's Odditor's moon. Why are we going back there?"

"The Syndicate won't work with us, but he said he'd be willing to."

"Yeah, but he wanted the database as collateral. We can't risk it, you know that. And besides, even if we did, someone still has to run his labyrinth."

*The labyrinth that no one has completed since... since I don't even know when.*

"Yep." Zelda nodded.

Kaiden scrunched up his eyebrows.

"What's that supposed to mean?"

"I'd never risk the database," Zelda said. "You know that."

"Then why is he going to let us run the labyrinth?"

"Because you just gave me a very good idea," she said. "One that might just work."

## Chapter Forty-Six

Just because they were level fifty didn't mean it was time to stop grinding. And considering the odds of them having to storm Warden HQ with an underpowered force, Kaiden made sure they picked up every mission they could on the way back to NC451.

They ground them out, rescuing hijacked ships and crews, shooting down pirates, and even making a quick stop in an asteroid field to eliminate a makeshift raiders' nest that had been set up. The ship and crew still needed to be leveled as well, and between the missions and the random PvE encounters that always spawned on a trip across the universe, everyone picked up a fair bit of experience, all the while plying Zelda for information on what she was planning. But by the time they arrived at NC451, no one had managed to get anything out of her.

"S.S. *Andronicus*," the voice of Whenstone, Odditor's constant companion, said over comms. "Have you reconsidered Odditor's terms? Ready to take a shot at the labyrinth?"

"Yeah, something like that," Zelda said back as she boarded the *Borrelly*.

"Buckle up," Ellenton said and Kaiden knew all too well to listen to her. Her flying had been tamer of late, but that didn't mean he was planning on risking anything going squish.

"Odditor says he'll see you, if you're ready to accept the terms he laid out during your last visit."

"We'll be right down, then," Zelda said. "And this time, we're not fighting our way through the jungle for your amusement. If he wants to speak with us, he's going to open a landing pad directly at his base."

"*The Madhouse,*" Whenstone corrected, a note of annoyance in his voice.

"If you're not going to tell us your plan, maybe the least you can do is not antagonize them?" Kaiden said to Zelda, careful not to broadcast it over comms where Whenstone could hear.

"Trust me on this," Zelda said. "I know what I'm doing."

Kaiden wanted to push back on that, but considering how things had gone with The Syndicate he wasn't exactly in any position to bash someone else's plan. After all, they were all in this together. If they didn't trust one another, then what did they have? Common purpose, he supposed, but after everything they'd been through, he liked to imagine they had a bit more than that. He'd trusted Titus to take down Maximus' tournament and he'd done exactly that. Was now the time to trust Zelda to carry the group for a bit?

"You're cleared for landing at pad oh-six," Whenstone said after a long pause during which Kaiden was sure he'd been speaking with Odditor. "That's at the base of the Madhouse. Odditor requests your pilot is careful on approach. Any damage to the structure or surrounding jungle will be most displeasing."

"We'll be down in a minute," Zelda said back, then gave the sign for Ellenton to undock from the *Veritas II*.

"Ah, so I see, uh, I see you're back," Odditor said, stumbling over his words in that way of his like he was constantly editing what he was going to say. Couldn't settle on one way to say it. He had no trouble settling on a smarmy smile, though, as they all walked into his office.

"I had, had a special show planned for today's stream but, well, I suppose I could bump it if..." He trailed off, then waved his hand. "If, you know..."

"If I run the labyrinth," Zelda said.

He smiled at that.

"I thought I might see your little, uh, group again," he said, then frowned in the least genuine way Kaiden had ever seen. "After what happened with the... the..." He paused, then looked back to his ever-present companion, the turenoid Whenstone. "What are they calling themselves these days?"

"The Syndicate, sir."

"Yeah! That's it." He turned back to them and resumed his fake frown. "After what happened with The Syndicate."

Kaiden felt his cheeks grow hot at the memory of the embarrassment. It was so recent he could still feel every bit of its sting. It reminded him all the more why they needed a win here today.

"I'd be willing to bet you were there," Thorne said, giving Odditor a sharp look. "Officially, you're not affiliated with any faction, but we all know that's just on paper."

Odditor just gave her a smile with his mouth half open by way of a response. Thorne didn't seem to know how to respond to that and Kaiden didn't blame her. Zelda cut back to the chase, though, mind on the goal as always.

"You offered the piece of the database Bernstein lost to you. If I complete the labyrinth, I want that piece and to have a reasonable discussion about your support of our efforts. We don't know the extent of your resources, but adding them to our growing alliance is a chance I don't think you want to miss. It'd be a shame to watch from the sidelines as we make history without you."

Odditor giggled at that.

"My dear," he said to Zelda. "Watching from the sidelines is, uh, exactly what I do." He gestured down to the labyrinth, then lowered his voice and leaned in close. "And I think we, think we all know the only reason those," he waved his hand as if tossing away something disgusting, "those Maximus brutes are on board is for the chance to bust some warden heads. You haven't convinced them of the, the, what it's called? The worthiness, yes! The worthiness of your cause."

*Nando might disagree with you on that account.* Kaiden stepped forward, commanding Odditor's attention. The man turned to him, eyes still a bit distant as if he was on the verge of being lost in thought.

"Are you in or not?" Kaiden gestured back to Zelda. "She's ready to kick your labyrinth's ass."

"Ha, heh. Well." Odditor shrugged but seemed pleased at the thought. "Many have tried. Maybe you'll join the few who, who actually have." He looked to the holotable that seemingly controlled the labyrinth and began interfacing with it, flipping through screens and menus at an impressive speed.

"Whenstone will serve as the middleman for our antes." He tossed the padlock he'd shown them last time – the piece of Bernstein's database he'd had all this time – over his shoulder with a casualness that pained Kaiden.

The turenoid caught it without looking, then extended a hand toward them.

For the database. For their sole leverage over the Party. The best chance they had at changing the world.

Kaiden looked to Zelda, but as he did, he felt no concern. 'Trust me,' she'd asked, and trust her he did.

"I can't offer the database," she said.

He had his back turned, but even still, it was impossible not to see Odditor's shoulders slump and hear his sigh. When he faced them again, he was pinching the bridge of his nose and there was a pained expression plastered across his face.

"I have something else to offer," Zelda said before the man could protest. She drew in a breath, hesitated for the slightest of moments, then spoke. "My account," she said and swallowed hard. But her eyes were determined. There was no doubt in her mind.

There was plenty in Kaiden's, however.

*What? Her account? That's...* He trailed off in thought, considering the implications of the offer.

"Why would I want your account?" Odditor asked.

Zelda gestured to the hallway they'd come from.

"You have many trophy accounts out there. Players who were first to explore new systems. Players who reigned supreme in

PVP tournaments. Players who were acclaimed pirates and criminals. But your collection is incomplete." She let the end of the sentence hang in the air for a long moment. "You see, my friends and I recently completed a Nova first." She changed something in a menu, and then all at once, the title they'd been awarded for what had happened at the Grinder appeared above her head.

**Zelda**
**Free Warden**
**Class: Blast Warden**
**Faction: Unaffiliated**
**Level: 50**
**Title: Destroyer of Worlds (record holder for most opposing players killed in a single battle)**

"Now, not only is my account among the most-wanted in-game, but it's tied to a game-wide first and has a unique title to show for it. But..." Zelda paused, and it was clear she had Odditor's interest now. He was leaning forward slightly and, for once, staring intently. "But this isn't just about that, is it? You have pretty much everything you could want in-game. My account may make a unique and rare trophy, but having it doesn't actually mean all that much to you. No, I've been thinking about this, and I think you ask for ante for a different reason. What has value to someone who already has everything?" She smirked, then answered her own question. "Taking value from others. You know the database is important to us and that's why you want it. You don't need it. You don't have interest in it. You desire it only insofar as it hurts us to lose it."

*She's right. Holy crap, she's right.* Kaiden's mind reeled as Zelda spoke, but everything she said made sense. Odditor had everything he could possibly want in-game, so why make people ante up? Because he enjoyed taking the things they valued.

"You don't want the database because it's valuable. You want it because it's valuable to us. But you aim too high. We'll never risk the database, period. So, I offer my account instead. You want the chance to take from us something valuable – priceless, even. Well, here it is."

Odditor had listened intently, eyes focused directly on Zelda. The rest of the world might as well not have existed in that moment for how focused he was.

"I had you, had you pegged as the smart one," he said, nodding, then all at once shook his head emphatically. "But you're wrong. An account is not priceless."

"No, most aren't. If a player loses their account, they can just make another. But there's more to an account than that, isn't there? There's a time investment. And time is something I really don't have the luxury of." Zelda was gaining steam as she spoke. Her words were confident, passionate, and above all, logical. She was just right, Kaiden couldn't deny. Odditor listened with rapt attention.

"It's taken months to level this character," Zelda continued, spreading her arms and looking down at herself. "To build this account into what we need it to be. If I lose it, I'll have to do all of that again. But that's time I don't have. Time *we* don't have. The Party will find us in the real world eventually. We're in the middle of a tenuous balance, frozen in a perfect moment where we have the potential to strike a killing blow against them. But any number of factors changing can ruin that. We don't have the luxury of waiting. If I lose this account, I'm going to be a detriment to the group, and above all, I'll be useless in the pivotal fight to come." She paused, eyes wet. "Everything I've done up to this point has been to finish what Bernstein started. To complete the task he gave his life for. This account is just as vital to that as the database because it's the means by which I can achieve my goal. Without it, all I can do is sit on the sidelines and hope." Zelda let her hands fall to her sides, then took a step forward and looked directly up into Odditor's eyes. "You want me to stake something that matters, something priceless. Well, here it is."

Odditor smirked ever so slightly, then bowed his head a fraction of an inch.

"I guess you are the smart one after all."

## Chapter Forty-Seven

*She did it! She actually did it!*

Kaiden fought to contain his excitement as they all moved into Odditor's broadcast room.

Monitors filled the wall in front of them, each showing the viewpoint from one of the dozen or so drones Odditor used to film every aspect of the labyrinth. Everyone was there except Zelda, who was making her way to the entrance to the labyrinth.

Odditor had accepted Zelda's account as ante instead of the database! Acting as the middleman, Whenstone now held both – the piece of the database and the login information to Zelda's account. In theory, he could break the terms of the agreement if he wanted to, but Kaiden didn't have much concern that would happen. In order for Odditor's ante game to continue with everyone who wanted to run the labyrinth, there needed to be a reliable middleman.

*She did it!* Kaiden thought again. *She did it.* It was only then that the gravity of the situation started to settle in. He'd been so excited he'd forgotten what came next.

"Huh. She's... actually doing this," Kaiden said aloud instead of through comms, not wanting to psych Zelda out. "She's risking her account. Everything."

"It's all on the line now," Thorne said with a nod. "Brave of her. She's risking a big sacrifice for us here."

"Don't mess up!" Titus said to Zelda through comms.

"Thanks…" she said back, turning to look up at the camera drone filming her. Her face filled the main monitor for a moment before the drone zoomed out, revealing the massive labyrinth in front of her.

It was a gargantuan thing, easily a couple square miles of high-walled corridors, twists, turns, and who knew how many traps and nasty surprises lying in wait. It was open-topped so the camera drones could get overhead views when needed, but from watching Odditor's streams, Kaiden knew most of the filming angles would be from right up close to the action.

All around the edge of the labyrinth there was a massive trench, its bottom far out of sight. A bridge stood in front of Zelda, spanning only half the distance across.

"You got this," Kaiden said to her through comms. "But we're going to be here to help however we can."

"Appreciated," she said. "I've got a few ideas I'd like to try out in there. But if you guys come up with anything on the fly, don't keep quiet."

"All right, all right," Odditor said from his commentating desk positioned directly in front of the wall of monitors. He clapped his hands together. "Let's get this underway, huh? The objective of this game of ours is simple. You must retrieve the flag at the center of my labyrinth and carry it to where you stand now."

"I'm ready if you are," Zelda said.

"Ah, but first, the rules! I know you all brought stimpacks, but their use is strictly forbidden in my labyrinth. Your stimulant chambers will deactivate once you cross the bridge, as will health regeneration. You have only the health points you take in with you."

"Annoying, but fair enough, I suppose," Zelda said.

"Secondly, as we discussed, streaming this live would likely bring that pesky Warden Corps down on us. Since this, this is a… special occasion, and I cannot abide interference, I will broadcast your run tomorrow." He looked pained as he said that, but carried on. "Thirdly, while many speculate otherwise, I do not control my labyrinth. My creation is a sentient, living thing. Or, well, a sentient, living *digital* thing." He waved a hand at the semantics of it all. "Suffice it to say, my job is simply to commentate. Everything the labyrinth does is a reaction to you, my little lab rat. This includes the mobs it releases, which will scale based on your level."

*Huh. That's interesting. I wonder how he managed that?*

"Now, aside from these rules," Odditor said, "it gives me great pleasure to say that, within my labyrinth... anything goes."

"I'll keep that in mind," Zelda said. The camera captured a close-up of her face as she did. She was smirking slightly.

*She has something in mind,* Kaiden knew. But knowing her, it wasn't just one something, but several.

"Well, then." Odditor leaned forward in his chair. "Let... let us begin." He flicked a switch on his control console and a little blinking red dot appeared in the corner of the main monitor.

*We're recording. No turning back now.* Kaiden made sure to turn his proximity chat off so he'd only be speaking to the others via comms.

"Well, uh, hello there," Odditor said to the viewers who'd be watching tomorrow. "The menagerie is hungry once again. It's time they were fed, wouldn't you, wouldn't you agree? Today we have a special challenger." The camera had been showing a wide shot of the labyrinth but now it began zooming in slowly on Zelda. As it did, she drew more and more into focus.

"You may have heard of, of her before. She's something of a celebrity right now and I don't think you've even heard the half of her story." Odditor was clearly in his element now, having too much fun building up the suspense.

At the entrance to the labyrinth, Zelda shifted from one foot to the other, looking impatient. Kaiden couldn't begin to imagine what was going through her mind as she waited.

"Today's competitor has taken a break from her seemingly full-time career of being a thorn in the Warden Corps' side to join us. She's a one-woman force of chaos." He paused, and the camera angle now showed Zelda's face clear as day. "Or maybe she's just grachnid lunch? Today's competitor is none other than

Zelda the free warden, and it's time to find out what she's going to be. Victor? Or victim?" With that, Odditor waved his hand over the holotable and the bridge in front of Zelda whirred and extended until it spanned the rest of the trench to connect with the entrance to the labyrinth.

Zelda didn't hesitate, leaning forward into a jog and making her way into the labyrinth.

"Titus," she said through comms as she crossed the bridge. "Do me a favor? Start a timer as soon as I set foot in there."

"You got it."

She stepped off the bridge and officially entered the labyrinth. Titus nodded and his eyes flicked off to the side, looking at a timer only visible to him.

Towering walls rose on either side of Zelda. From afar they'd looked like they were made of some sort of patchwork of stone. With a closer view now, however, Kaiden could see they were anything but. They were stone, but veins ran through them all along their length. And not veins of minerals, but veins of – well, it looked like blood. Or maybe oil? Kaiden didn't know how much was stone and how much was machine. On stream he'd seen them move – it was a fairly common trick of the labyrinth's to reconfigure itself – so probably they were mostly machine. Still, Kaiden couldn't deny there was an organic look to them.

The whatever-they-were-made-of walls guided Zelda ahead, forming a corridor that, like the rest of the labyrinth, was open to the sky. The sun of the star system they were in shone down with morning light that created long shadows from the towering walls of the labyrinth. And Zelda as well.

"Kaiden," she said as she jogged. "My shadow's off to my left, yeah?"

"Yeah."

"Good. Remember that for me. Or better yet, screencap it."

*Not sure why that's relevant, but sure.* He snagged a quick screencap of her in the corridor, shadow stretching off to her left side.

She continued down the corridor, then slowed as it came to an end at an intersection. She had two choices: turn left or turn right. Both directions just led to another corridor, each about fifty paces long before ending in intersections of their own. Zelda contemplated a moment then peeled off down the right-side corridor.

"Which path to choose? Which path, hmm?" Odditor asked to his stream.

"Thorne, make sure I take the right-most route at every inter-section I come to. I have a feeling things are going to get hairy down here, so you're going to be my navigator."

"Yes, ma'am," she said, her voice taking on the sharp, precise tone she'd used when she'd been a warden captain.

"This way, she doesn't get lost," Kaiden said, thinking through her plan aloud. "She's going to keep herself aligned with the same wall the whole way." *Work through the labyrinth slowly but surely.* He wasn't sure why he'd expected anything less analytical from Zelda.

"It'll work as long as this is a simple labyrinth. If it has islands – smaller sections that aren't connected to the exterior wall – then we'll have a problem. But we'll tackle that issue if it arises," Zelda said, then slowed as she reached the next intersection. She was staring down two options again. Not right or left, though. This time, both turns forced her to the left.

"Still gotta go with the right-most," Thorne said.

"A calm start so far, it seems," Odditor said. "But I think we all know that's not, not the way this game of ours goes."

As he spoke, Kaiden spotted something several paces in front and off to the side of Zelda. A rough spot in the dirt floor where the ground had been disturbed.

"On your left," Kaiden said, making sure Zelda saw it.

"I see it," she said then raised her hammer-gun and fired an Improved Warden's Bolt at the patch. It detonated with a burst of electricity and a series of piercing shrieks filled the air.

**Grachnid assisted kill – 1,000 EXP gained!**
**Grachnid assisted kill – 1,000 EXP gained!**

"Grachnid burrow," Zelda said, scowling at the now caved-in trap. "Thought as much."

"Nice!" Titus cheered.

"Ouch. Murdered in their sleep," Odditor said, his tone somber. "How, how rude."

*First trap down,* Kaiden thought. Though it hadn't been much of a trap. Not on its own, at least. But the labyrinth had far harsher tricks, Kaiden knew.

"Onwards, then," Zelda said and jogged forward, being sure to give the remains of the burrow a wide birth. "I know there's more difficult things in here than th—" She slid to a stop all at once, nearly toppling over, but catching herself at the last moment.

"What's up?" Kaiden asked as she backed cautiously away, eyes on the ground.

"Pressure plate." When she was ten steps back Zelda fired an Improved Burst Arrow at a spot on the ground. As it hit, there was an audible *click* and a series of spikes thrust up from the ground. Spikes as long as Zelda was tall.

"Ooh buddy," Titus said, frowning. "That was close."

"Good eyes on this competitor," Odditor commentated. "Doesn't miss much, does she, stream?"

As quickly as they'd shot up, the spikes slid back into the ground. The pressure plate popped back into place with a soft click.

"Maybe I'll try not to step on that," Zelda said as she eased around it, eyes to the ground in case there were others. Looking down as she was, she didn't see the little red light embedded in the wall beside her. Just as Kaiden was about to yell a warning she crossed in front of it and the wall beeped.

Zelda looked up sharply at the noise, and then twenty paces behind her one of the walls groaned and a door appeared near its base. It slid open and three monstrous forms stalked out.

**Grachnid Punishers**
**Level: 50**

**Quick facts: An elite member of the grachnid hive-mind, grachnid punishers are the preeminent hunters of their species. With maxed-out dexterity and strength stats, they excel in chasing down prey and pounding them to a pulp.**

Kaiden's visor read out some details on the punishers as Zelda raised her hammer-gun toward them. The grachnids Kaiden was used to were massive, insectile things with too many legs that each ended in sharp points perfectly designed for impaling. The punishers, however, were still insect-like, but in addition to their spear-tipped legs, they each had two chitin-covered arms tucked into their chests. At the end of each was a bulbous claw.

The punishers looked around for a moment, antennae on the tops of their heads working back and forth, until they spotted Zelda. They turned toward her in unison and a clacking, cracking noise filled the labyrinth.

*Their claws*, Kaiden realized. The punishers were punching their claws together with quick, almost hydraulic-like bursts of movement. With each impact, little shockwaves poured out from them and stirred up the dirt beneath the creatures' feet.

"Probably best not to get socked by one of those guys," Kaiden said.

"Can't say I disagree," Zelda said and began to back away. Then, all at once, the ground was moving. Dirt fell away with a hiss and a pit opened up at her back. At the same moment, the punishers screeched and charged as one.

"Go, go, go!" Titus shouted as Zelda readied to jump across the pit. It'd stopped expanding, but was still far too wide for a normal jump to cross; and, as more light illuminated the pit, Kaiden could see it was brimming with the same spikes that had been triggered by the pressure plate earlier.

"Uh-oh," Odditor said, letting out something that sounded suspiciously like a giggle. "I guess there're some fights you can't, can't run from."

Zelda sprinted toward the punishers and Kaiden heard himself gasp.

"It's three against one!" he shouted through comms.

"I'm not fighting them," Zelda said as she slid to a stop, then turned back toward the pit. "Just getting a running start."

The punishers were nearly on her when she started sprinting back toward the pit. Several clawed fists jabbed forward with explosive force, but stopped just short of her back.

Zelda reached the edge of the pit then flung herself forward in a jump. But there was no way she would make it. She was a blast warden, not an enhanced or power warden. She didn't have the movement abilities to clear such a distance.

What she did have was an Improved Kinetic Grenade on the end of her hammer-gun. Just before she hit the peak of her jump, she threw it downwards. It exploded against the bottom of the pit and a wash of flame along with a concussive blast carried Zelda up and flung her the rest of the way across the pit.

She came down hard on the far side, health down to eighty-seven percent, but still very much alive.

The punishers skidded to a stop on the far side of the pit and howled in anger.

"I had a feeling this one was clever," Odditor cooed as Zelda rose and dusted herself off.

"Close one," she said, but she was smiling. She looked directly into the camera. "Come on, Odditor. I expected a little more originality from your labyrinth. Is this all it's got?"

Chapter Forty-Eight

"Turn right, and right again. Yep, there it is," Thorne said, making sure Zelda always took the right-most passages as she ran through the labyrinth. Kaiden was pretty sure he'd lost track. Easy enough to do when grachnid ambushes and lethal traps were popping up every other minute.

The grachnid punishers were several turns back now and their angry cries were nothing but faint screeches in the distance.

"We're bound for a new trap any moment now," Zelda said, breathing heavy from the non-stop running.

"No burrows ahead," Titus confirmed.

"And I don't see any pressure plates," Kaiden added. Zelda had assigned them each a role in helping her keep a watch ahead. There was too much for one person to focus on. Odditor had let them use comms to communicate, so they were going to make the most of it.

Zelda tore around another corner, then paused as the whole labyrinth shook.

Odditor let out a maniacal peal of laughter.

"Ooh, this is always one of the best parts. You know what's coming, don't, don't you, stream?"

The labyrinth continued to shake and then, all at once, it was moving. All of it. The walls around Zelda slid into the ground, hissing and venting great plumes of steam and dust.

"Titus!" Zelda said as the tremors grew more severe and she fought to stay upright. "Mark the time!"

"Got it," he said. "Just about ten minutes since you started."

"Thank you," Zelda said. Kaiden could tell she was distracted. Her eyes were fixed on the wall closest to her. But no, not on it; *over* it. It sank all the way into the ground, as did the others, and for one brief moment, the entirety of the labyrinth was one flat plane. At its center, standing tall and unchanged, was the bright red flag Zelda needed in order to win. She took two quick steps toward it, unsure at first, then broke into a full sprint.

In the distance, Kaiden could see several grachnids and other mobs which must have been roaming the corridors of the maze. He made a mental note of that. *Good to know they're not just triggered as traps but sometimes roam freely.* The mobs had spotted Zelda and were charging toward her, including the grachnid punishers she'd left behind several turns ago. They were some distance away, though, and didn't make it far before new walls rose from the ground.

Zelda ran faster, sprinting straight toward the flag, but there were still two hundred paces between her and it – and the new walls were coming up fast.

"Damn it!" Zelda cursed as she tried to cut across one more quickly-forming corridor but didn't make it in time. The walls in front and behind her were too tall. She was trapped, back in another corridor.

The labyrinth stopped shaking as the last few walls settled into place, and then silence descended as the newly configured maze became inanimate once more.

"I think our 'always turn right' plan just got scrapped," Thorne said through comms.

Zelda nodded at that but stood unmoving, still facing the direction in which she'd last seen the flag.

"Left, right, right, left, right. I think," Zelda said, more to herself than anyone else.

"Come again?" Thorne asked.

"She counted the turns," Kaiden said as the realization struck him. "While the walls were rising."

"I tried," Zelda confirmed. "Not sure how reliable it was, though."

Thorne shrugged.

"As official navigator, I say go with it."

Zelda took off at a sprint toward the next turn. After Zelda took it, she skidded to a stop.

"That's going to make things a bit more difficult," she said, then cursed under her breath.

The corridor in front of her was not a usual one. It was split. One half of it continued as normal, stretching into the distance before running into an intersection. The other half, though, had sunk into the ground. The path sloped downward until it disappeared in a cave.

"Choices, choices," Odditor said. "But simply left and right gets so dreadfully dull. How about up and down?"

"Or backwards," Kaiden added. "Hey, technically it's an option!" he said as Titus gave him a look.

"I don't look the like of that thing," Thorne said, frowning at the camera focused on the deep darkness of the cave.

"Exactly why I'm choosing it," Zelda said and jogged forward. "It looks intimidating, which makes me think it's the route I'm not supposed to take. Unless this is reverse-reverse psychology, in which case I guess I'm getting outsmarted by a labyrinth."

"Into the cave?" Kaiden looked at the others. "Seems risky."

"What part of this whole thing isn't?" Thorne asked.

*Well, she has a point there.*

The darkness of the cave swallowed Zelda up and for a few moments Odditor's monitor showed nothing but blackness.

"This is not, uh, not a technical problem," Odditor relayed to his stream. "This darkness is intentional. After all, it's in the dark that we, that we learn to face our greatest fears. Or just get eaten by them." As he spoke, something moved in the dark. A light, faint and small. It came to life with a soft, warm glow.

Daylight, it almost looked like. Several long, curved stalagmites and stalactites were visible just at the edge of it.

Zelda stood silhouetted by the light as it pulsated and grew. No doubt in the deep dark of the cave it was a welcoming sight.

"Yeah, that's bait," Zelda said and turned away from it. "What else is down here?"

She flicked her shield on and its soft blue light splashed out through the dark, just enough to illuminate the area immediately around her. The glow reflected off of shiny rocks and puddles of still water. In other places it bounced from the slick surface of stalagmites and stalactites.

The entrance behind Zelda groaned, then slid shut, a wall rising to block it off.

"Well, that's comforting. Any ideas?" she asked, frowning at her blocked retreat, then reluctantly moving deeper into the cave.

"Probably don't go toward that pulsating light?" Kaiden said, eyes still glued to whatever it was.

"Yup, figured that one," Zelda said. And then something moved above her.

It was small and quick, fluttering across the ceiling, visible as nothing more than a flicker of movement. Zelda snapped up toward it, hammer-gun raised.

Kaiden's visor tried to give a readout on it but whatever it was disappeared too quickly.

"That's not creepy at all," Zelda whispered, but the flying creature was gone.

Right up until it wasn't.

It returned, flapping and fluttering, and dived down right at her face. Something slashed out from it and Zelda's health bar dropped by a percent – down to eighty-six.

"Ah!" she shouted in surprise, then pulled the trigger on an Improved Scatter Shot.

The attack blasted upwards and the cave was lit, if only momentarily, with a blinding light. In that moment, everything around her was visible.

The flying thing was some sort of bat or bird or... winged

nightmare. It was all fur and claws and wings, thrown together at seemingly random angles and with no apparent up or down, face or tail.

And it wasn't alone.

In that frozen heartbeat, where everything was alight, the camera drone revealed the entire ceiling to be *covered* in the creatures. They turned toward the light and screeched as one, fangs as long as one of Zelda's fingers arcing outward. The moment passed and darkness returned.

The brief flash of light had been enough for Kaiden's visor, though. It'd captured a good look at the creatures and was reading out their details.

**Abyssal Weevile**
**Level: 15**

"Visor just spotted them," Kaiden reported, reading the data as fast as he could. "Says they're called 'abyssal weeviles.' All around level fifteen."

"That's not so bad," Titus said.

"Except there's a couple hundred of them up there." Zelda raised her shield.

"Quick facts," Kaiden said, continuing to read from his visor. "Abyssal weeviles live only in the darkest caves in the universe and are fiercely photophobic."

"Well, they're on camera already…" Titus looked perplexed.

"Photo as in light," Zelda said, then held her shield higher above her head.

"Like photosynthesis," Kaiden added.

"This'll do it, right?" Zelda looked at her shield as she backed further into the cave. She was breathing hard and it was easy to see she was a bit shaken.

"I think so," Kaiden confirmed.

"Okay. Then let's figure out where I'm headed next—"

A screech tore through the cave. Hundreds of others followed, and all at once the darkness came alive with flapping wings, slashing claws and darting shapes. Zelda covered her head, ducking and running forward as hundreds of weeviles swarmed her. Her health dropped under a constant barrage of slicing blows and she made it several paces before running smack into a wall. Her health took another blow from that and she stumbled to one side, then fell.

"I'm afraid the caves around here are, well, a bit infested," Odditor said with an all too happy-sounding laugh.

Zelda held her shield above her, but she was a blast warden and not meant to tank attacks. The weeviles swarmed her all the more, several landing on her and sinking teeth into her armor.

"Gah!" she shouted, swatting at them to no avail. Her health was dropping worryingly quickly now. Down to seventy-six percent, then seventy-five, seventy-four.

"Enough! How's this for light?" Zelda screamed, then raised her hammer-gun and fired an Improved Warden's Bolt.

**Abyssal Weevile assisted kill – 300 EXP gained!**
**Abyssal Weevile assisted kill – 300 EXP gained!**
**Abyssal Weevile assisted kill – 300 EXP gained!**
**Abyssal Weevile assisted kill – 300 EXP gained!**

The cave lit up with Improved Warden Bolt's crackling electricity and the weeviles died en masse as the attack tore through their swarm, shocking one after the other as it jumped from target to target.

**Abyssal Weevile assisted kill – 300 EXP gained!**
**Abyssal Weevile assisted kill – 300 EXP gained!**
**Abyssal Weevile assisted kill – 300 EXP gained!**
**Abyssal Weevile assisted kill – 300 EXP gained!**

There were still too many weeviles, though. As soon as the light faded from the attack they were back, swarming and biting.

Zelda fired an Improved Burst Arrow, then another. With each blast of light, the weeviles screeched and died, but the light from the attacks never lasted long. As soon as it was gone the swarm returned, seemingly endless in number.

"They are terribly determined little creatures. They just... love biting so much." Odditor seemed positively gleeful watching the chaos unfold. Zelda, on the other hand, looked to have had enough. She'd been sprinting along the cave wall, following it away from the weeviles, though they pursued her every step.

"Toward the light, maybe?" Kaiden said, trying to figure out what to do next.

"That's the trap," Zelda grunted through the screeching weeviles. "The labyrinth wants me to run into whatever it is." And sure enough, as Kaiden looked back to the pulsating light he saw the stalagmites and stalactites around it move ever so slightly.

*Those aren't rocks. Those are teeth!* he realized with no lack of horror.

Meanwhile, Zelda curled up in a corner, her miniscule shield held in front of her. Weeviles swarmed around its edges, biting and clawing. Her health was down to sixty-six percent now.

"We need a plan!" Kaiden shouted. *Shit. Think, think!*

"I... I..." Titus cursed. "I don't know."

"I need a constant source of light," Zelda grunted.

"Flame?" Thorne said. "Improved Kinetic Grenade could make some, but it'd need to catch on something to burn."

"It's worth a try. Go for it!" Kaiden said and Zelda did.

She lobbed the grenade up into the swarm of weeviles. They dodged around it – right up until it detonated against the ceiling. The cave blossomed in an explosion of flame as the grenade went off. The weeviles fled again, but this time hesitated in returning.

Zelda peeked out from beneath her shield to find the weeviles were no longer swarming her. And then Kaiden realized why.

A pure, bright beam of light was shining down from above. Sunlight! The grenade had damaged the ceiling! Zelda saw it too and hurried into the beacon of safety. The weeviles swarmed just outside of its reach, but hissed and fled whenever their wings brushed the light.

"That's my way out of here," Zelda said, then wasted no time in firing into the ceiling again, then again. With each attack, dirt and debris rained down, and with it, more daylight. The hissing of the weeviles reached a fever pitch as Zelda fired a final shot and an entire section of the ceiling came down.

Zelda threw herself to the side at the last moment, narrowly avoiding the falling debris. Many of the weeviles did not and were crushed. Those that avoided the debris were left smoking and sizzling as pure sunlight beamed into the cave. What remained of the swarm dissipated, screeching as they frantically flapped into whatever remaining shadows they could find in the cave.

"Well. Well, now, that's just..." Odditor seemed at a loss. "Boo," he finally pouted.

"Get out of there," Kaiden said, all too relieved to see Zelda by the light of day once again.

"Working on it," she said, then began to climb the piled up debris from the cave-in. In no time she was back at ground level, emerging in another corridor.

"All that just to be back where we started," Kaiden said. "Or back in another corridor, which isn't much better."

"Grachnid burrow, on your right!" Titus shouted suddenly.

Zelda spun, spotted it, and fired an Improved Warden's Bolt into it before its occupants could emerge.

**Grachnid assisted kill – 1,000 EXP gained!**
**Grachnid assisted kill – 1,000 EXP gained!**

"Good catch," Zelda said through comms and Kaiden gave the big man a slap on the back. And then the labyrinth started shaking again.

"Mark time," Zelda said as she fought to keep her balance.

"Twenty minutes since you started," Titus reported.

Zelda nodded at that.

"So, the labyrinth reconfigures every ten minutes."

"I'm beginning to like today's competitor," Odditor said, and from inside the broadcast room, Kaiden saw him lean forward in his chair. "Let's not, let's not get too excited, stream, but she's doing all right, isn't, isn't she?"

All the while, the labyrinth continued to groan and shake. The walls around Zelda began to slide down into the ground with long, puffing hisses of steam.

"Look for the flag!" Kaiden shouted but Zelda was already on it. And as the walls around her slipped all the way into the ground it was right there. The flag. Not fifty paces away.

Zelda sprinted toward it as the walls began to rise again. She leapt and clambered atop the nearest wall, then tumbled down the far side and into a growing corridor.

"Come on, come on. One more!" Kaiden said, bouncing nervously in place as Zelda scrambled toward the next rising wall. She jumped and just got her fingers on it, then pulled herself up and over. The wall was high enough that she took five percent fall damage as she jumped off. But she came down not twenty paces from the flag.

"There you go!" Titus cheered.

The newly formed walls stopped moving around Zelda, leaving her in the same corridor as the flag. All she had to do was move forward and take it.

But the labyrinth wasn't done. Something swelled out of the ground in front of Zelda. Some sort of... plant? A thick hedge sprouted up, growing rapidly like some sort of massive chia pet – if chia pets came complete with finger-length thorns. It rose faster than the walls and in less than a second it bisected the corridor, separating Zelda from the flag. Kaiden could still see the red of its fabric, though. Billowing just beyond the apparent hedge.

"It's just a bush..." Thorne said. "There's no way it's that simple though, right?"

"I can think of a way to find out," Zelda said, then stepped back and leveled her hammer-gun at the hedge. She fired an Improved Burst Arrow into the hedge. The attack tore through it, punching a roughly human-sized hole.

"Huh." Zelda stepped toward the hole, but before she could get there, the hedge regrew and the hole swelled shut.

The new section of hedge bulged out toward Zelda, diminishing the already crowded space in the corridor. She paused at this and the camera zoomed in on her face as she frowned for a moment.

"It's going to take more than brute force to get through this labyrinth," Odditor said, glee in his voice.

Zelda fired at the hedge again, using Improved Kinetic Grenade this time. The explosive attack scorched the hedge and lit several fires all along it. For a moment it looked to be working, the fire burning through the vegetation, but then it began to regrow once again. This time it pushed even further into the corridor, forcing Zelda to back away as the finger-length thorns, now dribbling some sort of fluid out of them, jabbed toward her.

"The hydra hedge is a wondrous creation, is it not?" Odditor said with a low laugh. "I, uh, well, I made it myself. The more damage you deal to it, the more it grows. And those thorns, well, that's not fresh morning dew on them, if that's what you were imagining."

The fire went out after a moment and Kaiden sighed in relief as the hydra hedge stopped growing.

"Zelda, behind you!" Kaiden shouted as he spotted movement. She spun and brought up her shield in time for something wet to splash into it. Thick, black liquid sizzled and bubbled as it dripped down the face of her shield.

Zelda looked around to see where the attack had come from and Kaiden did the same, scanning the view provided by the camera drone.

"I saw movement on the wall," he said. "But it's not there anymore."

"There!" Zelda fired off an Improved Scatter Shot at a blank part of the wall. Something squealed, then fell to the ground with a heavy thunk. Kaiden saw the dirt puff up from the creature's landing, but there still wasn't anything there. As he watched, though, there was a flicker of color and then some sort of chameleon became visible.

It was frog-like in shape and texture, but with eight legs. It pulled itself up from the ground and its skin wavered and shifted in color, changing from the slate gray of the maze's walls to a vibrant green. The creature reared up on its hind legs and opened its mouth. A saliva-coated tongue whipped out and lashed toward Zelda. She just managed to sidestep and it hit the hedge behind her where more of the black venom sizzled and burned a small hole through it.

**Dilopoad**
**Level: 45**

**Quick facts: Native to the jungles of Felucha, dilopoads are infamous for their ambush tactics and impressive climbing abilities. As ambush predators they prefer to attack their prey from afar via their acidic venom.**

"Don't let the venom hit you," Kaiden said as Zelda squared up with the creature.

"Figured that much out already," Zelda said, glancing down to the face of her shield which was still wavering and sizzling.

"The venom of the dilopoads is, well," Odditor chuckled, "let's just say best not to touch it. Its numerous effects include reducing armor, slowing movement speed, and stifling health regen."

The dilopoad reared back to attack again but Zelda beat it to the punch, firing an Improved Burst Arrow. The attack caught the creature in the chest and bowled it over. But not for long. Eight frog-like legs pulled the beast up, then launched it at Zelda, tongue whipping forward.

Zelda took the attack on her shield, then dove to the side. The dilopoad landed where she'd been standing, its back to the hydra hedge.

"Crap," Zelda said, pulling herself to her feet and looking down at her shield. It was off.

"Overloaded," Thorne said. "Not good."

"Uhm, Zelda?" Kaiden asked. "You seeing what I'm seeing?"

"A freaky chameleon-spider-frog that's trying to lick me to death?" she asked as she raised her hammer-gun and took aim.

"Behind the dilopoad." Kaiden pointed, before remembering he was in the broadcast room and she was in the labyrinth. "On the hedge."

"Oh my god. Kai, you're brilliant!"

The dilopoad's venom had hit the plant earlier and burned through it a bit. And the hydra hedge hadn't regrown to repair the damage.

"Odditor said the venom stifles health regen!" Thorne said.

"You thinking what I'm thinking?" Kaiden asked, but Zelda was already in motion.

She charged the dilopoad, then fired off an Improved Burst Arrow. She was aiming to miss, though, and the attack hit the ground at the creature's feet. It hissed and scrambled away, creating just the opening Zelda needed to take its place next to the hedge.

"Come at me, frog boy," Zelda taunted.

The dilopoad seemed happy to oblige. It lashed out with its tongue. Zelda dodged to the side. Not quite enough, though. Some of the venom splashed down on her arm and set her health bar to flashing as it sizzled through her armor. Her health ticked down to fifty-four percent.

But the move had done its job. Zelda saw the majority of the dilopoad's attack had hit the hedge. The plant was squirming and seizing as if trying to regrow, but the health regen debuff from the venom was stopping it.

Zelda fired into the part of the hedge covered by the bubbling venom. The hedge burned back. Enough for her to rush through. She did just that.

Zelda clambered out of the far side of the hedge then turned to face the dilopoad, which was squealing and pushing through after her.

"Sorry. Tough luck, frog boy," she said, then hit the hedge with an Improved Scatter Shot. The other side of the plant had been covered in venom, but this side wasn't. The attack exploded and the hedge responded, repairing the new damage and surging out toward Zelda. The dilopoad was caught up in the rush and it squealed and hissed as thorns punctured through its body, skewering it inside the hedge.

**Dilopoad assisted kill – 3,000 EXP**

The creature stopped thrashing and there was silence for a long moment as Zelda turned around to face the flag.

## Chapter Forty-Nine

"It's right there," Kaiden said, unable to stop himself. "Yours for the taking!" *But no. Bad things always happen when you touch the flag.*

It was so close Zelda could have reached out and touched it. But she didn't. Instead, she crossed her arms and leaned casually to one side, like she was waiting.

"What's the hold-up?" Titus asked.

"Building charge," Zelda said bluntly.

"For...?"

She looked toward the camera, leaning into the drama a bit, and smiled.

"My grand escape."

"Aha! A flair for the dramatic!" Odditor cried, almost laughing as he did. "Why, this little lab rat is after my own, my own heart with lines like that. And look, she's so close to the flag." He drew out the moment. "So close to halfway done."

Zelda only smirked as Odditor's words carried out over the labyrinth. She pulled away from the camera drone to study the walls around her. They rose high into the air, just like all the others had.

"Titus, what's the timer at?"

"Twenty-six minutes."

"Great. And Kaiden, remind me, when I entered the maze, my shadow was on my left?"

"Yeah. It was on your left."

"Perfect." She looked down to the ground, then turned until her shadow was on her left again. When it was, she paused for a moment, then turned completely around to face the opposite direction. That done, she raised her gaze to the wall in front of her. She closed one eye and lined up her thumb, pointing roughly straight ahead.

"Getting to the flag is only half the battle," she said. "You also have to get back out. But the labyrinth changes its shape and layout frequently, which means trying to remember the route I used to get here is no good. The 'always turn right' plan was one idea to solve that, but not my only one." She smiled at the wall ahead of her, then raised her hammer-gun. "You see, I can't rely on the labyrinth to give me accurate information. But as sentient as this labyrinth is, and as controlling as Odditor is, there's one thing here neither of them can control." She nodded up to the sun, shining down on her and the labyrinth. "The sun."

She'd been standing still while delivering her explanation, and now Kaiden realized why.

**Ability: Sniper Mode**
**Warden must remain stationary for five seconds to activate or deactivate this mode. While in Sniper Mode, movement is locked and the warden's hammer-gun extends into a rifle. Range and damage dealt from all attacks are increased by 100%.**

Zelda's hammer shifted into its rifle orientation as she finished her explanation. At the same time, she began charging an ability.

"What's this?" Odditor asked, leaning forward in his seat.

"It was morning when I entered the labyrinth and my shadow was on my left. Thus, we can assume I was roughly facing north. The labyrinth changes, but the one thing that never moves is the flag. It was straight ahead of me when I entered the labyrinth. Straight north. So, to go back, all we have to do is turn south..."

The ability charging on her hammer-gun was just about done. She smiled. "And make ourselves an exit. You see, I noticed something in that cave. The ceiling broke when I hit it hard enough. Which tells me so will the rest of this labyrinth." She paused for another moment. "As long as I hit it hard enough."

Zelda fired the ability she'd been charging.

**Ability: Inferno Shot**
**You fire an explosive, superheated blast that ignores 50% of the target's armor. Deals 3x base damage to all targets in range (allies included). Takes 7 seconds to charge (must be stationary).**

Except she didn't just use Inferno Shot. She also activated her hammer-gun's special ability, Triple Threat. An Inferno Blast fired from the end of the weapon, and then another. And a third.

The first blast hit the closest wall and, with the damage boost from Sniper Mode, obliterated it. The explosion shook the entirety of the labyrinth and the whole wall came down in a crash of dust and debris.

The second Inferno Shot burst through the cloud and slammed into another wall which was also reduced to rubble. The camera drone recording it had to zoom out to keep the blast in frame.

The third Inferno Shot carried on even further, passing through the holes the first two blasts had created. The camera drone was forced to pan to follow the attack. The massive, glowing shot almost disappeared in the ever-thickening clouds of dust from the prior explosions – right up until it too struck a wall, this one almost all the way at the exterior of the labyrinth, and reduced it to dust.

Zelda was forced to stand still for five more seconds in order to exit Sniper Mode. While she did, silence settled over the labyrinth, broken only by the pieces of wall still crumbling and crashing to the ground.

Kaiden looked over to find Odditor stunned into silence at

the sight. *Now there's a rarity.* But even with shock plastered all across his features, the man was smiling.

"Admiring her handiwork?" Kaiden asked and Odditor turned toward him.

"She's a, a special one."

"That she is," Kaiden agreed, then looked back to the wall-sized monitor. It showed Zelda exiting Sniper Mode and regaining the ability to move again. The dust in front of her was settling, or at least most of it had been caught in the wind and whisked away to another part of the labyrinth. With it gone, everyone was free to admire exactly how much damage Zelda had done.

Three walls had been blown completely away. The gaping path of destruction where the wall had previously stood cut through several different corridors and created an impromptu path that led toward the exterior wall of the labyrinth. That one was still standing, but considering everything he'd seen so far, Kaiden was half convinced Zelda was going to find a way to bring that one down too.

She turned back toward the flag.

"Now, if you'll excuse me, Odditor, it's been fun, but I think it's time I headed out."

With a calm, smooth gesture, she reached out and wrapped a hand around the billowing red flag. It came free from its stand with the slightest of clicks—

And all hell broke loose.

If the labyrinth had any tricks left, it abandoned them in favor of releasing seemingly every mob it had.

Back in the direction of the cave, the ground erupted as a massive worm burst from below, its body as long as a corridor and its jaws gaping. Teeth that looked too much like stalagmites and stalactites were thrust forward as the worm surged toward Zelda.

**Angler Worm **Gargantuan****
**Level: 60**

Kaiden's visor began to read out quick facts but he didn't have time to pay attention as a flood of abyssal weeviles burst up like a geyser in the wake of the Angler Worm. They rushed forward, a screeching swarm of teeth and claws. Those at the top of the swarm burst into flame beneath the glare of direct sunlight, but their numbers were so great those on the bottom were shaded. Every few paces more and more of the weeviles burned up, but still the swarm came.

And then there were the grachnids. The monitors on Odditor's wall flicked from view to view as all across the labyrinth every burrow was vacated and every hidden door opened. Grachnids and grachnid punishers charged toward the center of the maze in a stampede of chitin and fury.

"The labyrinth reacts to your actions," Kaiden said, recalling Odditor's warning. "I, uh, don't think it cared for your grand finale."

"What makes you think that?" Zelda asked as her shield flicked back on, returning from being overloaded. At the moment, though, running was the best option by far, and she broke into motion. She sprinted toward the hole she'd created and clambered over the remains of the first wall just as the Angler Worm crushed the flag podium in its haste to follow her.

The abyssal weeviles caught up to Zelda first and the swarm surged around her, biting and clawing in a suicidal frenzy. Each one that broke from the shade provided by its dying siblings above soon burst into flame itself, but not before getting an attack in on Zelda. She forced her shield over her head but her health plummeted beneath their assault.

Fifty-percent. Forty-seven. Forty-four. By the time she descended the rubble of the first wall she was down to forty-one percent.

"Something to remember me by," she growled, then fired an Improved Warden's Bolt up into the swarm. Dozens of the weeviles dropped as she sprinted away.

She reached the remains of the second wall just as the army of grachnids rounded a corner. Zelda climbed frantically, pulling herself over the massive chunks of debris. The first of the grachnids reached the pile right behind her and began scampering up on unsteady footing. Several stopped to slash at her heels, most missing but a few connecting. For each of those that stopped, however, another rushed past it.

Zelda reached the top of the mountain of rubble and a shadow rose up to tower over her from behind.

"Jump!" Kaiden shouted through comms and Zelda flung herself forward into a bouncing slide down the rubble pile. Her health took a beating, but it was far less damage than she would have taken had she not jumped. Zelda clambered to her feet, then was thrown off of them again as the shadow behind her – the massive Angler Worm – came crashing down just short of her, crushing a dozen or so of the pursuing grachnids and more than a few abyssal weeviles.

"Get to the exit!" Thorne shouted, pointing to it on the monitor as if Zelda could see. But even as Zelda staggered to her feet and turned toward the last hole she'd blown through the labyrinth, the Angler Worm cut her off. It heaved its massive bulk forward, surging on countless legs like some sort of gargantuan millipede.

Zelda was forced to run in the opposite direction, following the corridor she was in instead of using the rest of the exit route she'd created.

The weeviles were still on her, chipping away at her health – down to thirty-five percent now – but most had finally burned up in the sun. The last of them took one more swipe at her, then collapsed in burning heaps on the ground.

The grachnids were not so easily lost, though. Those that hadn't been crushed by the Angler Worm were still hot on Zelda's tail.

"Pressure plate!" Kaiden shouted and Zelda spotted it just in time. She darted around it, then fired an Improved Scatter Shot over her shoulder. One of the lasers hit the plate and the front rank of grachnids were impaled as a row of spikes launched up from underground.

**Grachnid assisted kill – 1,000 EXP gained!**

**Grachnid assisted kill – 1,000 EXP gained!**
**Grachnid assisted kill – 1,000 EXP gained!**
**Grachnid assisted kill – 1,000 EXP gained!**

The others were undeterred, though, clambering over the corpses of their brethren and continuing the chase. They were faster than Zelda, what with their advantage of four extra legs. She couldn't keep ahead of them forever.

"They're gaining on you," Titus said, panic in his voice.

"Time check!" Zelda shouted back.

Titus looked perplexed, but glanced over to the timer.

"Twenty-nine minutes and forty-eight seconds since you entered."

"Thought so," Zelda said, and even from the shaky view of the camera drone Kaiden could see her smile. A moment later the labyrinth began to shake.

"It's reconfiguring again," Kaiden said. The walls sank into the ground, and for a painful few seconds, the whole of the labyrinth was one flat plane. Zelda was running along its edge now, the bottomless trench on her left and the exit just ahead. The Angler Worm was still guarding it. She ran right for it anyway.

The grachnids were on her, too. The swiftest of them slashed her across the back and her health dropped to twenty-nine percent.

She responded with a blind shot, blasting off an Improved Scatter Shot that left several grachnids screeching. But there were too many. She couldn't fight them off and she couldn't outrun them.

A moment later, though, Kaiden realized she didn't need to.

The labyrinth was finishing its reconfiguration and new walls were rising out of the ground. Zelda turned hard to the one nearest her – tanking several grachnid slashes on the way – and flung herself atop it. The wall carried her up as it rose and the grachnids were left behind, hissing and screeching as they swarmed around its bottom.

"Yeah!" Kaiden shouted. "That's what I'm talking about!"

"You got this!" Titus shouted.

Even Thorne joined in, cheering as Zelda stood, finding her balance as the wall came to a stop. It was an exterior one. At its base on one side the grachnids swarmed, climbing over each other in a living tower that was actually about halfway up the wall and rising. On the other side, the trench, bottomless and gaping. It was too wide for Zelda to jump across it to safety. No, she only had one option: the exit. The bridge she'd crossed to enter the labyrinth in the first place.

She was high above the maze now and could look out across its entirety. From such a height it was easy to see the exit – and the Angler Worm guarding it.

She charged toward it, sprinting along the top of the exterior wall as the camera drone zipped along beside her. Kaiden got a good view of her face. Focused. Determined. And maybe, if only a little bit, smiling.

As Zelda approached, the worm gave a great heave and stretched up as tall as it could. It rose above the wall, blotting out the sun for a moment, its millions of legs splayed out and ready to fall. And fall they did, in a rain of stabbing limbs and crushing weight.

But Zelda wasn't there.

Her eighteen percent health was enough for one last trick. A trick she'd used earlier, but that worked just as well here.

She launched off the wall, flinging herself diagonally over the trench and toward the bridge. As she did, she detonated an Improved Kinetic Grenade at her feet. The concussive blast washed over her and carried her over the empty expanse. She plummeted, then crashed down on to the bridge. Her health flashed down into the red as momentum forced her into a roll.

Finally, she came to a stop just beyond the edge of the bridge, the flag beside her on the ground, and the labyrinth behind her, defeated.

# Chapter Fifty

"Zelda! You absolutely brilliant maniac!" Kaiden couldn't stop himself from shouting as he ran out of the broadcast room to where she'd landed just beyond the bridge.

She got to her feet, wiping dirt and grachnid blood and who knew what else from her armor, but she was smiling.

"Well, not all exactly to plan, but I suppose it worked out—"

Kaiden hit her at a sprint and wrapped her in a hug. Hadn't even planned to do it, wasn't thinking properly, really.

She stumbled back, surprised but just managing to stay on her feet.

"That was incredible! I mean, the way you trapped the dilopoad in the hedge. And then the... oh." Kaiden realized he was hugging her. "Uh, ah. My ba—"

"That. Was. Insane!"

Titus hit them both from behind with a tackle hug that sent them all tumbling to the ground. The big man only laughed the louder for it. "I thought that worm had you for sure. I mean, that thing was massive!"

As he spoke, Kaiden looked up to find said worm was still lingering at the edge of the labyrinth and eying them with a look that went beyond malice. It wouldn't cross the trench and come after them, right? *It's probably not allowed to leave the labyrinth...*

Kaiden didn't hang around to find out. He helped Zelda up,

then led her and the big man back inside. Thorne was waiting for them, leaning against the doorframe, arms crossed.

"Not bad, kid." She gave Zelda a nod. "Pretty damned impressive, if I'm being honest."

Zelda blushed at the compliment, seeming not to know what to do with all the praise.

"Just doing my part," she said. "Group effort and all."

Titus slapped her on the back.

"Group effort nothing. That was all you."

"You guys helped," Zelda said. "I couldn't have done it otherwise."

"I could be wrong, but something tells me you'd have found a way," Kaiden said, then looked up to find Odditor waiting for them. His arms were crossed and there was a lopsided smirk on his face.

"I believe this is yours?" Zelda held out the flag. Whenstone stepped up and took it.

"The antes, please," Odditor said, holding out a hand.

Whenstone produced them. A tiny brass padlock – the piece of Bernstein's database – and a folded piece of paper – the visual representation of the login details and security questions for Zelda's account. Odditor closed his hand around them and in one smooth movement tossed them over to Zelda. Knowing Odditor, he'd probably hoped she'd snatch them out of the air dramatically. Instead she looked too shocked to move and the padlock bounced off her armor while the paper floated to the ground.

Kaiden dove down to grab the antes.

"You know, somehow I didn't think you'd actually give them up," Zelda finally said, her eyes wide as she watched Kaiden straighten, the padlock and paper in hand.

Odditor laughed at that. A laugh from deep in his stomach that set his whole frame to shaking. When he'd finished, he wiped what Kaiden was sure was an imaginary tear from the corner of his eye and smirked.

*I don't like the look of that,* Kaiden thought to himself, then began preparing his arguments. Zelda had beaten the labyrinth, but all Odditor had promised them for it was the antes and a conversation. He hadn't agreed to pledge his support. No. They still needed to win him over, and that was going to take fool-proof logic and sound arguments. Except, was it? What sort of argument persuaded Odditor? The dude wasn't exactly like everyone else.

Kaiden paused at that thought.

*How do we do this? I guess just give it our best. Convince him of the worthiness of the cause.*

Kaiden sucked down a breath, then began.

"Odditor, now that we've won your attention, if you just hear us out I'm sure you'll see the worthi—"

"Oh, do, do be quiet. I don't need your arguments, and more so, I never wanted them." Odditor cut him off. "What I needed was to know, to know you meant business. You see, Bernstein always talked of fixing things. Of fixing the world beyond Nova. A noble cause, I have to admit." He paused dramatically, drawing out the moment. Letting them hang on his every word and imagine what he was going to say next. "And one I happen, happen to agree with. The problem is, saying one thing and being prepared to do it are entirely different matters. You all say you want to take up Bernstein's cause. That's, that's easy to say. What I wanted to see, what I *needed* to see, was that you were willing to make the necessary sacrifices. That you were, were willing to do whatever it takes to succeed in this little... endeavor."

"This was a test?" Zelda asked "You had me risk everything on a test?"

"It wouldn't have been a very good test if nothing was at stake," Odditor said, and now he looked all too pleased with himself. "And the good news is, you passed. Beat my labyrinth too, which, truly, that's... that's something. Not even Bernstein managed that." Odditor paused for a moment, thinking. "You know, I'm sure my labyrinth is already itching for a rematch. Maybe you'll give it another go sometime, once this whole thing is over?" Zelda's expression provided a clear enough answer to that question. Odditor frowned, as if pouting, but kept speaking.

"We'll discuss that later. For now, though, you have proven, proven your commitment. Bernstein was my preferred partner in this undertaking, but you four..." He looked at each of them in turn. "Well, you'll do, I suppose."

*Well, isn't that flattering? Thanks.*

Odditor gestured to Whenstone. "Give them the terms."

The big turenoid cleared his throat – which did nothing to make his deep, coarse voice any easier to understand – and began to speak.

"Odditor stands ready to bring the full might of his forces in Nova Online to bear in support of your cause. I have prepared a document listing in detail the size and strength of these forces. Rest assured, they include no less than one dreadnought, eight large player-staffed guilds, three NPC factions, and, of course, the menagerie." As if on cue, several screeches and growls erupted from the now-still labyrinth in front of them.

*Holy crap. Eight guilds? Three entire NPC factions?* That was... an insane amount of strength for one man to control. And now it was available to support their attack? Kaiden could barely process the information. Maximus had been one thing, but this? This was so much more.

Whenstone continued with the terms as dryly as he might read the instructions to assemble a cabinet.

"A minimum period of twenty-four hours will be required to muster these forces. They will, of course, only accept orders from Odditor. All commands to them must be relayed to him and vetted first. If he agrees with the orders, then they will be passed along. Which brings me to the final and most pivotal point of these terms." Whenstone set his gaze on Kaiden and let it linger there a while, conveying the severity of what he was going to say next.

"Odditor and his forces will only move against the Warden Corps – and by extension, the Party – when a viable plan is in place. He has no interest in a prolonged conflict. Rather, if a blow is to be struck, it must be intelligent, precise, and final. His forces will not be mobilized for anything less than complete victory."

Silence followed the terms, but Kaiden knew there was no way they wouldn't accept them. Odditor had an army and they were going to put it to use. His mind reeled with the potential. An attack on Warden HQ wasn't a pipe dream any longer. With this force and Maximus', it might actually be possible. He hadn't run the numbers, would need to discuss with Thorne, but they had to be close in strength, right? Enough to match the forces the Warden Corps kept at their headquarters.

But, with the terms Odditor had laid out, that wasn't enough, was it? He wouldn't mobilize unless victory was assured. What exactly did that mean? They couldn't use his army unless they had an overwhelming advantage? The thought gave Kaiden pause, tempered the joy he'd been feeling at the sudden turn of events. He'd need to discuss with the others, figure out their next step, and what exactly Odditor would need to be convinced to put his army into action.

"This is all great," Titus said, breaking the silence, "but I'm still confused on something." He looked at Odditor quizzically. "If you needed to know that we were committed to taking down the Party, why make Zelda run the labyrinth? I mean, I understand making us ante up, but didn't that already prove our commitment? Why have Zelda still run the labyrinth and risk dying?"

Odditor waited a good long moment to answer, then smiled.

"Because it was, ah... fun."

## Chapter Fifty-One

The humming of the medbay had faded to an almost pleasant drone of white noise. In reality, it was helping Kaiden think – something he very much appreciated, considering how insane everything had been since the revelation of Odditor's support for their cause.

Since then it'd been all grinding and planning, grinding and planning. They had to level up as much as they could and figure out how in the world they were going to take down Warden HQ.

The last quest had been a tough one. Odditor had pointed them to the dilopoad home world and a chain quest there that had been – well, considering all of the dilopoads spat venom, rather messy. The EXP had been good but Kaiden had nearly left the boss fight with a week's vacation. He had taken a direct hit from the monstrous frog creature's Acid Spray and found the regen debuff from the higher level venom simply wouldn't go away. He'd needed to return to the medbay of the *Veritas II* to heal and remove the persistent status effect. The others hadn't waited up, pushing ahead to finish off a side quest.

Instead of questing, Kaiden had originally put forth the idea of grinding against Odditor's menagerie. The man had a seemingly unlimited supply of monsters for them to fight, so it made sense – a sort of miniature version of the Grinder. Kaiden hadn't counted on the fact that Odditor was thoroughly in love with his collection of monsters, so that idea hadn't really gone over well. And there was the minor issue that Zelda had appeared on Odditor's stream, so the Warden Corps was sure to show up at Odditor's base sooner or later looking for her. So, here they were instead, grinding missions in a hopefully backwater-enough sector to avoid notice. Everyone had picked up a few levels, but seeing as they were all above level fifty now it was slow going. The endgame wasn't designed to be rushed through, but time was a luxury they didn't really have.

"Watch your back!" Zelda shouted through comms. Kaiden could hear the sounds of laser fire and the piercing squeal of a dilopoad.

"Got it, thanks," Titus answered back.

Comms made it sound like they were right next to him, but they were actually quite distant, Ellenton having flown them down to the planet's surface and their mission while the *Veritas II* waited in orbit. Kaiden turned the volume down a bit. Not so much that he couldn't hear everyone, but enough that the constant battle callouts wouldn't interrupt his focus.

"All right, then," he said aloud, though he was alone in the room. Just him and the buzzing of the machines healing him back to full. "Let's figure out this puzzle, yeah?"

And puzzle really was the word for it. Warden HQ was a tough egg to crack. Thorne had told them so weeks ago, before they'd set out on this mad adventure, but back then there'd been so much to take care of before making an assault that he'd mentally put off considering how exactly to go about it. Now, though, they'd made enough progress that he was starting to realize just how daunting the task ahead was.

Warden HQ was located on the asteroid Custos, which circled the known universe on a fixed orbit. Not exactly the most realistic orbital mechanics, but in the end, Nova was a game and sometimes the 'Rule of Cool' displaced realism. Cool orbit or not, Custos was the site of Warden HQ and it was fortified as expected, which was to say: exceptionally well.

Thorne had shared 3D renderings of the base with everyone and Kaiden pulled one up now. It hovered in the air in front of him, the image only interrupted when the ring of the medbed passed through it, its white light still healing his wounds.

The heart of Warden HQ – and most of the infrastructure, really – was deep inside of Custos, protected by the rock. He gazed at the projection of the slowly spinning asteroid in front of him, wishing he could see down beneath the surface. Scans of the tunnels there were locked down so tight not even Thorne had access to them, but scans or no, it was safe to say the whole facility had been designed to repel intruders. After all, the heart of Warden HQ was its command center, and next door to it, the control room for the AFBS – their target. Fighting through to that room was going to be costly personnel-wise and take a herculean effort. But he was getting ahead of himself.

Kaiden turned his attention back to Custos' surface, back to what he could see.

Reinforced guard towers were visible first, with machine-gun nests built into them – positioned to provide overlapping fields of fire at any approach to the facility. Then came the armored hangars set into the rock with large anti-air batteries situated around them. While most of the Warden Corps' ships were on patrol at any given time, Thorne had assured everyone that a considerable force was always held in reserve on Custos. Looking closer at the surface, Kaiden could make out bunkers half dug into the ground and littered with gun ports and even some artillery. And at the center of it all, the gate. Though 'gate' wasn't really a proper word for it. It was more an armored wall that, even from the scan, looked so dense Kaiden could hardly believe it was able to move. But Thorne had assured them it did. And that it was the only way down and into Warden HQ.

So, then. Getting into Warden HQ was simple. They just needed a big enough fleet to occupy the Warden Corps' while a large enough ground force fought through the killzone of guard towers, reinforced bunkers, and presumably, an opposing army. Then they needed to blow the gate open, and fight their way through the defender-centric hallways and tunnels of Warden HQ until they made it to the control room for the AFBS.

"So yeah, no big deal," Kaiden said aloud and leaned back with a groan.

*The Warden Corps take their HQ's security seriously. It's almost as if they don't want any interlopers breaking in and hijacking their systems.*

Kaiden dismissed the scan of Custos and instead turned his attention to the documents Whenstone had prepared for them. As it happend, they listed not only Odditor's forces but also an estimate of those Maximus could bring to bear. A conversation with PlayaSlaya would confirm the numbers, Kaiden didn't doubt, but until that happened, he had a feeling Whenstone's information was accurate. He didn't seem the kind to speculate wildly.

According to the notes, Maximus could likely bring a bit over three hundred players to join the assault. Most of those would be max-level players, and even those that weren't would have PVP experience – an invaluable trait in the fight to come.

*So Maximus brings three hundred players, but not the ships to support them. They're largely a ground-based faction,* Kaiden thought, reading further through the notes. *Luckily, that's where Odditor comes in.*

Whenstone had briefly mentioned the sort of firepower Odditor had at his disposal, and it'd been impressive. Seeing the specifics now, though, it was even more impressive.

*One dreadnought fit for combat, twelve heavy cruisers, and twenty light cruisers.* Kaiden gave a low whistle at that. *Good numbers to make up the core of a combat fleet. Good enough to take on the warden carriers that'll no doubt be stationed on Custos.* Thinking back to the *Anakoni* and the forces it'd held, Kaiden knew each warden carrier represented a fearsome amount of force wherever it was stationed. Thorne expected Custos to have three or four of them in orbit around it.

Moving on from the core of Odditor's fleet, Kaiden found the document listed twenty-eight corvettes, thirty-two shuttles, and two hundred and thirty-one 'fighters / interceptors.'

*More ships here because they're smaller, but that doesn't mean they're any less useful. The shuttles can help ferry troops to the ground while the corvettes and fighters keep the battle going overhead.*

But so far these were all war ships, more tuned for combat

than anything. Kaiden ran the math in his head. Odditor's shuttles should be enough to ferry Maximus' troops to the ground, but even still, that was a risky plan. Shuttles were hard to defend and easy to kill. Each one lost before it landed would mean a hit to the total number of ground forces.

*Freighters – fourteen. Now we're talking,* Kaiden thought, a smile creeping across his face as he read further through Whenstone's notes.

The bulk of the troop transport, it looked like, would be handled by freighters. Not exactly quick-moving ships, but when they weren't loaded with cargo they had plenty of room for soldiers. A good thing, considering Maximus' warriors weren't the only ground troops they'd have.

Continuing through the document, Kaiden found specifics on the guilds Odditor ran – all of them secretly – and the forces they could be expected to muster.

**Player Guilds:**

**Explorers' Federation**
**Focus: Exploration**
**PVP-ready members: 35**
**Combat Effectiveness: Low**

**Merchants 'R Us**
**Focus: Freight Hauling**
**PVP-ready members: 14**
**Combat Effectiveness: Low**

**Boyd City Fence Repair**
**Focus: Manual Labor**
**PVP-ready members: 60**
**Combat Effectiveness: Medium**

Kaiden had serious doubts about the legitimacy of that last guild. *Fence repair? That's not even a game mechanic. Odditor's just being clever. 'Boyd City Fences,' more like.* It was no secret Odditor, like most powerful players in the game, dabbled in illicit goods. The profits were too good not to.

Kaiden continued through the document, taking in the guilds Odditor ran. Eight, all told.. Too many for him to oversee personally, no doubt, but it was known he ran them through proxy leaders. Easier to distance himself from them that way. Proxy leaders or not, Whenstone's document claimed they could all be counted on in the fight to come. That put the number of PVP-ready players and NPCs at around six hundred. Just about double that of Maximus, but looking at the focus of Odditor's guilds, they were all more economically oriented That meant they'd be less combat ready than Maximus' warriors, but still, numbers were numbers.

*So, we're looking at around nine hundred PVP-ready players with us.* He stopped to think about that for a minute. *That's actually insane.* When considered next to the approximately two hundred and fifty ships they'd also have with them, plus the *Veritas II* and the *Borrelly,* things were shaping up for them to have a rather nice army.

And still it wasn't enough.

Thorne had estimated Warden Corps forces at Custos would number approximately one thousand five hundred wardens. There were a lot more wardens in Nova than that, but with a game so massive they were often spread thin. And there were other important sites which required guarding. As such, the Corps never stacked too many wardens in any one place at one time – unless there was an emergency.

Of the fifteen hundred expected at Custos, not all of them would be max level, of course. And many of them were prisoners participating in the warden program, so there was a chance they were still fairly new to the game, their loyalty to the Corps far from cemented. The bulk of the wardens would be PVP-ready, though, as that was a core focus of the class. Looking at things from a sheer numbers game, their assault was dead in the water, Kaiden knew.

But sheer numbers weren't the only thing to consider. Time was also a factor.

Once the attack began, the Warden Corps would certainly call for reinforcements. Wardens from all over Nova would flock to Custos. If they were allowed to join the fight, it'd be over. Then there were Moran's thugs to consider. No one had any idea how many of them he'd recruited into Nova, but it was safe to assume warden numbers would be bolstered a least a bit by them, especially in places of power like the HQ. Ellenton's latest report on Dawson's activity had revealed he'd recruited a fair number of free wardens to their side, but would that be enough?

The only boon of the entire plan was that Moran wouldn't know it was coming. The element of surprise meant the warden leader wouldn't be able to amass troops before the fight, but more importantly, that he wouldn't be there himself. Thorne hadn't gone into the specifics of Moran's class, but Kaiden knew the basics. As commander of the Warden Corps Moran was allowed to be a special class: Warden Hierarch. Exactly what abilities that brought with it Kaiden didn't know, and didn't need to know. No part of this plan involved fighting Moran and he intended to keep it that way. In and out before the commander could react.

The whole plan hinged on the idea that neither the Warden Corps nor the Party knew this attack was coming. That was the only way it could succeed. The element of surprise was absolutely essential.

*So, we need more soldiers on our side, but we need to keep things quiet. And as soon as we attack Warden HQ, we'll be on a timer before reinforcements arrive.*

Kaiden felt his jaw clench. All of their efforts up to this point had felt like they were finally making progress. Like they truly had a chance at this thing. But now, sitting down and running the numbers, it wasn't looking good.

At least they didn't need to outnumber the Warden Corps force. Considering the plan was to infiltrate Warden HQ and blast Bernstein's database out to every player through the All-Frequencies Broadcast System, they didn't actually need to 'win' the battle. No, their victory condition came through reaching the system control room. Everything after that didn't matter. They could die in-game. Their forces could be defeated by Warden Corps reinforcements. All that mattered was sending the database out.

*That's something I can work with,* Kaiden thought as his mind began working through the possibilities. *We just need to get to that control room, which means the bulk of our forces are really just there to delay. An elite core of them will need to fight their way into the control room. If we can achieve that, we win.*

So, that was the game plan, obviously. Even before he'd run the numbers just now, everyone had agreed on that. The problem, and the reason he'd decided to run the numbers in the first place, was that their current force was still too small to achieve not even total victory, but just the smaller objective of fighting into the control room. If the Warden Corps fielded fifteen hundred troops in defense of the base Kaiden needed to have at least that number of troops just to hold out long enough to buy him and the others time to make it to the control room.

But they were fresh out of troops. Maximus was on their side, plus a good hundred or so free wardens thanks to Dawson, and now Odditor and his guilds as well. And still that wasn't enough.

So, what, then? Where could they find more support? Kaiden wanted his immediate answer to be The Syndicate, but they'd already said no. Even if PlayaSlaya or Odditor could arrange for him to speak before them again, what good would that do?

The problem remained. What could change the game in their favor?

That was the question he didn't have an answer for. The question no one seemed to have an answer for. Not Zelda, Titus, nor even Thorne.

Kaiden swiped angrily and the projection of Whenstone's document in front of him faded into swirling pixels.

"What about you, old man?" he asked aloud and opened up a copy of Bernstein's database. "You always had an answer." He began flipping through the files in the database, opening some, bypassing others.

But he'd been through all this before. So had Zelda. Together they'd combed every bit of Bernstein's database and all they'd found had been evidence of more crimes, video recordings of Bernstein's occasional ramblings, and in a few places, broken links from where the old man hadn't been able to finish his database.

Except…

Kaiden paused.

*This wasn't here before.*

Where once there had been a broken link, Kaiden now found it led to a new folder. And inside that folder were files he'd never seen before: more evidence of one of the Party's many crimes. Similar to some of the others, but as he read closely, Kaiden was sure – he'd never read this particular case before.

*Why is this here now all of a sudden?*

The thought rooted itself in his mind and he couldn't shake it. It didn't make sense. No one had altered the database.

*Hold up.*

The thought hit him all at once.

*Holy shit. How did I miss this?*

He navigated to the database's main screen and checked its change log. Sure enough, the most recent change was listed as today. A couple files had been added. But who did that?

*I did,* Kaiden realized as he checked his inventory.

Back at Odditor's, he'd scooped up Zelda's account information and the brass padlock representing the piece of the database Bernstein had lost to Odditor. He'd tried to open it – they all had – but it'd been password protected, and with no riddle to even hint at the solution. Zelda had been confident she'd figure it out sooner or later, but looking now, it seemed she didn't have to.

Seeing as Kaiden was trapped in the medbay for healing while the others finished the next quest, he'd grabbed the database from Braker, the NPC they'd entrusted it to, and now that he was looking at the changelog, he could see exactly what had happened.

He'd had Odditor's piece of the database as he'd added the rest of the database to his inventory. From the looks of things, having the two pieces in the same inventory had fused them back together. Kaiden looked closer at the changelog.

**14:09:06 Database detected nearby...**
**14:09:10 Database confirmed nearby.**
**14:09:11 Location check begun...**
**14:09:15 Location confirmed: Veritas II – Bernstein08-owned vessel.**
**14:09:16 Database reconnection begun...**
**14:10:52 Database reconnected. All files updated!**

Apparently, upon being in the same inventory, the two pieces had detected each other. And then... there was some sort of location check? Was that a safeguard Bernstein had built in? Kaiden hadn't even known that was possible in Nova. But as the changelog showed, all files in the database had been updated – including those that had only contained broken links before.

Kaiden gave the database a few commands and the newly completed files came to the forefront of his vision.

**Case file: evidence of corruption.**
**Case file: evidence of abuse of power.**
**Case file: suspected blackmail and abduction.**
**Case file: evidence of unlawful arrest.**

He read through them and they all appeared normal. That was, until he came to the last file in the list.

**Case file: Operation Killswitch**

"Killswitch?" he said aloud. He'd seen the folder before, but it'd never contained any useful information. Now, however, he saw it was flooded with files. He clicked the first one and read about three sentences before opening comms to the others.

"Guys," he said, trying not to panic. "You need to get back here, ASAP."

## Chapter Fifty-Two

"It was, was good you contacted me about this," Odditor said from where he stood with Kaiden and the others. Around them, the elevator hummed as they descended down, down, down into the deep. Down to where Kaiden's hope lay; to where The Syndicate waited, and to where maybe, just maybe, he'd find a chance to save Nova.

"We only found out about this because of the piece of the database you had," Kaiden said. "We had a file on Killswitch, but it was empty. When the database was completed, we learned the awful truth."

Odditor nodded at that. He'd changed since Kaiden's desperate call to him. He was still eccentric, still himself, but at the same time, the airy detachment he'd worn had fallen away. This wasn't a game anymore. The details Kaiden had found on Operation Killswitch had changed everything and even Odditor himself seemed to recognize that.

"The Syndicate will hear you out. I've made sure of it," Odditor said. "But however this goes, I'm already amassing my forces. Whenstone is seeing to it. As for your plan," he looked at Thorne, "it's sloppy and unimaginative."

"Gee, thanks."

"But considering the, the circumstances..." Odditor sighed. "Well, we're going to work with what we have."

The elevator clanked to a stop and the door in front of them slid open. The stale, damp air of the deep-water base flooded Kaiden's digital lungs but he hardly felt it. His mind was on the task ahead. He'd failed here once before, but that was no longer an option. Killswitch had changed everything. The attack on Warden HQ was moving forward immediately, with or without The Syndicate's help.

*There's just the small matter that we're all but doomed to fail without them...*

"Wait in the antechamber," Odditor said, pointing to the room ahead of them. "I'll be in my suite pulling some, some strings." With that, he strode off, quicker than Kaiden had ever seen him move.

Kaiden's nerves only increased as he entered the antechamber. The last time he'd been here he'd fallen on his face. Failed spectacularly.

"Hey, you got this, dude," Titus said, grabbing his shoulders and roughly massaging them like Kaiden was a boxer between rounds of a hard fight. "You're going to kick ass out there."

"You have to," Zelda added unhelpfully.

"I know, I know," he said, more to calm his own nerves than anything.

"Look, it's simple," Thorne said. "This is a threat like we've never faced before. We have to unite or we're all done. That's the bottom line. You'll make them see that."

She was right. That really was all there was to it.

*Titus took down the tournament and won us Maximus' support. Zelda ran the labyrinth and made an ally of Odditor. Now it's my turn. Everything's been leading up to this. So, uh, no pressure, yeah?*

The door at the far end of the antechamber slid open with a slight hiss and all at once Kaiden could see into the great room of The Syndicate once more. The calamitous results of his last experience there rushed over him. The memories swirled in his head and a panic began to rise in him.

*Oh shit. Oh shit. I'm going to mess this up. I'm going to screw up and we're going to be dead in the water. I'm—*

Titus slapped him on the shoulder, hard enough to jar him from his panic.

"Don't overthink it, man." He gave an easy smile that felt wholly inappropriate for the situation.

"He's right," Zelda said, stepping up beside him and leveling her gaze straight into Kaiden's eyes. There was confidence in her look. More confidence than Kaiden felt in his entire body at the moment. She stared at him as if she was going to pour that confidence into him with her look alone.

"Don't overthink it? That's strange advice coming from you," Kaiden said, trying to crack a joke. Zelda nodded stiffly, then broke her intense expression for the slightest of smirks.

"You're not wrong. But it's good advice. Get out of your own head. You know what you need to do." She nodded toward the open door. "So, go out there and do it."

Titus punched a fist into his open hand. "Give 'em hell."

Thorne crossed her arms and smiled. "What he said."

"I appreciate it, guys." Kaiden turned toward the door. "I won't let you down," he said and strode forward.

"We're all charging off to our deaths at Warden HQ soon, so even if you do, at least we won't be around to remind you of it for too long!" Titus called after him, and Kaiden didn't need to look back to know Zelda had given the big man a shove.

Kaiden found himself smiling as he stepped through the door and out into the great room of The Syndicate.

"You're wasting our time, Odditor!" a voice shouted from behind the opaque glass of one of the countless booths that surrounded the room.

"We've heard this rogue warden out before. He's just a delusional kid who thinks he can change the world."

"Get him out of here!"

A chorus of voices shouted down at Kaiden and echoed around the room. Doubts, annoyance, dismissal – it was almost all he could hear.

Almost. But there was something else. A voice inside that told him he couldn't fail. Not now. Not again. Too much was riding on this.

When he'd thought about stepping into the room, Kaiden had been nervous. But after that first step, after Titus' antics and everyone's confidence in him, the nerves had all fallen away. Let The Syndicate shout. Let them doubt. They were going to hear him out, and everything was going to change.

"Imagine the end of Nova Online," Kaiden said aloud. Few people heard him above the shouting, but those who did quieted. He couldn't see them through the glass that fronted each booth, but he could imagine them frowning at his words. He remembered how it'd felt when he'd first learned of Killswitch.

"Imagine a world without Nova," he said, speaking louder this time, and more voices quieted.

"Ridiculous!" someone shouted. "NextGen would never allow it!"

Kaiden opened his inventory and selected Bernstein's database. This was the first time they'd taken it off of the *Veritas II* and risked it in the open. But it was worth it. If they didn't risk it now, it wouldn't matter anyway.

Kaiden accessed the database and navigated to the folder entitled "Operation Killswitch." As he did, he reached out and touched the projector panel in the center of the room. A hologram rose in front of him and all at once his view was projected into the air above, clear for all to see.

"Operation Killswitch," Kaiden said, reading the words that had so recently become the focus of his every thought. The words that had changed everything.

"I'm sure you all remember the database I spoke of the last time I was here. Bernstein's database. Well, until recently, it was incomplete. Thanks to a good friend and ally of ours, Odditor, we have completed it. And discovered the single greatest threat any of us have faced."

There was a chorus of mumbling and sarcastic comments at

that, but less so than before. Maybe the namedrop had bought him some time. Or maybe The Syndicate was starting to listen. Kaiden wouldn't have blamed anyone for not believing him yet, though. He wouldn't have believed it himself it he hadn't seen the evidence. The evidence he pulled up now.

Internal memos stolen from the Party. First, rough ideas discussing the problem of Nova Online and NextGen games. The problem of Nova representing a space the Party couldn't control. A space that could be used for dissent, for rebellion. A place free of Party censorship.

"Since its creation, Nova has been a thorn in the side of the Party. It's lined their pockets, sure, but it's also always concerned them." Kaiden gestured up to the hologram hovering above him as he flipped through more and more memos, meeting minutes, and even a few video call recordings. Each bore official seals, timestamps, and were sealed with authentication certificates and once-secure but now cracked Party encryption algorithms.

"This is old news!" someone heckled.

"You're right," Kaiden said, turning toward the voice. "We all knew this. It's what led directly to the creation of the warden program and players like – well, like myself." He placed a hand on his chest. "But what if I told you the Party didn't stop there?"

"NextGen has held the Party at bay since day one," someone shouted and several other voices rose in agreement. "This is a non-issue. The Party has no power here."

Kaiden's only response was to flip through the Killswitch folder to a specific document, open it, and begin reading the text therein.

"'The game Nova Online, as overseen by the NextGen Games corporation, is a potential breeding ground for ideological dissidence. Such a space, if not brought under the rule of law, could serve as an echo chamber to encourage dangerous and violent actions. It is therefore the opinion of this council that a plan should be conceived to render such action impossible. Nova Online must become a completely Party-controlled space.'" Kaiden let that hang in the air a moment. Admittedly, it was nothing particularly surprising. Everyone knew the Party's distaste for Nova. It was what came next that was the bombshell.

"'On the authority of this council, and in the interest of the well-being of society, it is hereby ordered that Commander Moran will develop and oversee Operation Killswitch, which can be enacted to subdue Nova Online should the threat grow out of hand. Given the large revenue streams generated by the game, this will be an option of last resort. However, should the game or any of its players serve as a clear and immediate threat to the interests of this Party, military force is authorized to whatever extent is deemed necessary for the total and complete subjugation of NextGen and their creation Nova Online. Or, in the case that this is not possible, the termination of the game.'" Kaiden paused to catch his breath, then looked up from the document he'd been reading and out to the shadowy members of The Syndicate gathered around him.

Silence dominated the room.

*I have their attention now.*

"We know the Party doesn't like the freedom we enjoy in Nova. We've also known there isn't much they can do about it. There's the Warden Corps, sure, but they can only do so much. And thanks to NextGen, Nova has remained a safe space. Largely free from Party influence. Largely free from the mess they've made of the real world. But Operation Killswitch stands to change all of that."

Kaiden flipped through several documents again, focusing on them so the projection above would show them to the room.

"I will make these documents available to all of you. You are welcome to go through them for yourself, but let me summarize them for you.

"Operation Killswitch consists of three parts. Part one, the Party takes the internet offline for a few days. An unfortunate grid failure, they'll bill it as. Part two, military forces will storm NextGen HQ and forcibly take control of Nova Online. With the internet down, word might not get out for some time. Or maybe it will, but it won't matter, because by the time it does, the Party will control NextGen's servers. They'll turn them off, or maybe even destroy them. They'll rip the heart out of Nova, and in an instant, all data, all backups – everything – will be gone. We'll lose all of this." He spread his arms out to encompass the room. But not just the room, he hoped they realized. So much more. Every planet. Every player. All of Nova. "The international fallout will be massive, but the Party is desperate."

Kaiden took a deep breath.

"The last time I was here, I appealed to your sense of humanity. To your concern for the goings on of the world beyond Nova. But you weren't interested in that. You thought you were safe in here, in Nova. And you were right. Until now. These documents on Killswitch aren't new. The Party's been developing this plan for months now, which means if everything isn't already in place, it soon will be. The only reason they haven't initiated Killswitch yet is because they've been seeking a quieter solution. Taking Nova offline would represent a major financial loss to the Party, as they wouldn't be able to tax the in-game economy as they've done for so long. But when we make a move on Warden HQ, we'll be forcing the Party's hand. They'll begin Killswitch in response, and at that point, there'll be no turning back. We'll have eighty minutes before they can take the internet offline. And if they do that, it's all over. Nova as we know it will be dead."

Kaiden gestured to the projection above him, to the details of Killswitch laid out bare for all to see.

"I've vetted all of this information with Thorne, a former captain of the Warden Corps. Everything outlined in Killswitch is actionable."

Kaiden took a step forward and made a point of looking around the room, taking his time and letting his eyes slide from one booth to the next.

"The Party already controls everything else. Nova is our last escape. Our last gasp at a life not monitored and controlled by oligarchs. And now, even that is on the brink of destruction." Kaiden focused his thoughts and steadied his voice. "The plan I proposed last time is still in effect and our attack is set to begin.

We are not yet ready – my friends and I aren't even max level – but we cannot wait. If we do it may be too late. We're taking a stand to stop the Party. To save Nova. But we can't do it alone. We need your support."

Kaiden spread his arms out to the entire room and gave the next words everything he had.

"We're now fighting for the very life of Nova Online. Will you help us?"

Silence. And more silence. Silence for so long Kaiden began to feel ridiculous. And to realize that he'd failed. He'd given it his all and he'd come up short.

And then, a noise.

A light hiss and the opaque glass front of the nearest booth retracted. Odditor stepped out and walked across the floor to join Kaiden. In the middle of the vast room he looked small, but his stride was confident and his back was straight. He gave several booths hard stares as he approached. The shadowy figures in them seemed to shift in their seats.

"Nova is my home. My livelihood. It's where… where I keep my pets. I'm with you." Odditor came to a stop beside Kaiden.

The booths Odditor had eyed hissed open and several figures Kaiden didn't recognize stepped cautiously out.

Another hiss and another booth opened. PlayaSlaya emerged and joined them in the center of the room.

"You know I'm in," he said and cracked his knuckles. "No way Maximus is missing out on the fight of a lifetime. Let's kick some Party ass!"

Nando came next and gave Kaiden a slight but sharp nod.

"Let's make this count, huh?" he said. "Make a difference. One for the better this time."

A few more booths opened in response to the Maximus leadership showing their support. The group at the center of the room was, impossibly, growing.

*They're… they're with us,* Kaiden thought, seeing it but still having trouble believing it.

And then, one by one, the other booths opened and more and

more players emerged until the entire room seemed a flood of motion and bodies.

They gathered at the center of the room as one. There was no shouting, no exclamations, no cheers. But Kaiden had his answer.

The Syndicate was with them.

## Chapter Fifty-Three

With The Syndicate behind them, there was nothing more to do except assemble the biggest army possible, fine-tune the battle plan, then hit the Warden Corps with every single thing they had.

Maximus brought the elite fighters. Odditor brought the ships, the manpower of the guilds he led, and, of course, his menagerie of monsters. The Syndicate brought the rest, which was to say, all of the above and then some. Even with their full backing behind the endeavor, few members of The Syndicate actually turned up to fight themselves. Instead they sent ships and soldiers and a good legion or two of loyal NPCs. A hodge-podge army that, if Kaiden was being honest with himself, actually seemed to have a pretty good chance of pulling this whole thing off.

It'd taken two days to assemble all of the forces at – or more appropriately, above – The Syndicate's base on Aqukinho. With everything else in order, the wait was unbearable, but Thorne had suggested they grind as much as possible during that time. It was a welcome relief from nitpicking the battle plan over and over again, and in the end had paid dividends beyond just giving Kaiden's mind a much-needed distraction. He and Zelda had picked up two levels, putting them both at fifty-two, while thanks to his extra EXP from his heroics in the arena, Titus was almost even with Thorne. They'd also gained two levels each and were painfully close to fifty-three. No new abilities for anyone, but a search online revealed those would come with the next level. Kaiden had half a mind to push through and get the remaining EXP needed, but when it was a choice between that and delaying the now assembled fleet, well, that was a tough call. Every moment spent waiting was another moment the Warden Corps might notice the massive fleet – even if it was assembling in a backwater corner of the galaxy.

No; the element of surprise was more important than a few new abilities. The attack had to move forward.

"Thank you, Braker," Kaiden said. He'd taken the database back from the NPC several days ago – right before he'd discovered Killswitch – but he'd never properly thanked the mechanic. Technically he was an NPC and thus not sentient, but on the eve of such a monumental battle, Kaiden found himself feeling sentimental. He smiled and patted Braker on the shoulder. "You did a good job holding on to this for so long."

The mechanic gave a quick nod.

"Got a ship needs fixin', I'm your man."

"If we get through this alive, we'll promote you to head mechanic!" Titus said with a smile as he slapped the NPC on the back.

Braker gave another quick nod, indistinguishable from the first one.

"Ship's running just fine, Captain."

"All right, enough doting," Acton said. "Back to work." He snapped his fingers and shooed the mechanic from the cockpit. When Braker was gone, Acton returned to his co-pilot seat.

"Give them too much praise and they'll get big heads," he grumbled.

"Zelda," Kaiden said, turning to her and holding out the database. "Keep it safe. Though I know I don't need to tell you that."

She took it carefully in hand.

"It's the key to the whole plan," she said and looked down to the open padlock. She added it to her inventory, and the small thing – on which so much hinged – disappeared from sight. Zelda looked up to everyone around her on the bridge of the *Veritas II*. "I know you'll do your best to keep me alive, but if I go down, you loot me. Instantly. Custos is a PVP zone and we can't lose the database. It's more important than any of us."

"The database, your hammer-rifle, anything else of value you have on you. Couldn't pass up profit like that, after all," Titus said with a wink.

Kaiden knew he was joking but he punched the big man in the shoulder anyway. Though perhaps a bit harder than he'd intended.

*I'm on edge,* he realized. There was no pain in Nova, but even so, Kaiden could feel how tense he was. Every bit of him was coiled as if ready to spring into motion. But he wouldn't be doing that on the bridge of the *Veritas II*. Even if they were hurtling toward the coming fight as fast as their engines could carry them.

*Take a breath. We got this. We're as prepared as we can be.* He forced himself to take several deep breaths.

Somehow during all of the grinding they'd found time to send Acton and the *Veritas II* off to the nearest turen space station to purchase new upgrades. Defense drones had been the bulk of the purchase and they weren't even for the *Veritas II*, but for the *Borrelly*. Kaiden pulled up their information for one last review before things got crazy.

**Mk. 5 Proximity Defense Drone Launchers**
**Rarity: Rare**
**Durability: 100%**
**Capacity: 10 drones**

**Quick facts: With the push of a button these launchers will deploy autonomous defense drones around the perimeter of your ship. When active, these drones will engage any incoming hostile objects including missiles, torpedoes, and enemy ships.**

They'd loaded the drones with explosive ballistic rounds so they'd have a better chance at bringing down missiles and torpedoes in particular.

The second upgrade had also been for the *Borrelly* – a multifacing shield generator. Normally a ship had one health pool shared between all of its surface. This upgrade changed that.

**All Stop 6 Face Shield Generator**
**Rarity: Very Rare**
**Durability: 100%**
**+5 shield faces (individual overlapping shield generators**
**each protecting a specific part of the ship independently)**
**-30% capacity per shield face**

**Quick facts: Six faces are better than one. For the fast,**
**maneuverable ship on the go, this six-faced shield generator**
**allows clever piloting to extend the life of a ship's shields.**

If anyone was going to make use of clever piloting, Kaiden knew it'd be Ellenton. She'd be ecstatic at the purchase.

For the next upgrade Zelda had wanted another shield generator, but the *Veritas II* didn't have a strong enough core to support it. They needed a new one and there wasn't a shipyard close enough to get one. Thus, they'd settled on additional armor instead.

**Cetacean Hull Armor, Orca Class**
**Rarity: Uncommon**
**Durability: 100%**
**+10% ballistic resistance**
**+10% debris resistance**
**+20% explosive resistance**
**-10% speed**
**+15% radar signature**

Armor was similar to a shield, but it slowed them a bit and made them easier to spot on radar. All the same, though, the ship had good engines, so the speed debuff wouldn't be crippling, and it was well worth it when considered against the battle they were heading for.

And what was armor without offense? Their turrets had done a fine job so far, but an upgrade never hurt. Acton had insisted they change their turrets from the two-barrel variety to something a bit punchier.

**AP-EX Four-Barrel Slugshot Turret**
**Rarity: Uncommon**
**Durability: 100%**
**0-second charge time.**
**-10% damage to shielded targets**
**-20% fire rate**
**+60% damage to unshielded targets**
**+65% damage to critical components**
**+65% damage to crew**

**Quick facts: Forgoing the rapid-fire approach of many of its competitors, the AP-EX Four-Barrel Slugshot Turret fires armor-piercing, high-explosive rounds. Designed to penetrate enemy hulls, then explode on a timed fuse, these rounds specialize in damaging critical components and eliminating enemy crew.**

Lastly, they'd restocked on the munitions that had served them so well up until now. Particularly the torpedoes.

**Mk. 2 'Tumbler' Torpedo**
**Rarity: Uncommon**
**Durability: 100%**
**5-second lock-on required**
**+80% projective speed**
**+250% damage to shields and hulls**

**Quick facts: Once locked on to a target, the Mk. 2 'Tumbler' Torpedo rarely misses. Upon striking a target, the**

missile is designed to flip end over end and 'tumble' through shields and hulls alike, opening massive holes in each.

With upgrades and munitions covered, there'd just been the crew to think about. They were in peak condition as well; for the first time, there'd been enough credits to please Acton and hire actual turret gunners. Crewmen that'd be incredibly useful considering they were about to fly into what Dawson liked to refer to as a 'target-rich environment.' *Makes it easier to shoot the enemy when you're completely surrounded by them, right?*

Zelda had also loaded up as much as they could on boarding crew. Thanks to their soaring prestige with the Turen Geniocracy, turen marksmen were the best crew to hire for the cost.

Finally, in addition to the barracks now being fully stocked with crew, the pilot, Sias, had tiered up from all the grinding of the past week.

**Sias (Turen Pilot) – Journeyman, tier 5**
**+26% Dodge Chance**
**+10% Mobility**
**+5% Speed**

The tiering up had improved several stats, but mainly his ability to increase the ship's dodge chance. A good thing, too, considering there was about to be a whole lot of explosives to dodge, and soon.

The *Veritas II* was as prepared as it'd even been. Well equipped, well crewed, and in perfect condition. Despite all of that, Kaiden was still worried.

"You okay there?" Thorne asked, looking up from where she'd been leaning against a window. "Sounds like you're about to hyperventilate."

"Just... nerves," he said.

"I get it," she said with a shrug. "Big day ahead. And an even bigger battle. I mean, everything we've done before has been leading up to this. We have a chance to change the world." She said the words but her expression didn't match the gravity of them. If anything, she looked... relaxed?

"The secret to this sort of thing," she said, speaking to everyone now, "is just to relax. *Breathe.* Get out of your own heads." She tapped a finger to her temple. "The plan's in place." She nodded out to the ships in formation around them. "The army's assembled. " She gestured to the group of them. "And we're as prepared as we're going to be. I mean, a few more levels would be nice, but otherwise we're kitted up, finally restocked on stimpacks, and, if I'm being honest, there isn't a worthier group of troublemakers I'd rather be fighting beside today." She said the last part with a slight smile. Didn't make the nerves go away, but at least for a moment, they weren't at the forefront of his mind.

"Yeah, yeah, enough touchy-feely crap," Ellenton said from where she was leaning in the hallway leading out to the main compartment of the ship. "We've got some Party ass to kick before that begins."

"The lieutenant's right," a voice said and Kaiden couldn't help but smile even wider as Dawson appeared beside Ellenton. He'd joined them earlier while the army had been assembling, and Kaiden couldn't deny it felt good to have him on board.

"Not a lieutenant anymore," Ellenton reminded him. "I'm a free warden. Gone freelance, I guess," she said with a half frown.

"Good riddance," Zelda said. "It was just a tool of the Party anyway."

"The Warden Corps' not what it once was, there's no denying that," Dawson said. "I've turned a good number of free wardens to our cause. They're proof that the Corps isn't all bad. They produced some fine recruits. Luckily, being on the outside, they can also see how rotten it's gotten."

"What's the final count on them?" Kaiden asked.

"Hard to say for certain," Dawson said with a grunt. "Some who said they are with us may decide otherwise when the moment comes. And some who said they aren't, well, they may just find they're stronger than they think they are. We've one hundred and eighteen free wardens with the landing ships right now, though. Might be we can expect more on the way."

"Good," Kaiden said with a nod. "I'm thinking they're going to be the core of our force. Front and center on the battlefield."

"They'll prove their worth, wherever they're placed," Dawson said with no lack of confidence. He'd been so busy out of game that he hadn't had much time to grind. He'd managed to work his way up to level forty-two, which was impressive given the circumstances, but would hardly be enough once the fighting began. Still, the former sergeant had refused any discussion of not joining the attack. He was coming, and that, it seemed, was that. Admittedly, Kaiden would be glad to have him.

"Once we're spotted, there'll be no turning back," Kaiden said, as if anyone needed a reminder. "It won't take long for the Warden Corps to report our presence to the Party, and after that, Moran will start putting the pieces together. We might have gotten the jump on him in this battle, but he still has the off-button."

"Killswitch," Titus said with a grim nod.

"Eighty minutes," Zelda added. She did something on her UI and a timer appeared at the top of Kaiden's screen and no doubt everyone else's too.

"This is all the time we'll have. And not just to broadcast the message and database, but for the players to download it," Zelda continued. "So, we need to broadcast the database *before* this timer runs out. The actual download won't take long per player, but they'll each need time to decide to download it. As much time as we can give them."

"Right," Kaiden said. "If we're going to change anything, enough players need to have the database that the Party can't stop its spread. Once people realize what's on it, they'll share it. We just need to give them the power to do so."

Thorne chuckled at that.

"I love this plan," she said. "Wish I could see Moran's face when he realizes. I'm almost a bit sad the whole thing will be finished before he has a chance to get here."

"Attention SS *Andronicus!*" a voice rang out from the speakers on the dashboard. "This is the WCSS *Rimrock*. You are approaching restricted space."

Kaiden looked out through the windshield to see two Warden Corps light cruisers in front of them. They were still small, but growing larger by the moment as the *Veritas II* hurtled toward the airspace around Custos and Warden HQ.

"S.S. *Andronicus!* Change your course and—" The voice cut off suddenly.

"Looks like they just spotted the rest of the fleet," Acton said with just the slightest hint of a smile.

Kaiden looked out of the cockpit toward the port side of the ship, where half the fleet was formed up around them. Counting their number was near impossible, but that was what the command module was for.

Kaiden swallowed hard as he accessed it. It was just a program routed through his visor, but it came with a responsibility he wasn't sure he was ready for – command of the combined forces. He was leader of the group that put this plan together, so it followed he'd be leader of the whole thing. Or that had been PlayaSlaya's logic, at least. But there was no disputing it now. The others had mostly agreed, and it was done. The full force of the amassed army had been combined into one big group, and as far as Nova was concerned, Kaiden had been granted command status.

The command module opened up and Kaiden's visor was populated with details of the forces under his command.

To the port side of the *Veritas II* were some three hundred ships; the bulk of Odditor's forces. Most of those were fighters, but there was a core of light and heavy cruisers, corvettes, and the all-important freighters that would facilitate the ground assault.

To the starboard side were the combined ships from the rest of The Syndicate. The fact that Odditor rivaled their numbers on his own was impressive. Now, however, both sides were working in tandem. Some six hundred ships in total and more than twice that number in ground troops. Almost enough to match the Warden Corps forces they expected to encounter on the ground, and more than enough to take care of the two patrol vessels in front of them now.

The amount of fire that poured out toward the two unfortunate vessels painted the abyss of space bright as day, if only for a moment, before both ships' shields failed and their cores detonated. Nothing could stand up to that much firepower for more than a few seconds.

**Light cruiser destroyed – 0 EXP gained!**
**Light cruiser destroyed – 0 EXP gained!**

**-40 faction prestige with the Warden Corps**

Kaiden saw the notifications only because of the command module. He didn't receive any EXP because neither he nor his direct group of Titus, Zelda, Thorne, Ellenton, and Dawson had taken part in the brief fight. The whole army was really a collection of groups, all falling under the umbrella of Kaiden's command, but when it came to assisted kill experience, each group received its own based on their actions. The faction prestige, however, was a different matter. As commander of the army, Kaiden was directly responsible for their actions. He'd be surprised if his Warden Corps prestige didn't sink into the negative four digits before the day was out.

Kaiden went ahead and muted the assisted kill notifications from all the groups except his own. No need to have them cluttering up his notification feed. There'd be enough from just his little slice of the battle, he was sure.

The *Veritas II*'s shields lit up briefly as a few pieces of debris from the destroyed warden vessels whipped past.

"So, that's it then," Zelda said, staring straight ahead. At the top of Kaiden's vision, the countdown timer began, and in the distance he could just make out a vaguely circular object. An asteroid, he knew. Custos. Home of Warden Corps HQ and the place where the fate of Nova – and the Party – would be determined.

"They know we're coming now," Zelda said then walked over

to the control panel beside the pilot. She pulled up a menu and clicked a few times. A moment later a message flashed across the screen.

**Transponder deactivated.**

"No point in hiding anymore," she said. "We might as well fly true. Fly under the name Bernstein gave this ship."

"*Veritas II*," Kaiden said. "You know, I've never asked what it means."

"It's Latin," Zelda said. "And the name of the Roman goddess of truth."

Kaiden nodded at that. *A good name. Bernstein chose well – as usual.*

"Yeah, yeah. Dead languages and fallen empires are fine, but the *Borrelly's* named after a comet and that's way cooler," Ellenton said. "Now load up. We got some Warden Corps ass to kick."

# Chapter Fifty-Four



*Seventy-eight minutes and counting…*

Thorne couldn't stop her eyes from flicking up to the timer every few moments. It was strange to have everything laid out so… simply. But there it was. Seventy-eight minutes, or thereabouts, until Nova was offline. Assuming the Party had initiated Killswitch, which they no doubt had. Moran was probably screaming at someone about it now.

She smiled at that thought.

*Today's going to be a day you'll never forget, Moran.* If they were successful – if the database got out to the masses and spread like they expected – then Moran was certain to face much worse days than this one. But in the back of his mind, Thorne knew Moran would always think back to this day. Back to the catalyst that set everything in motion.

An explosion shook the shuttle and then everything was moving. Thorne flew through the cabin and face-planted into the wall, taking two percent fall damage.

"Told you to strap in back there!" Ellenton shouted over her shoulder from the cockpit.

Thorne looked back to the strap she'd been holding on to. In any other shuttle that would have been fine, but not with Ellenton at the helm.

She growled a curse up toward the cockpit then crawled to a jump seat beside Zelda and strapped herself in.

"I can't hear you over the sound of me keeping us all alive right now," Ellenton said, then there was an explosion outside and the game simulated all of the blood in Thorne's body rushing into her head at once as they pulled another high-g maneuver.

They must have been drawing closer to the asteroid because Nova's location announcement triggered in Thorne's vision.

*Well, that's one way to put it,* Thorne thought as a flight of fighters whipped by outside the windows, weaponry ablaze. One of the rear ships took a direct hit from one of the massive cruisers above and was vaporized instantly.

"Why are there so many of them?" Kaiden shouted, his face glued to the window beside his seat, watching the chaos without. It was a good question. Thorne peered out her own window, careful not to get too close lest another quick maneuver faceplant her into the glass.

The Warden Corps never kept more than two hundred ships at Custos at once, and most of those were fighters and shuttles. And yet here stood a fleet of five hundred, plus two additional carriers, to meet them. Except it wasn't standing; it was swarming. Roaring. Blasting away with everything it had.

A common critique of Nova was that the ship combat was unbalanced compared to individual player combat. When two players went at it, they ducked and dodged, hacked and slashed, and tore each other apart with abilities. When two ships fought it was a similar experience, just without the abilities. When a ship fought a player, though, it was wholly unbalanced. Some complained about this. Thorne just figured it made sense. That didn't make her feel any better, though, as she watched the landing shuttle next to them explode in a plume of blue flame, killing all onboard. Eight or so soldiers plus pilot – gone, just like that. The debris spun away in the direction of Custos, caught in the asteroid's limited gravity and pulled down to its surface.

As she looked down, she couldn't help but notice the

defenses on the ground. Anti-air turrets sprayed upward, their lasers coloring the darkness with lethal streaks of light. Among the guns she could make out bunkers, guard towers, and the massive reinforced gate that led down and into Warden HQ. Everything was just as it'd been when she'd seen it last. At least down there things seemed normal. Was there a chance the unusually large fleet above the asteroid had just lucked out? Happened to be stopping by when the attack had begun?

The *Borrelly's* shields lit up a brilliant blue as one shot made contact.

**Shield integrity: 96%**

Thorne near swallowed her own tongue as Ellenton rolled them to the side in a seemingly endless spin.

"I think the Corps got lucky," Thorne said, answering Kaiden's question from earlier. "I've never seen this many ships here before. We must have caught them during a shift change. Old patrol ships rotating out, new ones rotating in. Sometimes there's a period of overlap." *Though it's never more than a day or so long.* "Really bad luck on our part. I should have kept note of the schedule, but never thought I'd be breaking in to HQ..."

"Whatever the reason, it's bad news for us—" Titus' words cut off in a clenched-teeth groan as the shuttle rolled and shook again.

"It doesn't matter," Dawson shouted, seemingly unaffected by the chaos around him as always. Tough as nails, that man. "The fight in the sky is a distraction. All it has to do is give our landing forces cover. Might mean we get a few less troops on the ground, though. The number that ends up making it inside is going to be lower than expected."

"Hopefully everyone else is having an easier time of it than us." Zelda's face was scrunched up, her teeth gritted against Ellenton's high-g maneuvers.

"Everyone hold tight!" Ellenton shouted from up in the cockpit.

"What do you think we've been doing?" Thorne shouted

back. *No wonder Sola refuses to ever fly with this maniac again.* Something flashed up near the cockpit and Thorne spun to see a flight of fighters in formation and headed right for them.

"Ellenton!" Thorne shouted, but the woman seemed undeterred. She continued straight toward the fighters. They'd be in firing range any second now and they were decidedly outgunned.

"Ellenton!" Thorne shouted again, louder this time.

"I got this," she snapped back, then hit a button on the dash. The drone launchers that'd been fitted to the sides of the *Borrelly* clanked and clacked into motion. Through the window, Thorne saw several mechanical balls launch outward, then light up as their thrusters came online.

The drones were roughly spherical, but then they unfolded to reveal thrusters pointing in all directions, along with four Gatling guns mounted on their fronts. The drones hovered around the *Borrelly* in a tight formation, then reacted as one and opened fire on the approaching fighters.

Flashes of light were bursting from the wingtips and beneath the noses of the fighters now and Thorne realized they were firing back as the *Borrelly's* shields sprang to life.

**Front Shield Integrity: 90%**
**Front Shield Integrity: 83%**
**Front Shield Integrity: 71%**

"We can't take much more—" Thorne began to yell when Ellenton flipped a switch on the controls, decoupling the ship, and spun them hard to the side. They maintained their forward momentum but spun sideways. The shuttle's front shields were saved from the barrage of fire as the comparatively fresh port-side shields absorbed the shots.

**Port Shield Integrity: 90%**
**Port Shield Integrity: 86%**

And then the fighters were past, zipping by so quickly Thorne could hardly see them. She whipped her head around, looking across the cabin and out the starboard windows to see them turning around for another pass.

Then all at once a barrage of laser fire cut through them from above. Most of the fighters detonated instantly. Those that didn't tumbled out of control, trailing smoke and flame. A light cruiser blasted through the wreckage and pulled up behind them.

The *Veritas II!* Thorne recognized the ship.

There was a problem, though. All the fighters were gone, but as Thorne squinted, she could just make out five pinpoints of light blasting toward the *Borrelly*.

"Missiles!" she shouted. One of the fighters must have fired them before being shot down.

"Our drones will get them," Ellenton said from up front. "Probably."

They did, spinning as one and firing at the oncoming missiles. They went up in blasts of fire and smoke, none of them even getting close enough to threaten the shuttle.

"Man, my baby is even more ridiculously awesome now," Ellenton said from up front. "We'd have been fine even without Acton butting in."

As she said it, his voice come over the comms. "Escort the freighters, I know, I know," he said. "Those were my orders. But those fighters looked troublesome. And if you lot go down, this whole endeavor goes belly up." The turrets on the outside of the *Veritas II* were alive with blazing lasers, streaming in long lines after any targets that drew near.

"You can't take a cruiser down into this anti-air fire," Ellenton said back. "You'll get shredded."

"Takes their eyes off you though, no?"

"Acton!" Kaiden shouted, leaning forward in his jump seat. "You're not allowed to get shot down on our account." He paused. "But good thinking. The second we're below the anti-air fire you get back out of their range."

"Aye, sir."

Ellenton corrected their orientation, getting the nose pointed back toward the landing zone Thorne had designated from orbit – as close as they could get to the gate without having all the landing shuttles and freighters torn apart by defensive fire. Some would still go down, but most would make it. Or that was the plan, at least.

The lights in the *Borrelly* were flashing red now, indicating hull integrity had taken some damage. Some of the hailstorm of lasers and ballistics flying around outside must have found their way through the already over-taxed shields. Ellenton seemed unconcerned though, hurling them toward the ground. Enemy vessels slid in front of her guns but she never fired.

*Saving all power for the shields and engines. She's getting us on the ground first and foremost,* Thorne knew. *Then she's gonna tear a swath of wreckage and rubble through this sky.*

Blue light flared behind them and Thorne turned to see the shields of the *Veritas II* working overtime.

*The anti-air guns are targeting them.*

The cruiser took a beating, but it did its job. Only a few pieces were blasted off in the process.

"Godspeed, Captains," Acton said and Thorne could swear she saw him salute from the cockpit before the *Veritas II* turned hard and hit the afterburners. The anti-air fire followed it, but the ship's rear shields were fresh and did a good job keeping it mostly together on the retreat. Most ships didn't have separate health pools for each shield face – it was a top-tier upgrade. Thorne had made a considerable credit contribution to Acton and Ellenton, which they'd used to upgrade the *Veritas II* and the *Borrelly* with the best modifications on the market.

As the *Veritas II* shrunk away to nothing but the glowing light of engines, Thorne focused her attention back to their present situation inside the *Borrelly*.

There were a few sparks spitting from the ceiling and wall panels as Ellenton guided them below the firing arcs of the anti-air guns and slammed on the brakes. The retro-thrusters blasted to life outside the cockpit glass and Thorne felt her body doing its best to phase through her seat belt as the *Borrelly* went from stupidly fast to basically still in two seconds.

"Looks like this is your stop," Ellenton said from the cockpit, but the rear ramp was whirring down and everyone was already in motion, ripping off seat belts and jumping to their feet. Thorne wormed out of her own harness, grabbed her hammer, and sprinted toward the ramp.

"Remember to give your driver a good rating!" Ellenton shouted after them.

Thorne paused for just a moment at the start of the ramp. The pock-marked, crater-filled surface of Custos was a pace away but she turned back toward her fellow former warden in the cockpit.

"Good flying, Lieutenant," she said. "Now get up there and give 'em hell."

Turning around in her seat, Ellenton broke into a broad smile, then saluted.

"With pleasure, Captain."

Thorne leapt down to the surface. The *Borrelly* was gone before she landed. It arced up into the sky, drawing a hail of anti-air fire as it climbed. In moments Thorne had lost sight of it, unable to tell it apart from the thousand other streaking lines of light above. Was the *Anakoni* up there among them? She didn't know, and all at once she realized she didn't care.

"All right, then," Thorne said to herself as she brought her eyes down to the battleground around her. "Let's do this."

## Chapter Fifty-Five

*Seventy-two minutes and counting…*

Kaiden reached the cover of a small crater, threw himself down and out of the line of fire, and took a half second to glance up at the timer.

*Eight minutes?* Their hellacious descent to the surface had only been eight minutes long? It'd felt like half an hour, at least. But that was the past. Ellenton had gotten them down safely. That was objective one achieved. *On to the next, then.*

Kaiden raised his eyes to the reinforced gate that led down into Warden HQ. It wasn't more than three hundred yards away, but looking at it now, he couldn't help but feel daunted by everything that stood between them and it.

Chaos. Everywhere he looked. All around him the largest battle in Nova's history was playing out. Shuttles were landing anywhere they could find an open scrap of ground, their rear ramps dropping so the troops inside could pour out. And then came the freighters. Most were shot basically to pieces by the time they touched down, but they were getting the job done. By design, the anti-air turrets in Nova had a floor beneath which they couldn't shoot. Once the landing ships dropped below that altitude they were safe – from the anti-air, at least.

Kaiden ducked behind his shield as a Warden Corps corvette

managed to pull free from the fight above – one of the few that was able to thanks to the ferocity of the fighting. The plan was to use their ships to keep the warden fleet engaged so the ground forces were free to focus on the HQ's surface defenders. But occasionally a smaller vessel would break through to harry them briefly from above. This one came in low, weaponry blazing as it aimed to pick off a landed freighter. Return fire from the ground shredded the corvette's shields, but its own guns got the job done anyway. The landed freighter collapsed inwards as the hull was breached. Players and NPCs fled from the ship and moments later its core detonated, killing any left on board and many of those who'd been fleeing. The blast was big enough that even a hundred or more paces away Kaiden felt the concussion deep in his chest. His ears rang with the roar of the dying vessel and lights flashed in his eyes long after the ship was reduced to smoldering rubble.

Kaiden flicked open the command module to get a better grip on everything around him. Most of their forces were landed and more were coming by the moment. The module showed the current battlefield as a hologram, projected onto his vision. Wherever it could, it overlaid data over the real-time visuals he was seeing.

"Soon as they're on the ground, make sure your troops get to cover!" Kaiden said into the comm channel that'd been created for the commanders of the combined force.

"Will pass it along."

"Understood."

"Like we discussed."

A half-dozen or so voices replied. Some, like Odditor and PlayaSlaya, Kaiden knew. Others he considered friends, like Nando, Dawson, and Ellenton. The rest, he didn't personally know. But it was hard to know every commander in a force of a couple thousand. Especially with how quickly it'd been assembled.

"My uh, group leaders have been, have been notified," Odditor's voice replied next. "Ooh, that's a big one there," he said, sounding suddenly excited and distracted. His voice was more distant now, as if he was talking away from the mic. "Let's see if she's as tough as she looks..."

High above there was a resounding explosion as the guns of the *Veritas* – formerly Bernstein's and now Odditor's dreadnought – presumably tore into an opposing vessel.

"Maximus warriors know what to do. They don't need your commands." PlayaSlaya's voice came last. Sounded almost offended at the suggestion "This ain't their first landing under fire."

It took Kaiden a moment to realize the guild leader hadn't spoken through the comms channel, but out loud. Kaiden pulled his eyes from the raging battle to find PlayaSlaya next to him, face set in a grin. Looked for all the world like he was enjoying himself, huddled down in a crater as anything and everything exploded around them.

Burning soil rained down, hissing and thunking as it hit the ground, and PlayaSlaya only smiled wider.

*I guess this is sort of his thing...*

PlayaSlaya was wearing different armor than the last time Kaiden had seen him.

**Nihilist's Rage Powersuit, Warlord edition**

It was all spikes and painted metal and interlocking plates that moved with surprising fluidity. Some sort of end-game gear, Kaiden didn't doubt, but he didn't have time at the moment to pay much attention to it.

Nando was beside PlayaSlaya, as always. The familiar face was a welcome sight amidst the chaos unfurling around them. Maybe he'd always been a bit blunt, but if their heart to heart back on Kyraxis had proven anything it was that Nando had his reasons for being here. He harbored no love for the Party and he was committed to bringing it down.

"You ready to do this?" Nando asked.

"Can't really back out now," Kaiden said.

"No, I guess not." Nando chuckled. "Let's take these bastards down."

Kaiden agreed with a nod and turned to evaluate the situation around him.

PlayaSlaya and Nando, along with five of their elite guild members, had come down on their own landing ship. They'd made their way over to link up with Kaiden and the others, aka the 'bomb team.' Classic first-person shooters had always had a game mode where one team had to break through the enemy's defense and plant a bomb at a specific location. This was sort of like that, except the bomb they were carrying was the database – and it was going to do a whole lot more damage than just an explosion.

The *Borrelly* had brought the rest of the bomb team down to the surface: Kaiden, Zelda, Titus, Thorne, Dawson, and a few free wardens. Kaiden didn't know them, but he focused on them to recall their names.

**Eqokkhabone**
**Free Warden**
**Class: Shield Warden**
**Faction: Unaffiliated**
**Level: 55**

**Credwin**
**Free Warden**
**Class: Power Warden**
**Faction: Unaffiliated**
**Level: 53**

**AxeJacton**
**Free Warden**
**Class: Power Warden**
**Faction: Unaffiliated**
**Level: 60**

Friends of Dawson, Kaiden recalled. And part of the much larger free warden force the former sergeant had raised to help them. They would form the core of the ground force, but these three had been singled out to stay with Dawson as personal guards to make sure Kaiden and everyone else could do what they'd come to do.

Kaiden activated the command module and looked forward to the reinforced gate of Warden HQ. Getting through that was the next step. Then to navigate the maze that was the base – fighting the whole while, no doubt – and get to the AFBS control room. Then broadcast the database to everyone, then bring down the Party and—

Kaiden stopped himself. None of that would be happening if they didn't get through that gate.

*One thing at a time, dude.*

"Odditor," he said through the command channel again. "We're dug in down here. Ready for the gate busters."

There was silence a long moment, then Whenstone's voice came over comms.

"Afraid that's not going to be possible—"

*What?*

"There's too many of them up here. Far more resistance than we expected. The cruisers will never make it down there to take down the gate."

"Shit." Kaiden looked up toward the battle raging above. It was thoroughly impossible to tell how things were going, aside from violently.

"We need cruisers to blow open the gate and get us inside," Kaiden said. "That was the plan."

"We're losing cruisers left and right. Most of those still with us have less than half their hull integrity remaining. Anything we send down there is going to be picked apart—"

Whenstone was cut off as something exploded on his end. A moment later he was back, sounding considerably more desperate than before.

"I'm sending all we can spare. They're going to have to do."

"Understood," Kaiden said, feeling dread creep up inside of his chest.

He drew his focus to the ground troops around him. It looked like most of them were landed now. His earlier order to take cover had apparently reached the right ears. As he watched, the players and NPCs that made up the combined army were taking shelter wherever they could find it; in the various craters across Custos' surface, the rubble of destroyed ships, or just huddling up behind the nearest shield warden or tank-class player. But they couldn't stay there forever; they needed to break through the gate, needed to take the fight to the Corps inside.

Two large streaks of light broke from the fleet-on-fleet battle above – heavy cruisers, Kaiden knew from the size of their contrails. The gate busters, or what was left of them. They'd planned to have far more make the dangerous run to blow open the gate.

They made it all of halfway to the surface of the asteroid before a wing of Warden Corps corvettes intercepted them.

"No!" Kaiden shouted, but there was no stopping it. The cruisers took down a fair few of the attackers, but there were too many. They hadn't planned to meet so much resistance. It wasn't supposed to have been here. The first heavy cruiser exploded and the second went dark, losing power apparently and spinning off to one side. A few moments later it slammed into a smaller asteroid and spun away.

*The gate... the gate has a health pool, just like everything else in Nova, right?* Kaiden thought, desperately trying to piece something together. *That means we can destroy it. With ships or with the ground forces. Whatever it takes.*

Kaiden took a moment to swallow his own doubt. His fear that they'd come so far only to fail so early.

*No. There's no room for that. Not now.*

"Odditor, Whenstone, whoever's still alive up there, we need anything you can get down here to attack that gate. But if you can't, we're going to do it ourselves."

There was no response and Kaiden didn't have time to wait for one anyway.

*We need to get inside as soon as possible.*

"All right, everyone," Kaiden said through the commander-only comm channel, his direct line to the ear of everyone fighting on their side. "We're on the ground. Now the fun begins." He stepped above the rim of the crater and gestured with his hammer, jutting it toward the reinforced gate three hundred or so yards away. "The Warden Corps thinks that little thing's gonna keep us out. Let's show them how wrong they are, yeah?" He shouted that last part – partly to convince himself and partly to convince everyone else. As he did, above the explosions of downed ships, the roaring of engines, and the endless screams of firing weaponry, he heard a general, if faint, cheer go up from his forces.

*They're ready for this. They want this fight.*

He smiled to himself.

*So let's do it. Whatever it takes.*

"Stage two, then, everyone. Let's get that door open!" He gestured with his hammer again and the command module adapted, marking the gate as an area to focus fire – an order all of the troops in the force would see in their HUDs. As it appeared, the pockets of troops, huddled into cover all across the battlefield, burst into motion.

The gate towered in front of them like a boss at the end of some epic quest. Its health bar was the largest Kaiden had ever seen, and around it there were dozens of automated turrets – mini bosses in their own right with their own sizeable health pools – and a line of trenches and bunkers ready to defend it. Blast wardens moved among the trenches, preparing a defense.

"Form your ranks, move as one, just like we planned." Kaiden wished he could say 'practiced' but there hadn't been time for that. Luckily, with Maximus guild members sprinkled throughout the force, there were plenty of experienced PVPers to guide the less experienced. For the most part, the army moved as one, tank classes in the front, melee fighters in the middle, and ranged classes in the rear. There were holes in the formations here and there, but considering the circumstances it was good enough. On his command module they formed a wave of green dots, and arrayed before them was a sea of red opposing forces. In the middle, like a tiny arrow point, was the bomb squad, ready to punch through the defenses.

His own group was among them.

Titus and the free warden Eqokkhabone were both shield wardens so they took the lead, shields up and on.

"I've been waiting to do this forever," Titus said as he slid into place next to Eqokkhabone, then activated Shield Brother.

**Ability: Improved Shield Brother**
**Locking shields with another shield warden boosts absorption capacity of both your shields by +30%.**

The Maximus guild members PlayaSlaya had brought along were mainly DPS classes – Cybernetic knights and brawlers, plus one medic – so they took position just behind Titus and Eqokkhabone.

*Protecting those in the back. Protecting us,* Kaiden thought. And a weird thought it was. But he was important here. And so was Zelda. And Thorne. Each of them had a job to do and they needed to survive long enough to do it.

PlayaSlaya, Nando, Dawson and the other two free wardens joined up around Kaiden, Zelda, and Thorne, and then the whole unit was off. They rose from the crater that had been protecting them and into a spattering of fire from the Warden Corps defenses.

The good news was the majority of the ground defenses were designed to repel an air attack. The anti-air turrets couldn't aim down to ground level. The majority of fire that trickled in at the combined army came from the automated turrets and the small battalion of blast wardens who'd been stationed in the bunkers and trenches in front of the gate. Hardly enough of them to do much to the approaching army.

Kaiden's Intangible Defense passive was ready to blank the first attack that hit him. None did, though; not yet. Titus and the free shield warden, Eqokkhabone, at the head of the bomb team were enough to keep the rest of the group protected.

"That thing's got a health pool, like anything else in Nova. We can break it," Kaiden said, pointing to the gate as he spoke to his group.

"We'll see how it holds up to a corps of pissed-off free wardens," Dawson said.

"And the finest PVP guild in the game," PlayaSlaya added, not to be outdone.

Even as they spoke, though, something ahead of them moved.

*The gate*, Kaiden realized. *It's opening!*

*Oh*, he thought a moment later as he saw why it was opening. *Oh, shit.*

## Chapter Fifty-Six

They marched in a formation so tight, so perfectly in-sync, it would have been beautiful, would have been inspiring, would have given Kaiden the faith he needed that this battle was well in hand – if only those marching were his own forces and not Warden Corps reinforcements.

Though reinforcements wasn't the right word. This wasn't backup; this was their main force. The defenders of Custos come to do battle.

Kaiden had expected fifteen hundred wardens, but this force in front of him now was easily two thousand on its own.

The warden army deployed and Kaiden found himself facing a symphony of destruction set to unfold in four devastating acts.

The front lines came first. Ranks of shield wardens marched shoulder to shoulder with their massive shields glowing a burning blue. Custos shook beneath the sheer weight of their armor. With Improved Shield Brother they'd be an unbreakable force, ready to take the brunt of all damage and deal it back with Reflection and Karmic Reprisal. With their Intransigence, they were an immovable line of defense.

The next ranks were the sword behind the shield. Power wardens were arrayed in fighting groups of fours and fives, hammers the size of engine blocks and arms loaded with enough strength to put them to terrifying use. Their Earth Shatters and

Heroic Leaps when delivered en masse would rend even large groups of players asunder and their Gravity Sledges would wreak further havoc, sending players flying in all directions.

There were a few enhanced wardens sprinkled throughout as well, their forms lightning fast and glowing as they sped across the battlefield with ease. They would strike with pinpoint precision amongst the chaos created by the power wardens. Lightspeed. Enfeebling Strike. Onslaught. All would combine to devastating effect.

The blast wardens came last, hammer-guns at the ready. Like true DPS types they would already be soaking up charge, preparing to rain their most damaging attacks down upon their enemies in a storm of light and fire. Protected by the shielders, with opponents softened by the power wardens and information relayed by the roaming enhanced wardens, they would be the executioners. Their Improved Warden's Bolts and Inferno Shots would be death itself as they dispensed indiscriminate ruin to all in their path.

This was what the Corps was designed for, each class working in perfect unison. The Warden Corps' army was a machine built for war, designed that way, and ready to crush anything in its path. Kaiden now found himself and his army in that very path. It was terrifying.

"There are too many," Thorne said, awe in her voice as the reinforced gate closed behind the last ranks of the enemy army. She shook her head in disbelief.

"It's too late to worry about it now," PlayaSlaya snarled. "We don't have time to be distracted. No matter the number, all we need to do is punch a hole in that force, then another in that gate. They must have emptied out the bulk of their forces to put forth such a massive defense."

"He's right," Kaiden said, trying to shake the ever-growing dread that'd been brought on by the sight of the marching calamity they were facing. He'd thought they'd brought enough troops, but it was becoming increasingly apparent they hadn't.

*What happened? We had a good idea what sort of resistance to expect, but this... this far exceeds even our contingency plans—*

*No.*

He stopped the worrying right there.

"Analyze and adapt," Zelda said, likely seeing the concern in his features. "We can do this."

"Somehow," he agreed. "But yeah, we can." Kaiden clapped his hands together.

*Okay, okay. What do we do?*

The warden classes had basically been built to fight together in formation. Their abilities just went well together. Shielders in the front, blocking damage and using Shield Link to feed the blast wardens who'd be behind them, raining ranged damage down on the enemy. Then there were the power wardens, too adept at wreaking havoc in the enemy ranks. And the enhanced wardens, not to be forgotten, debuffing just about anyone they could reach which, considering their high dexterity stats and incredible speed, was pretty much everyone.

*So how do we beat this?*

The plan previously had been to take them straight on. Their army didn't need to win; it just needed to buy time to get the bomb team into the AFBS control room. Except...

The more Kaiden thought about it, the more he realized that was still true. *Right?*

*We don't need to beat this force. We just need to break through it. Break through it and hold long enough to get the gate open.*

Even as he concocted a plan, it seemed fate had deigned to grant him a bit of much-needed luck. One of Odditor's freighters, no doubt loaded with landing troops, was coming in late. The raging fires burning in its engines and spreading through the rest of the ship were a good indication of why, and based on its approach speed and angle, its maneuvering thrusters weren't exactly pulling their weight.

The front ranks of the warden army braced for impact as the freighter crashed to the ground. For a moment, Kaiden thought it was going to land on them, going to crush them flat and solve most of his problems in one fell swoop – but it missed. Came down just short and left a swath of rubble spread across the front ranks of the warden army.

And then that rubble started to move.

But it wasn't the rubble that was moving; rather, what was in it. Voidspawn, Kaiden realized as his visor brought up info on the hissing, chittering shapes rising from the wreckage of the ship. Kaiden had no idea how many had initially been on the ship but apparently a good number of them had survived.

"Odditor!" Kaiden called through command comms. "Did you bring a landing ship full of voidspawn?"

"Oh! Is that where that went?" his reply came, cracking with static. "I'd been wondering. Hey, uh, try not to get too close. They're not exactly tame."

*You think?* Kaiden couldn't help but think as the voidspawn charged the warden army. Some had noticed his own troops and were coming at them as well, but easily ninety percent of the creatures were bearing down on the front ranks of the wardens.

*This could be our window! We'll use the distraction to give us an edge in the attack!*

Charge. A simple command in concept. A bit more complex in execution. Kaiden gave the command verbally and from all across the battlefield his forces sprang from their cover and rushed forward.

Kaiden joined them, but his focus was on the command module. He flew through it, giving specific orders as quickly as possible. He selected the free warden battlegroup, one hundred or so members strong, and plotted a course for them. It cut in toward the middle of the battleground so they could form up as the center of the charging force. He confirmed the route and sent it out.

Off to the right, where the free wardens were charging from, Kaiden knew their HUDs had just updated with the order and a route was being projected into their vision. They moved with the precision expected of wardens – a phalanx of shielders in front, power and enhanced wardens in the middle, and blasters bringing up the rear – as they cut a diagonal path across the battleground.

Kaiden stumbled over some unseen obstacle, near toppling over, but a steadying hand from Thorne kept him upright. Lasers were flying in all directions now, exploding against Titus and Eqokkhabone's shields in the front, but he didn't have time to focus on that. He was too busy giving orders via the command module.

He sent the vast majority of his army to form up on either flank of the centerline of free wardens. What had once been a blind charge was beginning to take shape into something approaching a coherent strategy.

Next, Kaiden split the Maximus battlegroup between both flanks of the centerline of free wardens. As he confirmed the changes, he couldn't help but admire the efficiency of the PVP guilders. They didn't move in a tightly controlled formation like the free wardens, but they all followed the order immediately, breaking into a sprint to reposition as quickly as possible.

Lastly came The Syndicate soldiers, players and NPCs of all different classes and skill sets. What they lacked in individual skill they no doubt made up for in sheer numbers. Kaiden gave them no specific orders except to cause as much chaos as possible. For the enthusiasm with which they advanced, it seemed they were happy to oblige.

Kaiden looked up from his command module in time to see the battle had been joined– but not because of his army. The voidspawn had reached the warden force. And they were being decimated.

The front row crashed against the shielders in a tsunami of tentacles and teeth. The warden ranks held, however, and then the blast wardens opened fire. Five or six hundred Improved Burst Arrows all at once. They skimmed just over the heads of the front row of shielders and tore into the voidspawn horde.

Improved Warden's Bolts next, crackling and hissing in clouds of too-lethal electricity that jumped from one voidspawn to the next, frying them such that they screamed and burst into steaming puddles of molten ooze.

With the voidspawn thoroughly distracted, the shielders lashed out with Shield Slam. What was left of the voidspawn front rank was stunned motionless for two seconds. They weren't given the time to recover, though, as the shield wardens followed up with Improved Shield Charge and took off like charging bulls, plowing through their stunned and weakened enemies.

And then the power wardens joined the fray. Seemingly hundreds of them launched into the air as one, leaping from among the middle of the army and soaring into the enemy ranks. They hit the ground, each an earthquake all to him or herself. Bits of soil and voidspawn flew through the air as the power wardens began swinging their hammers.

What had once been a hissing horde was rendered to nothing more than a screeching, fleeing mass of mostly dead voidspawn.

The remains of the retreating foe were cut down by enhanced wardens who looked nothing more than blurs as they attacked at lightspeed.

"Now!" Kaiden shouted, urging his army forward as if his words could grant them all a speed buff. But they couldn't, and even as he spoke, the warden army moved with a practiced precision only possible in a military force. They pulled back together and reformed. Their pristine ranks were only sullied by splotches of voidspawn ooze on armor and the heads of hammers.

No matter. The voidspawn had been enough of a distraction. Now came the main event.

The two armies were only a few hundred paces from meeting as Kaiden finished sending out his last order.

Odditor's battlegroup – mainly consisting of the menagerie – was among the bulk of the army, but that was a waste of their potential. Grachnids and dilopoads and most of the other beasts Odditor had brought were bigger and faster than humans, and considerably more frightening. Kaiden ordered them to lead the charge and hit the warden lines first. Roars and screeches rose up from all around as the orders went through and then the beasts began to pull away from the army, sprinting at full speed and charging down the shielders at the front of the warden army.

"That's it," Kaiden said, looking around him one last time. "It's all in place. Now we just have to... do it. Just have to make it work."

## Chapter Fifty-Seven

"Here goes nothing, eh?" Titus replied from just ahead, shield held firmly in front of him. He and the free shield warden Eqokkhabone were leading their group. They'd moved to the middle of the army; the shaft of the spear, ready to plunge through the hole the front lines were supposed to blast through the warden ranks. While the attackers may have looked spread out, Kaiden had maneuvered the highest-level, most DPS-ready players to the tip of the spear. They didn't need to defeat this force. All they needed was a gap.

Any moment now...

The Warden Corps shielders were locked together with Improved Shield Brother and standing ready for the collision that was moments away.

*I'd have them using Improved Barrier,* Kaiden couldn't help but think. *It'd absorb the most damage from this charge.* Before he could think on it any further, the menagerie slammed into the warden force.

A handful of grachnids hit them first, plowing into the shield wardens in a crash of stabbing limbs and crushing bodies. Arcs of electricity lashed back at the attackers, Improved Volt Field doing its work. The massive insect-like aliens didn't seem to notice. They trampled a section of shielders and broke straight through.

Or so Kaiden thought at first. As he looked again, though, he saw the shielders had just been driven back. They were still linked to those beside them. A section of the front line had been pushed back, but it'd held together. It appeared the shield wardens who were high enough level to have Intransigence were acting as anchor points throughout the front line.

The grachnids stabbed and stomped in the bulge they'd created. A few of the higher-level ones even sprayed acid, the hissing liquid coming down in a sizzling mist that ate away at the armor of those it touched. The combined damage from the attacks had to have been massive and Kaiden found himself wondering again why the shielders didn't have their barriers up.

All across the front, more grachnids and dilopoads and even a baboulian manhunter slammed into the shield wardens. Some spots were driven back more than others, but everywhere, the line held. The charge ground to a stop. The warden line was still intact.

And then the wardens hit back.

The shielders lashed out first with a synced-up Shield of Rage attack. Their shields slammed into the ground almost in unison and concussions erupted all along their line, spreading outwards and dealing area-of-effect damage to the menagerie, which hissed and roared.

Then, all as one, the shield wardens turned off their shields and dropped to one knee. As they did, the blast wardens at the rear of the formation let loose a hail of fire. Improved Burst Arrows and Warden's Bolts, even a Kinetic Grenade or two. The menagerie disappeared in a cloud of fire and electricity and lasers. More abilities were fired off than the blast wardens should have had charge for, and as he saw that, Kaiden realized why the shielders hadn't used Improved Barrier.

*A shield warden can't build charge while using Improved Barrier, and the front lines were Shield Linked with the blast wardens behind them. They absorbed the hit from the menagerie and turned it into charge for the blast wardens to strike back with.*

At the edge of his vision, Kaiden's command module updated the status of the battlegroup to thirty percent.

*Seventy percent of the menagerie gone in that counterattack!*

The shield wardens flicked their shields back on and stood, then linked up with Improved Shield Brother again. Ready for the next attack.

What remained of the menagerie fought on.

*That was the one in our one-two punch,* Kaiden thought. *We have to break through with the follow-up. But hitting the shield wardens head-on only strengthens the force overall.*

"So we don't hit them head-on," Kaiden said aloud.

"What's up?" Zelda asked, running beside him.

"Blast wardens!" Kaiden called, jumping into the comm channel for the free wardens battlegroup. "Aim above their front line with Improved Kinetic Grenade. Don't hit the shielders; arc your attacks over them. Commanders, relay that to your ranged fighters as well. Anybody with arcing ranged attacks. We're not hitting these guys head-on."

He got the order off just before the bulk of the charge reached the warden front lines. A volley of grenades from the free blast wardens arched over and exploded among the ranks of power wardens and the few enhanced wardens. None died, but Kaiden could see waves form among them as they ducked away from the explosions.

Maximus' gravity slingers opened up with their ranged attacks and rocks flew through the air, raining down on the warden army with concussive force.

**Ability: Kinetic Velocity**
**A ranged attack that deals moderate damage.**

Other attacks that looked magical in nature and even some good old-fashioned plasma grenades soared across the front line and into the enemy ranks. Return fire from the warden ranks came right back. Improved Kinetic Grenades first, then a wave of Improved Warden's Bolts, and even a few Improved Paralyzing Shots. Lightning slammed into the front ranks, but then fizzled, finding only a few secondary targets. Kaiden had arranged his force in separated cells for just this reason, ensuring enough of a gap that the chain effect of Warden's Bolt was less effective. One of their few advantages was space; while their opponents were clustered around the gate, their own attack formations could be much more fluid.

And then the two armies met.

Shielders slammed into shielders at the center, and on the flanks cybernetic knights and brawlers, gravity slingers and even a few classes Kaiden had yet to identify crashed into the warden force. It was like two great waves slamming into each other, only instead of water, they were made out of armor and bodies and explosions.

The command module began frantically updating battle-group numbers as the first heavy casualties came in, mainly among the free wardens and Maximus elite. The flanks lit up as well, though, as the rest of The Syndicate force met the warden foe.

Abilities fired off on all sides. The Maximus members seemed to know what they were doing as their gravity slingers lashed out.

**Ability: Gravity Well**
**A crowd-control ability that creates a strong gravity field around an object within 40 feet.**

Kaiden's visor went wild trying to give details as a dozen Gravity Wells appeared in the air above the shielders. Many were sucked up toward them, leaving gaping holes in the line behind them. The power wardens and enhanced wardens directly behind the shielders were swept up too and sucked ten paces into the air by the swirling pinpoints of super density.

The warden formation broke in several spots, a large number of its soldiers suspended in the air amid swirling debris, discarded weapons, and the corpses of the menagerie. Then, all at once, the Gravity Wells dissipated and those caught in their grasp were dropped, slamming back to the ground and taking no small amount of fall damage.

The Maximus elite weren't stopping there, though. Kaiden

couldn't help but admire their proficiency as the brawlers and cybernetic knights leapt into the air.

**Ability: Launch**
**High dexterity launches the user high into the air.**

**Ability: Meteoric Launch**
**Player launches into the air. Landing deals AoE damage, and the next attack deals additional damage.**

They vaulted over the shielders, then landed among the ranks of the warden army – the cybernetic knights with explosive landings – and attacked anyone near them. Flames exploded outward. Magma oozed on the ends of weapons. The ground shook with the impacts of attacks on shields, attacks on armor, and sometimes attacks on exposed flesh.

**Ability: Fiery End**
**A high-damage attack. On a successful hit, the target is set on fire.**

**Ability: Melt**
**A powerful strike that bypasses armor and shields.**

A flood of damage poured into the backs of the shielders and the fronts of the power and enhanced wardens that had stepped up to engage the trespassers. The Maximus elite had the advantage of not needing to build charge before attacking, though, so for the moment, they had the edge. Kaiden watched as they landed attack after attack, looking for any gaps that would allow them access to the gate. Move too soon and they would be trapped in the middle of the warden force. The Maximus players fought on, many laughing as they threw out their attacks.

**Ability: Wind-Up Swing**
**A slow but powerful attack that requires a wind-up. Deals direct and knockback damage on a successful hit.**

**Ability: Concussive Strike**
**A forceful strike that travels along the ground for a short distance, dealing direct and knockback damage to any enemy in its path.**

The wardens without Intransigence were launched into the air, flung into the ranks of The Syndicate army where they were overwhelmed, or knocked backward to cause havoc for the Sniper Moded blast wardens in the rear.

The chaos in the warden ranks was a plus, but the front line, despite the holes in it, was largely still holding. Gaps appeared but were immediately plugged. The shield wardens finally activated Improved Barrier, creating glowing domes that held back any further attacks while the power wardens brawled with the Maximus members who'd broken into their lines.

**Ability: Mass x Acceleration**
**A high-damage melee attack that deals damage based on the user's level and dexterity.**

Several Maximus gravity slingers bold enough to be on the front lines lashed forward with their devastating melee attacks. In a couple of places, warden Improved Barriers shattered beneath the assault. Kaiden highlighted the weak points, and all around, free warden shielders burst forward with Improved Shield Charge. Just behind them the Maximus brawlers and cybernetic knights who hadn't launched in earlier followed with their own movement abilities.

The Warden Corps shielders were occupied – either focusing on maintaining their barriers, which meant not building charge, or desperately warding off attacks from their backs – and Kaiden could see them giving ground. They were driven backward, step by step. Kaiden was so far back among his own forces that few attacks made it to him and the rest of the bomb team, but already he could see the result of the warden lines giving. Those directly around the bomb team were surging forward, pushing into the bulge the front lines had created. With the center of the warden force distracted by the Maximus members among them, the shielders were left to hold the front on their own.

"We're pushing their line to the brink," Kaiden said. "We just have to break through."

"My boys are softening up their core," PlayaSlaya said. "If we can punch in there we'll cut right through that mess." Even as he spoke, though, Kaiden could see the fight just beyond the Warden Corps' front lines getting desperate – but not in the way he wanted. The enemy blast wardens in the rear had turned their attention to the chaos. Improved Burst Arrows and Improved Scatter Shots plunged toward the Maximus elite. Improved Kinetic Grenades detonated in blasts of lasers and flames.

Worse, the power wardens had charge now, and they were putting it to use. Kaiden's visor flashed abilities at him in a frenzy as it spotted them. Amid the chaos of it all he recognized a pattern.

**Ability: See Red**
**For the next 20 seconds your base damage is increased by 20% for each opponent slain.**

**Ability: Berserker**
**The warden does double base damage but also takes +50% damage for 20 seconds. Speed is halved for 1 minute following the ability.**

**Ability: Improved Chained Fury**
**Your combat prowess allows you to chain attacks together. For the next 5 seconds, each attack deals an additional 20% damage for every successful attack before it.**

The blast wardens were softening up the Maximus elite and the power wardens were mopping them up with a three-ability combo. Cybernetic knights and brawlers began to die with increasing frequency as the power wardens' See Red did its work.

Even as Kaiden watched, more and more of the Maximus

elite fell. The warden army had taken the full brunt of the attack and was on the verge of recovering. In a minute or two they'd be able to pivot onto the offensive.

If Kaiden's forces could just break the shielders in front they'd have a way into the warden ranks. The army could surge in and force the fight into the disorganized scrum Kaiden was aiming for.

With the fighting in so close it was likely most of his forces would have trouble recognizing they'd been given new orders, so Kaiden focused on the most reliable of them: the free wardens.

"Shielders, keep pushing forward. Power wardens, vault past their front line, then attack it from behind. Earth Shatter on landing, then follow up with Improved Shield Break as needed. Break the line!"

He'd hardly finished giving the order before the free wardens were in motion. Free power wardens launched into the air, less of them than Kaiden would have liked, but he'd only had a hundred free wardens total. An even smaller number of them were power wardens. Nonetheless, they came down like a meteor shower, exploding into the soil with a rain of shockwaves that crashed into the back of the opposing shield wardens' barriers.

*If they can break the shielders, the rest of our force can push in and reinforce the Maximus elite. Turn that fight in the middle ranks into a proper scrum. Just the kind of chaos we need to punch through to the gate.*

Several Improved Barriers cracked, then shattered entirely. The shielders were left with glowing auras around them – the personal force fields that persisted after Improved Barrier went down – but they didn't last long as the free power wardens struck with Improved Shield Break.

The combination of attacks left the very center of the warden line in shambles. Most of the barriers there were broken, and with Improved Shield Break hitting the wardens themselves, the front line was just about gone.

And still it wasn't going to be enough. The power wardens and blast wardens had all but eradicated the Maximus elite. The scrum Kaiden wanted in the middle ranks was almost gone and the Warden Corps forces were regaining their composure.

Suddenly, the Warden Corps middle ranks moved as one. They all split to the side to reveal a group of Sniper Moded blast wardens with abilities charging on the end of their hammer-rifles. Abilities Kaiden recognized all too well.

**Ability: Inferno Shot**
**You fire an explosive, superheated blast that ignores 50% of the target's armor. Deals 3x base damage to all targets in range (allies included). Takes 7 seconds to charge (must be stationary).**

"Oh hell," Kaiden said and then a half-dozen Inferno Shots tore through the Maximus elite and free warden core.

More players than Kaiden could keep up with were cut down as a scorching swath was burned through his army. His command module went mad trying to account for the losses. Commanders shouted through comms, trying to organize and compensate for having a hole blown straight through the entire force.

Kaiden heard them all, but for a moment, he was stunned.

As he watched, the rest of the Warden Corps blast wardens began to move. With the immediate threat gone from the army's middle ranks, they were forming up; had moved closer to the front line and were raising their hammer-rifles for some sort of mass attack. Kaiden cringed as his visor read out exactly what.

Inferno Shot.

## Chapter Fifty-Eight

Beside her, Thorne saw Kaiden flinch, then followed his gaze until she realized what he'd seen. The Warden Corps blast wardens were moving closer. As they set up, they held still, getting into Sniper Mode and no doubt planning to charge a second round of Inferno Shots. Many were still getting in place, but in moments they would all be charging, no doubt planning to fire at once to make it an almost AoE-level unavoidable barrage.

"We have to hit them hard. Now!" Kaiden shouted, but there was no way they could. Their own blast wardens could fire back, but they wouldn't be enough. The other ranged classes could help, but it was going to take concentrated assault to interrupt all the charging Inferno Shots. There was no way they could get a force back there in time.

"Ah, there it is," Dawson said suddenly through comms. "I was wondering when they'd go for the knockout punch."

"Why do you sound so happy about it?" Thorne shouted at him, but even as she did, a notification appeared in her vision.

**Lieutenant Sola has joined the comm channel.**

"Looks like you all are taking something of a beating over there," a familiar voice said.

Lieutenant Sola. Thorne hadn't even known she was in the battle, which meant... she was fighting for the Warden Corps. Thorne's heart sank at that. But who'd added her to their comm channel?

"Well, it's a mighty fine fighting force you've got," Dawson said. "My compliments to whoever trained it."

"Are you complimenting yourself again, Sergeant?" Sola asked.

"Might be," Dawson said. "Either way, those blast wardens have lined themselves up all pretty like, just like we knew they would. Once they're all in position, think you might be able to do something about that?"

"Already on it," Sola said.

"The hell is that about?" PlayaSlaya asked, shock plastered across his features. Kaiden looked about the same.

"What?" Dawson asked him. "You didn't think I was just recruiting free wardens, did you?"

Thorne felt a smile stretch across her face.

"It's a pleasure to have you with us, Lieutenant Sola," she said.

"Well, when you all defected and took Ellenton with you, that was just about the last straw," she said. "Tell her hey from me. Now, enjoy the fireworks."

Thorne looked back to the line of blast wardens. They were all in Sniper Mode now and charging Inferno Shots. Some were charged and just waiting for the order to fire. All were still, except for two. They suddenly stood, one on either end of the line. They already had fully charged Inferno Shots on the ends of their hammer-guns, having only feigned entering Sniper Mode. As one, they turned inward, placing the entire line of blast wardens in their sights, and fired.

The dual Inferno Shots tore through the line of squishy, low-HP blast wardens, then met in the middle with a blinding explosion that sent every warden within ten paces tumbling to the ground.

"Inferno Shot hurts enemies and allies alike..." Kaiden said, his eyes fixed on the aftermath. Nearly the entire line of blast wardens was dead. Those that still stood were just about one stiff breeze from dying as well.

"I think it's safe to say we can count Sola an ally," Thorne said as chaos erupted in the ranks of the Warden Corps army.

Five or so more blast wardens turned on their companions and began firing. Then, a few of the shielders in the front broke rank and Improved Shield Charged into their own force. A group of power wardens turned next, and as their hammers started swinging, scores of the still Party-loyal wardens were tossed into the air.

And then there was Sola. Nothing more than a blur, but a blur Thorne recognized. A blur that was tearing through the warden army and landing critical hits left and right.

"Ain't that a beautiful sight?" Dawson said. He made to wipe a fake tear from his face but his hand only clunked against the faceplate of his helmet.

"They had us in the first half, not gonna lie," Titus said with something approaching a laugh.

"But it's not over yet," Thorne said. "It's time for a knockout blow of our own." She looked to Kaiden. "Care to do the honors?"

He smiled.

"All battlegroups, push ahead. Tear through the center of their force and blow us a hole right through to that gate."

A list of names appeared in Thorne's vision – a file from Sola detailing those wardens who were working with her.

"And don't kill our new allies," Kaiden said. He must've added the file to his command module because a moment later Thorne saw a good fifty friendly markers appear within the chaos of the warden lines.

"Now let's get to that gate!" Kaiden sent out the 'all forces charge' order and The Syndicate army surged forward with renewed vigor. The surviving free wardens led the charge, and all along the front, The Syndicate army began to flow in, driven as if by an unstoppable current.

Even back in the center of the army, Thorne found herself and the rest of the bomb team sucked forward. The Warden

Corps' line was breached and now it was time to make the most of it.

Abilities fired off on all sides and Thorne found herself ducking behind her buckler shield, knowing it wouldn't do much good but unable to resist the instinct. This was a different fight than she was used to. The rest of the army was focused on fighting, on taking down any Warden Corps soldiers in front of them, but the bomb team had a singular objective: reach the gate and get through it.

Titus knew that, and along with the free shield warden next to him they pushed through the chaos of the battle. It'd devolved into an all-out scrum now, lines breaking apart as if they'd never even been there as combatants from both sides intermingled and had at it.

The Maximus elite and free power wardens who'd vaulted the enemy front line had softened the mid-section of the warden army enough that pushing through that part was relatively easy. Only a few enemies stepped in front of the bomb team as they surged forward, and those that did were quickly attacked by any surrounding soldiers. The army knew their objective and, thanks to their support, Titus was able to gain steam as he led them through the mid-section of the enemy force. Their path was kept relatively clear all the while.

A stray Improved Kinetic Grenade detonated in the air above them and Thorne ducked away as damage rained down. Beside her, Kaiden hissed as he took the bulk of it, his health bar falling a good eighteen percent. They'd all been taking glancing blows here and there. No one had made it this far unscathed, but Kaiden in particular was squishy. Enhanced wardens weren't made to tank damage.

Before Thorne could stop him, his health flashed back to near full as he popped a stimpack.

"Kaiden!" she shouted. "Let the medic handle that. Save your stims!"

"Shit. Right," he said. But she couldn't blame him. Between organizing the attack strategy and all the chaos going on around them it was a miracle he could even see straight.

She waved over to the medic, Skaia, and she shot Kaiden with a syringe, bumping his health the rest of the way back to full.

Thorne kept her hammer at the ready as the bomb team pushed through the battle, but she never needed to use it. Playa-Slaya, Nando, their Maximus guards, and Dawson and his free wardens had them covered on all sides. Anyone who got too close was beaten back. Not killed, usually, but attacked by several guards at once such that they were forced away. Combined with the speed Titus was keeping in leading them forward, they were away from most attackers in a matter of seconds.

They were deep in the warden lines now, and the fighters around them were changing from power wardens to blast wardens. Made it all the easier to keep pushing on as most of their opponents now tried to back away from them, keeping distance where they'd be more effective.

A quick glance behind told Thorne the free warden core of the army was bogged down in the middle of the defenders. Worse, it looked like the bulk of the warden army was closing in on the flanks now. Preparing for an encirclement, she knew. That was the problem with a spearhead attack like this. It could be absorbed, creating a churning mess of a battle in the center while the larger force – which was decidedly the wardens here – swarmed around the outside. The end result was the smaller force surrounded on all sides while the larger picked away at them until there was nothing left.

*We're not fighting the long game here, though,* she knew. That was Kaiden's plan, and she had to admit it made sense. *We need to move quick, take minimal damage, be ready for the fight that comes next,* Thorne thought, looking ahead to the gate. They were drawing closer to it. She looked up to the sky next. The battle was still raging there and it was impossible to tell who was winning. What was clear to see, though, was that no ships had been able to make it down to take shots at the gate.

*Are we going to have to do this ourselves? We'll never get through it that way…*

"Come on!" PlayaSlaya shouted from the front of their group. Kaiden had watched as he'd leapt past Titus, lashing out at any warden who drew near. His attacks were swift and savage. His axe cut through everything in its way, a blur of molten metal. Power and shield wardens had trouble standing up to him, but now the bomb team was in among the rear ranks of the warden force. Most blast wardens simply fled at the sight of PlayaSlaya charging them.

The gate was just ahead.

"Have a go!" PlayaSlaya shouted again, chasing down a fleeing blaster.

"Keep formation!" Kaiden said, trying to reel PlayaSlaya back in and sticking close to the others himself as they reached the gate.

*We made it*, he thought. *We made it…*

But now what? The fleet above was supposed to have been hammering the gate this whole time. The unexpectedly large force the wardens had mustered to defend the air space had cut that plan short, though.

"Odditor!" Kaiden called through comms. "Where are those ships? We're at the gate. We need someone to blow this thing apart!"

"Form up!" Thorne called, taking control of the situation as Kaiden tried to reach their air support. Thorne ushered everyone off to the side of the gate – towering, massive thing that it was – and formed a perimeter with shield wardens, Maximus guards, and Dawson and his free wardens on the edge. Zelda was blasting away from the interior, alongside another free warden blaster, and Skaia, the medic, was healing anyone who got hit as fast as her abilities came off of cooldown.

An enemy power warden sprang into the midst of their group with Heroic Leap. She came down with a vengeance, hammer already swinging. Kaiden raised his own to respond but a well-timed Energy Grip from Titus yanked the would-be attacker to the edge of the group where she was pounced on by the Maximus guards.

"Odditor!" Kaiden shouted again, staring up into the chaos above them. Still no response.

"We're holding, but we can't do it forever," Dawson grunted from where he was hammering away at a shield warden. "We have to get through that gate sooner rather than later."

"Can we do it ourselves?" Kaiden asked, turning to face the thing. His visor pulled up its health pool. It didn't give numbers, but percentage, as usual. Stray attacks and flying debris had likely hit the gate during the battle but it'd made little difference. The thing was still at ninety-eight percent health.

*If we can't get air support, we're going to need every fighter we've got to turn on this thing. It should be enough damage to bring it down. But it'll mean losing the army; while they're focused on the gate, the wardens will take over the battle. We have to get inside, though—*

Something exploded overhead and Kaiden ducked away as sparks rained down on him. He glanced up to see a line of ballistic rounds slamming into the surface of the gate, scouring dents and scars across its surface in flashes of fire.

"Let's see what this big bastard's made of," came a voice over comms.

*Ellenton!* Kaiden spun to see the *Borrelly* drifting over the battlefield. It was at full speed, though, drifting past impossibly fast and only able to keep firing on the gate for another second before it had to pull off. Three enemy fighters were behind it, guns blazing and lighting its shields up whenever they hit. The proximity defense drones looked to have had a rough time. Half of them were gone and those that were left were clearly damaged. They struggled to keep up with the *Borrelly* and fire back at the pursuing fighters.

"Can't slow down," Ellenton said as her engines carried her up to circle back. "But I can keep making passes. Probably." The fighters pursued her high into the sky before she pulled a hard turn and came back for another strafing run.

The second stream of bullets tore into the gate and Kaiden watched its health drop.

**89%...**
**82%...**
**76%...**

Good progress, but still not enough.

The *Borrelly* took a direct hit to one of its engines and veered sharply off course. Ellenton just managed to pull up before plowing into the ground.

"I'm here, uh, here," Odditor's voice suddenly sprang to life in Kaiden's ear. "Bit busy, though. Apologies." Crashes and explosions sounded as he spoke, crackling through the comm channel.

"We need this gate down. This whole thing fails if we don't get through this gate."

"Barricade the door!" Whenstone's voice suddenly shouted out. "We're dealing with a bit of a situation here. Boarders on the ship. I don't think we can stop them from taking the bridge."

"Bastards aren't taking, taking my ship!" Odditor cursed, more malice in his voice than Kaiden had ever heard before.

"Come at me, then!" roared Eqokkhabone, the shield warden who'd been beside Titus. He was very low on health, his shield was overloaded, and he'd obviously taken a massive hit to the side considering the state of his armor.

"I don't need a shield to tank for this par—"

He was cut off by an explosion as an enemy blast warden several paces away who'd been charging an Improved Kinetic Grenade was killed. The attack fired off anyway, though, falling to the ground and swallowing Eqokkhabone in its explosion.

**Party member killed!**

"I mean, he wasn't wrong..." Thorne said, frowning at the aftermath. "He did technically tank that..."

"Odditor!" Kaiden said again, turning away from the sorry sight and focusing on his desperate plan. "If you're going to crash... can you crash in this direction? Into the gate?"

The only response was the sounds of fighting and then, shortly after, no sound at all as the channel went dead.

"It was a good plan," Zelda said, frowning at him. "But we're going to need another one."

She was right.

"Ellenton, can you—" Kaiden began, but before he could finish, another voice cut him off.

"Captains," Acton said through comms. "This ship is insured, yeah?"

*What?*

Kaiden just managed to piece together what was happening as a blur dropped out of the sky.

The *Veritas II* was hurtling toward them. It was in a bad way, shields down, an engine and several turrets gone, but it was still flying – and directly at the gate.

"The ship's all paid up," Zelda said, her words heavy. She too had realized what was happening.

"Very good, then. Captains," Acton said, sounding far too cheery about the whole thing. "It's been a pleasure. I'll see you on the other side."

The remaining guns of the *Veritas II* blazed to life, hurling everything they had at the gate. A group of fighters was on the ship's tail, though. They chipped away at it, tearing chunks from its armor. But the armor was doing its job, because without it the shots would have been tearing components apart inside the *Veritas II*. As Kaiden watched, Acton fired what remained of the Tumbler torpedoes. They jumped from the ship all at once, falling for a moment before their thrusters kicked on. Several flipped over and hurtled back toward the pursuing fighters. The rest plunged into the gate in a series of rapid explosion.

Kaiden was cognizant of the gate's health dropping but he ignored it, flinging himself instead beneath the Improved Barrier Titus had thrown up.

He had just enough time for one last look at the gate before the *Veritas II* hit it at full speed.

The ground shook. Kaiden's ears exploded with a piercing ringing. Blinding light stabbed through his vision. Fire and debris swept across the battlefield in a shockwave so powerful it knocked everyone not under a barrier to the ground.

There was a moment of near-silence as the ringing faded from Kaiden's ears. The smoke began to clear, but he wasn't looking at that. No, he was looking at the flashing red text in the corner of his vision.

**8%...**
**8%...**
**8%...**

The gate was still standing. Barely, maybe, but it wasn't destroyed.

The *Veritas II* hadn't been enough. The gate was still standing, and the Warden Corps forces were closing in on all sides.

*So close, and yet so far. Damn it!*

"Kaiden! Look!" PlayaSlaya had waded out of the fighting and was gesturing wildly at the gate. "It's open!"

Kaiden squinted as the smoke cleared further. And yes, sure enough, the gate was ajar! The rightmost door was pulled back a bit, open just enough for a small group to slip through. The impact from the *Veritas II* hadn't been enough to destroy it completely but it had been enough to bust it open, it seemed.

"I didn't realize damage states could do that," Thorne said under her breath, frowning as she stared at the opening. "Normally it's an all-or-nothing thing."

"What are we waiting for?" PlayaSlaya shouted, pushing Kaiden toward the smoke clinging around the gate and the wreckage of the *Veritas II*. "Let's get in there!"

"One way or another, it's open," Kaiden said. "Let's go!"

He stumbled forward, running through the smoke and fire until the gate loomed in front of him. The gap was wide enough to slip through easily; Titus led the way, Kaiden went in after him, and then the rest of the group followed as well.

An Improved Burst Arrow came through the opening from outside and caught Kaiden in the shoulder. He spun to see the rear ranks of the warden army also charging in. They'd abandoned their fight with The Syndicate army to make a mad dash to defend the gate.

Dawson and his free wardens stepped in front of their charge.

"I got this," the former sergeant said. "You lot go with them!" he shouted to a group of free wardens that had fought their way to the gate. And with that, he turned back to the oncoming enemies and raised his hammer.

## Chapter Fifty-Nine

Warden HQ.

Kaiden couldn't believe it.

*We made it.*

And from an initial scan of the room they were in – a sort of lobby with hallways leading off to either side – it didn't seem there was anyone to fight them just yet. Probably that was on account of the massive damage to the space. In several areas the ceiling had collapsed and great chunks of stone had plummeted downward. Clearly many of the would-be defenders had been standing in the wrong places. Kaiden looked over them.

**TankerFlanker **Deceased****
**Warden Sergeant**
**Class: Power Warden**
**Level: 55**

**Harrison **Deceased****
**Warden Captain**
**Class: Shield Warden**
**Level: 58**

There were at least twenty dead wardens around the space.

He would have thought the HQ would be more resistant to damage like this, especially given the strength of the gate. But with the skeleton crew of defenders gone, their job was that little bit easier, so he wasn't complaining.

If it was calm inside the base, the fighting outside more than made up for it. Dawson and his free wardens were making a valiant stand. They needed to hold; if wardens caught them from the rear in close quarters like this, they would be doomed.

Kaiden pulled up his command module and redirected all their remaining forces to converge on the door.

"Help's coming, Dawson. And once they do, we'll storm this base. Secure it and broadcast the database," he started to say, but was cut off as something massive rumbled through the floor.

"The gate!" Zelda shouted, pointing at it.

And she was right. It was moving.

The damaged door that had been busted open was sliding along its track now. The gap leading outside was narrowing by the moment. And then Kaiden saw why.

Dozens of drones were buzzing around the gate. But these weren't proximity defense drones like they'd had around the *Borrelly*. These were repair drones. Their little arms and lasers were hard at work, and the gate's health was replenishing by the moment.

The free wardens Dawson had sent after them ran as fast as they could, but the gate rumbled closed with a resounding echo. Moments later distant bangs echoed through it and Kaiden could see its health rising more slowly. The free wardens were trying to fight their way in, but their damage needed to outpace the drones' repairs.

"Target the drones," Kaiden said through command comms. "Take them down, then beat the gate."

"Good thing we slipped through before that happened," PlayaSlaya said, staring at the closed gate.

"I don't think—" Thorne began, but PlayaSlaya cut her off with a gesture.

"We're here. Let's do this. Right, Kaiden?"

Kaiden nodded. He was right. They didn't have time to

waste. Having the rest of their forces with them would have been ideal, but they were inside the base now. Best to work with what they had. He used the command module to give an order for anyone that could to attack the gate, but based on how the battle had been going when the gate had closed, he doubted anyone would have time to follow that order anytime soon.

"I believe in this group," he said, pushing any thought of the battle outside from his mind. "We made it this far. Now it's time to finish this."

As he spoke, his eyes flicked up to the timer at the top of his vision.

*Shit.* In all the chaos outside he'd forgotten about it. It was down to forty-five minutes now.

"Ellenton, Acton, Dawson, The Syndicate... our allies got us this far, but now their hopes rest with us," he said, looking back to the group in front of him. "And the clock's still ticking. We gotta move. Thorne, which way to the AFBS control room?"

For a moment, doubt clouded her face. What was up with her? Something seemed off. The moment passed, though, and Thorne gestured toward a hallway.

"It's this way. Let's be prepared for resistance. I don't know why there's no one here to stop us yet, but I don't think we can count on that the whole way through."

"I've got a hammer-gun that's itching to be used if anyone steps up," Zelda said.

"Ha! That's the spirit," PlayaSlaya said.

*We made it,* Kaiden thought as Thorne led the group out of the lobby and into a maze of hallways. While they jogged along, their medic, Skaia, healed anyone who'd taken damage.

"We're closer now to victory than we've ever been," Kaiden said, resisting the urge to celebrate. The job wasn't done yet, but he could feel victory near at hand, so close he could almost reach out and touch it. "One last thing to do," he said.

"Find the control room and broadcast Bernstein's database," Zelda said.

"Then we bring the whole rotten Party down," Thorne added.

"Damn right!" Titus slammed his hammer against his shield with a cheer. "Let's finish this."

*Forty-one minutes and counting…*

Thorne checked the timer. *We're cutting it close, but we're almost there. And technically, the countdown represents the quickest the Party can enact Killswitch, which means, in theory, we could have more time than we think. Best not to chance it, though.*

She'd already been moving at a jog, leading the group through the maze of tunnels and closed-in passages that was Warden HQ, but now she picked up the pace even more, approaching a sprint.

She'd been expecting danger at every turn, but none had arisen. The Corps must have committed nearly their entire force to the battle outside. It'd certainly explain their surprising numbers. And then the cave-ins caused by the *Veritas II* had taken out most of those left behind. She'd spotted several side corridors on the way that'd entirely collapsed, no doubt trapping countless wardens in other areas of the base.

"Here. This is it," Thorne said, turning one last corner – into another empty hallway – and coming to a stop in front of an unmarked door. It was plain, gray metal set into the stone wall. It'd been carved out of the asteroid's heart, just like the rest of the base.

"This is the security checkpoint for the broadcast control room. I'll go first," Thorne said. "Nando, give me a hand?"

He nodded his agreement and she loaded up a swing of her hammer. He reared back as well, one of his brawler abilities active, his fist simmering with restrained fire.

They hit the door at the same time and it exploded inward in a burst of flame. The remains of it flew clear across the room. Thorne charged in after it, hammer at the ready.

But there was nobody in the room. Completely against proto-col, the security checkpoint was empty. There should have been at least five wardens guarding it. Preferably power wardens, seeing as they'd be extra effective in such tight quarters. Instead, a few computer terminals beeped quietly, their screens blank as they sat in sleep mode. An air vent hissed above. The lights flickered ever so slightly. The walls of the room were hewn stone, smooth but for the repetitive, swirling circles where the drill had bored out the room. Their dark color always made the space feel darker, even when it was fully lit. From somewhere far above, an explosion sounded and just the slightest bit of dust trickled down.

The room really was empty, Thorne confirmed, checking every nook and cranny again and looking close at each one. She kept her hammer at the ready as she inched around the room, prepared to lunge at the first hint of an opponent.

And still, nothing.

Empty.

"That's it, then?" Kaiden asked, too much excitement in his voice as he gestured toward a door at the far side of the room.

"That's it," she confirmed. Beyond it was the control console for the All-Frequencies Broadcast System, hidden deep at the center of the asteroid. It'd always spooked her going down there – seemed the game devs had had a bit too much fun making it a spooky space cave instead of the functional space it was supposed to be.

"What are we waiting for, then?" Kaiden asked.

"Something's wrong," Thorne said again.

Kaiden looked like he believed her, but his excitement won out.

"PlayaSlaya," he said. "Let's leave some guards here to cover our backs, yeah? Just to make sure no one surprises us while we're in there—"

A hiss shot through the room and Thorne snapped into motion, hammer raised once more, eyes scanning for the source of the noise.

The door to the broadcast control console. It slid open with a hiss to reveal a figure standing just inside. Its features were obscured by the shadows of the tunnel leading to the console room.

"So close," the figure said, and its voice echoed away down the tunnel behind it. "You almost made it, you really did." The figure took a step forward and Thorne cursed.

"You almost made it," Werner said, a too-pleased smile on his face. "Though that was our plan, after all."

Chapter Sixty

Werner10
Warden Captain
Class: Blast Warden
Faction: Warden Corps
Level: 60

Kaiden's visor brought up information on Werner as he walked out of the tunnel and the door to the broadcast control room hissed shut.

"What do you mean your 'plan?'" Kaiden snapped. They were too close to be stopped now. Especially not by one smug bootlicker.

"This," Werner said, stretching his arms and gesturing to the room around them. "And that." He nodded up to the ceiling and the battle above. "All of it. You didn't think you actually earned your way here, did you?" Kaiden didn't respond and Werner laughed in amazement. "It didn't seem suspicious that *your* landing shuttle specifically made it to the ground in one piece? That the gate opened without even being destroyed? That so little resistance stood in your way once you made it down here?" Werner shook his head, still looking far too pleased with himself.

"It was all planned and accounted for. And now here you are, right where we wanted you. And the database is as well."

"If this was your master plan, it seems you left out an important piece," Titus growled. "There's eight of us and one of you. Did your master plan account for that?" He delivered the line with a sneer.

"Eight against one, hm?" Werner nodded at that. "Those would be bad odds. Though I think you may have miscounted."

Kaiden clenched his hammer tighter as he looked around the room, ready to attack the moment Werner's reinforcements showed themselves. The rest of the group did the same, taking combat stances, their eyes wide and ready for whatever was coming. All of them except one.

PlayaSlaya stood nonchalantly, seeming entirely unconcerned about what was transpiring.

"God," he said suddenly, shaking his head. "Getting you all here was like herding cats. The battle outside was pretty epic. Enjoyed that. The rest was lame." He sighed, like a great weight had been lifted from him. He shook out his shoulders, then sucked in a deep breath. "Though this is going to be fun. Everyone thinks you're some hot-shit PVPers, but you've been lucky up to this point. You've never faced a real opponent."

*PlayaSlaya betrayed us. He's been working with the Party. For how long?* The realization blindsided Kaiden like a runaway hover-bus.

"This explains why he was so ready to charge in here without the rest of The Syndicate backing us," Zelda said, opening a private comm channel between her, Kaiden, Titus, and Thorne.

"Bastard," Titus growled.

"Should have trusted my gut, damn it," Thorne said, and Kaiden could hear the pain in her tone. He shared it. She'd been pointing out that things felt off but he hadn't listened. Had been too excited at being so close. Too distracted by the promise of victory to trust her instincts.

"That's why there were more forces above than there should have been," Thorne said, piecing things together.

"They made it just enough of a fight that our army would be bogged down," Kaiden said as everything started to make sense.

"Tricked us into leaving our reinforcements behind and coming here on our own."

"Form up on me," Zelda hissed, easing toward Titus and Thorne. "It's not a sure thing we lose this fight. If we can stay together, land a combo or two..." She trailed off, unable to convince even herself that they had a way to win the coming battle.

*Werner, PlayaSlaya, Nando, Skaia, and the last Maximus guard, Hurston, against us four. That's suicide,* Kaiden thought, evaluating the room. Every one of their opponents was max level, and with Skaia acting as a medic they'd have all the health they could want. No matter how he stacked it up, this wasn't a winnable fight.

Kaiden focused on PlayaSlaya for a moment and his visor brought up the man's stats.

*Cybernetic Knight, Level 60. I know all that.*

Kaiden moved his eyes to the new armor PlayaSlaya was wearing.

**Godslayer Armor**
**Rarity: Unique**
**Durability: 96%**
**+30% bludgeoning resistance**
**+30% explosive resistance**
**+20% stun resistance**
**Negates damage that would usually bypass armor**
**Wearer cannot be staggered**

*Oh jeez. That's a unique armor set. One of a kind. And look at those stats! Not exceptional in any particular way; just* every *way.* Kaiden almost feared to look at PlayaSlaya's weapon next. It was a massive axe – that much Kaiden had known – but now he was about to find himself facing the sharp end of it, he took a renewed interest.

**Star's Heart War-Axe**
**Rarity: Unique**

**Durability: 82%**
**+25% damage**
**+10% knockback**
**-5% dexterity when wielded**
**Deals burning damage per second on every critical hit. Does not stack.**

*Well. That's about the most terrifying weapon I've ever seen in Nova.*

"Kaiden," Zelda said through their new private comms channel. "Take the database from me. Use your speed and get out of here. You can go back topside, find Dawson, come back with reinforcements. It's our only—"

"No," he said, frowning now. Something still wasn't quite right. PlayaSlaya and Werner looked confident, assured of their victory. But Nando didn't. His expression was torn, conflicted. Like all of this was news to him.

Kaiden turned to Nando.

"Man, you really sold me on that 'the Party disappeared my father' story," he said. "Quite the actor, you are. What'd they promise you in return for betraying us?"

Nando frowned back at him.

"Nothing. Because I didn't agree to betray you." He shot an accusatory glare toward PlayaSlaya.

"I know, I know. I didn't tell you, blah, blah," PlayaSlaya said without a hint of regret in his voice. "All you need to know is there is a massive bonus waiting for you when all this is over. You can get, ah… what's her name, the kid, a bunch of new toys.'

Nando didn't look angry. He just looked disappointed. Kaiden could see it in his face, but PlayaSlaya continued on unawares.

"Anyway, who cares? It worked perfectly! We're here. Now let's finish it. I had my fun outside. This part was going to be a drag. Send out some database broadcast thing? Snore. Betrayal and a badass final showdown? Now that's the good stuff!" There was a fire in his eyes as he spoke. "Maximus always wins. And this will be one of our greatest ever!" He pumped a fist in the air, a gesture no doubt meant to fire up his guild mates. It seemed only to have the opposite effect.

"So this is what we do now, huh?" Nando's response came like an upturned bucket of ice-water, squelching the fire that'd been building in PlayaSlaya's expression. "We betray our allies and side with the Party?"

"What? Dude! You don't get it. Once we finish this, we'll be the undisputed top guild in the game. Not just PVP. We'll have the Warden Corps backing us, and the Party's support. Plus, if they do take over NextGen they've promised us early access to every DLC and alpha slots in all the upcoming game releases. Not to mention the hefty reward we'll be claiming IRL. It's all handled, my man. The hard part's done." He clenched a fist. "Now, let's have some fun."

Nando's only response was a blank stare, then a frown. A moment later, Kaiden saw why.

**PlayaSlaya has been kicked from the comm channel.**

"I didn't agree to this," Nando said in proximity chat for all to hear. "And I won't support it. My father once stood up to the Party. When he got taken away, it terrified me. I would never have stood up to the Party alone; I was too afraid. Didn't even think it was possible. But then I met you guys, with your crazy plan, and you convinced so many people. Then here we are, moments away from dealing the Party a mortal blow. I won't back down now. Not for Playa and his money. Not for anything. I can't."

Skaia and Hurston nodded at that and both took a step closer to Nando.

"This is wrong," Skaia said. "We didn't come here because we wanted to fight, because we wanted to win. We came here because Nando asked us to, and because it's what's right."

"What? No!" PlayaSlaya was panicked now, a pained expression creeping across his features. "I did this for you. For the guild. For all of us!"

"When have you ever done something not for yourself,

Playa?" Nando looked angry now. "Nova has always been just a game to you. Just a way to have a laugh or get a cheap thrill. You never realized there's more to it than that. Our guild is about fighting yes, but it's also an outlet for those who have been taken advantage of. Hurt. A place for them to work out their anger, to feel strong and to make friends. You would know that if you ever thought about anyone other than yourself. Did you even speak to Skaia? If you had you'd know her sister was arrested a couple months ago for breaking curfew. Never came back. That's why I asked her here. This means something to her too."

The pain in PlayaSlaya's face flared to anger at that.

"You don't understand. You don't get it!" Even from ten paces away Kaiden could see he was shaking with rage. "Fine. You don't have to. I'm your guild leader. I give orders and you obey. That's how this works! Hell, I pay your salary, Nando. The only reason you can afford to be in this game is because of me!"

"Not anymore," Nando said calmly. "And after today you won't be the leader of Maximus. You don't deserve it. Not after this. A lot of the members have been asking for new leadership, but I kept quiet so you would keep paying the bills. No more. I'm taking control. You can take your money and leave."

*Ouch.* That had struck a chord. Kaiden flinched but PlayaSlaya stumbled backwards as if he'd been physically assaulted. The anger in his face built to rage and he clenched his teeth so tight Kaiden swore he heard something pop.

"I built this guild. You're not going to take it from me. I am Maximus!" PlayaSlaya roared and moved so quick Kaiden didn't even have time to get his shield up.

## Chapter Sixty-One

PlayaSlaya had his axe out before anyone could react. In one smooth motion he lunged forward and brought it down on Skaia's head. She backpedaled, trying to get out of range, but the blow had already taken nearly a quarter of her health. Looked like it'd been a critical, too, considering Skaia was on fire – a fact made all the worse because her healing abilities were on cooldown from tending to the party on the way in.

**Ability: Concussive Strike**

PlayaSlaya brought his Star's Heart War-Axe down on the floor and a blazing trail of energy surged toward the already stumbling Skaia. She was a medic, extremely useful in combat, but rather squishy in one-on-one – and it showed. Concussive Strike took another chunk out of her health and its knockdown effect slammed her into the wall.

"I am Maximus!" PlayaSlaya shouted again and charged.

**Ability: Sucker Punch**
**A savage punch that deals 2x base damage. The first time this ability is used each combat it deals an additional 2x damage.**

Nando stepped into his path and scored a savage blow to PlayaSlaya's chin but was beaten aside by a counter attack in the form of the Involuntary Launch ability which flung him into the ceiling. PlayaSlaya continued forward, the blades of his war-axe glowing red hot.

**Ability: Fiery End**

The blow connected with Skaia and her health dropped to zero, her scream drowned out amid an explosion of flame.

**Party member killed!**

Skaia's corpse slumped against the wall, still flaming as the attack's damage-over-time ability continued.

PlayaSlaya wheeled on Zelda next and launched into a leap, axe raised. Titus jumped into its path and caught the blow on his shield, then lashed back with a hammer strike. PlayaSlaya was already gone, though, wheeling to the side, then spinning back in to get at Zelda.

*He's killed Skaia, taking away our heals. Now he's focusing on our DPS,* Kaiden realized. He moved to rush forward, hammer in hand, but Nando held him back.

"You handle this Werner asshole. Hurston and I got Playa," he said, then charged, fists lighting up with one of his brawler abilities.

"Keep Zelda alive!" Kaiden shouted to Titus, then joined Thorne in spinning to face Werner.

"Odds aren't on your side anymore," Kaiden said, advancing on him.

"Not exactly to plan," Werner retorted, looking entirely unconcerned. "But I'm max level and you two are barely into the fifties." He laughed. "This will be a cakewalk. I'm a blast warden, the best damage-dealing class in the Corps. I'll have you two dead bef—"

Thorne's hammer caught him under the chin and snapped his head back as his health bar dropped to the mid-eighties. The blow caught him by surprise and Werner fought to raise his hammer-gun and take aim, but Thorne gave him no room to breathe.

"You always were a snide asshole," she said. "But now you're a snide asshole who's out of his depth." She smacked him again, then landed another blow on his head, dealing critical damage. Her charge bar filled with each attack and Kaiden's visor brought up a line of text reminding him of the power warden passive.

**Ability: Improved Aggressive Mindset (passive)**
**Each successful attack you land will regenerate X charge where X is 15% of damage dealt.**

Werner retreated, eyes wide at the unrelenting aggression of the attack. He fired off an Improved Scatter Shot to cover his retreat but Thorne was ready for it.

**Ability: Improved Instigated Fury**
**The fervor of battle sweeps over you. For the next 8 seconds each time you take damage your base attack increases by 15%.**

The Improved Scatter Shot struck her right in the chest and Thorne looked down to the dozen or so scorch marks on her armor, then back up to Werner. He swallowed audibly as their eyes met.

"I earned my levels, Werner. You had some intern grind them out for you."

"Damn this game," Werner growled then charged up an Improved Kinetic Grenade. "PlayaSlaya! Take down Zelda and loot that database!"

His only response was a growl and Kaiden spared a glance back to see the guild leader unloading a barrage of attacks against Titus' shield. Hurston was already dead – Kaiden must have missed the notification – and PlayaSlaya still looked to be gaining steam. He was a hell of a fighter. His armor helped in no small measure, absorbing far too much damage than any suit of armor should. And his Star's Heart War-Axe was flaming brightly, boiling from deep within as if there was an actual star inside. Combined with PlayaSlaya's max level and obsession with PVP he was a near unbeatable opponent. Somehow, though, Nando seemed almost a match for him. With the support of Titus – harassing PlayaSlaya with Energy Grip and Shield Slams – and Zelda – blasting away with every ability in her arsenal – Nando was just barely keeping pace with PlayaSlaya.

"PlayaSlaya!" Werner shouted again, then in a panic, threw the grenade at Zelda.

"Zelda! Look out!" Kaiden shouted but Thorne was already in motion. She stepped into the path of the grenade and tanked the damage from the ensuing explosion – and her base damage increased by another fifteen percent.

**Ability: Gravity Sledge**
**You channel a massive amount of charge into your hammer. Your next attack deals 250% base damage and on a successful hit knocks the target into the air. They take fall damage on landing.**

"You're a criminal and a murderer," Thorne growled, then swung her axe into Werner's chest with a rising blow. A shock-wave burst out at the impact and he was flung into the ceiling. He slammed into the rock there then thudded back down to the floor. From the attack and the fall damage combined, his health dropped down to forty percent – and Kaiden hadn't even thrown a blow yet.

"I've been waiting to beat you down for a long time, Werner," Thorne said, advancing on the stunned man. The expression on his face said he was totally out of his depth.

He scrambled to his feet, then retreated across the room, back toward the door he'd come in through.

"Let me in!" he shouted as he ran toward it.

Kaiden burst into motion and ran him down with his increased dexterity.

With no charge yet, he led with a hammer strike to Werner's back, then raised his weapon to attack again.

Werner spun and fired a quick Improved Scatter Shot into Kaiden's chest, but Intangible Defense nullified any damage from the shot.

"I've got this under control," Thorne's voice came from behind. It was calm but seething, like a fire that'd burned down to coals but when disturbed revealed a far more intense heat beneath. And then she flew past him, launched into the air with Heroic Leap. She landed between Werner and the door with a shockwave that crashed into Werner.

He stopped dead in his tracks, seemingly frozen.

"You're right," Thorne said, advancing toward him slowly. "Blast wardens do deal the most DPS of the warden classes – when at range. Power wardens, though," she said, looking down at her hammer, "are specialists in close quarters."

**Ability: Hammer Sweep**

Werner's health dropped further.

"And blast wardens are pretty shit up close. Something you would have known if you'd actually leveled your class. Actually cared about this game. But you didn't. It was just a means to an end for you, wasn't it? Just a way to keep working your way up the corrupt ladder of the Party."

"I should have killed you when I had the chance," he growled. "In the real world. Not in this child's game."

"There are a lot of things you should have done, Werner. But instead you made me party to your corrupt investigation into Zelda's parents. Instead you killed innocent civilians then blamed it on the resistance. Instead you lied and you cheated. You abused your power and lorded over the world like it was your plaything." Thorne clipped him with a hammer strike. Not enough to kill him. Just a wounding blow.

"You thought you were untouchable. Thought you were safe in your corrupt power. How do you feel now, little man? Do you feel powerful?" She hit him again and he cursed.

"If I ever see you again, I will end you," he snarled.

"Oh, we'll meet again," Thorne said. "Once the Party is in ruins and justice comes calling. And you better believe, Werner. Deep down in your blackened little heart, you better believe I'll be there. I'll be the one who brings you in."

With that, she wound up for one last attack. Werner didn't even try to resist.

"Damn you," he snarled.

"You first," she said.

**Ability: Gravity Sledge**

The blow connected and Werner flew clear across the room. He was dead before he hit the ground and rolled to a stop.

**Blast Warden Werner10 assisted kill - 8,000 EXP gained!**

"You, uh, handled that," Kaiden said, still in awe at the onslaught.

Thorne shook out her shoulders and her hammer hand, then smiled.

"That felt good." She craned her neck to one side, then the other. "I needed that."

An explosion from behind caught his attention and Kaiden spun to see Zelda firing away at PlayaSlaya. Titus' shield was overloaded but Nando had PlayaSlaya thoroughly occupied, the two of them near the exit and trading a brutal flurry of blows back and forth.

Abilities fired off one after another with no thought for defense, the cybernetic knight and brawler duking it out in a straight damage race.

**Ability: Mano A Mano**
**A 'trap and scrap' ability, Mano A Mano locks the user and one target together for three seconds plus X, where X is 1% of the user's total strength stat.**

Nando activated the ability and the chains around him unwound, then lashed forward and caught PlayaSlaya tightly.

The guild leader retorted with Wind-Up Swing, a slow but powerful attack that would have knocked Nando back had the two not been chained together. Nonetheless, the blow connected with an explosion of force so strong it shattered the floor beneath their feet.

Nando's health dropped into the red but he seemed unconcerned as he replied with a Frenzied Barrage. The attacks fell in rapid succession, each dealing more damage than the last as Nando's blazing fists punched through his opponent's armor.

"I'll never forgive you for this," PlayaSlaya growled, then broke away with his own health in the red as Mano A Mano ended. "You ruined it. Ruined it all. We could have had everything we've ever wanted!" PlayaSlaya shouted.

"Everything *you* ever wanted," Nando said back, slow and sad. "And think of the cost. How could anyone live with that?"

"Damn you!" PlayaSlaya screamed and sprung forward. He reared back with his axe for a killing blow.

**Ability: Cataclysmic Unmaking**
**An attack that deals massive damage, bypasses armor, and knocks the target back. On a critical hit, damage from this attack and any fall damage is doubled.**

Nando reacted with his own attack, raising two flaming fists above his head.

**Ability: Untimely End**
**Deals 2x base damage, staggers the opponent and deals burning damage per second equal to your base damage. On a critical hit, this ability deals 3x base damage.**

Nando's fists came down on Playa's head at the same time as Playa's war-axe rose up into Nando's stomach. Cataclysmic Unmaking hit far harder, bypassing Nando's armor. He crumpled inward at the blow and his health dropped to zero as he flew up into the ceiling

**Party member killed!**

PlayaSlaya staggered backwards, his health down to single digits.

"Damn you, Nando," he said, looking down at the corpse. "We could…"

Magma from Untimely End was seeping down from his shoulder and over his chest. It sizzled and hissed, eating through his armor and boiling his health away.

"We could have had it all, man. We could've…"

The damage-over-time effect of the magma did its job. Playa-Slaya's eyes rolled up in his head and he collapsed to the floor with a thud.

**Cybernetic Knight PlayaSlaya assisted kill - 8,000 EXP gained!**

**Level 53 achieved!**
**Max health and stamina increased**
**+3 stat points**

**Ability Unlocked!**
**Dual Wielding**

More text followed, explaining the ability. Kaiden snapped a screenshot of it on instinct but he really wasn't focused on it because it didn't matter. Relief was flooding through his body. They'd won, and this time, for good. The battle was done, and with – he checked the timer – thirty-five minutes to spare.

"Guys," he said, looking at them across the chaos of the room. Five dead players, a host of busted floor tiles, a cracked ceiling, and a rapidly cooling pool of magma. It was chaos, but they'd won.

"We did it," Kaiden said, letting a smile stretch across his face. Werner had set the trap but it hadn't mattered. PlayaSlaya had misjudged his followers. Nando had stayed true, and together they'd turned the tide. Reversed the trap on those who'd set it.

"We did it," Kaiden said again.

"No." Thorne was frowning sharply. There was no humor in her eyes. As Kaiden watched, he saw Zelda had the same expression.

"What?" he asked, looking between them both and swallowing the dread rising inside him.

"PlayaSlaya betrayed us. He worked with the Warden Corps to set this trap, to lure us in."

"Yeah, and we just kicked their ass for it," Titus said.

"No," Thorne said again. "Werner isn't smart enough to act alone. He doesn't think for himself; he just obeys. It wasn't his idea to set this trap." She turned her eyes toward the door that led to the tunnel, and beyond, the broadcast control room.

"There's one last person standing between us and victory." She grimaced as she spoke, and suddenly, Kaiden understood why.

The name echoed in his thoughts and sent a shiver of fear down his spine. Their plan had hinged on not fighting him. On surprising the Warden Corps and the Party with their attack here. But PlayaSlaya had sold them out, and that meant the Party had been ready for them. Meant the one person they had intended to avoid at all costs had been ready for them.

"Moran," Kaiden said, then swallowed hard. "Shit."

Chapter Sixty-Two

"You really think he's here?" Titus asked, leaning forward and peering down the tunnel ahead. It was long, dark, and revealed nothing of what awaited them.

"He's here," Thorne said. "This whole thing has his handiwork all over it."

Kaiden couldn't help but agree.

"He's down there," he said. "Waiting right next to the broadcast control console, I don't doubt. It's the best way for him to make sure no one uploads the database."

There was some comfort in that knowledge. A chilling, frightening sort of comfort. It was the undeniability of the fact that everything had led up to this. One final confrontation, and for all the marbles. Lose, and Killswitch would take down Nova. Win, and – well, win and maybe they'd change the world.

There were no more ifs or ands or buts. Just the certainty of what needed to be done.

"We're gonna kick this guy's ass, broadcast the database, and bring down the Party," Kaiden said, and he knew it was true. Memories of everything they'd been through flashed through his mind, all starting with the day he'd found Bernstein murdered and been blamed for it. From prison to the resistance. The attack on their base to being harbored by King Street. Eventually kicked out of there, then living out of a damn van, then... Thorne. And from there, everything had changed.

*We've come too far to fail now. People have died to help us get here. Lives have been ruined. But no more. This ends today. Now.*

"No part of this is going to be easy," Zelda said. "We need to be realistic about that. Moran is the Warden Hierarch. He's stronger than any one player has a right to be."

"Should we go back for reinforcements?" Titus asked, half turning to look back at the exit.

"There's no time," Zelda said. And she was right. The timer was still ticking down. Thirty-two minutes to go. That was it.

Kaiden's quick check of the command module revealed the battle up top was drawing to a close, both sides depleted from the fighting, but it still wasn't clear who the victor would be. He didn't have time to wait around to find out.

It didn't matter anyway. The army had done its job by getting him and Zelda and Titus and Thorne here. They couldn't expect any more help. All they had now was each other, and that was going to have to be enough. *Was* going to be enough.

"We're each at full health," Kaiden said, looking them all over even though he knew what he'd find. Nando taking down PlayaSlaya had been a gift in two parts. One, it removed Playa-Slaya from the equation, but two, the experience from it had leveled them all up. Full health, then, and level fifty-three each. It was far from max level, but it would have to do. They'd also looted stimpacks from the remains of the last fight, bringing them each to a full three.

And then there were the new abilities.

Kaiden pulled up the screenshot he'd snapped of his newest ability then sent it to each of them.

"Study up as we walk," he said, taking his first steps into the dark of the tunnel. "We're going to need every advantage we can get."

**Ability Unlocked!**
**Dual Wielding: For a duration of 1 minute your shield reforms itself into an energy hammer, which you may use**

alongside your normal weapon. While Dual Wielding you cannot block, your charge capacity is increased by 50%, and the effect of your Slayer passive is doubled, meaning each critical hit restores 10 charge.
**Cost: 0**
**Cooldown: 10 minutes**

Admittedly, it was one hell of an ability. Sounded like fun, if he was being frank. He paused for a moment, salivating over the thought of burying Moran under a stream of critical hits from two hammers at once. The pleasant daydream was interrupted as Titus' screenshot arrived.

**Ability Unlocked!**
**Center of Attention: For the next 30 seconds, a target of your choosing must target you or take 2x base damage for every second they don't. You must be standing still to use this ability.**
**Cost: 80 charge**
**Cooldown: 15 minutes**

"Finally, the recognition I deserve," Titus said with a nervous laugh. "In all seriousness, though, this is a nasty ability. It'll either force an opponent to focus on me instead of y'all, or it'll just pump damage into them. And two times my base damage, so those would actually be respectable attacks."

Kaiden nodded along.

"Most people want to go around the tank. This'll stop that plan dead in its tracks."

"Yeah, keep all the attention on you," Thorne said as sent her screenshot. "That'll tie in nicely when I come back from the dead with a vengeance, eh?"

**Ability Unlocked!**
**Improved Last Rites (passive): When you reach 0% health this ability triggers. You have 30 seconds to kill all opponents in a 50-foot radius of your point of death. Every kill**

made during this time extends the kill timer by 3 seconds. Should you succeed, you will be given 1 HP back. If not, you will die. Kills made during this time earn no EXP. Abilities *can* be used during Improved Last Rites.
Cooldown: 6 hours

"Anything that increases our survivability is going to be a huge asset," Zelda said, stepping carefully through the dark of the tunnel. "Even if it only keeps you up for an extra thirty seconds, every one of those counts."

"And what about you, Zelda?" Kaiden asked. "What new trick are you packing after that level-up?"

Her screenshot arrived with a *ding*.

**Ability Unlocked!**
**Pain for Gain: You may sacrifice 25% of your max health to make your next attack deal 2x damage. If you sacrifice 50% of your max health that attack will deal 4x damage instead.**
**Cost: 70 charge**
**Cooldown: 5 minutes**

"Holy crap," Kaiden said, his mouth falling open. Blast wardens really did get all the insane DPS abilities. Though this one came at quite a price.

"I'm pretty sure that ability officially gives me glass cannon status. If I use it, that is. Can't imagine I'd have much health left."

"So, uh, don't miss, I suppose?" Kaiden smirked.

"Real funny," Zelda shot back, but there was slight smirk on her face as well.

Kaiden made to respond but the tunnel pulled a tight turn, and as they rounded it, he stopped in his tracks. The path ahead opened into a large cavern and at the center of it, Commander Slaen Moran stood waiting for them.

~

Slaen Moran
Class: Warden Hierarch
Faction: Warden Corps
Level: 60

Quick facts: The Warden Hierarch is a unique class only available to the leader of the Warden Corps. The progenitor of all warden classes, the Hierarch is a dangerous adversary and a very valuable ally.

*Something tells me Moran is going to lean more on the adversary side of things,* Kaiden thought.

Moran greeted them each with a gentle nod, eyes sliding from one to the next. Finally, they came to rest on the last member of their party.

"Thorne." There was a clear note of distaste in his tone.

*So, this is the fearsome Commander Moran?*

To be honest, Kaiden was surprised by the man in front of him. Like all warden accounts, his avatar was locked into a realistic representation of what he looked like in the real world. He had light brown hair, kept close in a military cut and parted too neatly down the side. His eyes were equally brown and rested high above a nose that was crooked, as if it'd once been broken. But that wasn't what caught Kaiden's attention most. Instead, it was the expression on his face. The slight frown at the corners of his mouth. The sadness in his eyes. The disappointment evident in every wrinkle and fissure of his clearly stress-strained face. He looked nothing like the fearsome tyrant Kaiden had always imagined. Instead, he just looked... sad. Tired. Like he'd expected better of all of them and had been sorely disappointed.

Whatever unexpected emotions Kaiden found in Moran's face were immediately overshadowed, however, as he took in the commander's armor. It was clearly warden armor – with mechanical veins and tendons running across it to carry charge throughout – but it seemed older somehow. Heavier and thicker than the sleek suits most wore today. At the same time, it didn't look old in a dusty, relic sort of way. No, it looked old like a mountain looked old. A monolith of days long gone by but standing tall and proud still. Resilient, defiant until the end. As Kaiden stared, his visor brought up details on the armor.

**Warden Hierarch Power Suit,**
**Rarity: Singularly Unique**
**Durability: 100%**
**+10% charge gained from Atmospheric Charge**
**+10% charge gained from critical hits**
**+10% AOE damage resistance**
**+10% melee damage resistance**
**+10% ranged damage resistance**
**+10% charge regeneration**
**+80% charge capacity**
**Stimulant Cooling Slots: 0**

*No stimulant cooling slots,* Kaiden noted. That was a boon. Everything else he saw was not. It left him swallowing hard.

In contrast to his armor, the weapon Moran held was far from impressive. It looked for all the world like a regular old Warden Corps hammer. Could easily have been the standard hammer given out to all ensigns.

"Thorne. I am truly sorry to see you here." Moran's voice echoed through the cavern. The place was smaller than Kaiden had expected. It was a simple space lacking any decoration or adornment. A simple room with a simple purpose: to house the All-Frequencies Broadcast System. As Kaiden looked closer, though, he realized there was no console in the room. Instead, it was off to one side in a room of its own, half the size of the one they were in now. Almost as if it'd been an afterthought.

Afterthought or not, the control panel was nestled into its room, a sleek console jutting from the otherwise jagged and scarred core of the asteroid.

"Yeah, gotta admit I'd be a lot happier not seeing you here," Thorne said back. "It'd certainly make things a lot easier."

Kaiden kept his hammer held tight and his shield at the ready as they spoke. It'd been long enough since the fight against

Werner that Intangible Defense was active again, but all the same, he preferred not to lose it to just any old surprise attack.

"There was no eventuality in which this story ended without me here," Moran said, and he didn't sound the least bit happy about it. "After all, this isn't a new story, is it?" He shook his head at that. "Once again, the world stands on the brink of chaos and it falls to me to stop it. To protect everything we've built." He gave Thorne a stern gaze. "You were there during the Great Test, Thorne. I thought for all our differences of opinion that you would at least understand this. This business with the database, with broadcasting it to the world – it's playing with matches. It's going to start a fire none of us can put out."

"That's the idea," Thorne growled. Kaiden saw her fist clench on the grip of her hammer.

Moran shook his head and tutted at that.

"You have a problem with my methods? Fine. Then oppose me," he said, and there was a hint of anger in his voice now. "Challenge me. Take me down and claim my spot at the top. Honestly, that's what I always hoped you'd do. Or if you're not strong enough for that, then fine. Take your toys and go home. But this isn't either of those options. You're not just refusing to play; you're threatening to burn down the whole playground. It's childish, and it's dangerous."

"We're doing more than threatening," Titus snapped. "We're going to see it through."

"Titus, right?" Moran turned his attention to him. "The murderer. The petty criminal who took a fall for his boss. Loyal to a fault, I hear. But not too bright." He didn't say it cruelly, just as a calm statement of fact, devoid of emotion.

Titus growled deep down in his throat but Moran had already moved on, looking at Kaiden now.

"And Kaiden, I presume? The leader of this little operation. But are you really? Or are you just the convenient puppet they're propping up? Real power doesn't lie with the figurehead. Everyone knows that. If you're not pulling the strings, you're the puppet."

"No strings here," Kaiden said, stretching his hands out. "But you'll learn that soon enough."

Realistically, it wasn't a very good threat. Kaiden had never been particularly good at sounding intimidating. He didn't delude himself about that, but Moran seemed so unconcerned he didn't even bother to acknowledge anything had been said. Instead, he looked at Zelda, and for the first time since they'd met, a smile pulled at his lips.

"Zelda." He drew out the name, let it hang in the air, echo through the chamber a moment. "Now, you're the interesting one of this bunch of rabble rousers. The brains of the operation. There's potential in you."

"Who killed Bernstein?" she snapped by way of response. "Who ordered it? Who carried it out?" She raised her hammer-gun and took aim at him. "They will answer for it."

"Does it matter?" Moran asked. He looked genuinely surprised. "Bernstein's dead. He's not a factor in this anymore. No longer able to affect the outcome. That was, admittedly, the point of having him killed."

"It was you, then?" There was an edge to her voice Kaiden had never heard before, but in the moment, he welcomed it. He agreed with it, could feel his own anger rising inside him. They'd never learned who killed Bernstein – one of the mysteries even his database couldn't solve. But someone had been responsible. And from the looks of things, Moran was the odds-on favorite.

"Would it make you feel better if I said it was me? Would that bring you peace? Let your mind rest thinking you've avenged him?" Moran looked genuinely curious.

"It'd be a start," she snarled.

"No, it wouldn't. Don't lie to yourself." Moran took a step forward and everyone tensed, raising hammers and flicking on shields. "Bernstein's death will weigh on your heart for the rest of your life. Just like every serious mistake you've ever made. Every decision you regret. Every person you love that you've failed. These transgressions, these weaknesses – they never go away. They weigh us down. They hold us back. The only way to be truly free of them is to keep moving forward."

"What, and become like you?" Kaiden snapped.

Moran frowned.

"Boy, you don't know the first thing about me."

"I know you're standing between us and the broadcast control console. In this moment, that's about all I need to know."

"Damn straight," Titus added. "It's about time we did something about that, don't you think?"

Moran sighed and closed his eyes. Kaiden almost charged him then, almost took the moment to strike first. But then Moran's eyes were open again and he looked genuinely frightened.

"If that database goes out to the masses, chaos will follow. Upheaval. Violence. Death. You will be responsible for throwing the world back into unchecked violence and bloodshed. Back into the darkness we fought so hard to defeat during the Great Test." Moran drew his hammer. "And if I fail to stop you, I'll be just as responsible." He shook his head at that thought. "I buried friends. Brothers. People I loved. I won't see their sacrifices made meaningless."

"Your actions have already done that," Thorne said. "How do you not see it? The Party is built on violence. Upheld by abuse, injustice. You encourage people like Werner. Bullies and sadists propped up by the very system you cherish."

"Werner is a useful tool. A hammer, say. Crude, perhaps, but effective." Moran paused then and scowled. "We could debate these points ad infinitum, I fear, and never see eye to eye. You just don't understand. Thorne, I thought you did. I thought the Test had shown you the hard truths of our world. I see now that I was mistaken. You don't see reality. But I do. And I'll do whatever I must in order to protect it."

"He's stalling," Kaiden said. The thought hit him like a freight train. Of course he was. Did Moran believe what he was saying? Was he really that deluded? It didn't matter. They were on the clock and every moment they spent debating him was a moment lost. A moment closer to Killswitch taking Nova offline.

*Twenty-seven minutes on the timer…*

"You're buying time for Killswitch to complete," Kaiden said, and for the first time since the conversation had begun, Moran looked surprised.

"Maybe there's more to you than I thought," he said.

"Let's find out," Kaiden said.

"Let's." Moran waved his hand in the air. A door in the wall that Kaiden hadn't noticed slid open and a dozen max-level wardens strode out, hammers raised and shields on.

"Shit," Thorne said, backing up a pace and setting her feet in a combat stance.

Kaiden's heart fell through his stomach, but there wasn't time to worry. Only time to act. The battle had just become unwinnable. They needed a new plan, and fast.

"I let Werner have his moment," Moran said. "But he screwed it up. I'll be doing no such thing." He gave a signal and the wardens charged.

Something exploded behind Kaiden and he spun to find more wardens behind them.

"Behind us, too!" he shouted, but something was wrong. The wardens charging down the tunnel weren't looking at them. They were focused on Moran and his men. And their armor was bent and bloodied, as if they'd just fought through hell itself. Which they had, Kaiden realized as he recognized the two wardens leading the charge.

"Dawson! Sola!"

"Got a bit delayed up top," Dawson grunted.

"Better late than never, though, right?" Sola flashed past, Lightspeed active. The rest of the rebel wardens followed her and the room exploded into chaos. Abilities fired off on all sides and it was all Kaiden could do to usher Zelda out of the line of fire.

"This is our chance," he said, eyes fixed on the console in the side room. "Get to the console!"

Thorne and Titus followed as the previously dark cavern blossomed with explosions and laser fire such that it was bright as day. But the wardens were too busy focusing on each other. An initial volley of Improved Kinetic Grenades and Improved

Warden's Bolts had filled the cavern with fire and dust and particle effects so much that it looked more like a rave than a fight to the death.

"Go, go!" Kaiden shouted, ducking through the chaos then sprinting toward the console room. Zelda slipped in first but Kaiden was a step behind. Then Thorne, then Titus.

"Send the message, quick!" Kaiden shouted, then positioned himself next to Titus. "We'll keep you covered."

"Don't waste your effort," a voice said.

Kaiden squinted into the smoking mess of explosions and debris as a figure strode forth.

Moran.

Kaiden retreated a step as the warden hierarch reached the doorway. Moran tossed a look over his shoulder, and when he turned back to Kaiden there was doubt in his eyes.

"What, not liking the changing odds?" Kaiden asked.

"No." Moran pressed a button on his armor and the ceiling rumbled. A thick steel door descended just behind him and before Kaiden could react it'd cut them off from the battle raging without. They were left alone in the console room with Moran.

"These odds, on the other hand, are much better."

## Chapter Sixty-Three

"All right," Kaiden said, switching to group comms. "This guy's like some sort of souped-up power warden, right?"

From his appearance, that was the best he could figure. Moran didn't have the massive shield of a shield warden, nor the sleekness of an enhanced warden, and definitely not the hammer-gun of a blast warden. That just left power warden. Power warden with a small hammer, maybe, but Kaiden wasn't under the illusion that it took a big hammer to do big damage.

"We'll deal with this asshole like we would any other high-level enemy. Titus, try to tank his attacks. Thorne, deal all the damage you can. I'll harass him. And Zelda..."

"Charge up and hit him with everything I got. I know the drill," she said, then fell back toward the rear of the room. It was a relatively small space, no more than twenty paces across, and Moran watched her as she went.

*Eyes over here!* Kaiden darted in, hammer raised. He went in fast, sprinting with everything he had and everything his stamina would allow. Moran turned to face him just as Kaiden brought his hammer down on the man's head. Except – no. The attack had missed?

Moran was a step to the side. Kaiden swung again. Another miss. Moran had moved again. He'd waited until the last possible moment, then simply stepped out of the way of the attack.

"How high is this guy's dex stat?"

Kaiden didn't have long to ponder the question as Moran lashed back with a hammer strike. The blow slammed into Kaiden's Intangible Defense bubble and shattered it. Kaiden's health was spared, though – right up until Moran's second attack caught him in the jaw. Kaiden's health bar flashed down to ninety-two percent.

He growled, then kept swinging as Titus and Thorne joined the fight. Neither had any charge yet so they came in with a flurry of hammer strikes. Thorne needed to connect with her hits to build charge while Titus needed to block attacks. Moran backpedaled, facing all three of them at once.

Thorne lashed out with a downward hammer strike, then quickly followed with a rising blow. Moran ducked around the first then leaned back on his heels to let the second slip right past his chin. As he did, he landed a hammer strike on Thorne's shoulder, then another in her ribs. Her health flashed down to eighty-five percent.

Titus took advantage of the moment to attack from the side. Moran spun and caught his hammer strike on his shield, absorbing the blow. There was a window for Moran to counterattack but he held back instead. Titus swung again but his attack found only Moran's shield once more.

"He's trying to charge-starve us," Kaiden shouted as he realized what was up. *Why else would he dodge Thorne's attacks then block Titus', but not hit him back?* "He's playing to our classes' weaknesses."

"Play to this," Zelda snarled. A light bloomed at the corner of Kaiden's vision then an Improved Burst Arrow flashed toward Moran. He caught it on his shield.

"Focus on getting into Sniper Mode," Kaiden called to Zelda. "Then hit him with a Paralyzing Shot or something. We need to slow him down!" But Zelda was already firing another ability.

**Ability: Improved Scatter Shot**

Blasts detonate on impact, causing a small explosion that deals an additional 10% damage and blinds the target for 3 seconds.

Moran shot straight into the air, so high he almost hit the ceiling, and the flurry of lasers passed well below him. He raised his hammer, and as Kaiden watched, it stretched, growing to the size of a power warden's sledge.

**Ability: Earth Shatter**
**You channel charge into your legs and leap into the air.**
**Upon landing, a shockwave bursts out from around you.**
**Opponents within 10 feet of you are knocked down.**

Moran and his newly massive hammer came back down like a one-man earthquake. The ground exploded around him and Kaiden saw Titus go down before he himself was bowled over by the attack.

"That was a power warden attack," Kaiden called, struggling back to his feet. "He's a modified power warden, like I thought. Look at his hammer."

Moran made a go for Zelda but Thorne cut him off and set her feet.

"Gonna have to go through me, Slaen."

"With pleasure, Ava."

**Ability: Improved Chained Fury**
**Your combat prowess allows you to chain attacks together.**
**For the next 5 seconds, each attack deals an additional 20% damage for every successful attack before it.**

Moran lashed out with a series of hammer strikes, each stronger than the last.

"Where is he getting all of this charge?" Titus shouted.

"Improved Aggressive Mindset, probably," Kaiden said back. "Power warden ability. He gains charge for each successful hit."

"But not this much charge," Thorne grunted, dodging and

ducking his assault. "Screw this." She leaned in, letting the attacks land on her armor so she could strike back. Moran disengaged at the movement, though, sidestepping away and rushing toward Zelda who was now in Sniper Mode and charging an Inferno Shot.

"Not so fast," Titus snarled. His Energy Grip whipped forward and caught Moran around the ankle. A good yank and he was dragged back. Kaiden sprinted over, hammer at the ready. Titus raised his hammer as well to tear in to Moran.

**Ability: Heroic Leap**
**You direct charge into your legs and hammer. Your next jump will carry you 20 feet and if you attack as you land it will deal area-of-effect damage equal to 200% base damage.**

Moran flew up before either could land a strike. He landed and slammed his hammer into the ground. Damage washed out over Kaiden. His health fell to seventy-seven percent. Titus took damage too and his health bar flashed, then stabilized at eighty-five percent.

"Jeez. For a power warden, he's fast as an enhanced warden," Kaiden said. "We need to get some stuns or a slow on him."

"I have a better idea," Zelda said.

**Ability: Inferno Shot**
**You fire an explosive, superheated blast that ignores 50% of the target's armor. Deals 3x base damage to all targets in range (allies included). Takes 7 seconds to charge (must be stationary).**

Kaiden rolled away as the attack exploded against Moran in an blast of superheated plasma. Stifling heat washed across the room and Kaiden's eyes burned at the blinding light. Nonetheless, he felt himself smile.

*Let's see how you stand up to that, huh?*

The light faded to reveal Moran was standing still and his health was untouched – still at one hundred percent.

*What?!*

A faintly glowing bubble surrounded Moran. Cracks were shot through its surface, and not a moment later it shattered and fell away.

"That was an Intangible Defense bubble," Kaiden said. "An enhanced warden ability."

"Okay..." Thorne said, cautiously approaching. "So, he has power warden abilities *and* enhanced warden abilities?"

"Well, that was a good shot," Moran said, turning to face Zelda. "It might've tickled even if it'd hit me."

"Gah!" Thorne cried as she charged in. Moran smiled.

**Ability: Shield Bash**
**The warden strikes out with their shield, dealing no damage but stunning the target for 2 seconds.**

Moran slammed his shield into Thorne and her body went rigid as the stun took effect. Zelda fired an Improved Burst Arrow from Sniper Mode but Moran was already in motion again. Except there wasn't one Moran; there were three.

"Improved Blur!" Kaiden shouted as he recognized the ability. "How many abilities does this guy have?"

Zelda's attack had been aimed at the center-most Moran but as it phased through him it became apparent that was one of the body doubles.

The three Morans lashed out at Thorne, bashing great chunks of her health away with each hit. Only one of them was actually doing damage but through Improved Blur it was impossible to tell which it was. The stun wore off with Thorne's health at fifty-two percent, and she swung at the Moran on the right. Another body double.

"Stimpack!" Kaiden shouted at Thorne and her health swelled back to seventy-seven percent as she used the first of her three. He popped one as well and his own health was back to full as he sprinted forward to attack Moran from behind.

He still didn't have any charge but Zelda had identified one of the body doubles and Thorne the other, so Kaiden managed to surprise Moran and land a hammer strike on his back for base damage. Moran's health dropped by less than a single percent and Kaiden recoiled as a jolt of electricity jumped from the hierarch's armor and zapped him for four percent damage.

"Improved Volt Field?" Titus asked. "Now he has shield warden abilities? What, does he have every melee warden ability?"

Kaiden wasn't focused on that, though. He lashed out again, and this time landed a critical on the back of Moran's head.

**Critical hit!**
**+50% damage (Headshot)**
**+5% damage (Chrono Sledge ability, extra damage on crits)**
**Moran is slowed by 30% for 2 seconds**

Improved Volt Field bit back at Kaiden for another five percent and at the same time, the warden hierarch's health dropped by two percent. Not a good sign, Kaiden knew. His Chrono Sledge hammer had triggered on the hit, though, slowing Moran by thirty-percent for two seconds. And even more importantly, Kaiden's Slayer passive had triggered because of the critical, so he'd gained five charge. An idea popped into his head at that.

"You won't give me charge? Then I'll make my own," he said.

Five charge wasn't enough to do anything, really, but it was enough to activate an ability that didn't require any charge.

**Ability: Dual Wielding**
**For a duration of 3 minutes, or until you cancel this ability, your shield reforms itself into a second hammer, which you may use alongside your normal weapon. While Dual Wielding you cannot block, your charge capacity is increased by 50%, and the effect of your Slayer passive is doubled, meaning each critical hit restores 10 charge.**

He activated the ability and his shield warped and resolved

into a mirror image of his hammer. Moran raised an eyebrow as if impressed. Kaiden gave him a wink.

Moran's response came immediately.

**Ability: Dual Wielding**

His shield formed into a replica of his own already massive hammer.

"Have at it, then," he said as Kaiden charged forward. Moran was just as fast. They met in the center of the room in an exchange of hammer strikes.

Kaiden swung his hammer in a downward blow from the right and Moran ducked under it – straight into the rising blow from the energy hammer Kaiden had sent in from the left.

The blow connected with Moran's elbow.

**Critical hit!**
**+25% damage (Shattered Elbow)**
**+5% damage (Chrono Sledge ability, extra damage on crits)**
**Moran is slowed by 30% for 2 seconds**

The hammer flashed as it made contact and Kaiden also saw his own charge bar fill by ten. A good amount considering he hadn't yet had to tank an attack on his shield – a bit difficult to do with his shield currently in the form of a hammer. His health dropped again from Improved Volt Field. This wasn't a winning strategy, but Moran had no stimulant cooling chambers on his armor, which meant he didn't have stimpacks.

*I can afford to eat some damage here if it means building charge.*

Moran lashed back and Kaiden dodged to the side, slipping around the blow, then barely ducked under the follow-up strike.

**Riposte x1 gained!**
**Riposte x2 gained!**

Was that surprise on Moran's face? The debuff from Chrono Sledge must have caught him off-guard.

With a double riposte stack, Kaiden attacked back. He aimed for Moran's head and just managed to land the hit. The extra damage from riposte poured in on top of the critical hit damage and Kaiden's base damage

**+50% damage (Riposte x2)**

**+50% damage (Headshot)**
**+5% damage (Chrono Sledge ability, extra damage on crits)**
**Moran is slowed by 30% for 2 seconds**

Moran's health dropped by a little under three percent this time, but Kaiden smiled to himself anyway as his charge bar jumped by another ten.

"If I keep landing crits, he'll stay slowed," Kaiden shouted through comms. "Hit him while we can!"

Kaiden and Moran exchanged more blows while the others charged in. Titus and Thorne joined the fray and between the three of them and the speed debuff, Moran started actually taking damage.

**Ability: Improved Paralyzing Shot**
**Fires an electric blast that confuses the electrical impulses in the target's muscles, deals 110% base damage and slows target's movement by 60% for 10 seconds.**

"How's that?" Zelda asked as her shot caught Moran in the back and sent spasms through his body. She was the only one of them with any significant charge, thanks to Improved Atmospheric Charge, so she was the only one with access to consistent abilities. "Now you can really tear into hi—"

"Enough!" Moran shouted. He ended Dual Wielding and his energy hammer morphed back into a shield, which was immediately put to use in a Shield Slam that left everyone stunned for two seconds.

**Ability: Embolden**

An aura of rage surrounds you. For the next 5 seconds, you and allies within 20 feet deal double damage on melee attacks and take 50% more damage.

Ability: Gravity Sledge
You channel a massive amount of charge into your hammer. Your next attack deals 250% base damage and on a successful hit, knocks the target into the air. They take fall damage on landing.

Moran hit Thorne and her health dropped to fifty-four from the blow, then forty-nine as she crashed to the floor some distance away.

Ability: Improved Shield Break
You channel charge into your hammer. Your next attack ignores armor, staggers the target, and deals 250% of base damage.

Moran hit Titus next, dealing a massive dose of damage. The big man's health settled at fifty-nine percent and he stumbled backward, trying to recover from the suddenness of the assault. Moran hit him again with a Debilitating Blow that sent his health reeling down to forty-six.

"Heads up, asshole," Zelda said then hit Moran in the back with an Improved Warden's Bolt. With Embolden active he took an additional fifty percent damage from the attack and his health dropped to seventy-eight percent.

"Hit him again!" Kaiden shouted, ducking a hammer strike and backing out of Moran's range.

"You're annoyingly slippery, you know that?" Moran growled and pointed his hammer at Kaiden's face, but he was well out of arm's reach.

Ability: Improved Scatter Shot

The end of Moran's hammer opened with a faint click and

Kaiden found himself staring down the barrel of a hammer-gun. A flash of light, and then a shotgun blast of lasers burst out. Kaiden lunged backwards but there was no avoiding the flurry. The individual lasers exploded on impact and he was left reeling, vision blinding bright.

"That was a blast warden attack!" Kaiden shouted as his health fell to seventy-two percent. He retreated, trying to avoid any follow-up attacks. "He has abilities from all of the classes. The Hierarch is every warden class combined." His stomach fell through his feet as he said it. *How do we beat that? How do we compete with every warden ability at once?*

"Every class at once?" Thorne asked. There was doubt in her voice. "How is that possible?"

"He'll die just like anyone else will. We just have to hit him enough," Zelda said through gritted teeth.

Moran advanced on Kaiden, then reared back to attack again, but an Improved Burst Arrow from Zelda caught him in the back. The laser exploded against his torso in a spray of blue sparks. Zelda charged up another shot but Moran swung his hammer in her direction.

**Ability: Energy Grip**

A lasso of energy whipped from the end of his hammer and, before she could move, had wrapped around her leg. Moran gave a yank and Zelda was ripped out of Sniper Mode and dragged across the floor toward him.

"Gah!" Titus shouted as he charged to protect Zelda.

Moran met him with a hammer strike, raising his weapon high then bringing it down in a blur. Titus caught the blow on his shield – finally gaining some charge – and a shockwave burst out at the impact.

**Ability: Hammer Smash**

The big man slammed his hammer into the floor, creating a mini-crater and sending a rolling burst of energy out in all directions. It washed over Moran and set his health bar to flashing. Titus followed up with a Shield Slam, smashing his shield into the already formed mini-crater and stunning all enemies in a ten-foot radius.

But Moran wasn't within ten feet of him. He'd used Kick-back, dealing base damage to Titus and launching himself fifteen feet away.

He landed with a smirk. Titus looked up with a frown but Moran was already in motion again.

## Ability: Earth Shatter

His hammer had grown in size again; it was now as large as a power warden's as he launched forward, then came down right in front of Titus. The mini-crater was obliterated as Moran hit the ground with enough force to completely shatter the floor. Stone and tile whipped through the air, carried in a shockwave that washed over Titus and dumped him to the floor.

Zelda was on her feet now. She spun, leveling her hammer-gun at Moran.

## Ability: Improved Scatter Shot

From so close, Zelda's attack should have dealt a fair amount of damage, but Moran had been ready.

## Ability: Karmic Reprisal
**Your shield glows brightly, infused with charge. You may expend X% of max charge to reduce damage from a single attack by that percentage. Additionally, your next attack deals base damage plus additional damage equal to the amount this ability negated.**
**Cooldown: 3 minutes.**

He'd abandoned Dual Wielding and his hammer had reformed into a shield now. But not just a regular shield. It'd grown and stretched so it was large as a shield warden's. Its glow swelled and brightened and Zelda's eyes went wide as it absorbed her attack. All of one percent damage trickled through to Moran's health.

"Ooh. I almost felt that," he said then struck back with a hammer strike. The additional damage from Karmic Reprisal exploded against her chest, cracking her armor and dealing a massive hit. Her health plummeted to fifty-eight percent and she wheeled backward, teeth gritted against the damage flowing through her.

"Does this guy ever run out of charge?" she growled through comms.

"He's using Slayer, so every critical hit is restoring five charge for him. Plus his armor buffs that by another ten percent," Kaiden said, recalling what his visor had shown him.

"And he has Improved Atmospheric Charge generating seven charge per second *and* Improved Aggressive Mindset giving him charge equal to fifteen percent of all the damage he deals," Thorne added, pulling herself from where Moran had flung her.

"And he's building charge the normal way, through blocking attacks with his shield," Titus said, sounding none too happy about it.

"So no, then." Zelda scowled. "He's not going to run out of charge."

Kaiden's Dual Wielding had fizzled out now and his energy hammer shifted back into his shield. As it did, he took a half second to glance at everyone's health.

*Zelda's at fifty-eight. Titus, forty-six. Thorne, forty-nine. And I'm down to fifty-four already. Meanwhile, Moran...* He turned his focus on the hierarch. *Moran is sitting pretty at eighty-two percent.*

"We've put a grand total of twenty percent damage on this guy between all of us," he told the others. "This isn't working."

"We still have the numbers advantage," Zelda said. "Attack as one. He can't stop all of us at the sa—"

Moran darted in and swung a hammer strike at her head. Her voice cut off as she flung herself away from it.

"I'm not going to let you sit there and conspire," Moran said, shaking his head. "This is a fight, you know." And then he was in motion again, charging Zelda.

Thorne charged in, hammer raised high and ready to bring down on Moran's head. He stepped calmly forward and spun under her strike, then activated an ability.

505

**Ability: Gravity Sledge**

His energy hammer bashed into Thorne's rib cage and flung her into the air. Her health flashed from the blow, then again as she slammed into the floor ten feet away.

"Really, now," Moran said as he stared at them scattered about the room. "I expected more from you four."

## Chapter Sixty-Four

"Pop your stimpacks," Titus said as he threw up an Improved Barrier around himself and Zelda.

*We can't beat Moran head-on. Is there an alternate win condition here? We don't need to kill him. Just distract him long enough to get the message out, right?*

"Over here, you tyrannical asshat!" Kaiden shouted, scrambling for a ridiculous insult in order to draw Moran's attention. As he shouted, he charged the hierarch, hammer raised, then switched back to private comms.

"Zelda! Can you get to the broadcast control panel? Send out the database while we distract Moran?"

Even from across the room he could see her eyes light up at the idea.

"Keep me covered. I'll do what I can," she said, but Kaiden was only half listening, staring as he was down the barrel of Moran's hammer-gun.

**Ability: Improved Paralyzing Shot**

The shot exploded from Moran's weapon. Kaiden spun, then activated Kickback. His hammer slammed into the ground and he exploded up, over the oncoming attack and Moran's head in one motion.

He came down behind the hierarch and began charging an ability.

**Ability: Flash Bang**
**Discharge an intense light from your shield that blinds opponents within 10 feet for 5 seconds. Has a 3-second cast time.**

"Cover me!" Kaiden shouted but Thorne was already on it. She came in from the side and as Moran loaded up for a no-doubt crippling blow on Kaiden, Thorne landed with an Earth Shatter.

Moran was knocked onto his back. He stood up just in time for Flash Bang to go off in his face and blind him. He wasn't stunned, though, so he was still free to attack.

**Ability: Through the Breach**
**You channel charge into your armor. For the next 10 seconds all damage taken is reduced by 30% and your attack speed is doubled.**

Moran popped the ability then attacked wildly, his massive hammer swinging in long, looping blows. One caught Kaiden in the shoulder before he could duck away and sent his newly replenished health back down to seventy percent. Thorne had other plans, however, and she stepped in swinging.

"We need to buy time," Kaiden said, glancing to where Zelda was now interfacing with the console.

"I need sixty seconds for it to upload to the broadcast system," she said.

"You heard her. Don't focus on damage. Focus on delaying him."

"I can do that," Thorne growled.

Moran blinked a few times, then winced as Flash Bang's blind effect wore off. He raised his hammer toward Kaiden, but Thorne grabbed him.

**Ability: Improved Grip Like Iron**
**You channel charge into your shield hand. The next oppo-**
**nent you grapple will be held in place for 5 seconds plus X**
**seconds, where X is 3% of your total strength stat. A grap-**
**pled opponent can be attacked and deals 20% less damage**
**when attacking.**

"Interesting approach," Moran grunted, then took advantage of the grapple to land several attacks on Thorne. He had the twenty percent debuff to his damage but still his blows fell with incredible force. The grapple came to an end with Thorne at forty percent health. Moran broke free and stepped away – just in time for Titus to hit him with the full force of an Improved Shield Charge.

Kaiden had all too good a view as the force exploded through Moran, sending his eyes wide and rocking his armor to its core. But Intransigence kept him standing, though it didn't protect him from the damage of the attack. His health was down to eighty percent now.

The tides were turning; Kaiden could feel it. Moran was strong, but who could take on three opponents at once? And Zelda was at the broadcast control panel now, working it with hands a blur.

*Thirty more seconds…*

"Oh, so that's where you went." Moran's voice boomed out, echoing off the floor and walls and ceiling such that it resounded through every nook and crevice of the chamber. Moran reared back, aiming at Zelda, and Kaiden didn't need a visor to tell him an Energy Grip was coming.

He darted forward and caught Moran in the back with a Shield Bash, stunning him for two more seconds. The hierarch growled, but Kaiden scored two more hammer strikes on him. The stun wore off quickly, though, and Moran ignored Kaiden, aiming up the Energy Grip again.

**Ability: Energy Grip**

**Ability: Lightspeed**

Moran flung his lasso at Zelda – and Kaiden darted in front of it, carried by the unnatural haste of Lightspeed. The lasso wrapped around him instead of Zelda and Moran howled, then yanked Kaiden toward him.

"Not what you were hoping to catch?" he said as he climbed to his feet, then got a hammer strike to the chest for his trouble. Kaiden darted away before he could get hit again, his health bar already flashing. When it stopped, he was down to thirty percent health. But he'd bought Zelda a few more moments.

*Just fifteen more seconds…*

Moran charged Zelda.

Thorne cut into his path but was promptly bowled over by Improved Shield Charge.

"Hey punk," Titus shouted. "Might want to rethink that." He fired off his newest ability.

**Ability: Center of Attention**
**For the next 30 seconds, a target of your choosing must target you or take 2x base damage for every second they don't. You must be standing still to use this ability.**

Moran hesitated for a moment, then scoffed and spun toward Zelda, his health ticking away by the moment.

*Seventy-eight percent, seventy-six percent…*

"I said get back here!" Titus lashed out with an Energy Grip but Moran slammed his massive shield down and blocked the ability as it reached him.

"Just about got it—"

Zelda was cut off as Moran reached her and ripped her from the console.

"No!" Kaiden shouted as she was flung backwards.

Moran hit a button and the progress bar on the console reset.

"Almost had it there," Moran said, a look of relief on his face. "Now, Titus. I believe you wanted some attention?" Moran fired off a combo of abilities all at once.

**Ability: Berserker**
The warden does double base damage but also takes +50%
damage for 20 seconds. Speed is halved for 1 minute
following the ability.

**Ability: Improved Instigated Fury**
The fervor of battle sweeps over you. For the next 8
seconds, each time you take damage your base attack
increases by 15%.

**Ability: Lightspeed**
Dangerous levels of charge are channeled into your leg
implants, increasing movement speed by 200% for 10
seconds. You will take double damage if hit during
Lightspeed.

**Ability: Lethal Precision**
Your knowledge of the enemy increases the chance of you
and your allies landing critical attacks. For a duration of 15
seconds, all attacks from you or your allies (within 50 feet)
gain a +20% chance of becoming critical attacks.

*Double base damage, damage increased every time damage is taken,
insane movement speed, and an increased chance to land crits.* Kaiden
could barely keep up with all of the abilities as they flashed in
front of him.

Moran went for Titus first. Lightspeed did its thing and he
was a blur. Right up until his hammer came down on Titus' head
with a resounding crack and his health bar went wild with flashing. Nineteen percent health evaporated in the blink of an eye.
Fifty-two left.

Another blow landed on Titus, echoing through the chamber.
His health plummeted. Another attack or two and he was
done for.

**Ability: Improved Burst Arrow**

Zelda fired the attack but Moran was moving far too fast to be hit by it. He sidestepped it then turned back toward Titus, looking to deal a lethal blow.

**Ability: Improved Scatter Shot**

Lightspeed made Moran near impossible to hit as long as he kept moving, but Zelda was so close it was almost impossible for the shotgun blast of her Improved Scatter Shot to miss. She blasted Moran with the attack from mere steps away. The laser exploded against him, biting away at his health and dropping it to seventy-five percent.

**Ability: Lock On**
**You direct charge into your hammer-gun. For 5 seconds, as long as the last target you damaged is within your line of sight, your attacks will not miss. You cannot attack any other target. If you take damage this effect deactivates.**

"Your speed won't help you now," Zelda said, then fired an Improved Kinetic Grenade. With Lightspeed and Berserker active Moran was looking at some serious penalties for getting hit, as became painfully evident when Zelda's grenade went off at his feet with a resounding boom.

His health flashed down to sixty-four percent, and as it did, something strange happened. He doubled over, growling and cursing. His armor began to glow and vibrate. Whatever was happening spread to his hammer, and as it did, the hammer changed. It'd been the size of Thorne's, clearly a power warden's weapon. Now, however, it was shaking and moving as if it were liquid. As Kaiden stared, Moran's hammer shrunk in size until it was back to that of an enhanced or shield warden.

**Power warden abilities removed.**
**Berserker, Improved Instigate Fury, and associated effects ended.**

The system message flashed in Kaiden's vision, but he didn't understand it.

*What does that mean?*

"He's lost the ability to use power warden attacks?" Kaiden asked aloud.

"How did that happen?" Titus asked, stepping in front of Zelda with his shield up.

"He lost more than twenty-five percent of his health!" Zelda exclaimed all at once.

"And...?" Titus asked.

"Oh my god. You're right!" Thorne said, and Kaiden knew it as well. Suddenly it all made sense.

"The Warden Hierarch is a special class, right?" Zelda said, staring at him with a new appreciation. "Almost like he's part player, part boss. So, what if his class works like a boss? What if he has stages? Every twenty-five percent health he loses, he loses the abilities of one of the four classes he's made from?"

It all made perfect sense. And for the first time in the fight, Kaiden started to piece together a path to victory.

"Guys!" Kaiden shouted. "I know how we win this. We need—"

Moran wheeled on him and began swinging, cutting him off mid-sentence. The attack came blindingly fast and Kaiden didn't have time to dodge. The blow came down as a critical strike and his health dropped to eighteen percent.

He backpedaled, shield up to protect himself.

Moran charged an Improved Kinetic Grenade then slammed it into the ground at Kaiden's feet. It detonated with an eardrum-rupturing bang in the confines of the chamber. Even with his shield blocking most of the damage, burning bits of ground and razor-sharp fragments of tiles blasted past Kaiden as the fire overtook him and a massive chunk of his health evaporated once again.

*Thirteen percent health now.*

Kaiden grunted as he regained his balance, blinking through the stinging in his eyes from the blinding attack. He drew his vision back into focus in time to see a hammer swinging into his face.

He ducked under it and slipped past Moran, scoring a critical hammer strike on his knee as he passed. Lightspeed had expired now and the speed debuff from the Chrono Sledge kept Moran away for a moment. Kaiden had just enough time to catch his breath.

"Every time we strip one of his abilities, he gets weaker," he said. "If we can take them away, we can beat him. Right now he can counter our attacks with whatever warden ability is best for it. If we take that away, he'll be more predictable and we'll know what to expect." Kaiden used his last stimpack. His health swelled to thirty-eight percent.

"Pop stims," Kaiden reminded everyone, staring down Moran. "There's a lot of fight left in him."

Moran must have seen it coming because he chose just then to unleash a volley of attacks. A Paralyzing Shot that slowed Thorne. A Hammer Toss that sent Zelda dodging to one side. And then an Energy Grip toward Kaiden.

Moran lashed out and the lasso caught Kaiden around the leg, then ripped him to the ground and dragged him forward. Zelda fired an Improved Burst Arrow but Moran ducked it, then leveled his hammer at Kaiden and unleashed an Improved Scatter Shot. Kaiden's armor cracked and a few pieces were blown away as the attack hit him square in the chest.

His health dropped to twenty-four percent. Moran above him, raising his hammer, was the last thing Kaiden saw as the Improved Scatter Shot's blind effect kicked in.

**Ability: Matter Shift**

He activated it on instinct, unable to aim it, but teleporting anywhere was better than staying beneath Moran's oncoming attack.

Even through the blind effect, lights flashed in Kaiden's vision and he felt the ground disappear from beneath him. It reformed a moment later in time for him to hear what must've been Moran's hammer slam into the spot he'd just occupied.

The blind wore off and Kaiden saw Moran turning toward him. Zelda hit him in the back with an Improved Warden's Bolt that dropped his health to sixty percent but Moran was fixated. Bent on killing Kaiden.

"What is this little group of yours without their leader?" Moran roared as he used Kickback to launch through the air and land above Kaiden, then raise his hammer.

*Screw this*, Kaiden thought and grabbed an item from his inventory. The Matter Insubstantiator. He activated it with a click, and all at once, he was insubstantial. Moran's attack passed right through him. Kaiden looked down through his own transparent chest to watch as the hammer thunked into the floor.

Moran cursed as Kaiden rolled to his feet, then stepped forward and directly through him. The hierarch spun and raised his hammer, but he seemed unsure what to do. *Hard to hit a target that has no mass.*

But the ability wouldn't last long. Kaiden turned to run, to regroup with the others.

### Ability: Improved Shield Charge

Moran's shield hit him with the force of a meteor just as the Insubstantiator wore off and then Kaiden was flying backwards, driven across the room.

His health flashed down to six percent from the initial impact. And then the walls of the chamber shuddered with an echoing boom as he was driven into them. Moran's shield crushed him, drove him a foot deep into the wall as stone was pulverized to dust around him. Kaiden's health was likewise pulverized and the last thing he saw was his health drop to zero before it all went black.

## Chapter Sixty-Five

**You have been defeated**
**Respawn available in: 6 days, 23 hours and 59 minutes.**

Kaiden stared at the text. It was the only thing he could see, and even still, he couldn't believe it.

**You have been defeated.**
**Respawn available in: 6 days, 23 hours and 59 minutes.**

*I had a plan. A way to beat him. It was all there; we just had to execute it. I just... just had to live long enough to pull it off. But I didn't. I failed.*

Could the others do it without him? They had to now. The three of them had to be enough or else that was it; they lost. Killswitch would take Nova offline and then... then what? Before he could come up with an answer, a light flashed in his vision.

*Huh?*

It was distant, but growing larger. As it did, he could see what was inside it. Zelda. Thorne. Titus. Moran and the chamber, the broadcast control console. The light was an image of them all and it was resolving itself by the moment.

And then text flashed in his vision.

**Ability: Saving Grace**
**You have been revived! Welcome back.**

Kaiden stared at the text blankly. Uncomprehending. And then he was back in the chamber. Back in his body. He looked down to find one hand clutching his hammer and his shield glowing in the other.

He blinked dumbly as his brain caught up to what had happened. He was alive and he had ten charge. But why?

Titus, he realized. Titus had revived him!

Pebbles clattered off his shoulders and dust rained down around him as Kaiden pulled himself up from the pile of rubble Moran had left him in and took in his surroundings.

The warden hierarch was attacking Thorne. Her health was down to seven percent, but as Kaiden watched, she used her last stimpack and rose to thirty-two percent.

Zelda was focused in, unloading a barrage of attacks into Moran's back. Plenty of them must have already connected as his health was down to fifty-five percent.

And then there was Titus, off to one side. He was slumped over, like Saving Grace had taken an incredible amount of physical exertion. And as Kaiden looked closer, he realized the big man's health was down to thirty-three percent.

He pulled up the text of the ability and realized why.

**Ability: Saving Grace**
**You expend a massive amount of charge to save yourself or an ally from death. If a target within 100 feet has been reduced to 0% health in the last 5 seconds, they return to 50% health instead.**
**Cost: All of your charge and 50% of max health if targeting an ally. If targeting yourself, all of your charge but no health and you resurrect with only 5% health and 5% charge.**
**Cooldown: 6 hours**

*All of your charge and fifty percent of your* max *health,* Kaiden realized. Titus had nearly killed himself to pull the rez off.

"Titus!" Kaiden said through comms. "You're almost dead!"

"Well, you were fully dead," he said with a shrug. "Had to do it."

"Use a stimpack!"

He shook his head.

"Used my second one a bit back, then my last one just now to survive Saving Grace."

"I need you alive to win this."

Thirty-three percent health was far less than ideal, but Kaiden was only at fifty percent himself. But at the moment, it was a far sight better than the zero percent he'd been moments before.

"All right," Kaiden said through comms so he would get everyone but Moran's attention. "Let's finish this punk." He was painfully aware of the timer at the edge of his vision, still ticking down as ever. Fourteen minutes left. If they were going to do this, they needed to do it now. He did a quick mental rundown of everyone's abilities, then compared that against his knowledge of what Moran was capable of.

*How do you beat someone who can use nearly every warden ability? He can counter nearly all of our attacks. But he's outnumbered. He can't counter all of our attacks at the same time. And he doesn't know I'm here.*

"Combo time," Kaiden said to the rest of the group. "We're gonna blow this asshole away. Titus," he said, pointing to the big man. "Shield Link with me, then block any attacks you can – but stay alive!"

"Will do my best," he said, then charged into the melee, joining Thorne and Moran where they were exchanging blows. He slipped in next to Thorne and together they fought as one, Titus blocking and Thorne attacking. It wasn't long before charge was flooding into Kaiden from the attacks hitting Titus' shield.

"Zelda," Kaiden said next. "Hit Moran with a Paralyzing Shot when you see me going in."

She nodded.

"After you hit him with that, get into Sniper Mode and start charging the biggest attack you've got."

"I'd love to," she grunted, still firing at Moran.

"Thorne," Kaiden said last, turning his attention to the belea-guered power warden. She'd been doing the bulk of the fighting against Moran and it didn't look like she had much more to give.

"Stay alive," Kaiden said simply. "We're going to need your DPS to pull this off. Just… stay alive."

She nodded by way of response and eased off her attack, pivoting to lash out only when Moran took swings at Titus.

Having been caught in the middle of the assault for so long up until now, the warden hierarch was bleeding damage left and right. Fifty-four percent health left. But Thorne and Titus had been taking a beating as well. Thorne was in the red again at twelve percent health, Titus holding for the moment at thirty percent. Even Zelda seemed to have weathered an assault, down to fifty-five percent from the rather high total she'd been at earlier. Not much health left across the team, but Kaiden had been given fifty percent when he'd been resurrected.

And his charge bar was brimming thanks to Titus.

## Ability: Lightspeed

## Ability: Dual Wielding

"Thorne, get his attention!"

She roared and made a show of winding up for a Gravity Sledge. Moran raised his shield.

"Zelda, hit him!"

## Ability: Improved Paralyzing Shot
**Fires an electric blast that confuses the electrical impulses in the target's muscles, deals 110% base damage and slows target's movement by 60% for 10 seconds.**

It caught Moran in the side while he was busy with Thorne. And then Kaiden darted forward. Lightspeed carried him with unnatural swiftness and he was on the slowed warden hierarch in the blink of an eye. Lightspeed against a slowed target wasn't quite fair, and the disparity was made all the greater as Kaiden landed a critical hit and his Chrono Sledge further debuffed Moran's speed.

Critical hit!
+25% damage (Kneecapped)
+5% damage (Chrono Sledge ability, extra damage on crits)
Moran is slowed by 30% for 2 seconds

Critical hit!
+25% damage (Kneecapped)
+5% damage (Chrono Sledge ability, extra damage on crits)
Moran is slowed by 30% for 2 seconds

The text flashed twice, once for each hammer, and Kaiden's charge bar jumped by twenty. Moran grunted as his health dropped from the attack, but Kaiden was far from done. Next, he brought both hammers around in wide, arcing swings, then smashed them together on either side of Moran's head.

Critical hit!
+50% damage (Headshot)
+5% damage (Chrono Sledge ability, extra damage on crits)
Moran is slowed by 30% for 2 seconds

Critical hit!
+50% damage (Headshot)
+5% damage (Chrono Sledge ability, extra damage on crits)
Moran is slowed by 30% for 2 seconds

That got his attention. Moran's health lost another chunk and his eyes went wide as he spun to find Kaiden alive and already attacking again. Two more critical hits and then Kaiden couldn't help but smile as Onslaught activated.

Ability: Onslaught
Following 6 consecutive critical strikes, you may enter

onslaught mode for 5 seconds. While in Onslaught mode you deal double base damage and have double current movement speed. Onslaught may be triggered twice before cooldown.

With Onslaught active and plenty of charge in the tank, Kaiden had some options open to him. He wanted to dump fifteen charge into a Shield Bash, but his shield was currently a hammer – another downside to Dual Wielding. No matter, though.

**Ability: Hamstring**
**Charge is redirected into your hammer. On your next successful critical attack this charge cripples your opponent. Their movement speed is reduced by 50% for 10 seconds.**

Kaiden was moving far too fast for Moran to keep up with now. It was like fighting an opponent who was half asleep.

*That's the window we need,* Kaiden thought as he ducked under an attack from Moran and landed a critical hit on the back of the man's knee, triggering the crippling effect of Hamstring. Moran's health fell to fifty percent and a lash of damage slapped Kaiden back for five percent.

Seeming desperate, Moran cursed and swung in with an attack but his slowed movement speed meant Kaiden easily avoided it and stacked a Riposte. He responded with a hammer strike to the man's head and the commander's health dropped to forty-six percent just as Onslaught wore off.

"Damn you," Moran growled as he bent double, energy glowing inside him once again. It flowed out over his arm and then his shield shrunk in size from that of a shielder's to that of a regular warden.

**Shield warden abilities removed.**

"Just blast warden and enhanced warden left," Kaiden said through comms. "He's getting weaker."

*It's time*, Kaiden thought. He would have liked to get Moran lower, but the timer was still counting down and Thorne wasn't going to hold out against much more damage. None of them were, for that matter. No, it was time to end this fight.

"You know, Moran," Kaiden said, ducking under another of his attacks. "You're strong, I'll give you that. And you're smart, too. But your past has ruined you."

Another attack, another dodge.

"You can't accept that your worldview might not be the right one."

"Oh?" Moran scowled at that. "Do go on," he said, then lunged forward and landed a hammer strike on Kaiden's shoulder. Kaiden let the force of the blow carry him to the side, then came around with a return hammer strike that buried the Chrono Sledge into Moran's side.

*Forty-three percent health left on him.*

"You think others are just puppets to be played. Strings to be pulled."

"They are," Moran growled.

"I'm sorry you feel that way," Kaiden said, then snapped his eyes over to Thorne. "Improved Grip Like Iron!" he shouted and she sprung into motion. Moran tried to turn to meet her, but she got there first and activated the ability.

**Ability: Improved Grip Like Iron**
**You channel charge into your shield hand. The next opponent you grapple will be held in place for 5 seconds plus X seconds, where X is 3% of your total strength stat. A grappled opponent can be attacked and deals 20% less damage when attacking.**

She wrapped her arms around him and squeezed tight, locking the hierarch in place. Moran screamed, veins straining in his neck as he fought to break free.

"All right, now Titus," Kaiden said, turning to him. This next part was going to be critical but they had to finish the combo before Thorne died. Then her damage would push them through to the win.

**Ability: Matter Shift**

Moran disappeared from Thorne's grasp, fading into nothing. He reappeared a moment later.

"Behind you!" Kaiden shouted but the hierarch was already attacking.

One, two critical hits to Thorne's back and the last bit of her health slipped away.

**Party Member Killed!**

Thorne collapsed like a bag of rocks, armor clanking to the ground as she went down in a limp heap.

*Shit! The combo doesn't work if we can't root him first.*

Kaiden stepped up to distract Moran, to keep him in place, but it seemed he'd caught on to what was happening.

**Ability: Improved Last Rites (passive)**
**When you reach 0% health this ability triggers. You have 30 seconds to kill all opponents in a 50-foot radius of your point of death. Every kill made during this time extends the kill timer by 3 seconds. Should you succeed, you will be given 1% HP back. If not, you will die. Kills made during this time earn no EXP. Abilities can be used during Improved Last Rites.**

Thorne's ultimate ability kicked in and she came back from the dead – like Kaiden had known she would – but Moran was too clever. He activated Lightspeed and darted away, easily clearing the fifty-foot radius Thorne was bound within. She was alive for thirty more seconds and could deal damage, but not if Moran stayed outside the radius of her death, which she couldn't leave.

Zelda had slipped into Sniper Mode now and she activated

her hammer-rifle's special ability, then fired three Improved Kinetic Grenades at Moran, trying to drive him back toward Thorne. They detonated in bursts of laser and flame, but with Lightspeed active Moran was too fast. He took glancing damage as he slipped out of their range and further away from Thorne.

Titus followed him as well, but he might as well have been a toddler chasing a cheetah.

Even with a partial hit from her multiple grenades Zelda was able to use Lock On so her attacks wouldn't miss Moran, which was a start, but it wasn't going to force him into Thorne's radius, which had quickly become the most important part of the plan.

*We can't access the broadcast controls while Moran's alive, and he knows that. We leave ourselves too open if we do. He's going to delay until Thorne's Last Rites wears off, or Killswitch is complete. That's his plan,* Kaiden knew. It was clear the tide of the fight was turning, but Moran didn't need to kill them and everyone knew it. If he simply harassed them long enough, Killswitch would ensure his victory.

Still moving too fast to see, Moran weaved in and out of the group, striking with critical hits whenever he was close and blasting away with ranged attacks when he wasn't.

Kaiden's Dual Wielding was over now so at the least he was able to block several of Moran's blazing-fast hits on his shield. Titus was forced over to Zelda to keep her alive. Everyone took damage, though. Everyone except Thorne, who was technically unkillable while Improved Last Rites was active.

*All right, new plan. Or rather, an alteration on the old.* Moran was fast – too fast to hit. But that didn't mean he couldn't be caught; it just meant Kaiden needed to move at the same speed as him.

**Ability: Lightspeed**

Kaiden body reverberated with energy as the ability activated. And then everything seemed to slow down. Titus spun in slow motion, hefting his shield around to block an oncoming attack. Zelda pulled the trigger on an Improved Burst Arrow and Kaiden watched as the laser oozed out of the barrel of her hammer-rifle. Moran moved to dodge it, but Lock On made sure it hit.

With Kaiden's Lightspeed active, Moran was the only other person in the room moving at regular speed, and he just had time to turn to look as Kaiden tackled him from the side.

They tumbled to the ground and the double damage debuff on Lightspeed set both of their health bars to flashing. Kaiden's health dropped even further as Moran caught him with a sloppy hammer strike. Kaiden lashed back.

*Twenty-three percent for me, thirty-eight for him.*

Moran snarled, then attacked again, and Kaiden fell away, narrowly avoiding the blow. With both of them taking two hundred percent damage on any hits – thanks to Lightspeed – it wouldn't take many blows to reduce either of them to zero. Moran knew this just as much as Kaiden and he stormed forward now, ready to kill him – again.

Kaiden blocked the attack on his shield, then fell to the side, inching toward Thorne. Moran pounced, swinging once more. Kaiden rolled away from that blow but it still caught his shoulder and his health dropped to eight percent.

Moran could feel victory looming. It was obvious in his eyes. He was transfixed. Obsessed.

Moran swung his hammer for a killing blow.

Kaiden threw caution to the wind and lunged forward. He slipped just under Moran's blow and danced away. Moran growled, then spun to chase him.

*Yes, come on. Chase me. Chase me!*

But Moran pulled up short. He paused, then looked down to his feet. He was one step from entering the radius of Thorne's Improved Last Rites. Kaiden's panicked retreat hadn't been so panicked after all. It'd been intentional, but Moran had caught on.

"Ah, well." Kaiden shrugged. "Close enough." He lunged forward.

**Ability: Shield Bash**

The stun caught Moran full in the chest. It didn't deal any damage, but it locked him in place for two seconds. And two seconds was just enough time.

"Titus!" Kaiden shouted but the big man was already on it.

**Ability: Improved Shield Charge**

He came in like a bus, slamming into Moran from behind and driving him several steps forward. Several steps into Thorne's reach.

"Improved Grip Like Iron," Kaiden shouted. "Let's give it one more try."

Thorne lunged forward with the ability and grappled Moran. He kicked and flailed, landing hammer strike after hammer strike on her, but in Improved Last Rites she couldn't be killed. How did you kill what was already at zero percent health?

**Ability: Enfeebling Strike**
**Loads charge into your hammer. On a successful hit, this charge floods into the target's nervous system, making them more susceptible to pain. Increases damage taken by target by 50% for 10 seconds.**

Kaiden lunged forward and slammed his hammer into Moran's ribs, then reeled back before a counterattack could kill him.

"The thing I pity you for most," Kaiden said, pulling his eyes up to Moran's, "is that you've forgotten what it means to have allies you can rely on. *Friends* to have your back." He backed away.

"Boom," Zelda said, then pulled the trigger on the ability she'd been charging. She was in Sniper Mode, and Moran hadn't touched her, but her health was down to five percent. It became apparent why as Kaiden's visor read out the abilities she'd chosen for the finisher.

**Ability: Pain for Gain**

You may sacrifice 25% of your max health to make your next attack deal 2x damage. If you sacrifice 50% of your max health that attack will deal 4x damage instead.

**Ability: Inferno Shot**
You fire an explosive, superheated blast that ignores 50% of the target's armor. Deals 3x base damage to all targets in range (allies included). Takes 7 seconds to charge (must be stationary).

The attack was like nothing Kaiden had ever seen before. Inferno Shot on its own was a terror to behold but this was something else entirely. When the Warden Corps army had marched out what felt like forever ago Kaiden had thought they were the most frightening thing he'd seen. An asteroid about to destroy a planet, a natural disaster given shape and purpose – but this, this was more. In every way. It was like staring into the heart of a star as it went supernova. An asteroid could take out planets, but this would take out solar systems.

Kaiden's eyes burned like nothing he'd felt before as Zelda's supercharged Inferno Shot tore across the room. The explosion as it hit Moran shook the room so hard Kaiden toppled over and dirt and debris rained down from the ceiling. He wouldn't have been surprised if the impact was felt all across the asteroid, shaking all of Custos to its core.

In the midst of the nuclear inferno, Thorne was laughing madly. She was invincible for two more seconds while Improved Last Rites finished up and she watched firsthand as Moran's health drained away to nothing. His health pool was massive and he'd tanked pretty much everything they'd thrown at him so far, but there was no tanking this. His health drained to nothing, then his armor burned off, then his body entirely. When the attack ended, Thorne was left standing, her arms wrapped around nothing but a faint scorch mark on the floor.

**Warden Hierarch Slaen Moran killed – 20,000 EXP gained!**

**Achievement Unlocked!**
**Harbinger of Upheaval – 10,000 EXP!**
**You've toppled the leader of all law and order in the universe and brought about a new age. It's time for change to take root in Nova... and beyond. A new age is on the horizon.**

"That's what's up!" Titus said, pumping a fist in the air.

*We did it. Holy shit. It... it actually worked.*

"No time to celebrate," Zelda said, and she was right. The timer was down to four minutes now. Far less time than Kaiden would have preferred.

Moran's death had fulfilled the 'kill all enemies within fifty feet of your place of death' condition of Thorne's Improved Last Rites and she was fully alive again, if one percent health could be considered fully alive. But it was enough to do what she'd come to do.

She rushed to the broadcast control console and began working the controls.

"Every extra second we can give people to consider the broadcast is needed," she said as she worked. "No time to waste. We need as many downloads as possible. Spread this bad boy far and wide. Titus," she said over her shoulder. "Come here, hold this down." She gestured to a touch screen and he stepped up and pressed his hand to it. "Takes two people to do this part."

"But I was able to do it with one—" Zelda began before Thorne cut her off.

"One can upload but It takes two people to activate," she reasserted, then shot Zelda a look. She turned to Titus who had his hand planted on the screen. "Good, keep that there." She moved a step to the side to an identical control panel. She repeated the procedure she'd done on the first one, then pressed her hand to that console's touch screen and looked back to Zelda. "It's ready," she said. "Database?"

Zelda produced it from her inventory, the opened padlock appearing in her hand as she ran up to the console.

"There," Thorne said, nodding toward a slot in the front of the console. Zelda held the padlock up, then gave it a quick kiss.

"For Bernstein," she said and slid it into the slot. The console accepted it with a faint whirring.

"Good, good." Thorne said with a nod. "All right, it's ready to go." As she said it, a button rose from inside the console. It wasn't huge and red. Didn't look intimidating. Didn't even look important. Instead, it was just a simple button with one word written across its face.

'Send.'

Titus stood on one side, holding his hand to the touch screen. Thorne was on the other, and for a moment, everyone seemed frozen. Then Zelda looked over her shoulder and met Kaiden's eyes.

"You should do it," she said.

"I guess, uh, this is it, then? Huh?" Kaiden asked. He stepped up to the button and in one smooth movement, pressed his thumb to it. It depressed with a soft click. A moment later, a message appeared in his vision.

****Full System Alert! Full System Alert!****
**This is a Warden Corps All-Frequencies Broadcast.**
**Players of Nova Online:**

**The Party has been lying to you.**

**The Party has been abusing its power.**

**You've suspected it for a long time, but anyone who brings it up is silenced. Silenced, like our friend, Fred Bernstein.**

**He was killed for his work uncovering evidence of the Party's abuse of power. In his memory, we send you this file. It's his life's work: an extensive database chronicling the Party's crimes.**

If you're tired of living in fear, then now is the time to take action.

We won't tell you what to do with this information. The truth should speak for itself. All you have to do is listen.

- Kaiden, Zelda, Titus, and Thorne

\>> Download file?

**End Full System Alert**

# Epilogue

It was seven o'clock in the evening on a warm summer's night when Kaiden Moore sat down at his desk. Outside, the cicadas were singing and a cool breeze slipped through his cracked window, bringing with it the smell of the woods; of earth and pine, and just a tinge of damp. Just enough to send his thoughts back to those last few days in what had once been their home sweet swamp bunker.

It hadn't taken long for Bernstein's database to saturate through every level of media. A day to go viral online. A week to dominate the newsfeeds. Two weeks and it'd flooded into every home, every head, every mind. There'd been no escaping the database. It had been all anyone was talking about.

The injustices of the Party had been laid bare to the people, and then the people had passed judgment. There'd been protests, of course. In some areas they'd turned to violence as the Party had fought to subdue them. But in most areas, there'd been no such resistance.

Kaiden had seen it himself. Thorne had always said it, but he'd never quite believed it – not until he saw it himself. The Party hadn't been rotten to the core. The majority of it had been made up of honest people. Just people doing their best to earn a salary and live their lives. When the news came out, when they'd learned what had really been happening, there was no other option: they'd turned on those responsible and the Party had collapsed. From within and from without. Kaiden had never expected it to go so swiftly, but then again, he'd never expected a lot of what had happened in the past year.

In the chaos that'd followed, some of the higher-ups had tried to hang on to power. But they hadn't lasted long. Then there'd been others who, like Werner, had fled. Some, like Moran, had simply disappeared. An unfortunate reality of the chaos of the transition. The Party had fallen to pieces, and in the mess that followed there was no time for a coordinated effort to arrest those responsible for its injustices. But they hadn't been forgotten.

It'd taken some time, but when things had finally settled down – when the country had achieved a semblance of stability and a transitional, democratic government had begun to emerge – one of its first actions had been to begin the investigation to track down Werner, and Moran, and everyone else who'd been in their inner circle.

Thorne had insisted Kaiden and the others stay with her at the bunker until things had truly settled down, and until the official word had come down that they were all unanimously cleared of the crimes the Party had accused them of. The charges had been dropped and their records cleared. In the eyes of the law, they'd once again become ordinary citizens. Or something like that.

Kaiden leaned back in his computer chair and smiled at the memory. Not because of what they'd been offered, but because of what they'd chosen to do with it.

After the world learned their story, their futures had looked set for fame and fortune. But they'd turned it down. They'd each asked to be spared the spotlight, declined the interviews and book deals. After all, they hadn't been heroes. They hadn't been rebels. They'd just been people who, when given the opportunity, had done what was right. They'd been ordinary citizens in extraordinary circumstances, they'd insisted. But if one thing was certain now it was that they would never be 'ordinary citizens' ever again. Especially not in Nova Online.

By the time NextGen had brought the full – and Party warden-free – game back online, Kaiden, Titus, Zelda, and Thorne had become legends. They'd also never logged on to those accounts again.

Kaiden had seen the rumors, of course. They'd run rampant. Hardly a week had gone by without someone claiming to have seen them in a far corner of Nova. Battling against a voidspawn army all on their own, or picked up just on the edge of a scanner's range, flying the *Veritas II* off into uncharted space. But those were just rumors, and he knew better than anyone that they weren't true.

To the outside world, it seemed as if their accounts had simply disappeared. Or, Kaiden thought, perhaps some suspected that something else had happened. That the accounts had quietly been turned into trophies and sold for a hefty sum each to a well-meaning if slightly odd collector.

Out of game, their stories were a bit harder to keep secret.

Titus had gone back to his family to help support them and be a role model to his errant brother – a task that had been made much easier when NextGen Games offered him a role in their motion capture department. Working on combat fluidity in character movement, and on the development team for black-market gameplay. A job he excelled at, Kaiden knew.

As for Zelda, well, her first priority had been to find her parents after they – along with thousands of others who'd been wrongly imprisoned – had been released from Party prison.

Once reunited with her parents, Zelda had returned to her work with Bernstein's database. The whole of it had been released online and was available everywhere, but it wasn't complete. With the Party in ruins, their data and records had been abandoned – and would likely have been forgotten – if not for Zelda. With the help of a special grant from the transitional government, she'd established the Fred Bernstein Foundation for Human Rights. With her at its head, they'd begun work to piece together the remains of the Party's data; clearing the records of the wrongly accused, solving missing persons cases, and bringing closure to the families of those who'd been disappeared into Party black sites.

And then there was Thorne. Kaiden took a sip from his glass of iced tea as he called her to mind.

She'd been asked to run for elected office in the transitional government. It'd been an offer she'd declined. Declined in favor of taking a spot on a special investigative task force. The very same task force, as it happened, that'd been assigned the job of tracking down Party criminals in hiding. Under her leadership they'd already brought many to justice, among them one former Agent Werner and his boss, the disgraced Commander Slaen Moran.

And then there was Kaiden himself. The leader of the band that'd brought down the Party, people liked to call him. But he still disagreed on that point. What he was going to do next was, well, still unanswered. He'd never really had the freedom to choose before. But now, with a new government in place, and his bank account full for some time thanks to a transaction marked "sale of digital goods," he wasn't in any particular hurry to figure out what came next.

No, Kaiden wasn't sure where the future would take him. Wasn't sure what *he* wanted to do next. And for the time being, that was okay.

The only thing he was sure of was that twice a week he was going to log into Nova Online. Log in on a new account where he and three other players were very excited to play through the game. And maybe, this time, they'd take it a bit slower. Maybe they'd bypass overthrowing any tyrannical governments or uncovering databases of buried crimes.

This time, they'd play at their own speed and enjoy themselves.

Yeah, that sounded good, Kaiden thought. Inside a modest house somewhere on a nondescript street, he pulled a VR headset over his head and logged in. A smile stretched across his face as a line of text projected onto his vision.

**Welcome to Nova Online.**

It was followed thereafter by a less familiar line.

Kaiden Moore didn't want much out of life, but this? Well, this was a good start.

534

**Create new character?**

# Afterword

Hello, Alex Knight here.

If you're reading this, then you've finished the Nova Online Trilogy! I hope you've enjoyed it. These three books have been the primary focus of my life for the last two years and I can't overstate how grateful I am that you've read them!

Being an author is my highest aspiration in life and I still have to ask myself just about daily "is this real life?" Readers like you help make my dream a reality and I truly can't thank you enough!

The trilogy is finished, but that doesn't mean your adventures in the world of Nova Online have to be. I've written a short story, *Survivors: Nova Online,* which you can get for free when you sign up for my publisher's mailing list. Included with the novelette is 60,000 more words of LitRPG stories from my awesome fellow authors at Portal Books. They're all very talented folks who are creating some amazing stuff. You can find *Survivors: Nova Online* and the rest of the free story bundle here:

https://portal-books.com/sign-up

Plug in your email on the landing page and my publisher will get the bundle to you straight away!

As well, I have something of a favor to ask. Reviews make a huge difference to authors. More reviews mean more readers will discover my books, which gives me the support I need to dedicate more time to writing.

If you've enjoyed the Nova Online Trilogy it would mean the world to me if you would consider leaving a rating and a short review on Amazon or Goodreads. I love hearing from my readers and this is a direct way for you to send me feedback!

For those of you that want to discuss my books further, you can check out the Portal Books Facebook group:

www.facebook.com/groups/LitRPGPortal/

Thank you again for taking a chance on my trilogy. I hope you enjoyed reading it as much as I did writing it!

Keep grinding,

Alex Knight

P.S. Look out for Hellbound (Saga Online #2), coming soon!

It's available on Kindle Unlimited and Audio.

**Dungeons of Strata (Deepest Dungeon #1)**
When Martin's guild joins the race to complete Strata Online, he finds an impossible task. A 100-floor dungeon, filled with an ever-shifting ecosystem of monsters.

It's available on Kindle Unlimited and Audio.

**God of Gnomes (God Core #1)**
Reborn as a god, Corey must guide a village of bumbling gnomes as they build defences to defeat an invading army of kobolds.

It's available on Kindle Unlimited and Audio.

**Warden: Nova Online.**
Imprisoned for a murder he didn't commit, Kaiden's only hope of early release is in serving as a Warden in the game-world of Nova Online.

It's available on Kindle Unlimited and on Audio.

**Mastermind (Titan Online #1) - A Superhero LitRPG**
Karna was just like any other comic book fan. He dreamed of fighting alongside colorful heroes and taking down dastardly villains. In Titan Online, the most popular VR MMORPG going, he finally got the chance to live out his cape-donning fantasies.

It's available on Kindle Unlimited and Audio.

**Battle Spire: A Crafting LitRPG Book.**
Battle Spire is a meeting of *World of Warcraft* and *Die Hard*, using crunchy LitRPG mechanics with a heavy focus on crafting. Readers can expect to find in depth item and spell descriptions, along with stat tables and profession recipes.

It's available on Kindle Unlimited and Audio.

For more general discussions about the genre, these groups may be useful to you.
www.facebook.com/groups/LitRPGsociety/

www.facebook.com/groups/LitRPG.books/

www.facebook.com/groups/LitRPGGroup/

## Acknowledgments

This book and trilogy are the product of the hard work of a corps. of talented and hard-working individuals who each helped me through the long process of bringing it into existence.

In no particular order, thanks of the highest degree are owed to: Laura Hughes, editor extraordinaire, for her support and endless courage in correcting my grammatical errors; Graeme Penman for his support, ideas, and game theory consulting; Brook Aspden-Li for his excellent work in structural editing and for letting me blow up his phone with plot and mechanics questions at all hours of the day; Rocket League, for distracting me when I needed to be distracted (and just a few times when I didn't); my wonderful wife Erin for dragging me – when necessary – through the inevitable rough patches that come with writing; and to the awesome guys at Portal Books who not only published this book, but were always available to reminisce about classic MMOs or chit chat about the newest LitRPG releases.

I can hardly begin to state the extent of thanks that are owed to each of you – so I'll continue to do it how I always have, via random, tangentially related gifs on Twitter. Be excellent to each other.

# About the Author

Alex Knight is, at any given time, leading a zerg rush in StarCraft II, or crushing opponents in Rocket League.

In the real world he's the author of the Nova Online trilogy and spends his days filling good books with bad jokes one sentence at a time. When he isn't writing he's likely clawing his way through champion rank in Rocket League or slinging burn spells in Magic: The Gathering.

Though he's lived in many places around the world, he currently lives along the Gulf coast of Texas, in a bayou near Houston. You can find Alex online at:

Website: http://authoralexknight.com/
Twitter: @AlexKnightBooks
Facebook: Alex Anthony

# Join the Group

To learn more about LitRPG, talk to authors including myself, and just have an awesome time, please join the LitRPG Group.